21/5709

CW00518868

BRON, FLAMES OF PROPHECY

The Story of Bron
Part II

Iris Lloyd

Pen Press Publishers Ltd

First published in Great Britain by
Pen Press Publishers Ltd
25 Eastern Place
Brighton
BN2 1GJ

ISBN 978-1-906206-23-9

Printed and bound in the UK

A catalogue record of this book is available from
the British Library

Cover design by Jacqueline Abromeit
Photograph Sarah Cook

Praise for Bron, Part I, Daughter of Prophecy

'The book makes for a most entertaining read.'

Daily Mail

'This is a gripping first novel and, as it is part of a series, I eagerly await the next instalment.'

Diane Morgan
Newbury Weekly News

'Congratulations to Iris Lloyd, whose new book (the first in a series of wonderfully accomplished historical novels) is now published. Gripping, insightful, funny and inspiring - unreservedly recommended.'

Jacqui Bennett
Writers' Bureau

'Quite simply a superb read. The story was a real page turner and the gritty realism brought early Britain to vivid life. I can't wait for Part II.'

A reader in Sydney, Australia

'I enjoyed Bron very much and could not put the book down. In fact, the sites of Crete were put second best to reading the book. I cannot wait until the next instalment.'

A reader

Born in Clapham, London, before the war, at the age of five Iris Lloyd moved out to a new estate in Queensbury, Middlesex, with her parents and her brother. They were caught at her grandmother's in Clapham on the first night of the Blitz, and soon were all evacuated by her father's employers to Chesham, Buckinghamshire, returning to Queensbury when she was 14 years old. Her sister was born during the post-war baby boom.

When 17, she joined a superb church youth club, and wrote eight annual pantomimes for them to perform (usually directing and choreographing as well, as she has been dancing since the age of three), then nine more scripts co-written with a friend for his drama group. Three have been published by Cambridge Publishing Services Ltd. and are performed regularly by amateur companies.

In the 1950's, Iris also wrote the script of a romantic musical set in 1730, which was performed by a church group. Recently, she entered two full-length plays for competitions at her local professional theatre, the Watermill, in Newbury.

Two years (1959-61) were enjoyed as secretary to the Editor of Children's Books at Macmillan's publishers in London, where she met author Ray Bethers, and later she line edited for him five of his short children's books.

In recent years, she wrote and performed, one Sunday morning on Radio Oxford/Berkshire, a dramatic monologue and (with a friend) a two-hander between Barabbas and the mother of the thief on the Cross. She has written sketches and plays for stage, church and parties. Two of her poems have been published in anthologies.

A correspondent for many years for the Newbury Weekly News, her local independent newspaper, she had several half-page and full-page articles on various topics published. And in her last parish, she was chief editor of the church magazine and of a prestigious village book which was produced for the millennium. Having moved to Hungerford, Berkshire, two years ago, she has now taken on sole editorship of the monthly parish magazine.

Iris was married to Denis, who for 27 years was self-employed in the construction industry, and was widowed 19 years ago. She is the proud mother of two daughters and grandmother to three lively grandchildren.

For exercise, she still teaches tap dancing to adults.

Author's contact: iris.lloyd@virgin.net
www.irislloyd.co.uk

CONTENTS

Roman Towns, Villages and Rivers mentioned in the story

Aetheling - Eling
Byden – Beedon, north of Newbury, Berkshire
Calleva Atrebatum – Silchester
Camulodunum – Colchester
Durnovaria – Dorchester
Eboracum – York
Lambburnan – Lambourn
Londinium – London
Pegingaburnan – Pangbourne
Portus Dubris – Dover
River Chenet – River Kennet
Spinis – Speen, Newbury
Stan stream – no longer flowing
Stanmere – Stanmore, Beedon, Berkshire
Venta Belgarum – Winchester
Verulamium – St. Albans

Reminder List of Characters (Cont'd)

Romans

Julius Gaius	Roman official
Lucilla	His wife
Flavia	Their daughter
Adrianus Maximus	Ex-governor of Eboracum
Aurelius Catus	Junior Roman officer
Decimus	A young legionary
Lysander	A young legionary
Naseem	A sentry

At Calleva Atrebatum

Luenda	Owner of brothel
Jannica	A prostitute
Gift	A baby born in the brothel
Asher	A Christian pilgrim
Chrystella	A woman of Christian faith

Foreigners

Cullum	A Catuvellauni man
Ziad	His emissary

In the Wood

Umbella	Clairvoyant, herbalist, abortionist

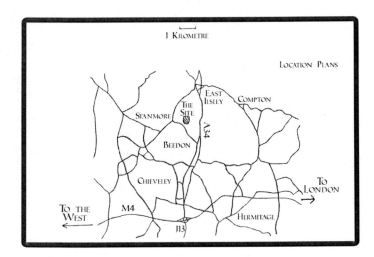

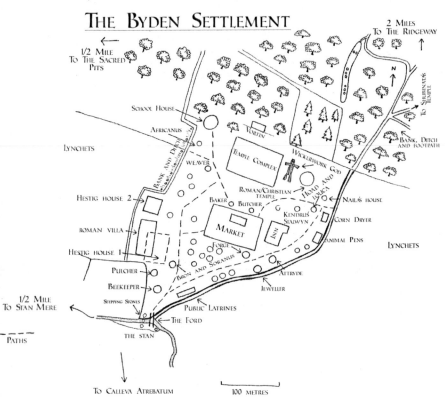

THE BYDEN SETTLEMENT

Reminder List of Characters

Bron's Family

Bron
Soranus   Bron's childhood friend and husband
Campania   Mother of Soranus
Hestig   Bron's father
Trifena   Bron's mother
Hestigys   Bron's brother
Trifosa   Bron's sister
Aelia   Bron's baby sister
Storm   }
Layla   }
Alon   }   Bron's children
Darius   }

Temple

Vortin   High Priest
Iraina   High Priestess
Nobilianus   Their son
Sharma   Priest
Selvid   Priest
Jeetuna   Priestess
Veneta   Priestess
Brocchus   Eunuch
Sunina   Temple prostitute

Reminder List of Characters (Cont'd)

Temple Children

Sorin   }
Naila   }   Bron's friends
Edreda   }

Villagers

Pulcher   Neighbour, a dwarf
Stalwyn   Midwife and nurse
Kendrus   Doctor, husband of Stalwyn
Africanus   Schoolteacher, of African origins
Hoad   Shepherd
Louca   Hoad's wife
Catterina   Their eldest daughter
Attryde   Blacksmith's wife/widow/
                    employer of Soranus
Obrina   Attryde's daughter

The Story So Far...

This story is set on an archaeological site on the Berkshire downs at Beedon, north of Newbury, that I help excavate.

Part I Daughter of Prophecy
AD 385

Trifena and Hestig, slaves of the Roman Governor of Eboracum, were released from bondage upon their marriage. We first meet them as they walk through the wood on their way to Byden, ancestral home of Trifena's tribe, the Atrebates. Trifena is pregnant.

The couple are accosted by Umbella, an ancient clairvoyant who lives in the wood, who prophesies that the birth will unleash "Sword, fire and total destruction" on the settlement.

In the great Temple of the sun god, Ashuba, High Priest Vortin and Iraina, his High Priestess, have produced only deranged Nobilianus.

To appeal to their god for a consort for their son and heir, Vortin has arranged the sacrifice of a girl baby at the great Midsummer festival. The sacrifice will take place at the temple in the wood dedicated to the goddess Shubinata, wife of Ashuba.

Trifena's baby, Bron, is born at the exact moment of the sacrifice, and Vortin claims her as his daughter, consort for his son, and demands she will enter Temple life at the age of three.

For nine years, Bron is trained for her priestly role by the priestesses, kindly Veneta and jealous Jeetuna, and the black schoolmaster, Africanus. Bron and Nobilianus detest each other but Vortin becomes obsessed with her so is not concerned when High Priestess, Iraina, mysteriously vanishes in the wood.

Bron's parents intend to buy her back from the Temple when she reaches adulthood at the age of twelve. To prevent this, Vortin arranges for their house and pottery business to be burnt down, impoverishing them. However, surprisingly, they present him with a valuable amber and pearl necklace as her purchase price.

Thwarted, on the day she is due to leave the Temple, Vortin conceals Bron in a cellar below his house and rapes her moments before she becomes twelve, so breaking Temple law. She is rescued by her father and Pulcher, a neighbour and dwarf. Bron becomes pregnant.

An attemped abortion by Umbella is not successful, and when Vortin learns of her predicament, to hide his duplicity, he decrees that she should marry. Her childhood friend, Soranus, is chosen as her husband. Vortin intends that Bron and their baby will enter the Temple, she as his High Priestess, once the child is three years old.

At her marriage ceremony, Bron comes face to face with her natural father, Adrianus Maximus Brontius, her mother's late master. Bron is dumbfounded but the likeness between father and daughter is irrefutable. It was he who had given her mother the necklace on learning that she was expecting Bron.

Vortin has by now returned the necklace among other wedding gifts, indicating that he has bought Bron back for himself. The gifts were accompanied by a love letter, which Bron tears up but which her mother saves.

Adrianus Maximus takes Bron on a sightseeing visit to Calleva Atrebatum, south of Byden, where he introduces her to a legionary, 18-year-old, handsome Aurelius Catus, whom he asks to oversee her welfare when the young man returns from military duty abroad.

Bron's life is played out against a background of dramatic events in Byden, including rape, murder, theft and plague, which killed three of Bron's Temple friends while she was being kept safe in a cell in the wood. She also witnessed secret sexual activity between Sharma, a priest, and Brocchus, who posed as a eunuch.

On a happier note, a pilgrim arrives to tell the villagers about the new Christian faith, and Soranus accepts an offer from Attryde, a widow, to become an apprentice in her smithy.

At the end of Part I, Bron is left awaiting the unwanted birth of Vortin's baby.

Now read on…

Prologue

Byden, AD 398 – A February Afternoon

Trifena couldn't explain, even to herself, why she felt so restless and, now that she was out in the wood, why so nervous? Her stockings and leather shoes were already saturated and she lifted the hem of her thick woollen cloak away from the oozing mud. Drops of February rain slid along bare branches and dribbled down her neck, making her shiver.

She sniffed, detecting a faint malodour among the misty trees and tried to recall where she had come across that smell before. It was not until she sensed movement among the tangle of undergrowth and raised her eyes from the mud that she remembered.

"Umbella?"

The hag materialised through the grey veil that hung between the trees and stood as she had, thirteen years ago, blocking the path. As usual, she was swathed shapelessly in black, her straggling grey hair, wrinkled face and scrawny body hidden beneath the folds of cloth, only her piercing dark eyes visible, but they were penetrating Trifena's soul.

"So, Trifena, our paths cross yet again," she croaked. "How is Bron?"

"My daughter is well – no thanks to you!" Trifena accused her.

"I did what you asked, but there was a power greater than mine at work that day," countered the hag. "Didn't you feel it?"

"All I felt was the pain you caused her with your clumsy attempt at abortion!"

"I wasn't the cause, as you well know. It was Vortin's lust and Vortin's pain." The old woman cackled. "Our venerated High Priest wants Bron, and Ashuba, our great sun god, wants that baby, Vortin's heir. She might as well get used to the idea."

"Bron's married now."

"I know. But do you think that will make any difference?"

Trifena was nonplussed. "Thirteen years ago, you told me –"

" 'Sword, fire and total destruction' – I remember. What of it?"

"Your prophecy hasn't come true."

"How impatient you are for catastrophe! My prophecy *will* be fulfilled, make no mistake – but not yet. There are other fires to burn first."

"What other fires?" Trifena asked.

"Fires will rage where they should never have been lit. Your daughter –"

"Bron?"

"You have two daughters," Umbella reminded her.

"Trifosa is still only a child."

"Children grow up. You should inflict more discipline on that one. And what flames burn in your heart, my fine lady?"

Trifena's cheeks flared. "They are quenched!"

"Spent fires can be rekindled," Umbella cackled with relish, now in full flow. "Soranus, your son-in-law –"

"What about him? He's a good boy."

"When Bron burns, that handsome young blacksmith husband of hers will light more than one consuming fire in the forge."

"You speak nonsense. You talk in riddles. I'm going home."

"Go – but you will have cause to remember that old Umbella isn't as crazy as you'd like to believe. Go, Trifena, go, and enjoy your peace while it lasts because there is coming a time when you will burn… all of you… burn… burn ..."

Trifena turned and fled, her shoes slipping and sliding in the mud, her cloak flapping against her legs, the old woman's insane cackling reverberating round and round inside her head, the warning jangling in her ears, until she was dizzy.

That ugly old hag! That wicked old woman! Trifena was crying her thoughts out loud, but there was no one in the wood to hear her.

She slowed down a little when she reached Byden settlement, and before entering by way of the eastern ditch and boundary bank, tried to tidy her hair, pushing the bone hairpins back into its thick coils. Then she drew several deep breaths to calm her thoughts and steady her pounding heart.

Hurrying past the untidy huddle of round houses and on between the market place and the wide stone Temple steps, she reached home. Once inside, she discarded her wet clothing and flung herself down on the mattress and lay still, gazing up at the roof, watching smoke from the fire in the central hearth seeking a way out through the twisted branches and interwoven turfs.

Then she touched her still-burning cheeks with the tips of her fingers and recognised that the perspiration on her forehead had nothing to do with her flight through the wood. She knew, and Umbella knew, that her own fire was the burning passion she had nursed for Bron's father – a yearning she had at last succeeded in banishing from conscious thought.

She was determined to tell Hestig about her meeting with Umbella and all that the hag had said – at least, most of it, perhaps not quite all.

Until he came home from his pottery stall in the market place, she would fill her time by walking down the hill to call on Bron, and make sure she was all right.

There was still a month to go before the birth of her baby. Vortin was delighted at the prospect and had assured the family that their god, Ashuba, was also very pleased.

So, until the baby reached three years old, there was nothing to fear…

Section IV

SORANUS

CHAPTER 1

AD 398 – March

Bron was screaming when she woke, dark eyes wide with fear and her long black hair, falling over her neck and shoulders, damp with perspiration.

Her waters had just broken and were saturating the cover of their mattress. Soranus shouted in panic for his mother, but she was already there in the doorway.

"Hush, hush, dear." Campania crouched by her daughter-in-law, stroking her cheek. "All is well."

Bron clung to her. "I'm so afraid," she whispered.

"Son, go and fetch Stalwyn!" Campania ordered him.

Soranus looked relieved at being given something to do and ran from the little round house to make his way across the market place towards the eastern edge of the settlement, where Byden's midwife lived.

"She'll be here soon, Bron. Just lie still. You must lie still. Vortin will wreak havoc on us if anything bad happens to you and his baby."

At that hated name, Bron began to cry and whimpered that she wanted her mother.

"Your mother will come as soon as your labour begins. In the meantime, can you make do with me?"

"Don't go away! Please, don't go away!"

"I'm here for as long as you need me," Campania reassured her.

Bron drew comfort from the arms around her and the shared, though unspoken, loathing for their High Priest, her baby's father.

Soranus soon returned with Stalwyn, who advised Bron to spend a quiet day about the house.

"I'll come back when your contractions start in earnest," she promised.

The storm began early evening. They could hear a low rumble of thunder in the distance and saw faint flashes of lightning in the sky to the north, above the hill on which the settlement stood. Bron's labour started at about the same time.

"But it's not a pain," she explained to her mother-in-law. "It's like the heavy monthly ache coming and going."

"Good," smiled Campania and sent Soranus to Stalwyn again, and to Bron's mother, with news that her labour had begun.

Bron stood in awe at the open doorway as thunder sped through seething black clouds, ever closer and louder. It brought with it lightning, intermittent at first but then almost continuous – great swathes of blue-white light, which washed the sky from east to west revealing, as if by daylight, flashed views of the settlement with the great white Temple dominating the brow of the hill. These sheets of light sometimes gave way to jagged streaks, great luminous branches, joining sky to earth. Then the overawing display was washed out by a curtain of rain that turned the beaten paths into quagmires.

Bron's mother, Trifena, arrived and Soranus was sent from the house to keep Bron's father company. However, Pulcher called not long afterwards to say that he had found Soranus wandering the paths near the house. The lad was drenched to the skin so Pulcher had taken him home, where he now was, drying off.

Pulcher would have lingered but was also sent away.

As the storm grew in intensity, so did Bron's pains. The three women took turns to sit with her, calming her and wiping the perspiration from her face as she lay on the pile of covers that had replaced the soiled mattress. They passed the hours by timing her contractions, just as they counted the pause between the lightning display and crash of thunder.

As it was a first pregnancy, Stalwyn said she didn't think anything would happen until morning and was surprised when the pains surged progressively stronger, became more frequent and lasted longer, until they exhausted Bron without remission. Stalwyn said it was time to sit her in the birthing chair. In a short interval between two strong contractions, they helped her into the seat. It was the chair in which all Trifena's babies had been born, including Bron herself.

She was now in great distress, crying over and over, "I don't want this baby! I hate this baby!"

Trifena cradled her daughter in her arms. "There's nothing you can do about it, Bron. The baby will come whether you want it or not."

"But I don't know what to do!" she wailed.

Stalwyn smiled as she sat down on the stool in front of her. "Your head may not know, Bron, but your body does. Relax and let yourself be carried along in the flood tide. It's the most natural happening in the world for a woman and you'll be fine."

Campania moved to the back of the chair, ready to clasp her arms round and under her daughter-in-law's armpits – a restraint during Bron's final exertions.

Just before midnight there was one explosive clap of thunder directly above the thatched roof, which made them all jump, and at that moment Stalwyn pulled Bron's baby into the world – a healthy boy.

"And considering his mother's age, he looks a good weight," she pronounced as she cut the umbilical cord with a sharp knife.

Trifena, too tearful to answer, drew her young daughter's head to her breast.

"I'm so proud of you," she whispered.

Campania peeped at her grandson in Stalwyn's arms, smiled broadly, then hurried out into the rain, which had eased off a little, to call at Pulcher's house next door and tell Soranus the good news.

Bron's brother, Hestigys, who was lodging next door with Pulcher, breathed a loud sigh of relief.

"I'm certainly glad that's over!" he said. "Soranus and Pulcher have been pacing the room like a couple of demented beings – you'd never know that neither of them was the father!"

Campania shivered. "I suppose somebody had better inform Vortin," she said.

"Can't that wait till morning?" asked Soranus. "There's time enough to upset everyone."

There was no need to inform Vortin, however, because as Campania came back down the hill, having given Bron's father and sister the good news, she was startled to come face to face with Brocchus. Dressed all in black, as sinister as always, he was lurking in the shadows, but a dull glimmer of lightning revealed his hiding place.

"Well," he asked, "what is it?"

"A boy," replied Campania, "and healthy."

"Vortin *will* be pleased," he said and slunk back into the shadows.

"How on earth did Vortin know?" Campania wondered when she was once more inside the house.

"Vortin knows everything," mumbled Bron, who had been washed and was back in bed. "He doesn't need to be told."

Stalwyn had cleaned the baby briefly and swaddled him, as was the custom. Campania bent over the cot. "He's a little beauty," she enthused.

"But Bron won't look at him," Trifena whispered, "though she'll have to soon because he'll need feeding."

Bron overheard their whispers. "I won't feed him!" she said. "He can die, for all I care. All he's done is cause me a lot of pain and misery."

Trifena gazed at her daughter, looking completely helpless. "But none of it's his fault, Bron," she reasoned, but Bron was adamant.

"All I can do is offer you a wet-nurse," Stalwyn told Trifena.

By now, the menfolk and Bron's younger sister had arrived. They peeped at the new member of the family, but no one, not even Soranus, seemed to know what to say to Bron in the face of her obdurate rebellion, and they stood around uncomfortably.

"Don't all look at me like that!" she complained bitterly and retreated under the covers, pulling them over her head so that she couldn't hear their whispered concerns.

Several minutes passed, and when she decided to emerge, only Pulcher was in the room, waiting patiently till she was ready to look at him. When she did, he came and sat down awkwardly beside her and took her hand in his.

Gently, he told her about his own childhood, of how much he loved his parents, especially his mother, but of their disappointment and embarrassment at his freakish appearance; how he had always tried to please them but never could; and how, when he was eight years old, they had crept away during the night and left him to fend for himself, not caring whether he lived or died.

"But not my fault, Bron, not my fault," he said over and over again, remembrance of the pain sending tears running down his weathered cheeks.

Bron touched his face and wiped the tears away with her fingers. He caught hold of her hand again and held it against his cheek.

"Bron, I love you," he said fervently, "always have, always will. I die for you."

"I know," she said, bending her head towards him, so that their foreheads touched and her tears were mingling with his on their hands.

Eventually he put her hand back on the coverlet. "No child suffer," he said simply.

She lowered her head and nodded. He went across to the cot and picked up the bundle as gently as his clumsy hands could manage, and laid it in her arms.

For a moment, Bron still did not look at her son, only at Pulcher.

When she did finally gaze down at the baby lying there so peacefully, his new blue eyes now wide open, she was taken completely by surprise at the sudden rush of maternal love that surged through her like a strong autumnal wind blowing everything dead before it. She didn't notice Pulcher creep from the room nor the family come back, but when she did realise they were there and glanced up, the radiant look on her face told them everything.

"I'm going to call him Storm," she said happily. "He was conceived by storm and was born in one."

Looking at her then, Soranus was consumed by jealousy, thinking of the pillow they had agreed to place between them each night until her body was purged of Vortin's seed. He resolved to take it away as soon as Bron was ready. Then he would give her a baby of their own.

However, when she held her son out to him and he took him awkwardly into his arms, neither could *he* find any quarrel with the new member of their family, and resolved only to do his best for the boy until it was time to give him up to the Temple at three years old, as the High Priest had decreed.

He pushed to the back of his mind the thought that, when the child went, Vortin intended that Bron should accompany him.

CHAPTER 2

Next day, Jeetuna arrived from the Temple with Vortin's gifts. The priestess had recently taken to bedecking her beautiful face and body and golden hair with flamboyant jewellery, which she must have decided befitted her position as the intimate companion of the High Priest. However, Bron was vaguely aware that, by sending Jeetuna with the gifts, he was using her as an errand boy and putting her firmly back in her place.

Bron began to unwrap the first of the two sealed packages. Hearing a noise, a slight choking sound, she looked up. Jeetuna quickly turned her head away, but not before Bron had seen the venomous look in her eyes, accentuated by the charcoal-blackened lashes and eyelids. Bron was shocked and returned quickly to her task.

For the new mother there was a heavy gold ring decorated with a motif of clasped hands. Bron removed her plain iron wedding ring, which had been her mother-in-law's and had now been made smaller to fit her finger, and tried on Vortin's ring. The size was exactly right and it looked magnificent. Suddenly, aware of the implication, Bron snatched if off and replaced the ring Soranus had given her.

For Storm's neck, there was a small torque, a sign of authority, created from twisted gold strands with hollow finials that each contained a gold nugget that rattled when shaken.

To Bron, the implications were obvious. Vortin was admitting in private that he was the father of this baby. The ring was a betrothal ring, leaving no doubt about his intentions towards herself. So what was supposed to happen to Soranus, her young husband?

And where did that leave Jeetuna? The priestess must be writhing inwardly at the thought that one day Bron might usurp her place in Vortin's bed. She could not guess that Bron had no intention of doing so.

When Jeetuna had gone, Trifena bundled up the gifts and said she was taking them home to join the others hidden under her mattress. Vortin had started sending presents to Bron as soon as he had learned about her pregnancy and the ineffective attempt at abortion she had suffered at the hands of Umbella.

Bron knew that she would have to present Storm at the Temple when he was eight days old, and there was no way she could avoid it without bringing Vortin's wrath down on someone's head.

So, on the eighth day, family and friends left the house to attend the short ceremony.

Both assistant priests were also officiating and Sharma, the senior, had two young Temple boys running around him, obeying every word of command.

Vortin was grinning from ear to ear as he took their son from Bron's arms and looked down into the tiny, innocent face. Bron shuddered. Soranus put his arm round her waist and held on to her tightly. Her parents, Hestig and Trifena, closed in behind her while other members of their party formed a tight, protective semicircle around them.

"Well," Vortin said, still looking at his son, "I'm pleased to say he closely resembles his father."

Bron was indignant, but in all honesty could not deny it.

"But I hear," now looking insolently at Trifena, "he is one-quarter Roman. However, we won't hold that against him."

Bron saw her mother blush as she looked down at the mosaics on the Temple floor. Hestig gently took hold of his wife's hand.

Vortin raised the baby up towards the yellow stone figure of their great god, Ashuba, who towered behind the altar. He introduced his son by the name Bron had chosen, Storm.

Ashuba stood firm on parted shapeless legs with arms folded across his chest, blatant in his naked masculinity. Above jutting jaw, unsmiling mouth and thin nose, his eyes glowed ominously red. Bron and her mother had seen those eyes glow red on other occasions, and always it meant that Ashuba wanted something from them and was drawing them into his will.

"Mother, he is calling to me and Storm!" Bron whispered in agitation.

"Don't look at him!" Trifena instructed her daughter.

Vortin intoned the words of purification and dedication. He accepted the gift of four horseshoes made by Soranus in the forge, and handed the baby back to his mother, managing to fondle Bron's full breasts as he did so. She flushed bright red and turned on her heel and marched out of the Temple.

With the pillow that had separated them finally thrown across the room, Soranus and Bron began gently to experiment physically with each other's bodies, enjoying the deepening sensations being awakened, and by Bron's thirteenth birthday she knew she was pregnant again.

CHAPTER 3

AD 399 – January

Soranus came home to Bron with the news that Attryde, his employer, had left her job as a prostitute at the inn and was back again in her own house, opposite the forge.

"She obviously thinks Soranus is making a success of the smithy," Hestig said to his wife.

"And he is trying so hard to be a good husband and caring stepfather to Storm," Trifena commented. "He and Bron certainly seem to be very happy."

"Even I can see that," agreed Hestig.

Trifena would have been a little less complacent if she had been aware of a small incident that had occurred a few days previously.

It was January, grey, cold and wet. Bron, eight months pregnant, was standing in her doorway, gazing down the slope towards Pulcher's house, waiting for him to bring Storm home after they had spent part of the afternoon together, when she saw a rider galloping down the opposite hill toward the ford, his cloak flying out behind him.

Even from that distance, it was obvious by his authoritative bearing and dress that this was a Roman, and she was taken quite unawares by the sharp thrill in the lower part of her abdomen. Her thoughts flew to the inn in Calleva Atrebatum where her father had introduced her to Aurelius Catus and had given the young man a scrolled letter of recommendation to ease his way up through the junior ranks. Bron remembered how the torches high up on the walls danced golden highlights among the legionary's dark blonde curls.

Her father has asked Aurelius to keep an eye on her when he returned after an imminent tour of duty in Gaul, and Aurelius had readily agreed. She hadn't seen him since that meeting, fifteen months ago.

It was soon obvious that the horseman was not Aurelius Catus, and the sharp pain subsided. She wondered whether he was still alive and prayed to Shubinata, their goddess, for his safekeeping. The memory of the griping sensation and her surprise stayed with her for several days afterwards.

The rider was, in fact, Julius Gaius, recently appointed a decurion of the ordo, the governing council of Calleva. He had been to Byden before and was now visiting during the winter, to make sure that building a country house there was what he and his wife and daughter really wanted to do. At present, they had all settled in Calleva.

During the following month, February, Bron gave birth to a daughter, Layla, and then was too tired to think of anything other than establishing a feeding routine, changing napkins, coping with baby colic and trying to get sufficient sleep.

Trifena watched with pride as her husband, Hestig, began to build up his pottery business again after the devastating fire that had destroyed their home and most of his stock. His determination to succeed was earning increased respect from the people and confirming his position as leader of the settlement's council.

By the end of the midwinter festival of Unvala, he had saved sufficient capital for Trifena to come to him with a request.

"Trifosa would really like to go back to school, Hestig, until next October, when she's twelve."

He agreed to ask permission for this to happen, his request was granted, and it was not long before Trifosa was again enjoying her days at the round school house under the tutelage of Africanus, a big man with a heart to match, assisted by priestess Veneta.

Late one afternoon, as Trifena was on her way back from the Stan stream with a basket full of washed clothes, her younger daughter came running towards her in a panic and flung herself into her mother's arms.

"Whatever's the matter?" asked Trifena in alarm, trying to put the basket down and hold on to Trifosa at the same time.

"It's Nobilianus!"

Trifena looked up, and saw the boy lurking in the distance. He was now about seventeen years old, tall and strong.

"What about Nobilianus?" Trifena asked sharply.

"He's been following me to and from school every day."

"Why didn't you tell somebody, you silly girl?"

"Because he always kept far enough away, but today he came really close, and I got frightened."

After that, Trifena made sure her daughter was escorted to school by a member of the family or Pulcher, and was brought home by one of her teachers.

"I like Africanus with me best, as he makes me feel safe," Trifosa told her mother. "He's so big that Nobilianus stays further away, and I think Nobilianus is afraid of his black skin – but near or far, he's always around."

On the occasions when Africanus arrived at their door, Trifena invited him in, sometimes for a meal, during which she and her young daughter, and Bron if she was present with the children, listened wide-eyed to his stories.

Often Africanus would still be there when Hestig came home. The two men formed a close friendship and would spend hours in each other's company, discussing the affairs of the settlement and matters of wider concern.

It was peaceful in southern Britannia but news had filtered through of successful assaults on the great wall by Picts and Scots from the north and Saxons from the sea, and their subsequent domination of parts of the island.

As they went about their chores, Trifena and her young daughter overheard talk of their Roman masters, hard pressed on all borders of their empire.

"Who are these people, Father?" asked Trifosa. "Visigoths, Vandals and –" She paused.

"They're nothing to worry your head about, we're safe here," Trifena was quick to reassure her.

"Burgundians," Hestig said. "They're barbarians all, and they're sweeping south towards Rome, and more and more troops are being withdrawn from Britannia to fight them."

"The end of Roman rule in Britannia is in sight," stated Africanus. "Perhaps not this year or next, but certainly within a decade."

"Do you really believe that?" asked Trifena.

"Sadly, yes, I do."

Hestig was thoughtful. "Then what will happen to Britannia, to us?" he asked. "What will become of us when the legions leave?"

"If we aren't careful, we will enter a dark age of our own making," replied the African. "That is why it is so important to teach the children."

By the beginning of June, with Bron's fourteenth birthday approaching, Soranus learned from her that she was pregnant yet again with her third child. Running after Storm, who was now toddling about, trying to feed Layla, and coping with nausea and exhaustion, she became very depressed. On many mornings, he went to the forge, leaving her crying.

"I don't know what to do to help you," he agonised.

Often, he came home to an empty house, with no meal cooking for him, and discovered that Bron had taken the children to Trifena's for the day, or had been wandering round the settlement, gossiping with anyone who would stop to talk to her. Not even Pulcher could cheer her up.

Soranus spoke to his mother-in-law about his concerns and Trifena sent her daughter to Stalwyn, who gave her a tincture of St. John's wort to cure her melancholy. Campania suggested to her son that Bron was too young to have a baby every year and sent him off to Kendrus, the settlement's doctor, for advice.

Nobilianus had begun to frequent the inn and consort with the prostitutes there, although Temple law forbade it. Priestess Jeetuna guessed this was due to frustration caused by his inability to get anywhere near Trifosa. Whatever the reason, he had become a byword for perversion and the girls dreaded his visits, although the innkeeper did not feel able to complain until a serious incident forced her to speak to Jeetuna.

"Last week, one of my girls was so badly beaten and cut about that she almost died," she informed her. "I had to call in Stalwyn yet again and she said this can't go on. So I've decided it's time to ask you to plead with Vortin to do something about his son."

Having seen the interest Vortin was taking in Bron's son, Storm, Jeetuna believed that Nobilianus now had little chance of inheriting the High Priesthood, and it was time she withdrew her pretence of friendship and loyalty to him.

She spoke to Sharma, who she knew had priestly ambitions far in excess of any he should have allowed himself, and between them they cunningly devised a plan to rid themselves of both of Vortin's sons. Accordingly, Sharma did as the innkeeper asked and reported Nobilianus to his father.

That evening, when there were no worshippers in the Temple, the High Priest called his son to his office. Jeetuna hung about outside the closed door, trying to hear what was being said. Vortin's voice was thick with disgust.

"I suppose you've spent another night and day drinking and carousing at the inn! Just look at the state of you!"

They argued loudly for five minutes, then Vortin lowered his voice. Jeetuna strained her ears to hear.

"You will never succeed me as High Priest – I've made sure of that. I don't care about that girl you nearly killed, but neither you nor any of your bastard children will lord it here."

Nobilianus sounded beside himself with anger. "Yes, you've made sure. Don't tell me that Storm is the son of that convenient marriage – I know who the baby looks like, and it isn't Soranus!"

"You *are* observant, my son!" Vortin's sarcasm cut into the tirade and Jeetuna could imagine the self-satisfied smirk on his face.

"I thought it was strange the way you fell down the steps and broke your jaw at the Midsummer Festival two years ago," Nobilianus continued, hardly pausing to take breath. "You took her then, didn't you, your young priestess-in-training, after she had been bought back from the Temple by her parents, and before she had reached twelve years of age? You broke Temple law on both counts and someone beat you up for it! My guess is, it was her father and that monstrosity, Pulcher, who she's so fond of –"

"Prove it!" challenged Vortin. "From now on, you do not exist as my son! Storm will be renamed Nobilianus, and as soon as he is three years old, he will enter the Temple in your place, and his mother with him! Now get out of here!"

Jeetuna guessed that Nobilianus had not moved, because a moment later, the door was flung open and Vortin appeared. He was pinning the right arm of Nobilianus behind his back and grasping the boy's left ear with his other hand. He frog-marched his son into the corridor, gave him a push then banged the door shut.

Nobilianus could not speak because of his humiliation and rage, and when he began blubbering like a baby, Jeetuna took his hand and led him behind a cluster of pillars and pulled him down beside her on to the cold stone floor. She put her arms round him, hushing him and rocking him like a baby.

He was soon aroused and she let him fondle her intimately while she whispered to him about the threat that Bron and her baby posed. That baby was obviously Vortin's son, half brother to Nobilianus, and was going to usurp the office of High Priesthood unless Nobilianus did something about it. She insinuated ideas into his head, as Sharma had instructed her, which became inextricably woven into his passion.

"You won't forget what we've planned, will you, when morning comes?" she wheedled. "Just keep reminding yourself – he stands in your way, and without Storm, Bron has no place here, either."

"Yes, I'll remember," Nobilianus promised. "But now I have other things on my mind."

Jeetuna reproached him. "No, Nobilianus, take your hands away! Not now, not here!"

Sharma had been lurking near and appeared opportunely with a full goblet. Teasing the boy's mouth open with her tongue, she managed to pour the liquid down her would-be lover's throat and he soon passed out. Together they carried him to his room and laid him on his bed.

"In the morning, he won't remember whether he took you or not," said Sharma with a grin. "You can tell him he did, against Vortin's instructions to keep his hands off the priestesses. That will make him feel like a man! Then, hopefully, he will do what he promised. That way, we should be able to dispose of both heirs – the baby and this disgusting creature."

"I'll ask one of the girls to clean him up," said Jeetuna. The Temple prostitutes on the second floor loathed Nobilianus as much as the village girls in the inn.

"Make sure she doesn't accidentally strangle him while she's doing it!"

The conspirators left the room, laughing together at the joke.

It was not long before Bron realised that, inexplicably, Nobilianus was shadowing *her* and her children. It seemed that, wherever she went, Nobilianus was never very far away. For a while it unnerved and further depressed her, but she gradually became used to it, attributed it to his crazy ways, and felt safe as long as she was within sight of one of the family or Pulcher.

Now that he could walk and was into every kind of mischief, Storm had to be watched constantly to make sure he didn't roam too far and come to harm.

He resembled Bron very little, being much lighter in colour and complexion, though with very dark eyes. Some people, not perceiving any likeness to her, imagined and commented how much he favoured his father, meaning Soranus, but Bron saw only Vortin in him – in his expressions, in the way he sometimes held his head or used his slender baby fingers. She wished it were not so, but couldn't deny it.

She was worried about his future, mapped out for him by his father – the Temple at three years old, to be trained as she had been. It was also Vortin's intention to take her for his High Priestess. Perhaps she could submit to this degradation if it meant she could stay near her son, but she knew that she would be allowed no input in his upbringing from that point onwards, and that they would grow apart and he would probably become as maladjusted and as full of loathsome excesses as Nobilianus.

Of course, if Nobilianus realised the truth of Storm's parentage, and perhaps he knew it already, he would be a constant threat to her son, who for evermore would stand in the way of that young man's accession to the highest office in the Temple, with all its attendant luxuries.

And what would happen to Soranus, who loved them so, if they were taken from him? And would Vortin allow her to take Layla with her, as well as the baby she was now carrying? The future looked black for all of them.

In the meantime, Storm had to be watched and protected.

However, in spite of her care, one afternoon the toddler went missing. He had been playing in the dirt outside Pulcher's house one minute and the next he had disappeared.

"Bron, I swear, left him seconds," Pulcher told her. "Seconds, only seconds."

They searched the pathways in the vicinity without success, then Bron took Layla to her mother while Pulcher ran to fetch her father and brother from their pottery stall and Soranus from the forge. They all scoured the settlement, anxiety increasing. There was no sign of the toddler. Bron was wild-eyed with fear.

Someone said he thought he had seen Storm by the sheep pens, but that proved a fruitless search. Then the beekeeper's wife said he had been playing down by the Stan. Bron flew down to the stepping-stones, Soranus following her, but there was no sign of him there, either.

She began to sob, with Soranus trying to comfort her, when he looked down and saw Storm's sandal in the clear water. The men scattered in all directions, while the beekeeper's wife stayed with Bron.

After about ten minutes, her companion cried with relief, "Look, Bron, look! They've found him! Hestigys is carrying him home!"

In the distance, Bron saw her brother walking down the grassy slope towards her, Storm sitting astride his shoulders, chattering non-stop in his baby language, with Pulcher hobbling along beside them.

She splashed across the stream, through the tall wild grasses and flowers along its edge, and ran up the slope. As she drew near, Storm held out his little hands, reaching towards his mother. Bron flung her arms round both of them, sobbing and laughing at the same time. Then she took Storm from her brother and hugged him tightly to her.

"Where?" she asked.

"He was playing up at the mere," said Hestigys.

"On his own?" asked Bron.

"Yes, right by the water, so near he could have toppled in."

Hestigys went off to tell Soranus and the other searchers that the toddler had been found, while Pulcher escorted the beekeeper's wife, Storm and his mother home.

"How could he have got there?" Bron wondered. "He couldn't have walked all that way on his own, and so quickly."

"Bron," said Pulcher, anxiety deep in his voice, "Nobilianus."

A chill ran down Bron's spine and her breathing became shallow and fast. "Where?" she asked.

"Among trees."

"Are you sure, Pulcher?"

"Certain sure," he said.

CHAPTER 4

Bron happily settled down for a couple of days but it was not long before her depression took hold again, and her increased fear of Nobilianus plunged her into deeper gloom, though he now seemed to be keeping out of her way.

The same could not be said for Vortin. She had not been taking Storm to the Temple and, if he desired to see more of his son, his only option was to come down into the settlement. He took to walking about near her home or in the market place or anywhere else where she and Storm might be. At first he found excuses to be wherever they met, but soon abandoned that pretext.

"He's neglecting his duties," Sharma complained to Jeetuna one morning. "He's never here."

"We all know where he is, of course –" she replied, looking at the priest with her big dark-blue eyes, "– mooning around Bron and that baby of theirs."

"That stupid Nobilianus fouled up again," he said. "One would think it was quite a simple matter to abduct a baby and –" He did not finish his sentence, but added, "Brocchus would have done the job properly."

"But it's Nobilianus we want accused and out of the way, not Brocchus," Jeetuna reminded him.

"It's a dangerous game we're playing, my beautiful Jeetuna," mused Sharma, "and we must be very careful."

"It just needs a little patience," she said. "In the meantime, Vortin's down there and you're up here taking over his duties – which you are doing with great distinction, may I add – and people will begin to notice."

"And meantime, you're still playing the field," he laughed.

"You can't blame a girl," Jeetuna smiled back. "We have to do the best we can in a world run by men."

"Not a girl any longer," Sharma reminded her unkindly. "You're forty now, my sweet."

Her smile faded, but to get her own back, she snuggled her body hard against his, and feeling the response she wanted from him, laughed and drew away. Now the teasing changed direction.

"Jeetuna," he said, reaching for her.

"Not in the Temple," she scolded him. "You haven't yet acquired the discipline of Vortin, my dear," and with that she turned and left him.

One evening, Soranus answered a knock at the door.

"Veneta's come to see you," he announced to Bron, and ushered the priestess inside. "I'll be at Pulcher's if you need me." He left quickly.

Bron held out her hands in welcome.

"He's anxious about you," Veneta said, her brown eyes large with concern, "and asked me to call."

"Bless him, he's quite out of his depth with my problems," Bron answered, with only the hint of a smile. She was reassured by the familiar music of Veneta's voice, which her mother always said reminded her of a warm summer afternoon.

They talked together for a long time, the priestess trying to find out what troubled Bron and to give her all the comfort she could.

Then, to give Bron something to think about other than her depression, she told her that she and Selvid, Temple priest, had just returned from a few days spent in Calleva, both on Temple business. Selvid had accompanied the wagons carrying the settlement's taxes – corn and cash. He was trusted to hand this over in the basilica to Tebicatos, a civil servant and member of the local Irish community, then explain both sets of accounts in minute detail. This had been scheduled to take two or three days.

Veneta was accompanying one of the girls the Temple had sold. She had passed her twelfth birthday many months previously and had been bought by one of the brothels in Calleva, but the money had not been forthcoming. Sharma had run short of patience and had instructed Veneta to deliver her and sit in the brothel until she had collected the promised payment.

"Poor Victorina," sympathised Bron, who knew the girl very well. "During my visit to Calleva, I saw the prostitutes walking up and down outside that particular brothel."

"I know you can keep a secret, Bron," said Veneta. Bron nodded. "I found Asher, the pilgrim who once came to Byden to preach his gospel, and he took Victorina and me to the home of one of the Christian women, Chrystella –"

"I know Chrystella," interrupted Bron. "She was a good friend to me when I visited Calleva with my father. How is she?"

"Very well," said Veneta. "She took us in overnight while arrangements were made."

"Arrangements for what?" asked Bron.

"Asher knew a woman who was looking for a nanny and tutor for her two young daughters and was willing to pay the same amount as the brothel offered."

"So she is safe?" queried Bron.

"Thankfully, yes," replied Veneta, "it all worked out very happily."

"I'm glad," said Bron. "She will be a very good friend to the children, I'm sure."

"You've heard one secret, my dear. Can you keep another two? I'm bursting to tell someone I can trust." Bron nodded again, intrigued.

"It's a matter of life and death, Bron, you understand," warned Veneta.

"Yes," said Bron, eyes wide. She seemed to have forgotten her own troubles for the moment.

"Selvid was staying with one of the Roman officials but came to Chrystella's for supper on the first evening. Asher was also there, with a few more friends, and we talked far into the night."

"About their Christian faith?" queried Bron.

Veneta nodded. "As you know, Selvid and I have been thinking

40

seriously about it since Asher's first visit to Byden and later during our secret meetings with him in the wood. We are increasingly disillusioned about what's happening at the Temple – most of which you know, but not all –"

"You mean what I watched them doing in the wood – Sharma and Brocchus?"

Veneta nodded. "Brocchus, the eunuch who is not a eunuch, so you tell us. And the rest – the disappearance of our High Priestess, for instance. So much intrigue! But the Christians provide what we need."

"And what is that?" asked Trifena. She had come into the house quietly, unnoticed.

"A god of love," Veneta replied. "A god who does not demand human sacrifice, or any blood – except his own – who does not want us to fear him, who makes no threats –"

She looked through the open, unglazed window, and their eyes followed hers. The wickerwork god still towered above the settlement from his position beside the Temple wall, a constant reminder of the power Vortin wielded over any miscreants in the settlement who disobeyed him, which he maintained was the same thing as disobeying their great god, Ashuba.

"A god of love?" asked Trifena. "But what does that mean? It's only words."

"No," answered Veneta, "it's more than words," and she recounted all that Asher and Chrystella believed about Jesus, who had been God walking the earth, and who had affronted the authorities, which eventually led to his torture and death.

"But there have been many martyrs since the world began," argued Trifena.

"Maybe, but Jesus suffered instead of us. Our wickedness causes death – but his, not ours."

"But what are his rules?" asked Bron who, having been brought up in the Temple, knew there were lists and lists of rules and regulations to follow.

"Only two," said Veneta, "and you've heard them before – love God and love your neighbour."

"Sounds too easy," commented Trifena.

"It's not," smiled Veneta. "It's the most difficult task in the world. Could you love Vortin?"

"Of course not!"

"There you go," smiled Veneta. "I said it was hard."

At that moment there was a knock at the door and Bron opened it. Selvid stood there.

"Are you looking for Veneta?" Bron asked him. "She's here."

"Vortin's asking for you," Selvid explained as he came in.

"Is he angry?" asked Veneta.

"No, not when I told him where you were. Anything Bron needs she gets, as far as he's concerned."

"I was just telling them what happened at Calleva," said Veneta. Selvid looked surprised.

"It's all right, Selvid – our secrets are safe here."

"But you haven't told us what they are yet," Bron reminded her impatiently. "You said there were two more."

"We thought long and hard about it, and we decided –" Veneta paused.

"We decided," continued Selvid, "to be baptised into the Christian faith. We are now both Christians!"

Bron and Trifena gasped simultaneously.

"Early in the morning, after that supper I told you about, we were baptised at the font in the courtyard in front of the Christian church," explained Veneta, "and we're both so happy about it! We know it was the right thing to do. But that's not all." She smiled at Selvid and went close to him and took hold of his hand. "That afternoon their priest married us. We took our vows before the Christian altar, with Chrystella and Asher as witnesses."

Bron stared at them and Trifena sat down hard in the nearest chair and looked from one to the other.

"Married?" she repeated, stupefied. "But priests and priestesses can't marry. It's against Temple law."

"We're not bound by Temple law any more," said Veneta quietly, "only our God's law, and by that we are now husband and wife."

"Our honeymoon was short," smiled Selvid. "Chrystella gave us her home for the night, then we had to come back to Byden."

He drew Veneta close to his side and put his arm around her waist.

"But you are still working at the Temple," argued Bron.

"For now," said Veneta. "We may be able to curb some of the excesses going on up there if we stay. We can also keep our eyes out for any further danger threatening Storm. But their evil time is running out and when God wants us to make a move, we will be there waiting and ready."

Lying in bed later, first having asked their permission, Bron told Soranus all that Veneta and Selvid had confided that evening.

She expressed a wish of her own, and he gave his consent, not because he understood what was happening, but because he hoped that getting her own way would help lift her dark mood.

One evening a week later, Asher slipped into the settlement without attracting attention and disappeared into Campania's house. Next morning, with the whole family and a few trusted friends present, and Veneta and Selvid as witnesses, Storm and baby Layla were baptised into the Christian faith. Bron hadn't yet reached the stage when she could commit herself.

CHAPTER 5

Jeetuna was inspecting the heavy hangings around the altar in preparation for the Midsummer Festival, to be celebrated a few days later. Vortin had allowed the settlement's orgy to continue but had never reinstated the impregnation ritual on the altar slab since the mysterious disappearance of his High Priestess.

Jeetuna thought about that disappearance and wondered yet again what had happened to Iraina, who had gone into the wood to prepare for the festival and had disappeared into thin air. No amount of searching had found her. However, Vortin seemed not to care any more.

Each year, Jeetuna hoped that he would bring her to the altar slab but it had never happened due, she realised, to the strength of his growing obsession with Bron. He had long ago abandoned all pretence of marrying that girl to his son. Jeetuna knew he was waiting till Storm was three years old, when he could bring him and his mother to the Temple and install Bron in Iraina's place.

The priestess writhed with resentment and jealousy at the thought of Bron in authority over her, but didn't know what to do about it. Vortin seemed impervious to all her seductive wiles and she had no trump card to play, as Bron had with their son. She knew she was losing her looks to middle age, whereas her rival was only now entering full womanhood.

True, Bron had never been seen wearing the gold betrothal ring Vortin had sent her, preferring to wear the cheap and nasty iron ring given by Soranus. The one slight hope was that the girl's hatred of Vortin would lead her to take some disastrous action that would cast her out of his favour.

That Midsummer night, Bron was alone in the house with the children. Soranus and her brother were out late roaming round the settlement, assuring her that they would not be taking part in any sexual activity, but just enjoying the drink and the spectacle.

Pulcher had joined them, although he was not feeling at all well. He said the clamour of his voices was giving him a headache. Pulcher often heard his voices. However, tonight he could not understand what they were trying to tell him, though Bron knew.

"I wish I had listened more carefully," he confessed afterwards.

Dawn was approaching, at which time Bron would become fourteen years old. She had been sitting by the side of Storm's cot for over an hour, watching him sleeping peacefully, her hands folded on the pillow on her lap.

She thought at that moment that she loved her son more than anyone or anything else in the world. It was because she loved him so much that she had to do what she had planned, to keep him from being corrupted, to protect the rest of the family from pain, and to save her own sanity.

The night was hot and he had pushed his covers away. He was lying quite still on his back, his breathing shallow and slow, his plump baby arms stretched above his head, hands relaxed, a smile on his lips. She wondered if he were dreaming. His long lashes fringed the eyelids that were hiding his dark eyes – clones of Vortin's or hers? Both had those nearly black eyes.

Bron continued to watch his every unconscious movement as he stretched a leg or turned his head this way and that, sometimes almost awake, but then returning to the deep innocent sleep of his babyhood.

It was almost dawn. She remembered the storm of Vortin the night he raped her, exactly two years ago, and the thunder and lightning on the night their son was born, and she knew that, if he lived, there would be nothing but storm for all of them for evermore. She could not let him bear that responsibility, when none of it was his fault.

Picking up the pillow, she stood above him. She touched his face

45

lightly with the tips of her fingers, careful not to wake him, then bent down and kissed him – kissed him so much that she disturbed him and nearly lost her resolve.

Then she took the pillow in both hands, bent over him again and pressed it down hard against his face. There was only a faint struggle and then he lay still. She kept her weight on the pillow until she was sure there was no life left in him, then took it away and laid it on the floor.

At that moment dawn broke over the eastern hills, Bron became fourteen years old, and had she known it, Pulcher's voices silenced.

She brought her son's arms down to his sides. She fetched a flannel to wipe his face, a soft brush to smooth his hair, and changed his wet napkin. Lastly, she covered him gently with his lightweight cover. All that done, she sat in the chair to await the return of Soranus.

CHAPTER 6

While Bron looked on, they buried Storm in a grave dug by the front door. She would pass it every time she went in and out of the house.

Looking up towards the Temple as they lowered the little bundle into the hole, she saw Vortin watching from a distance, and turned her eyes back to the grave, anguish smothering her elation at being freed from his clutches.

That Vortin was suffering, she had no doubt. She had seen the look in his eyes – the astonishment, the pain, the grief – when Soranus had taken her to tell him that their son had died in his sleep during the night.

She could only guess his utter frustration when he realised that, not only had he lost the only perfect son he had sired, but once again he would have to rely on Nobilianus to succeed him, and worse, Bron was finally out of his reach.

She thought that no one would suspect her because everyone knew how much she had loved her baby son.

However, there was no chance of hiding the deed from her family, because Pulcher had finally understood his voices, which made plain her guilt. Appalled by what she had done, they watched her hour by hour, and for a while would not leave her alone with Layla. But her mood lightened daily, until the bouts of depression disappeared altogether, and eventually she began to enjoy her daughter and anticipate with confidence the birth of the next baby.

She was also more affectionate towards Soranus, and clung to him at night with a need she had never shown before.

"We're all safe from Vortin now," she whispered to him, "you and me, Layla and the baby inside me – untouchable – because of the death of my beloved Storm. He's safe, too."

"I love you, I love you," Soranus whispered to her over and over again, "and I'll never forget what you've done for us."

His work at the forge had improved with practice and gradually he built up the stock of kitchen utensils and household items, farm tools and equipment, horseshoes, nails and harness decorations, and his own design of personal adornments for both women and men.

Bron's pride increased as the people began to refer to him as "the young blacksmith", and she spent more time visiting him during the day, or worked in her kitchen, preparing dishes she knew he enjoyed.

In January AD 400 Alon was born to the young couple and their happiness seemed complete. He was baptised into the Christian faith by Veneta as soon as he opened his eyes, but Soranus insisted that he also be presented at the Temple at eight days, according to settlement custom.

Bron had abandoned all thought of becoming a Christian herself. Instead of trying to forgive Vortin, as Veneta had suggested she should, she rejoiced at his pain and humiliation. Often she caught sight of him loitering in places from which he could see his son's grave. He continued to follow her wherever she went. There were times when she blatantly ignored him and others when she stared him out then tossed her curls and turned her back.

One summer afternoon, she was crouched on the stepping-stones, collecting fresh water in a pitcher for their evening meal. The Midsummer Festival was approaching and, if Storm had still been alive, she would have been facing the ordeal of being forced to split the family and enter Temple life again.

Hearing a slight noise behind her, she turned.

"Vortin!" She gasped in alarm at his sudden appearance, hurriedly rising and ready to take flight.

"Bron, please don't run away! I only want to talk to you," he pleaded.

"I know what you want, and it's not talk!" she threw back at him.

She was nearly fifteen now, no longer a child but developing into a beautiful young woman. He made no attempt to hide his raging desire for her as his eyes travelled from the curve of her hips to her narrow waist, and higher to the firm fullness of her milk-laden breasts. She blushed. He licked dry lips and his words came in short gasps.

"My life is cold and empty without you," he told her. "I can't concentrate, I can't sleep, I'm not eating. Sharma takes over my duties while I walk the settlement, hoping for a glimpse of you, a smile, a kind word. I feel less than a dog at your heels. Please, Bron, let me love you again."

"Love!" she cried scornfully. "You don't know what the word means! My parents love me. My children love me. Pulcher loves me and so does Soranus – every night. Do you hear that? While you are mooning about in the dark outside our house, Soranus and I are in bed, loving each other."

The hatred Bron felt for this man poisoned the barbs on her words and the High Priest staggered back under her onslaught.

"Why so surprised? You forced our marriage, though we were so young. Did you think we wouldn't find out how to bring pleasure to each other?"

Before she could draw breath, Vortin had collapsed to his knees, the water swirling his cloak around him, though he seemed unconscious of the discomfort. He reached out towards her and she allowed him to catch hold of her tunic then fumble beneath it to caress her bare leg above the knee. Then she jumped deftly out of his reach and threw her pitcher at him. He dodged it and fell sprawling into the water. Bron laughed and sped past him, back across the stepping-stones to the safety of the grassy bank.

She ran to seek the comfort of the warm forge and the protection of her young husband's arms. Elated at the extent of her revenge, she also felt ashamed. She had teased Vortin as if she had been a common prostitute.

Soranus warned her that she was playing a dangerous game, but she laughed and said that Vortin had no power over her now that the only link between them, their son, had been removed. Then her tears flowed again.

Meanwhile, Vortin stood on the bank, humiliated and angry, his cloak clinging heavily around his legs, wet and cold. He was now even more resolved to crush Bron's swingeing arrogance and contempt for him and bring her, subdued, to his bed, to fulfil all his fantasies.

From that moment he ceased yapping at her heels, resumed his duties at the Temple, and laid his plans.

Bron, relieved by his absence, hoped she was at last rid of his attentions.

CHAPTER 7

AD 400/401

Hestig regarded his younger daughter with pride as she sat shelling hazelnuts at the kitchen table, her head bent so that her long chestnut hair fell over her mischievous face.

Trifosa was approaching thirteen years of age. Her days were now spent in helping her mother with household chores. She shared the husbandry of fruit and vegetables grown on the lynchets, looked after the animals living around the house, and harvested nuts and berries as, with various friends or family or Pulcher, she roamed the woods and fields – not alone for one minute because Nobilianus was never far away.

Having left school almost a year ago, Trifosa had elected to continue her studies with Africanus. She especially wished to increase her familiarity with the Latin language.

Hestig knew that his friend's black skin was the direct cause of a lonely, bachelor life, with few close associates except Veneta and the schoolchildren, and was glad that this caring and intelligent man found, round this welcoming hearth, the loving family atmosphere he obviously craved.

The two men still argued and discussed late into the evening the political and social climate of the time.

AD 400 was the year that news reached Byden about the liberation of Britannia from all her invaders, brought about by the Romanised barbarian Stilicho, who had been sent by Emperor Honorius. However, it was northern news that hardly affected life in the settlement.

Of much more interest was the arrival in the autumn of Julius Gaius with his wife and daughter. They were booked into the inn and that evening invited Hestig to meet them over supper, then stay late to discuss business. The Roman wished to purchase the valuable plot of land on which the shell of Hestig's derelict house still stood and to demolish it and build another, in Roman style, as his family's summer residence.

Proudly, he introduced his womenfolk to Hestig. His wife Lucilla must have been a pretty woman when in her twenties, not too many years ago, but she looked tired, with lines on her forehead and darkness under her eyes, and her skin was paper thin and sallow. She excused herself after the second course of their meal and went to lie down. Her husband sighed.

"Your grey skies and unfamiliar food don't agree with my wife," he told Hestig. "She's been sick ever since arriving in Calleva. I had hoped the summer might brighten her, but that's not been the case. The doctors don't know what's wrong. I'd like to take her home to Rome but she won't entertain the idea because it would mean I would have to resign. Besides, my daughter loves it in Britannia."

Hestig smiled at Flavia. "I'm glad to hear it," he said. "You must miss your sunshine, but it's not all bad here."

"I have much more freedom, away from Rome," Flavia smiled. She had been taking lessons in their local language and her accent was enchanting.

"My children are looking forward to meeting you," Hestig told her. "They are about your age. Bron is fifteen and married with two children, and my younger daughter, Trifosa, is thirteen. Hestigys helps me in the pottery. He's fourteen later this month."

"I'm fourteen this month, too!" exclaimed Flavia.

"I hope you'll all be good friends as well as neighbours," said

Hestig. "You'll probably meet them tomorrow. My wife is looking forward to getting to know your mother."

Flavia nodded and thick strands of her short blonde hair fell over her forehead. She had a lovely round face with well-spaced features and a pale complexion as smooth as cream. Her mouth and frank light blue eyes smiled all the time. She reminded Hestig of a pale yellow rose and he foresaw that his son stood little chance of keeping his heart intact once they met.

After she retired for the night, he and Julius Gaius agreed terms. The contract included building the large house for the Roman family and a smaller property on the site for Hestig and his family.

Demolition work and clearance would commence straight away with a view to having both houses ready to move into by the end of the following year. The two men shook hands on the deal, and Julius said he would have the legal document drawn up in Calleva for both to sign.

Hestig knew that he was again climbing the achievement ladder and would soon be back on the rung he had reached before the arson, perhaps even higher.

The families were introduced to each other the following day. Lucilla had many questions to ask about life in Byden, and Trifena answered them all. Enchanted with Bron's children, Lucilla confided to Trifena that she yearned for more babies herself but the doctors had advised against it.

Clearly, Trifosa and Flavia took an immediate liking to each other, and as Hestig anticipated, when the Gaius family arrived at the pottery, Hestigys gawped at Flavia. He had never been much interested in the girls in the settlement, preferring the rough and tumble of the boys' games, and his parents were amused now to witness their son's complete capitulation before this lovely Roman girl. After she returned to Calleva with her parents, he was preoccupied for days, and no one could get more than monosyllables out of him.

"I remember what it was like," smiled Hestig, kissing his wife. "It's tumultuous and confusing, and it hurts. It would be a good match."

"But too early," protested Trifena. "He's not old enough to be thinking seriously about girls."

The building site was cleared and work continued apace. People expressed surprise when they saw two sets of foundations being dug, and said they admired Hestig for his sharp business sense and persistence in clawing back all he had lost.

Julius Gaius was often in the settlement, checking on the progress of the work. Sometimes, he joined Hestig and Africanus in their late-night discussions, and brought news from Calleva of the ongoing withdrawal of their troops back to Rome to defend their homeland. At these times he looked troubled and wondered if, though a civil servant, he would also be recalled and for how long his family would occupy their new house in Byden.

One morning in March 401, Vortin summoned his priests and priestesses to his office behind the high altar. Jeetuna wondered what to expect.

"I have been up all night," he began, "in communion with our great god, Ashuba." He was standing behind his large oak desk and leaning forward, his weight on his hands, which were set apart, fingers spread.

Jeetuna commented, "It has invigorated you, Vortin – you don't look a bit tired!"

She doubted that he had been up all night consulting Ashuba, and guessed that the others were thinking the same, but all decided it was imprudent to say so. She usually considered herself less vulnerable than the others, because of Vortin's occasional need of her, but this morning, he ignored her. He continued, leaning further forward and speaking with animation.

"Ashuba has indicated that he desires the appointment of a High Priestess before the Midsummer Festival. He confided to me that he has waited long enough – five years since Iraina's desertion – and the time has now come."

"But who?" asked Jeetuna excitedly.

"Our great god will choose," Vortin told her. "He orders that I gather all the people together in front of the Temple on the evening of May Day and then he will come to a decision."

They all looked at each other, nonplussed, trying to read into

Vortin's words what he intended. For months now, he had been hard at work in the Temple, carrying out all his duties, and seemed to have relinquished his infatuation for Bron.

Jeetuna admired Sharma for hiding the anger he must be feeling, as once again he saw the office of High Priest slipping from his grasp – he had made such an exemplary effort while Vortin was spending time out and about the settlement in Bron's shadow.

However, Jeetuna hoped that, at last, she was about to be the recipient of Vortin's favour, and the privileges and possessions that went with it.

Her expectations were given some credence when Vortin spoke again.

"Veneta, you are working too hard as it is, caring for the children in addition to your other duties, so I have to look to you, Jeetuna, for help in preparing for this appointment."

"Whatever you say," agreed Jeetuna wholeheartedly.

"I want Iraina's suite of rooms cleaned from top to bottom – hire help from the settlement, if necessary – then redecorated and completely refurnished, fit for their new occupant. I will abide by your choice of colours. May I leave all that to you?"

"Of course, Vortin, it will be my pleasure," Jeetuna agreed breathlessly, her eyes sparkling and cheeks flushing.

"Good," he said. "Then we shall require a new wardrobe, fit for my consort's high position, and jewellery – we mustn't overlook the jewellery, eh, my dear?"

"Jewellery, yes," repeated Jeetuna ecstatically.

"Good," said Vortin again. "Of course, I will need to be kept informed of what is going on. You may come to me late each evening to report, Jeetuna."

Jeetuna was speechless. "Bron, eat your heart out!" she exalted gleefully, though silently.

Later, Veneta approached her. "Vortin is playing with you," she warned. "I don't think for one minute that he has finished with Bron."

Jeetuna's voice was acid. "Let's wait and see, shall we?"

She threw her heart and soul into the work Vortin had entrusted to her. A small contingent of women came up from the settlement, armed with brooms, brushes of every description and dustpans, dusters, bowls and cloths.

They were followed by a gang of men who burned off old paint, filled cracks, skimmed and replastered as necessary, and applied colours according to Jeetuna's directions. Vortin had objected to a cheerful red with black areas she had first chosen, saying the colours were fine for the women's rooms on the second floor but not for the High Priestess.

They then settled on a strong forest green for the wall behind the mattress and a gentler, relaxing green for the other walls. The woodwork was painted white. Even the thick green glass in the window overlooking the courtyard was replaced by thinner glass panes that were more transparent and less flawed.

Then Jeetuna revelled in choosing new furniture, some made locally and some ordered from Calleva. Vortin spared no expense. First a mattress, pillows, and embroidered and tasselled cushions, with thin sheets, and a bedspread woven in brown and green with a design of trees, branches and leaves. There was a white basket chair, natural wood box footstool, bleached sheepskin rugs, bronze oil lamps and one candelabra, metal tripods supporting washing bowl and brazier, a rectangular Kimmeridge shale table, and two wooden chests for storing bedding and new clothes.

Jeetuna chose the clothes to suit and fit herself. After a particularly successful shopping trip, she called on Vortin at his house during the evening, as he had suggested she should, to show him her purchases.

"This is a Menimane, Vortin, which I am reliably informed, by merchants from Calleva, is a fashion that the wives of the German mercenaries in the Roman army are wearing."

Vortin inspected the garment. It consisted of a bodice with long tight sleeves over which was worn a loose tunic pinned at the shoulders by a pair of chained brooches, and drawn in at the waist by a girdle. On this occasion, he approved the deep red colour she had chosen.

"And these," Jeetuna continued, shaking fine white linen from its wrappings, "were chosen especially with you in mind, Vortin."

He fingered the undergarments sensually, then smiled in approbation of all she had bought, and said she could stay the night.

They went together to Calleva to choose jewellery. Jeetuna held her breath as rings, necklaces, bracelets and earrings in precious metals and stones were displayed before them, and Vortin made his choice, ordering some special designs and asking to bring other pieces away with them.

As an afterthought, he wanted to see some fine gold chains, then unexpectedly knelt and clasped one around Jeetuna's left ankle.

"A 'thank-you'," he said, "for all your hard work and enthusiasm. It expresses how I feel about you."

Jeetuna was mystified at his words, as she expected to be the recipient of everything chosen, but was grateful anyway for his expression of appreciation. For weeks after that, right up to May Day, she took every opportunity of displaying her bare left ankle encircled by the gold chain.

CHAPTER 8

Lucilla was very unwell. Julius Gaius decided to bring her and Flavia to the settlement for a few days' refreshment in the country and to show them the building progress of their new house, which was just being roofed.

On May Day, a crowd of young girls assembled as usual at Shubinata's temple in the wood to bathe their faces in the early morning dew, Trifosa among them. Flavia had obtained her parents' permission to join this traditional celebration.

No boys were in sight in the wood but the girls knew they were hiding with their cow horns, waiting for the moment of chase. Hestigys was among them, but not Nobilianus this year. Hestigys had strict instructions not to let either of the girls out of his sight.

The girls, dressed all in white and carrying hoops of flowers and leaves bedecked with coloured ribbons, came warily along the twisting path, giggling in anticipation. Suddenly, through the trees, resounded the low notes of the cow horns and the boys broke through the undergrowth, intent on catching whichever girls caught their fancy.

As the exuberant and noisy chase began, Flavia and Trifosa became separated. Flavia kept to the path, which she recognised, but Trifosa struck out through the trees, hotly pursued by one of the boys Hestigys knew well. Her brother hesitated momentarily, but decided that Flavia was their guest and a stranger to the woods, whereas Trifosa knew her way around. He surrendered to his inclinations and went after Flavia.

He caught up with her a quarter of a mile from the edge of the wood and they walked back to the settlement, talking shyly but comfortably together about their lives, so different up to that point.

It was not until he had returned Flavia to the inn that he wondered about his sister, and retraced his steps. None of the young people he met and questioned had seen her since she left the path. Neither had they seen his friend.

Hestigys was not unduly worried, as he knew the boy well enough to be sure that his sister would come to no harm. However, he dare not go home and tell his parents that she was missing, so when he met Africanus wandering through the trees, collecting together items of interest for a class next day, he enlisted help to look for her.

They set off in different directions and it was Africanus who eventually heard the shouts and laughter ahead of him. When he drew closer, he saw Trifosa and her friend precariously balanced in the branches of a large horse chestnut. Her hair was flaming among the leaves as if autumn had come to the tree too soon.

"Trifosa, you're such a tomboy," he shouted up to her. "We've been worried about you."

"She's all right, Africanus," called the boy from an even higher branch. "I've been with her the whole time."

Africanus smiled. "I'm glad about that," he said, "but both sets of parents will be wondering where you are. Come on down, now. Mind how you go. Don't fall! I wouldn't be able to carry you both back with broken legs!"

The boy began scrambling down, branch to branch. Trifosa waited for him. When he reached her, he helped her down in front of him. Africanus looked up, admiring their agility, still advising them to take care.

When the muscles at the back of his neck ached, he bent his head forward and rubbed them, then looked up again. Trifosa was now directly above him and he found he was looking straight up her tunic, between her legs. Embarrassed, he looked away. She was nearly fourteen and maturing, though one wouldn't have thought so to see her clinging to the swaying branches. As her teacher and friend of the family, he had always been there to protect her and she was too innocent to cope with anyone's prying eyes, let alone his, when there had only ever been trust between them.

She called to him, and reaching up his arms he caught her as she jumped down, then moved away to give the boy space to land. He escorted them both home, finding Hestigys on the way, and no one else was any the wiser about the escapade.

Later that May Day, messengers hurried from the Temple, calling at every house in the settlement to 'invite' all the people to gather at sunset in front of the steps to hear an announcement of great importance to the whole assembly.

There was speculation all day as to the nature of the 'important announcement'. Vortin's staff, of course, all knew the reason for the summons. He had decided that he had been without a High Priestess for long enough, and this evening he was going to choose Iraina's replacement.

Jeetuna was so excited that she had not eaten a thing since yesterday. Veneta and Selvid looked apprehensive, and Sharma was plainly angry. However, there was nothing to be done but obey Vortin's orders.

At the time appointed, the High Priest commanded his retinue to follow him and led them to the top of the steps.

Jeetuna's eyes swept along a row of seating that had been arranged in a large semicircle, facing the Temple. As people arrived they were directed by the eunuchs, either to stand behind the chairs or, if of sufficient importance, to sit on them.

As leader of the council, Hestig had been allocated a seat facing the steps, slightly off-centre of the semicircle. Trifena and their two children, Trifosa and Hestigys, sat to his left and Bron immediately on his right, with Soranus next to her. Layla, nearly two and a half, and Alon, a year younger, were asleep on their parents' laps. Africanus and other members of the council sat further round the semicircle. Sufficient light was thrown by torches held by Temple staff, who were standing at intervals around the area.

There was a general hubbub of voices until Vortin began to descend the steps, then everyone fell silent.

Jeetuna noticed then that Bron had been placed conspicuously centre front. She saw Vortin stare directly at the girl, once, then he

60

adjusted his position slightly to avoid looking at her again.

A sudden, sharp suspicion took hold in Jeetuna's mind, which unconsciously propelled the priestess down the steps until she was standing below Vortin. She brushed the thought aside as soon as she was aware of it.

No, he wouldn't, she told herself. He hadn't been near Bron or spoken of her for a whole year – except (she remembered suddenly) sometimes at night in his dreams.

Vortin addressed the assembly from his position halfway down the flight of steps.

"Dear people," he began, "I have called you together on a momentous occasion. As you know, I – we – have been without a High Priestess for five years since Iraina was spirited away." The people murmured agreement.

His expression became mournful and his voice reached a lower register. "I have waited all that time, celibate, for her return."

Nearby, Nobilianus sniggered quietly. Jeetuna choked and was overtaken by a fit of coughing. She turned her head and found Vortin glaring at her.

Those who believed him looked sympathetic.

"Some weeks ago, our great god, Ashuba, summoned me to his altar and we spent the whole night in mystical communion. He revealed his innermost thoughts to me – a great privilege and honour, and I would die rather than ignore them – in fact, he would probably kill me for disobeying him." The people understood and nodded their assent.

"Ashuba told me –" he paused for greater effect, "– that he wished me to choose a new High Priestess on the evening of May Day, to serve him faithfully in the Temple and stand by my side as my comfort and consort, and to provide us with heirs from the altar at the great Midsummer Festival. That girl – woman – whoever she may be, is here tonight. I do not know who she is, but Ashuba will reveal her identity before you all go home. He will do this by means of a divining stick held in my hands."

One of the eunuchs handed him a short willow wand, forked at one end. Vortin took that end in both hands.

Jeetuna saw Bron quickly stretch out her hand towards Soranus. He took it, drawing closer to her. The priestess reflected that they were all helpless in the face of Vortin's absolute power.

She then detected, out of the corner of her eye, a slight movement on the path into the settlement from the eastern bank and ditch. She turned her head in that direction. People were standing aside as a tall figure silently made its way forward and stood a few rows behind the front edge of the crowd. Vortin was intent on his purpose and was quite unaware of the interloper.

"I am going to move among you all," he called to his audience, "until Ashuba shakes the wand before a girl or a woman, whereupon I shall claim her as my High Priestess. Men, please stand clear and let the women come forward."

Some of the women with families moved closer to their husbands and gathered their children to them. It was inconceivable to Jeetuna and, she guessed, to Vortin, that any woman would not gladly abandon her family to take her place by his side.

There were others – women from the inn, slaves, those wishing to escape unhappy liaisons, and young single girls – who pushed forward to the front. Vortin smiled indulgently.

He went down the steps now and walked towards the edge of the crowd to the far left of Bron, behind the row of seats, both hands clasping the wand erect before him, unconsciously revealing the thoughts in his head and the desire in his body.

The people moved back as he approached, making a clear path for him, though some of the eager women blocked his route so that the eunuchs had to ask them politely to stand aside. The wand remained erect, not moving.

Minutes later he had passed behind Bron and her family and had reached the eastern end of the semicircle. Still the wand had not moved in his hands except when he was jostled. On those occasions, the eunuchs spoke sharply to whichever woman had dared touch the High Priest.

Then he started back in the opposite direction, walking in front of those sitting on the chairs, making his way towards Bron. She looked sick with fear. Soranus was still tightly gripping her hand.

However, when only three seats away from Bron, Vortin paused and walked back towards the Temple steps. Jeetuna hurried down to meet him, her face expectant, but he passed her by as if she were not there, and moved across to the other end of the seats, once again making his way along the row towards Bron in the centre.

Jeetuna stood stunned, ignored and uncomprehending.

"What did you expect?" Sharma hissed at her. "He's played you like a fish on a hook. It's still Bron he's after. Watch!"

But Jeetuna couldn't watch and bowed her head, the whole of her being cursing him, Bron and herself for the fool she had been, the crushing shame and hurt filling her eyes with tears and her mouth with bile, which she spat into the dust.

The spittle lay in bubbles beside her left foot and the ankle chain came into focus. Suddenly, she knew what Vortin had meant when he said that it expressed how he felt about her – he regarded her as no better than a street girl. She impulsively crouched and with frantic fingers tugged and pulled at the gold chain until it snapped. She clawed it from her ankle and threw it away from her as far as she could. Her delicate skin was left cut and bleeding.

Vortin was drawing nearer to Bron. Jeetuna watched again, mesmerised, in spite of her anger. She understood now that Vortin had been prolonging and savouring the anticipation of standing before Bron, the wand shaking in his hands, a symbol of the overwhelming passion he still felt for her.

Again, he was only three seats away, and standing in front of Trifosa. Now it was Nobilianus who involuntarily took a step down in protest, but the wand remained still.

Then a voice called Vortin's name, a voice so familiar, but one that Jeetuna could not immediately attach to a person.

Vortin turned to see the tall, elegant figure crossing the intervening space between them, a thin veil hiding her face. A slender arm covered in gold bangles to the elbow moved up to the edge of the veil and slender fingers pulled it away, revealing a pair of large violet eyes. The High Priestess! Iraina!

Vortin hesitated. He had been only seconds away from claiming Bron for Ashuba, for the Temple, for himself. Jeetuna knew he could still deny Iraina the position she was reclaiming – all he had to do was turn towards Bron and point the wand at her and begin to shake it – but someone – it was Soranus – was already shouting "Iraina! Iraina!" and the people were cheering and chanting over and over again, "Ashuba has chosen! Ashuba has chosen! Blessed be Ashuba, great sun god of Byden!"

All eyes were focused on the wand held in Vortin's hands. He looked down and seemed surprised to see it pointing directly at Iraina and vibrating violently.

No one noticed when Jeetuna fainted.

CHAPTER 9

Iraina had not expected her return to be accepted so readily. She was prepared for opposition from many quarters, but found none. All was quiet.

She wondered whether Ashuba *had* chosen her once again to take her place by Vortin's side. She had certainly returned at exactly the right moment, and the wand *had* vibrated, whether shaken by Ashuba or not.

Her explanation to the people, that she had been spirited away by nymphs to a world of amnesia, and had found herself, five years later, in the wood outside the settlement, was universally believed.

Vortin was morose but accepted her return, probably not knowing what else to do. She told him her story, which he acknowledged, though she doubted he believed it. Whatever the real reason for her disappearance and return, he seemed not to care.

So Iraina settled in as if she had never left. She revelled in the luxury she had voluntarily abandoned five years ago, and was especially pleased with her newly decorated and furnished suite of rooms and new clothes. They were a little loose on her and too short, but she sent them to a woman in the settlement to have them altered. Only the new jewellery was withheld from her, but her own was returned from its place of safety in the cellar beneath Vortin's living room.

Five years of penury had been enough for Iraina. It was true she had been very happy for a time in the settlement on the far side of the great Ridgeway, until poverty ceased to be a novelty and began to grind into her sinews, crippling every moment of her day.

She still loved Cullum, her Catuvellauni boy, now grown into a handsome, mature man, and adored their children, four in number – but not enough to stay with them in the small round house for the rest of her life. She knew he would take care of their sons and daughters, assisted by the matrons of the village. One day he would marry one of their daughters, any of whom, she knew by their admiring sidelong glances, would be glad to have him.

She had abandoned her family as suddenly as she had abandoned Vortin five years previously, without saying goodbye or leaving a message. In time Cullum would forget her, as would the children.

She could not have been more mistaken.

Jeetuna guessed that Vortin's next problem would be the Midsummer ritual. He was now sixty-one, Iraina forty-three years old, and there no longer seemed to be any physical attraction between them, or any pretence of it.

On Midsummer Eve, after the traditional pageantry of Iraina's ride through the wood in the chariot drawn by the two white oxen, and her entry into the Temple, he ordered the doors shut and let the onlookers outside make of it what they would. He was in a bad temper and went to bed and left everyone else to their own devices.

Iraina shrugged and went up to her suite of rooms.

Jeetuna watched as Selvid sent the musicians home and set about preparing for the children's service later in the day, while Veneta ushered her charges to bed. Then Veneta bid Jeetuna goodnight and left for her rooms in the schoolhouse. Selvid checked that the eunuch on rota was on duty, then snuffed out the unwanted candles and torches and hurried after Veneta.

Jeetuna was mystified. For years he and Veneta had made great efforts to keep each other at arm's length. However, one could always feel the tension between them, as if each held one end of a rope that was being alternately tugged and resisted, one way then the other.

Lately, however, resistance seemed to have given way to ease and familiarity, and they were never very far apart from each other. She was sure they seldom spent their nights alone any more, though they were very discreet. This puzzled Jeetuna, because as priest, Selvid had a right of access to both Veneta and herself whenever he wished. However, he never looked at her as if he considered she was available to him – indeed, he treated her with the utmost respect and courtesy at all times. He was about the only man around who did.

Sharma was ignoring her and spending most of his free time with Brocchus and two of the Temple boys, who were looking more and more like girls with their dyed blonde hair and curls and simpering attitudes. Jeetuna was highly suspicious about what was going on between the four of them, but had no proof.

One morning, she had capriciously ordered the boys to take the Temple's night buckets down to the public latrines for emptying, but Sharma had intervened and rescued them and sent two others to carry out the unpleasant job.

Now she looked around her. She had been left alone in the Temple. Not feeling sufficiently tired to go to bed, she decided to take a stroll round the settlement to see who she could find. As priestess, she was forbidden by Temple law to consort with any man other than the priests, but Vortin had cruelly let her know that he considered her no more than a common prostitute, so a common prostitute she would become.

Without letting the eunuch on duty see or hear her, she slipped out of the side door and into the morning light. Her route took her past the towering wickerwork god, which straddled its legs next to the Temple, Vortin's ever-present threat. She looked up past all the ladders and platforms that gave access to the interior, up to the hollow head and grinning face, and shuddered.

Making her way to the inn, she spent a couple of hours gossiping with the girls there, pampering herself in the baths, watching them operate, enjoying the relaxed and convivial atmosphere among people who had little conscience and followed their own inclinations.

When the sun was several hours old and she judged it was time to return to the Temple to prepare for the children's annual service, she dressed and made up her face. She knew she was still a great beauty.

Looking her best, in spite of missing a night's sleep, feeling refreshed and relaxed and smelling of sensuous forest perfume, she stepped through the "No entry" door into the hall of the inn.

It was then that she saw Julius Gaius for the first time. He was emerging from his room, coming to breakfast. His wife followed him, pale and slightly stooped, and they stopped to knock at a door on their way past.

Jeetuna pretended to be consulting the breakfast menu she had picked up from a table, and studied him from beneath her blackened eyelids.

She judged him a few years younger than herself. He was taller, muscular, with a fine physique, and light brown hair. If his well-cut fashionable brown tunic and proud bearing had not betrayed his origin, his lean Roman features would have done so immediately.

She noticed the gentle way he treated his wife, who did not look at all well, as he sat her at the meal table and ordered breakfast for her. If the lively blonde girl who joined them was their daughter, it was a wonder that the woman had had the strength to carry, let alone birth the baby. In fact, Jeetuna's assumptions were remarkably accurate. She learned later that Lucilla had undergone a caesarean operation after two painful days of premature labour.

The priestess continued to stare.

"Jeetuna, you're gawping," the innkeeper whispered as she passed her.

Jeetuna motioned her outside.

"Who is he?" she asked.

"Julius Gaius – he's the Roman who's building the house on Hestig's plot. They've come to choose colours and measure up for hangings. And they've brought a furniture maker with them and an artist who is designing their mosaic floor."

Jeetuna made her way back to the Temple, slipping in unnoticed through the side door. She could not understand why her heart was banging about so noisily and irregularly inside her chest. Of one thing she was certain – she wanted to see Julius Gaius again.

Iraina had been back for more than two months when a stranger called at the Temple late one afternoon and asked to see Vortin. Sharma was on duty and went to find the High Priest, taking with him a gift of a fine unbleached and embroidered sheepskin surcoat without sleeves, which reached to the knees.

Vortin stroked the fine wool lining and tried the coat on. It fitted perfectly.

"Someone knows your size," commented Sharma.

"Who is he?" asked Vortin.

"He didn't say, except that he comes in peace, and his mission is private, for your ears only."

"I will see him here in my office," said Vortin. He draped the coat across the back of a chair.

Sharma showed the stranger in and left, shutting the door behind him.

The man was tall, over six feet, and Vortin would have felt intimidated if it had not been for the man's smile and raised right hand, palm facing him, a sign of friendship.

He was dressed in a grey coarse cloth tunic fringed along the bottom edge and at the side edges from shoulder to hem, held in place by a wide leather, metal-studded belt. His feet were encased in sheepskin shoes, and leather thongs from ankle to untidy knots at the knee kept his loose cloth trousers under control.

Vortin returned the greeting and asked his guest to sit down.

"Thank you for your gift," said Vortin. "It is very fine. Who sent it and what is your errand?"

"My name is Ziad," the man began. "I have to tell you things you will not wish to know, but I tell only the truth and I trust you will hear me out. I come in friendship, without threat, and only with requests for your consideration."

"Speak on," invited Vortin. "You have my attention. You need not fear me."

He listened for half an hour or more in silence, except to give the speaker an occasional prompt. Eventually the stranger paused and asked for a drink of water, which Vortin brought him. Impatiently he waited while his guest emptied the beaker and cleared his throat.

"Continue," he said grimly, "and don't stop until you have told me everything."

Ziad spoke at length until he had said all he had come to say, then he looked expectantly at the High Priest.

"It is late in the day," Vortin said. "We will talk of this again tomorrow. I have to think what is best to do."

"Of course," agreed his visitor.

"You will stay the night at the inn, at the Temple's expense, and in the morning perhaps you will attend on me again. Tell no one why you are here. Be discreet. The inn has many temptations."

"I do not indulge in full-bodied wine or full-bodied women while I am on duty," Ziad assured him, and laughed.

Vortin summoned Sharma. The emissary stood, bowed and left in the company of the priest.

Vortin spent the evening pacing his office floor, then ate alone in his house. When one of the girls from the second floor knocked tentatively at his front door he sent her away, then spent a sleepless night going over and over in his mind all that he had learned, marshalling the facts in order.

Ziad had told him that he came from a Catuvellauni village many miles to the north of the Ridgeway. He came on behalf of his friend, Cullum. Cullum and Iraina (he called her Irene) were partners to a marriage blessed by the Catuvellauni gods. Their eldest daughter was eight years old. He said that Vortin should realise that Irene had been visiting Cullum, and he had been visiting her in her private cell in the wood, for many years.

Under the table, Vortin's nails cut deeply into the palms of his clenched hands, but did not pierce as deeply as Iraina's hitherto unsuspected treachery. His trust, the love he once had for her as a lover and before that as a father, the memory of the wonder he had shared with her mother at the moment of her birth – everything that he had believed in, that he had trained her to be – all betrayed.

Above all, she had mocked their god, Ashuba, and his goddess wife, whom she had served, not with humility and faithfulness as he had thought, but with arrogance and duplicity.

But Vortin had betrayed none of his feelings and had said nothing except, "Go on, I am listening."

Ziad's tale continued to unfold. Cullum had been overjoyed when, pregnant with their second child, Iraina had left Byden and come to live with him. They planned to stay together for the rest of their lives, and now had four bright and healthy children.

At this news, something deep inside Vortin snapped. She had never given him a bright and healthy child – but there was someone who had.

However, Iraina had missed – *and Vortin had leaned forward then. Perhaps, at last, there was some thought for him* – but no, the emissary said she had missed the luxury of her life at the Temple. One day she had disappeared from the village, leaving her husband and children without a word. They were distraught. Cullum had grown thin and the children cried every day for their mother. It was not that she didn't love them, Cullum knew, but that she was weak and vain and missed all that Vortin gave her. Except that he hadn't been able to give her any wholesome babies. If he had, Ziad said, she might never have left him.

By morning, having had little sleep, Vortin had determined that the Catuvellauni should have her back, whether she wanted to go or not, and she would be sent penniless. Ashuba would be avenged and he would be avenged, and with Iraina out of the way again – suddenly his dark thoughts were replaced with his fantasies of a life spent with Bron, which he had kept in storage since Iraina's reappearance.

As arranged, Ziad returned.

Vortin enquired about his comfort overnight then said resolutely, "I will deliver her back to you," and added, "I imagine you have not come entirely alone?"

The emissary laughed. "That would have been foolish! Two friends are waiting for me in the wood, close by the temple of your goddess."

"Then wait there with them," said Vortin. "Iraina will be delivered to you by midnight. Then take her away. I don't care what happens to her as long as she never returns. Tell her she is lucky that I have taken this merciful step, but if she ever comes back, I will show her no mercy. Tell her that, because I shall not converse with her again."

"I'll tell her," said the man. "Till midnight, then."

"Till midnight," repeated Vortin, and Ziad left.

CHAPTER 10

Bron still dreamed of one day going back to find the Ridgeway. It was eight years ago that she had followed Iraina to the mighty highway, and had seen her welcomed and embraced by a stranger, a Catuvellauni man.

It was at the time of the plague, when Bron had been sent to live in Iraina's cell in the wood for safety. One day, the High Priestess had appeared from nowhere, had checked that the plague was still virulent in the settlement, and then had gone back to her own place of safety, wherever that was. Noticing her thick waist, Bron had decided that she looked exactly as her own mother had looked when expecting her baby sister, and had followed her. She had not been back to the Ridgeway since.

When Pulcher suggested going with her that afternoon, and Trifena offered to look after the children, Bron accepted with alacrity.

She knew that Pulcher would be happy spending this time with her. He would have her all to himself. She also anticipated the walk with pleasure.

They started along the path into the wood and soon reached Shubinata's little temple.

"If you will wait a few minutes," she said to Pulcher, "I'll go in and speak with the goddess. I have an iron brooch Soranus has made for her – we want to thank her for bringing Iraina back."

Pulcher understood. They all knew what could have happened the evening that Vortin stood before Bron with the willow wand in his hand.

"I'll wander," he said. "Legs hurt to stand long."

Her feet bare, Bron entered the temple and momentarily closed her eyes. She remembered vividly the hours she had spent here during her flight from the plague, cleaning and polishing and arranging flowers in their pots. Now she flicked an errant leaf from the praying stool, upholstered in green at this time of year, and ran her finger along the wooden altar, checking for dust. Finding none, she smiled up at the naked figure of the pregnant goddess.

"I'm glad they're looking after you well," she said and knelt on the stool. "I have come to ask you a favour. Soranus is a dear, and I love him very much, and he loves me even more, and he makes love to me whenever he has the chance, and I don't mind because he makes it such fun, but –" She paused. "He doesn't want any more children – he says two is enough and I am too young to be burdened with a baby every year – and Kendrus has told him how to protect me when – you know – but I would like another baby, I really would, and it sometimes makes me unhappy. I still miss Storm so much. Can you do anything about it for me?"

She thanked the goddess for listening to her, laid the brooch on the altar, and went outside. Pulcher was waiting and approached her with his finger to his lips.

"What's the matter?" she whispered.

"Men – strangers – three," he whispered back. "They talk bad things. Come!"

Quietly they crept further into the wood until Pulcher stopped and motioned her to crouch down. The tall, abundant nettles and yarrow quite hid them from view.

Three men lounged under the trees. All were dressed in grey cloth tunics and loose trousers, bound to the knees with leather thongs, and sheepskin shoes. Their long, decorated wooden shields and long-handled spears lay by their sides. One man lazily stood up to relieve himself against a tree, and Bron and Pulcher could see how tall he was.

They stayed hidden and listened.

"Time drags," said one, a younger man, speaking a dialect they could understand. He turned onto his back, hands behind his head, and placed a sheepskin cap over his face so that his words were muffled. "I could be at home repairing my thatch."

"And listening to the wife nagging me about not poking my nose into other people's dirty washing," added the other man.

"Then you're both better off here." The tall man laughed and, returning to the circle, sat down. "Make the most of it, having nothing to do but wait."

"Do you believe the old priest?" asked the muffled voice. "Will he bring her here before midnight?"

"I'm sure of it," replied the tall man, who seemed to be their leader. "He didn't say much but I could see he was angry. He's dumping her. Can't blame him. I'd do the same."

"How will we get her back to Cullum if she's not willing?" asked the second man.

"Truss her up and sling her over our shoulders – take it in turns to carry her," said the tall man. "Not to hurt her, though. Cullum's a good friend of mine. He'd do the same for me if my wife ran off."

"He'd be better off without her, if you ask me," said the first man, removing the cap and sitting up, leaning back on his hands, his legs thrust out in front of him.

"Maybe," said the tall man thoughtfully, "but don't forget there are four children, decent young 'uns. You haven't got any of your own yet –"

"I'm working on it," grinned the younger man. "It's not for want of trying."

"You're right," agreed the second of the group. "I'd fight to get her back if she was mine."

Bron and Pulcher looked at each other and silently made their way back to the path and the temple. He beckoned her to follow and led her towards the settlement.

"Not Ridgeway today," he said. "Trouble, Bron, trouble."

When they had almost reached the edge of the wood, Bron asked Pulcher to sit down and tell her what he thought was going on.

"Catuvellauni," he explained. "Iraina. Vortin sending her back." Bron nodded slowly.

"Not matter except for you, Bron."

The danger was obvious.

"We warn Iraina," he said. "I find her. You go home."

She kissed him lightly on the cheek. "I must tell Soranus, then I'll go home."

Pulcher nodded and they separated.

The dwarf learned from one of the Temple women that Vortin and Sharma were in consultation in Vortin's office. Iraina was resting. He climbed the spiral staircase and was about to head for her suite of rooms when he saw Brocchus loitering about at the other end of the corridor. Hurriedly he pulled back against the wall and retreated down the stairs. He realised they were keeping her under observation and was at a loss to know how to approach her without being noticed.

He paused at the entrance doors, beside the large bronze warning gong. Fortunately, no one was around at that precise moment. Picking up the heavy stick with both hands and raising it above his head, he brought the cloth-covered end crashing down against the gong. It produced a low, hollow boom. He raised the stick again, and again crashed it with all his strength against the gong, followed by a third strike and a fourth. Then he dropped the stick and hobbled out of the doors and through the vestibule to the entrance.

By now, people outside had heard the warning gong, and were looking up towards the Temple. He slid along the front outer wall, round the corner, and back in by the side door. He was small, and such a common sight around the settlement, that no one took any notice of him.

Once inside, he joined the throng of Temple staff and worshippers who were gathering at the entrance. The gong, in its wooden frame, was still swinging from the chains. Everyone was looking puzzled. Vortin and Sharma arrived and despatched the eunuchs to search the ground floor for any signs of fire. Brocchus was there, a bunch of keys jangling from his belt, and was sent by Sharma to look in his room and Selvid's. Veneta ran upstairs to check the children's accommodation while Selvid went outside to ask the people passing whether they had seen who had banged the gong. Nobody had.

Iraina came downstairs and said something to Vortin. He did not answer and walked away. She was left standing on her own, looking perplexed at being ignored.

Pulcher took advantage of the general confusion to approach her.

"High Priestess," he said. She turned towards him. "Great danger," he told her.

She raised a hand, about to gesture him away, but his serious grey eyes and the fresh memory of Vortin's rebuff must have made her change her mind. She looked around. No one was watching.

"Where?" she asked.

"Not here. Follow me. Hurry."

Without questioning, she followed him past the altar, past Vortin's office with its open door, and out through the High Priest's private exit that led to the path to his house. From there the dwarf led her into the wood to the north, in the area of the plague pits.

Once he judged it safe, he stopped and turned to her.

"Tell me," she said.

So he told her of his walk with Bron, of the three men, and the conversation they had overheard.

"Describe the tall man," she ordered, so he did. She was left with no doubts. "His name is Ziad," she said.

She stood, looking undecided whether or not to explain. "Since you've risked your life for me –"

"No, not you – for Bron," he said.

"How Bron?" she asked, then understood. "If I go, Vortin takes Bron for himself?" Pulcher nodded.

"Anyway, you deserve an explanation."

"We know –" he said, "– the Catuvellauni. Bron once followed, through wood, to Ridgeway."

Iraina swore. "The little cow!" she said.

Pulcher was offended. "Never told Vortin," he said. "Eight years – Bron never told."

Iraina's shoulders relaxed and she looked at him.

"You love her, don't you?" she asked. He blushed. Iraina continued, "She is very lucky. I know – I am loved, too. But it isn't enough."

"No," Pulcher agreed quietly, repeating her words, "not enough."

"So what do I do now?" asked Iraina. "I don't want to go back.

I can't live in poverty. I've tried, and I can't."

"Hide, past midnight," he said.

"But where? Vortin will search."

Pulcher had an idea. "Not his own house," he said. "Room under floor – mattress there."

"How do you know that?" she asked, then added, "But there isn't time for explanations." She continued, "I don't have the keys of his house, but I know where there is a set – hanging in his office."

Together they hurried back to the Temple. On the way, Iraina voiced her worries.

"If I'm not returned tonight, Cullum will come for me. I realise that now. There's going to be big trouble."

Pulcher left her hidden behind Vortin's house and entered the Temple through the back door.

All those who had been in the building at the time the gong sounded were still assembled. Vortin had not let anyone leave until a thorough inspection had been carried out. Pulcher saw that Vortin's office door was still open, but he passed it and followed the shadows along the massive walls and joined the crowd. He spoke briefly to a couple of people, to establish his presence there, then returned unnoticed the way he had come. He knew he had to hurry as the eunuchs had already returned from their search and only Veneta was awaited.

Iraina had told him where, in Vortin's office, the keys were hanging and he slipped them off their hook and hurried out to the house. As he unlocked the front door, Iraina joined him. They stepped into the living room and Pulcher raised the carpet that hid the trapdoor. Iraina put her foot on the first rung of the ladder.

"Sorry, dark," apologised Pulcher.

"Safer," said Iraina and disappeared into the blackness. Reaching the bottom step, she called back, "Whatever you do, don't forget to let me out in the morning!"

Pulcher promised then closed the trapdoor, replaced the carpet, left the house and locked the front door.

Inside the Temple, he turned right towards Vortin's office, intending to return the keys to their hook, but was dismayed to find the door now shut and voices coming from inside – Vortin's and Sharma's.

For a moment he panicked. How long would it be before Vortin noticed that the keys weren't there? Pulcher could only hope that, as they were a spare set, the High Priest wouldn't miss them straight away.

Then he had an idea. Mounting the spiral staircase to the women's rooms, he sought out Sunina, a trusted friend.

He apologised for asking a personal question but said he had good reason – was she in favour with Vortin? She was a pretty girl, chosen for her mass of naturally blonde hair and bubbly character, and she answered as Pulcher expected, that she was one of the High Priest's favourites among the women.

"Except that he turned me away last night," she said ruefully, "when he had specially asked me to visit."

Pulcher then hesitantly made another request, again apologising.

"It's all right," she smiled. "It's my job."

She took the keys from him and slipped them down the front of her tunic.

Then he left the Temple. The crowd had dispersed.

Sunina walked along to Iraina's rooms and plumped up pillows in her bed to make it appear that the High Priestess was there, but asleep. As she reached her own room, she met Brocchus at the top of the staircase.

"Have you seen Iraina?" he asked casually.

"I think she's in her room," she replied.

"Come with me and check," he ordered.

He followed her along the corridor and knocked at Iraina's door. When there was no reply, he knocked again.

"Open the door," he ordered Sunina. She did so and he walked through the living room and peered into the bedroom.

Satisfied, he nodded and went downstairs again. He was still hanging about there when Sunina came down later in her nightshift, which revealed more of her feminity than it hid, a shawl about her shoulders. She made her way towards the back door of the Temple and so to Vortin's house.

CHAPTER 11

Not long afterwards, Sunina heard Vortin turn his key in the lock of his front door and enter the living room. She heard him kick off his sandals and then nothing more as he walked about on the soft pile of his red carpet.

She coughed briefly, which brought him into the bedroom, obviously amazed to find her lying naked on top of his coverlet.

"Sunina!" he said in surprise. "What are you doing here?"

The girl sat up. "You sent me away last night and I wasn't going to let it happen again!" she told him.

"You're so right, it won't happen again!" he exclaimed. "But how did you get in?"

"I stole the spare set of keys from your office while the door was open, when everyone was looking for the fire." She held out the keys that Pulcher had given her. "Forgive me?" she asked beguilingly.

"Every time," he said, with evident pleasure.

An hour later they were interrupted by a furious banging on the front door. Without hesitation, Vortin threw on a robe and left the bedroom.

"She's not there!" Sunina heard someone say. It sounded like Sharma.

The front door closed and, though she strained her ears, all she could hear was the mutter of low, urgent voices outside. Sunina guessed that it was something to do with Iraina and hoped she herself wouldn't be in trouble. She wished now that she hadn't been so ready to help Pulcher with whatever problem he had.

However, Vortin had been pleased with her tonight and only once had he gasped "Bron!" Sunina didn't mind. She and the other girls knew where his inclinations lay and were used to being relegated to a lower place.

Suddenly the door was flung open and Vortin strode into the bedroom, followed by Sharma and Brocchus. Sunina covered herself modestly, though she realised they had other matters on their minds at that moment.

"You told me that Iraina was in her room!" accused Brocchus.

"You saw her yourself," she countered.

"I saw a pile of pillows!" he shouted at her. He had been duped and was in deep trouble with Sharma and Vortin.

"What made you think she was there?" asked Sharma evenly. "Did you see her?"

"I saw her in the crowd," said Sunina. "She had been resting in her room before the gong summoned everyone, and I assumed she had returned there."

"All that is by the way," insisted Vortin. "What you've got to do is find her and deliver her by midnight, which doesn't leave you very much time. Get everyone out of bed to search, if necessary, but find her!"

"And if she's 'disappeared' again?" sneered Sharma.

"Send Brocchus out to those men to explain!" ordered the High Priest. "Now go!"

When they had left, Sunina asked if she might stay the night. She knew she still had to be there in the morning after Vortin left, to open the trapdoor and let Iraina out.

"Yes, you can stay," agreed Vortin, "but I need some rest. Be a good girl and go to sleep," and he turned over and was soon snoring loudly.

When Iraina could not be found, Sharma had to order a reluctant Brocchus to meet the men in the wood and explain that she had completely disappeared. Brocchus set off into the wood, but went no further than the first line of trees. The Catuvellauni were no friends of the Atrebates and he knew that, as soon as the men saw his black robes and realised his role at the Temple, they would have their sport with him. He was usually willing for such pleasures, but with those ruffians it could get out of hand and he could lose his life.

So he crept back to the Temple and hoped the men would just go home.

Vortin left the house early and threw the spare set of keys over to a still-sleepy Sunina.

"Lock up when you go," he said. "Hang the keys back in the office – and don't take it on yourself to steal them again. It was all right this time, but beware of taking me for granted.

"Yes, Vortin," replied Sunina meekly.

Some time later, Iraina wandered into the Temple.

"Where have you been?" Vortin shouted at her.

"I spent the night in the wood – it felt safer out there than in here." Vortin looked at her sharply. "The gong that bangs its own warning," she explained.

There was not a blade of grass or leaf or twig in her hair or clothes to give credence to her story. However, Vortin was not about to say why he was so put out about her disappearance. In fact, he was still so angry with her that he didn't feel able to string a sentence together in her presence.

He pondered how she frustrated his plans every time she disappeared or reappeared, but there was nothing more he could do now, and he hoped that the Catuvellauni had given up and gone home, though he feared the worst.

"If they come for her, I shall let them take her," Vortin told Sharma, "but I'll not let her go without some pretence of a fight."

"Quite right," agreed his priest.

Accordingly, he began to make preparations for defence without alarming the people. The gong was dragged outside and positioned under the portico, for use as an early warning by anyone passing. The eunuchs, by rota, now patrolled the covered walkway around the Temple, in addition to their daily duties inside.

Vortin recruited one of the men from the settlement, who had had some military experience when younger, to drill squads of men and boys in the market place during the evenings. He said it was to make sure they kept fit and had something to occupy their time as well as visiting the inn. Most of the men were enthusiastic, and enjoyed the novelty of practising unarmed combat, also attack and defence using heavy, whittled branches.

"At the very least, they'll crack open a few heads!" mused Sharma.

CHAPTER 12

Jeetuna was bored but found some excitement in watching the men training, as did everyone else.

There were some like Hoad, the shepherd, who excelled, and others, like the ropemaker, who caused no end of amusement by his clumsiness and lack of co-ordination. Even Nobilianus took part and was strutting about in front of the women, showing off his limited prowess, as if he were the emperor himself.

'The general', as the instructor was nicknamed, had a difficult time keeping order, but all the barracking was good-humoured and no offence was caused.

For some years, at intervals, Jeetuna had been displaying more than a friendly interest in Hestig. At first he had seemed flattered by her attentions but on one dark evening when she confronted him along a settlement path, he had told her plainly, "No chance, Jeetuna. I'm not going down that road!"

Recently, she tried waylaying him after several of the training sessions but he would have none of it and ignored her. When she persevered, Trifena took to wandering along to meet him after training, and they would walk hand-in-hand to look at the building progress of their new house. Eventually, Jeetuna gave up.

However, in retaliation, she mischievously turned her attention to their son and Hestigys was no match for her seductions. He was fifteen, almost, and she was twenty-eight years his senior.

At first she observed him from a distance until she knew everything about his movements – where he went, what he did, times and places – and they began bumping into each other, seemingly by chance.

Because Hestigys was living partly with his family in their rented house and partly with Pulcher, no one realised the extent of the developing association.

That she had chosen *him* for her attentions flattered him and surprised his friends. She attracted him initially because she was a priestess and forbidden fruit but he knew she must have a wealth of sexual experience and that, together with her beauty, drew him to her like a fly to the spider's web.

He bragged to his friends about the money she spent on him and showed them the trinkets and love tokens she had given him – in short, he told them, Jeetuna knew her way about and was going places and he was going with her.

They encouraged him in his liaison, enjoying his experiences vicariously as he reported back to them her suggestive comments, the increasingly intimate touching, the maturing kisses, which at first were all within their own knowledge, their own youthful experience, and within his control.

Then he stopped reporting to his friends – in fact, they saw very little of him, and he seemed to have matured out of their reach. That was when Hestigys became a man and began to understand the ways of men and women together. He only weakly resisted the sweet, sticky trap set for him, and Jeetuna was bored no longer.

"You're very moody lately," commented Hestig one day at the pottery. When his son made no answer he sympathised, "Is it Flavia? Calf love can be very painful. But you're worrying your mother. She thinks you look wan and need building up – that's why she piles your plate high at mealtimes."

Pulcher was more observant and tried to warn Hestigys off the priestess, reminding him that she should not be associating with anyone other than the priests, and the affair could cause serious trouble. However, Hestigys brushed his friend aside, saying airily that Pulcher knew nothing of such things.

The day came when the large house was finished and furnished and the Roman family took possession. Julius said he was retaining the town house in Calleva, but his wife had decided that their house in Byden would become their home and she would live there permanently with Flavia, while her husband travelled to and fro as it suited him.

On the same day, Hestigys helped his mother and father and Trifosa move into their new house next door. It was similar in design to their previous home, but smaller.

Hestigys went with his father to retrieve the household gods from their storage place in the Temple and install them in their niche in the triclinium. Trifena had hand-sewn the curtain to pull across the shrine when it was not in use. Hestigys was amused that, this time, his father had got his own way and the mosaic on the floor was a simply-worked geometric pattern in white, black, yellow and red.

The two wives were ecstatic and Hestigys watched their enthusiastic and delighted embrace when they met halfway between houses, each on the way to wish the other family every happiness and prosperity. He was glad that his mother was so happy to be in her own house again, and Lucilla said she thought that the fresh country air would revive her own failing health.

Both house-warmings took place on the same occasion and became part-Roman and part-local celebrations.

Hestigys had told his mother that he would continue to sleep at Pulcher's, but after meeting Flavia again at the ceremonies, he moved back in with his family the same evening.

He permitted one more meeting with Jeetuna, which took place at the mere. He remained strong and calm in his resolve, and in spite of her wheedling and other well-practised arts, he refused to make love to her or allow her to take the initiative, as she often had. He handed back all her gifts, and with difficulty extricated himself from her embraces and kisses and tears.

"No!" he said emphatically. "No, Jeetuna! No more!" and turned and left her where she lay on the grass by the side of the water.

Having officiated at the house-warmings, she knew the reason for his change of heart – the graceful, young, blonde and blue-eyed Roman girl. Flavia!

For a while, she looked down into the dark waters, shrinking from the rejection of a mere boy, which seemed worse than other rejections. She contemplated making the greatest sacrifice of all to her goddess by wading out into the deepest part and becoming one of the many offerings lying on the muddy bed.

Instead, she stood up, rearranged her dress, wiped her eyes, and in the absence of a comb, dragged her painted nails through her hair. However ripe Hestigys had been, and he had, like a juicy peach, she knew she would get over her obsession with him. She always got over her obsessions with men, eventually.

And, of course, there was Julius Gaius. Her spirits suddenly revived and, as she thought about him, her heart again thumped hard inside her chest. Hestigys faded from her mind. Could it be that she was falling in love for the first time? Could it be that she was falling in love with *a Roman*?

She dismissed the notion, but her heart was still pounding as she made her way back to the settlement. That he had a wife never bothered her conscious thought for a moment.

CHAPTER 13

The attack came unexpectedly from the wood behind the Temple. About fifty Catuvellauni men, fearsome in their iron helmets, came running out of the trees, screaming and yelling and shaking long spears and wooden shields.

"Find Iraina and hold on to her!" Sharma ordered Brocchus. "And this time, don't lose her!"

Brocchus found her at the altar. He forced her arms behind her back and dragged her to one of the pillars, where he and another eunuch tied her fast. She screamed and pleaded with them to let her go.

"It's for your own safety," Brocchus told her. "It's no good shouting, as there's no one to rescue you. Veneta has gone to the schoolroom to be with the children, and Jeetuna has been told to ignore you. So be quiet, or the Catuvellauni will know where you are!" Then he left her.

Outside, hidden by pillars, he watched the fight that was no fight. The eunuchs were quickly struck down. They sought refuge with Brocchus, having been told by their attackers to keep out of the way or they would be abducted and taken back for the pleasure of the Catuvellauni men.

Someone had been banging the gong and men from the settlement were arriving excitedly from the market place, fields and houses, ready to try out their newly acquired skills. They could not help but be discomfited to see that the attackers were taller than most of them and obviously experienced fighters.

Several skirmishes took place around the Temple but the

Catuvellauni appeared to be amusing themselves, playing with the Byden men.

There were a few broken limbs and ribs and noses and some bloodied heads, and one of the farmers died when he fell and hit his forehead on the Temple steps, but the attackers had come only to take Iraina back with them.

"We have no quarrel with the people of the settlement," one of them told the frightened eunuchs. "In fact, we've been given instructions to cause no more injury or damage than is absolutely necessary."

About twenty of them, led by a tall man Brocchus thought must be Ziad, ran up the Temple steps.

"She's inside," the eunuch shouted, making himself heard above the commotion.

"Show me!" ordered the man, and Brocchus led the way into the Temple.

Once inside, the men ceased their yelling, lowered their spears and shields and looked round, blinking in the low light.

"There!" shouted one, pointing to where Iraina was struggling to free herself from the pillar.

There was a rush towards her and Brocchus took the opportunity to escape.

"See what trouble you've caused us!" Ziad said, drawing a knife to cut the ropes binding Iraina to the pillar. "Come quietly now, or I'll have to knock you out!"

"What will you take instead of me?" she asked them breathlessly.

"What are you offering?" asked Ziad.

"Gold!" she said. "Jewellery! Much treasure!"

"Where?" he demanded.

"Let me go first," she said.

"What do you say, men?" he asked them and laughed.

"Yes!" they shouted back, also laughing. "We'll take the gold!"

He loosened his grip on the ropes and she shook herself free of them and darted towards the entrance doors.

"Where?" he demanded again, as she put distance between them.

"In Vortin's house, behind the Temple. There's a trapdoor under the carpet in his living room. The cellar is full of treasure!"

"Off you go, men – ten of you!" Ziad instructed. "Collect what you can! Take your tunics off to bundle it all up if you have to!"

He called to his companion, who was still sporting his sheepskin cap. "Stay with me! The rest of you go outside and collect the men together! We're going home!"

Iraina was almost bowled over as the men rushed past her to the doors and tumbled outside to recall their companions.

Ziad made a sign to the young man in the cap and together they bore down on Iraina. She saw their intent and tried to get through the doors but they were upon her and eventually she gave up struggling and went quietly with them.

She made one more break for freedom as they left the Temple, so the young man punched her on the jaw, knocking her into unconsciousness, and Ziad slung her over his shoulder as if she were only a hare.

In small groups, the fifty Catuvellauni headed for home, carrying with them bundles of Vortin's looted treasures.

"At least she won't be living in poverty any more," commented Ziad, as they made their way through the wood. "Perhaps now she'll stay with Cullum and the children."

The younger man grinned. "They'll sort her out," he said. "Did I tell you my woman's pregnant? Makes a difference, doesn't it?"

"Soranus, what have they done to you?" cried Bron when he returned home from the fight with one eye closed and blood coursing down his cheek. When she had cleaned him up, however, she was relieved to find only a deep cut and bruising where he had been caught accidentally by a glancing blow from the shaft of a spear.

"I winded him, though, and put him down," Soranus said proudly. "He said no woman was worth it and he'd had enough for one day and was going home!"

They both attended a special celebration service Vortin arranged for all those who had taken part in the battle. Kendrus and Stalwyn had been busy, and splints and bandages, wounds now healing and black eyes became medals of honour for those who bore them. Their number did not include Nobilianus who, it was rumoured, had been cowering upstairs in his rooms throughout the skirmish.

During the service, Vortin bemoaned the abduction of Iraina but told the people about her treachery and that Shubinata did not want her back.

He was not grieving for Iraina but had been devastated when he realised the extent of the looting. Returning to his house after the fight, he had found the trapdoor open, and with trepidation descended the steps.

The Catuvellauni had almost stripped his cellar bare. Not much was left except the mattress, an overturned table, a few smashed glass vessels, empty boxes and some vestments embroidered with pure gold thread. Diligently searching around, he had found on the floor a few gold coins and some scattered items of jewellery.

He wondered how they had found his secret hoard. Only a handful of people knew what the cellar contained, or that there was a cellar at all. Someone had talked.

He employed craftsmen to repair the damage to the Temple building and his front door, but said nothing about the looting that had taken place.

CHAPTER 14

AD 402

For the rest of his life, Hestigys remembered year 402 as one of sunshine and laughter, and of a growing love between himself and Flavia.

Trifosa and he were constantly in her company, wandering the footpaths around the settlement, paddling along the Stan and teaching the Roman girl to swim where the stream widened and deepened further down the valley. Brother and sister introduced her to the woods with all their wildlife and variations in growth and colour, and she in turn entertained them with descriptions of life in the Roman world of Calleva and Eboracum.

Hestigys had already experienced the intensity of a previous, more intimate relationship but was content for the love each felt for the other to take its own natural and unhurried course, and he respected Flavia's virginity. He was pleased that no man had taken that from her, and however much he wished it, would do nothing to devalue her until, as he fervently hoped, their relationship was established on a more mature and recognised footing.

Unfortunately, Flavia also attracted the attention of someone else in the settlement – Nobilianus, now twenty-two years old. When he followed Trifosa, he was following both girls, and on one occasion shouted after them, "Two for the price of one!"

The year 402 was a victorious one for the Romans. General Stilicho pursued Alaric and his Visigoth forces, and drove them out of Italia after a great battle at Pollentia. To accomplish that, he had been forced to recall a further part of the British garrison and it was not unusual to see legionaries frequenting Byden's small Roman temple, the inn and baths as they passed through on their way to the coast to set sail for their homeland.

Free-thinkers like Africanus and Hestig were extremely concerned at the depletion of the Roman garrison in Britannia. They continued to hold political discussions in Hestig's new house during the evenings, and Julius Gaius joined them when he could. It was not long before he, too, was invited to serve on the village council.

Jeetuna was at a loss to know how to meet Julius socially, as his family did not, of course, attend Ashuba's Temple. She solved the problem by asking Vortin's permission to take over, from Veneta, responsibility for the Roman temple. She suggested that it must be kept ready at all times for any passing Romans, who brought their money to the market, inn and brothel, and sometimes gave large donations to Ashuba's Temple. Vortin expressed surprise at her zeal but granted her wish and left her to get on with it.

She was very conscientious in carrying out her duties and was often there with one of the Temple girls, supervising sweeping out the snow or rain, bird droppings, occasional dead spiders and field mice, summer blossom, and autumn leaves. The emperor's bust and both Roman and Christian altars were dusted and polished, the floor and pillars washed, and the flowers changed almost every day.

Consequently, she often met the Gaius family there, sometimes together and sometimes individually. She made a friend of young Flavia, and smiled self-deprecatingly when Lucilla told her, "We are so grateful to you, Jeetuna, for keeping our temple sparkling."

On one occasion, Lucilla asked, "Do you think Honorius" – and she nodded towards the bust of the emperor – "understands women's problems? I know he is a god, and I am sure he listens to Julius, but does he listen to me when I ask him... other things?"

"I don't know about your gods," Jeetuna replied, "only ours. Shubinata, our mother goddess, would listen to you. Her temple is in the wood and only women are allowed in it. Ask Trifena to show you, some time."

"Thank you, Jeetuna, I will," and Lucilla smiled at her again. Jeetuna hated that smile. It made Lucilla look almost pretty. *But she's still too pale and thin,* thought Jeetuna with satisfaction, looking down at her own full curves.

Sometimes she managed to be in the temple when Julius came on his own. On those occasions she would apologise, lower her eyes demurely and withdraw until he had ended his prayers.

She had to be careful this time. Here was no boy, no rustic, but an intelligent and powerful man who cared about his family. He did not venerate the gods of the Atrebates and their priests and priestesses, as did the local people. In other words, she had to make him take notice of her not for the position she held but for herself as a woman. This was a new challenge and would take time and careful management.

With surprise, Jeetuna realised that she was indeed in love with Julius. It had never happened to her before and she was completely bowled over by the feeling – not so much the passion, though that was present, but a desire to care for him and look after him, to share her days with him as well as her nights. She imagined herself cooking and cleaning for him in a house of their own.

These thoughts she shook from her head. What was happening to her? She had never cooked and cleaned since finishing her Temple training at the age of twelve! She was fantasising like any silly schoolgirl. Such a relationship was a non-starter. He was Roman and she an Atrebate, besides which he was married and was a father and she was a priestess.

It was all very inconvenient, but those were the facts. She knew there was only one way she could have him: the usual way. She sighed. It would not be enough this time, but would have to do. But she would take her time and enjoy gazing at him and talking to him and sometimes dreaming about him. Anything else could wait. He wasn't going anywhere and neither was she.

One day she asked him, "Does he answer your prayers, your emperor god?"

"News reaches Calleva very slowly and often very late," replied Julius, "but it does seem that General Stilicho and his army are defeating our enemies and driving them out of our homeland. We are all very anxious, though, that withdrawing so many troops leaves Britannia very vulnerable."

"Do you speak to your wife about your concerns?" asked Jeetuna innocently.

"No," he replied slowly. "She is very delicate and I don't wish to worry her."

That was the beginning of many conversations. Jeetuna told him about her life since being taken as an orphan into the Temple at the age of three years, not knowing who her parents were, and he spoke to her about his boyhood in northern Italia and his life since.

As the days went by she fell more and more in love with this strong, gentle man, so devoted to his faded wife who, Jeetuna felt sure, could not be supplying his physical needs in the way she knew *she* could. He was the first man who treated her as if she had a brain as well as a body. In fact, he seemed surprisingly impervious to her body, no matter how she dressed to try to attract him.

One day at harvest time she saw Trifena in the market, buying Kentish oysters as a special treat for Hestig, and stopped to speak to her about Lucilla.

"Yes, she told me of your suggestion," Trifena informed the priestess, "and I'm taking her to see Shubinata tomorrow, mid-morning."

"I'm glad," said Jeetuna. "I hope her prayers are answered."

When Trifena took Lucilla into the temple in the wood, they paused for a moment to adjust their eyes to the dim interior. One large candle was burning on a pedestal. As they approached the altar, a sudden draught disturbed the curtains behind the goddess and flickered the candle flame.

The wooden altar was covered with red and bronzed leaves, scarlet rose hips and red and black berries picked from the woody and black nightshade.

Lucilla walked barefoot along the red carpet and gazed up at the stone figure of Shubinata, over-heavy with pregnancy, and began to cry. Trifena hurried to her friend and put an arm round her shoulder and eased her down on to the praying stool, kneeling beside her. Lucilla bent her head but was silent.

"You can tell *her*," Trifena encouraged.

"There's no need," whispered Lucilla. "She is a goddess of fertility so she knows."

She turned and sat on the stool, with Trifena beside her.

"We've been in our new houses almost a year," observed Lucilla.

"I don't know where the time has gone," agreed Trifena.

"In all that time, Julius has never once made love to me," Lucilla confessed miserably.

Trifena was appalled. "But why not?" she asked. "It's obvious to everyone that he worships you."

"I had a bad time carrying Flavia," explained her friend. "I nearly died. You can see I am never in good health – that's why we have moved to the country."

"Have you been to the doctors?" asked Trifena.

"Many, of all sorts, and I have taken pills and potions and followed all their advice, but I am no better."

"I thought you were looking a little stronger," encouraged Trifena gently.

Lucilla brightened. "Do you really think so?"

Trifena nodded.

"I wish Julius thought so," continued Lucilla wistfully. "You see, he is so afraid that if we have another child he will lose me, that he hardly touches me. It's killing me, and I think it is killing him."

"Do you want another baby?" Trifena asked her.

"Yes, almost more than anything," Lucilla whispered, her voice so quiet that it would have been inaudible if it had not been for the silence in the temple. "But above all, I want my husband," and she began to cry again. "What can I do, Trifena?"

"Stop worrying. You know he loves you. In spite of what you've told me, he never looks at any of the other women in the settlement – and he doesn't visit the inn of a night, does he?" Lucilla shook her head. "Then just concentrate on getting stronger. Go for long walks and get some sun on your skin – and a little rouge on your cheeks wouldn't hurt."

"Thank you, Trifena, you are a good friend," smiled Lucilla.

"Then one day, he'll think 'Lucilla is looking much stronger these days' – you'll see."

"Right!" agreed Lucilla, with sudden determination.

She laid a leather pouch of coins on the leaves on the altar and the two women left the temple.

A few moments later, a draught of cool air displaced the curtains again, extinguishing the candle flame, and there were only disturbed leaves where the pouch had lain.

CHAPTER 15

AD 403

One afternoon in early December 403, a day that was bright and sunny and unusually warm for the season, a covered wagon drawn by two mules approached from the direction of the Stan. The driver brought the wagon to a halt in the market place. Everyone stopped whatever they were doing and watched as a group of young men and women tumbled from the back.

It was about the time that the children were coming out of school and excitedly groups of them rushed over to find out what was happening, surrounding the entertainers as they hauled their musical instruments and other paraphernalia from the wagon. Last of all, a child of about three years was helped down.

To Hestig it all seemed rather familiar, and he left Hestigys busy at the wheel, throwing a tall pot, and wandered over.

"Yes," said the driver, "we've been here before – must be about fifteen years ago."

"I remember," said Hestig. "There was an old man driving then –"

"My old father," said the man. "He's been dead long since."

"– and a child who walked the tightrope –"

"My daughter," explained the man. "She's over there – got a child of her own now, my little granddaughter. She's a quick learner, but not quite up to the tightrope yet."

Hestig looked at the wagon. It was brightly painted and the company looked altogether more affluent than before.

"Performance tonight!" shouted the man with the drum. "Fire eating and flame-throwing, magic, conjuring and juggling, tightrope walking and – are you ready for this? – a display of mind-reading and mind-suggestion!"

The crowd that had gathered gasped, while the children asked urgently what all the long words meant. The market place soon cleared of shoppers as people hurried home to prepare early evening meals, and the traders had to close before time.

Later that evening, Hestig and his family joined those assembling to watch the performance. As before, all Temple staff were excused their duties.

The presentation had improved and the programme expanded over the years and the crowd seemed even more enthralled. The tightrope walker had developed her act and walked the rope carrying a long, flexible pole made of a lightweight wood unknown to Hestig. Her daughter danced daintily and went round the crowd, hat in hand, returning to her grandfather every time the coins thrown in became too heavy to hold.

Jeetuna looked for Julius in the crowd and saw him standing with Lucilla and Flavia, who was holding hands with Hestigys. Hestigys saw her watching them and turned away.

"Not interested, young man," she thought. "I have in mind a tastier meal than you ever were."

At that point, Lucilla said something to her husband. He spoke to her but she shook her head and left his side. Jeetuna watched as she wove her way through the crowd towards their house. Julius stayed to watch the demonstration of hypnotism.

Jeetuna was a willing volunteer. The hypnotist was a little man with piercing blue eyes and restless hands. His act was not faked, as she believed had been the mind-reading demonstration that preceded it, and she 'lost' all consciousness throughout the ten minutes that he worked with her, as she carried out his requests and answered his questions.

He had promised that he would not ask her to do anything that made her look foolish, and she could not be made to do anything of which she disapproved. Standing next to her, Sharma had muttered that, if she had such a list, it was very short.

Once the man had put her into a hypnotic state by talking to her quietly, she told him her name and her position at the Temple, even her age, at which everyone roared with laughter as Jeetuna usually kept that a secret.

Two chairs were brought and he asked her to lie across them, then passing from chair to chair, he gradually widened the gap between them until her head rested on one, her feet on the other, and her body lay rigid between them without support.

When he had reversed the process, he asked her to sit on one of the chairs. He then asked her to remember back to her childhood, before she entered the Temple.

The audience's surprise was audible when, from her mouth, came a child's voice, calling for her mother by name. The crowd hushed. She had always maintained that she did not know who her parents were.

She became distressed and said her mother was cold and would not get up off the floor of the hut. She said she had searched for food in the house but could find none, and had to eat berries from the wood, and she showed how she cried and slept and cried and slept, until somebody found her and took her to the Temple. The crowd was quiet and did not laugh.

The hypnotist told her to close her eyes and said she would wake after three clicks of his fingers, and then she would find a bald head to kiss. He clicked his fingers as he counted, "One, two, three," and she opened her eyes, but they were glazed over. She left her chair and moved to the crowd, silently and intently searching, until she found a man with a bald head, which she kissed soundly. Everyone cheered and laughed. Her vision cleared then.

Confused, she returned to the little man with piercing eyes. He thanked her for taking part in his demonstration and took both her hands in his and kissed them. Jeetuna was surprised at the warmth of his action and did not know the reason.

The hypnotist's act concluded the performance and the crowd clapped the entertainers for several minutes before beginning to disperse.

Julius was talking to Hestig and Africanus. Bron and Soranus were there with Pulcher, and close by Trifena was holding the hands of Bron's two children. Eventually, they all moved away, Hestigys escorting Flavia, followed by sixteen-year-old Trifosa, who was chatting animatedly to Africanus and her mother.

Hestig walked across to where the performers were packing up, to ask them to leave the pitch clean and indicating where rubbish should be dumped, then he too left.

Jeetuna had sat down on one of the chairs, feeling as if all energy, mental and physical, had been sucked from her. Julius noticed her sitting there on her own and went across to her.

"Are you all right, my dear girl?" he asked her.

She smiled up at him and he sat on the other chair facing her.

"I feel quite shattered," she said.

Julius, used to weak women, became as protective and reassuring towards her as he always was towards his wife. Jeetuna understood that this was quite an unconscious reaction on his part and had nothing to do with her charms.

"Do you know what happened under the mind-suggestion display?" he asked her. She shook her head, so he told her gently what she had said about her childhood. Jeetuna closed her eyes and passed the back of her hand across her forehead.

"Tell me again," she asked him, and he repeated it.

"I remember now," she whispered. "We were in a hut. The fire had gone out. She lay on the floor and I shook her but I couldn't wake her."

Everyone had gone, except the entertainers, who were still packing up, and no one was taking any notice of the couple, but their conversation was too public in the middle of the market place under all the flaring torches.

"Come," he said, "we'll walk, if you feel able."

Jeetuna nodded and they set off along the path down to the Stan stream.

The sky was clear and starry, the moon new, but it was cold and Jeetuna shivered. Immediately, Julius put his arm around her shoulders, then obviously realised what he had done, and withdrew it.

"It's all right," she told him, but he made no attempt to return it.

"I have such a headache," she said.

"Do you want to talk?"

"I feel I need to," she replied, and described all that she was remembering, which wasn't much more than when under hypnosis. "How could I have forgotten her all these years?" she asked with remorse.

"Do you remember your father?"

Jeetuna shook her head. "There was never a man around."

They walked in silence and Julius began to suggest that they should return when she started to cry, quietly at first, then with loud sobs. She reached for him and he took her in his arms and began to soothe her, kissing her hair, stroking her cheek, trying to calm her with soft, gentle words.

It was plain that he was not prepared for her response. She suddenly threw her arms round his neck and would not stop kissing him, and pressed her body close so that he would feel her heart thumping against his.

At first, he tried to move away but she guessed he would not be able to struggle for long against all his pent-up passion, and it was only seconds before he capitulated to her desire and pulled her to him.

She was exultant as his hand strayed, heavily crushing then roughly massaging her left breast as he returned her frenzied kisses, and his body pulsed and rose hard against hers.

Then he stopped as suddenly as he had responded.

"No!" he said. "No! Jeetuna, I apologise, it was all my fault – and you're not yourself tonight."

"But I am myself!" she cried. "This is me, the real me. I love you, Julius!"

"You don't know what you're saying. You're beautiful and you're desirable, but you're a priestess and I love my wife. I must go home. I'll take you back to the Temple."

"No, I can find my own way back!" she retorted, tossing her head and gathering together what pride she had left, then finding it was very little, pleaded with him to stay with her, or at least to let her be part of his life, if only occasionally and in secret.

"No! Never!" he said and turned and walked swiftly away.

Reeling from his rejection, her thoughts were dark as she sobbed and stumbled her way back to the Temple, to spend a night that left her with resolve but such a headache that she could not get out of bed next morning.

Meanwhile, the entertainers were delighted with the pile of donated coins that the child tipped from the hat onto their table. That was until Vortin decided to exact an on-the-spot performing tax, which they paid resignedly. After the women had wisely helped themselves to a share of the balance, the men drifted across to the inn and baths and spent the remainder during the night.

Next day, leaving later than intended, they took away little more money than they had brought with them, except that a few pieces of jewellery, a leather pouch or two, eggs, chickens and even a pig had found their way into the wagon, hidden under a pile of costumes.

Along the path, they were joined by Julius and Lucilla, who were out walking in the morning sunshine. The couple accompanied the wagon to the top of the ridge, then down the other side, before finally waving the company out of sight.

Trifena had been thinking that Lucilla looked much better of late, but did not know whether it was the effect of the phial of liquid obtained from Stalwyn, or the long walks, or the unobtrusive rouge, or all the remedies combined.

Now, seeing the couple returning home with their arms around each other and Lucilla's head resting against her husband's shoulder, she stopped tossing seed corn and waved. The chickens clucked and squawked around her feet, complaining at the delay. Lucilla's contented smile said it all, and Trifena chuckled.

I don't know how, but it seems you've done it again, Shubinata, she thought.

103

CHAPTER 16

AD 404

It was the end of March when Lucilla confided to Trifena that she was pregnant. Trifena kissed her friend.

"I'm so pleased for you both," she enthused. "How far?"

"I'm about four months gone," Lucilla said. "We wouldn't tell anyone before this, in case I miscarried. I'm thirty-six, you know."

"Have you told Flavia?" asked Trifena.

"She was the first," Lucilla smiled, "and she can't wait." Her eyes twinkled. "It will be good practice for when she is expecting her own."

It was not long before the news reached the Temple. Jeetuna did her sums and raged silently. She could not be sure, but guessed that she had provided the foreplay and Lucilla had reaped the benefit.

Julius had not spoken to her since that night and she had not sought him out. The Roman temple became neglected and the flowers decayed and stank in their vases. She believed the only reason he had fled from her was that he honoured his marriage vows to his wife. The resolve she had made that night had not left her and now she purposed to put it into operation.

"Come inside, come inside, my dear," Umbella invited, straightening up from her inspection of the contents of the cauldron and wiping her hands on her skirt. "Always glad to see you. Have you brought me more baby business?"

Jeetuna followed her through the doorway, into the dark interior of the hovel.

"In a way," she replied, and briefly explained the reason for her visit. "It goes without saying that you will be paid well."

"Horsebane – an abortion by another name," cackled the old woman. "Wait here." She hobbled to the far end of the hut, to a table on which Jeetuna could just make out a small cabinet of wooden drawers, sealed jars of richly-coloured liquids, and bunches of dried plants dangling overhead from grass strings.

Jeetuna was invited to sit down but, recoiling from the soiled seat of the only chair, preferred to stand and wait as, with a pestle, the old woman pounded root and stem in a mortarium.

Uncorking a bottle, Umbella tilted back her head and slurped down a mouthful, then wiped the back of her hand across thin, sore-encrusted lips, sighing contentedly as she did so.

A small amount of the liquid was poured on to the mashed-up plant, stirred well and strained through a piece of cheese cloth, and finally poured into a green glass phial. Finally, with yellow-stained fingers, Umbella held the phial up to a ray of sunshine that had bravely ventured in through the roof branches, and shook it vigorously. She brought it over and gave it to the priestess. Jeetuna looked critically at the liquid fizzing lazily in the phial.

"Is there enough there?" she asked.

The old woman was affronted. "Of course there's enough. You're not poisoning an army!"

Jeetuna handed her a small bag with drawstring neck.

"Is there enough here?" Umbella asked in turn, grinning and showing the gaps in her blackened teeth.

Jeetuna smiled. "Of course there's enough, even though your charges keep rising."

The woman cackled. "We've all got to live," she said.

"Not all," commented Jeetuna, hiding the phial in her shoe, and went out, leaving the woman raising a large jug of beer to her ugly mouth.

Jeetuna waited a couple of weeks until she next saw Trifena in the Temple. She guessed that Julius would not have told anyone of their encounter under the new moon, and took a chance.

"I hear that Lucilla is pregnant," she said, and Trifena nodded. "That's very good news," continued Jeetuna. "Her visit to Shubinata was not a waste of time, then? Tell her she can go back anytime to take her thank-offering – better to come on her own – just let me know and I'll make sure the candle is lit and everything is as it should be."

"I'll tell her," promised Trifena.

Jeetuna waited impatiently for two more weeks before receiving a message that Lucilla would be taking her thank-offering to Shubinata on the following day.

Next morning, Lucilla crossed the market place and stopped by the stall of a pedlar of jewellery and fashion items such as combs, manicure sets, pill boxes and eastern perfumes in phials, all advertised as 'What fashionable Roman women are using'. As she stopped to look at the goods in his tray, Bron approached.

Bron looked harassed. Layla, now a lively five-year-old, was running to and fro, chattering non-stop to her mother, and Alon, a year younger, had just fallen over his sister's feet, grazing his knee, and was yelling loudly, though without tears.

"Bron, dear," Lucilla greeted her, "not a good morning?"

Bron pulled a face. "I've threatened Soranus I'll take them to the forge! He can look after them while I spend the day being pampered at the baths!" she spat out.

Lucilla smiled and offered to take them off her hands for a couple of hours later on. Bron looked relieved and the children were delighted to be invited to the large house where they could run and play, splash in the shallow end of the bathing pool, and consume large quantities of honey cakes.

"But first you must be quiet and let your mother help me choose a present for the goddess," she told them. "It's for my thank-offering," she explained. "Have a look, Bron. I'm not sure whether to choose this pendant or the necklace."

They discussed the matter for a few moments and decided on the necklace. Strung along copper wire were clear glass beads with gold foil gleaming inside them.

"Julius has given me an offering as well – a pouch of money – but I wanted to take her something for herself," said Lucilla. "This will look lovely round her neck."

When Lucilla arrived at the temple in the wood, the interior was lit and smelling of wild narcissi. Jeetuna was waiting, concealed in the shadows behind the altar.

Lucilla dropped to her knees on the stool, bowed her head and silently thanked the goddess for hearing her prayers.

"But I'm terrified of the birth," she confided aloud. "I'll need some help to get through that."

"We're all here to help you, Lucilla." Jeetuna's voice was soft and overly sweet. Lucilla jumped and raised her eyes.

"Jeetuna!" she said, "I didn't expect you to be here."

"I have only just finished filling the pots with flowers," explained the priestess. "I'll go if you wish."

"No, that's not necessary," Lucilla assured her. "Would you like to see the gift I've brought her?"

She stood up and took the necklace from a linen pouch slung from her girdle and laid it on the altar.

"May I?" asked Jeetuna, picking it up and holding it towards the light. The gold foil reflected the flicker from the candle flame. "It's lovely," she murmured, thinking how well the necklace would look round her own neck.

"I bought it especially this morning, from a pedlar in the market. He's only there today before he moves on, so I was lucky to find him."

"Very lucky!" agreed Jeetuna, committing the information to memory. "I am sure Shubinata is delighted with your gift. Look, I will hang it round her neck straight away. There!" she enthused, "See how it glows."

"I have also brought money from Julius," said Lucilla and laid his leather pouch on the altar.

"You are both so generous," Jeetuna flattered her.

Lucilla smiled. "We are both so happy," she said.

"Last time you came, you were in tears because your husband was being cold towards you." Lucilla looked surprised that Jeetuna knew.

"Shubinata keeps no secrets from me," smiled the priestess. Lucilla accepted the explanation.

"That's all past," she blushed. "He's making up for it now."

But not for much longer, thought Jeetuna. Aloud she said, "Lucilla, you were asking for help to get through the birth."

"Yes, I was. I'm not very brave."

"Perhaps I can help you." The offer sounded guileless. "Shubinata is asked for such assistance many times and, under her direction, I mix a special potion. It looks like water, but has magic that will quicken your baby and bless him – you do want a son, don't you?" Lucilla nodded. "He will grow perfect and strong inside you, and the delayed effects of the tincture will deaden the pain when your time comes and ensure the birth process is easy."

"How I long for that!" Lucilla exclaimed fervently.

"Then will you take the tincture?" asked Jeetuna.

"Yes, I will," agreed Lucilla readily.

Jeetuna laughed to herself. *What a fool the woman is!*

She took a while, pretending to search for the phial in the recesses behind the altar, and exclaimed with pleasure when she brought it out. Then she found a chased goblet, which she placed on the altar. Into this, she poured the liquid from the phial and watched it sparkle and fizz against a silver surface that was as cold as the hatred in her heart.

Turning her back to Lucilla, Jeetuna then histrionically raised the goblet towards the statue of the goddess, turned round and touched it briefly with her own lips, then handed it to Lucilla across the altar. Lucilla took it, apparently suspecting nothing.

"Do I have to drink it all?" she asked.

"Every last drop," replied Jeetuna lightly.

She watched as Lucilla lifted the goblet to her lips and drained it. Then, without remorse, she waited.

She did not have to wait long. Suddenly, Lucilla gasped. "I felt the baby quicken," she said, smiling, but then her face drained of the little colour it had and she dropped the goblet.

"I have such a pain," she cried, clutching her stomach, and collapsed on to her knees. "Help me, Jeetuna, please." Jeetuna didn't move. "Jeetuna, help me!" Still Jeetuna didn't move.

Lucilla stared at the priestess without comprehension then rolled on to her back, shuddered and began to convulse, screaming in pain.

"Quiet!" Jeetuna ordered. "Do you want the whole settlement to hear you?"

The priestess turned her back on the writhing woman and faced Shubinata. "Thank you," she said above Lucilla's screams, looking up at the goddess.

She turned again towards her victim and stood and watched, without emotion, then observed, "As Umbella said, it's abortion by another name."

After half-an-hour, the screaming and senseless babbling turned to moaning and heavy panting, then there was silence.

The priestess walked round the altar and knelt by Lucilla's body. The wife of Julius was lying still, her face contorted with pain. Jeetuna looked down at her, a smile on her lips.

But suddenly, Lucilla sat bolt upright and grabbed hold of Jeetuna's tunic! Then it was the priestess who screamed in fear. But it was the last supreme effort of a dying woman, and she fell back, pulling Jeetuna down on top of her, and did not move again.

The priestess unclasped Lucilla's fingers, so releasing her hold, and threw her arm to the floor, then straightened up. She tried to make the body look as natural as possible by closing Lucilla's eyes and mouth, smoothing away the lines of pain as best she could, rearranging her legs and laying her arms by her side. When she was satisfied, she stood up and again looked down at the body.

"I wonder who your widower will take to his bed now, Lucilla," she said aloud. "Certainly not you any more! Now he's free to look in another direction!"

She set about collecting together the goblet and phial, and wiped up the liquid spilt on the wooden altar, all the while planning the future. He should be allowed a decent time for mourning, of course, then she would indicate that she was anxious to help him recover from the loss of his beautiful wife and their unborn son – and he would soon forget this pale, limp creature, Jeetuna determined. Of course, she would play a little hard to get at first, but would quickly give in to his pleas for loving.

She left by the door behind the altar and made her way back to the Temple without being noticed.

Julius was distraught when they came to tell him later in the day that Veneta had found Lucilla's body on the floor of the temple in the wood. Apparently, she had gone there to take a thank-offering to the goddess – the pouch of money was still lying on the altar where she had placed it – and she must suddenly have had a pregnancy convulsion, which killed her. She looked quite peaceful, they told him. They were bringing her body back to the house.

"It's all my fault, it's all my fault!" he accused himself over and over as he sat with his head in his hands. "If it hadn't been for me and my lust she would be alive today," and he thought of Jeetuna and cursed her for rousing him that night and himself for coming home with desire in his body.

Lucilla was buried in the wood with her jewellery and other treasured possessions. Julius placed on her breast a blue glass bottle. It contained a tear from each of her mourners, then had been filled to the brim with his, collected one night when he was alone in their bedroom.

At first, Flavia was in denial and would not accept that her mother was dead. Then she ran to Trifena for comfort, and later to Hestigys. Not long after the funeral, by the side of the new grave, they became engaged.

"Your mother would have been so pleased, and so am I," smiled Trifena, and hugged her future daughter-in-law.

CHAPTER 17

Julius devoted more and more time and energy to his work in Calleva. When he was in Byden, his leisure was spent at the home of Hestig and Trifena, discussing and debating with his host and Africanus and other members of the village council, sustained by the meals cheerfully served by Trifena and her young daughter.

He took upon himself as much planning and organising of settlement affairs as he could – anything to keep his mind and body active and occupied, so he had less time to think of the wife he had loved so completely and mourned so deeply. Above all, he wanted to make sure he was able to sleep as soon as he crawled into bed.

Sunk in his own grief, he scarcely thought about Flavia on her own in the house, with only the slaves for company.

Trifosa was glad on the occasions when her mother took pity on Flavia and invited her to stay the night with them or, at other times, allowed Trifosa to sleep in the Roman house to keep her friend company.

The two girls were about to leave for Flavia's house one evening when Hestigys offered to take Trifosa's place. His mother looked at him knowingly and said she hadn't sprung up overnight with the bluebells, that she felt responsible for Flavia's welfare until her father made other arrangements, and Hestigys had better stay in his own bedroom!

That same night, when the girls were sharing Flavia's bed and chatting together, a soft tap sounded at the bedroom door and one of the women slaves stood there in her night attire, candle in hand.

"What is it?" asked Flavia.

"I'm not certain," replied the slave, "but I have the strangest feeling that there is someone creeping about the house."

Trifosa sat up. "What makes you say that? Surely that can't be?"

"I've felt it on several occasions, but only when you're both sleeping here. I hear noises –"

"What noises?" asked Flavia.

"Breathing, and footsteps, but when I take one of the men with me to look round, there's nothing, except –" She paused.

"Well?" asked Flavia.

"Shadows that move – here, there, gone when I blink –"

"Now you *are* imagining things!" exclaimed Flavia. "What does the other slave say about it?"

"He doesn't see anything," mumbled the woman, probably feeling as foolish as she sounded.

"How could anyone get in here? You're mistaken, go back to bed."

The woman left, still looking troubled.

"We could go to my house," suggested Trifosa.

"If I let shadows frighten me, I'd never sleep here again," replied her friend with determination. "Let's cuddle up together."

Trifosa lay awake a long time, listening to Flavia breathing quietly beside her. Eventually she too fell asleep, and dreamed of fleeting shadows, of a face yellow in flickering candlelight, and bluebells, and a pattering like rain, and someone calling her name.

She woke with a start. It was light but Flavia was still asleep, her blonde hair tousled round her face. Trifosa crept quietly out of bed and made for the door, intending to get a drink of water. However, hearing her friend murmuring, as if she too were waking up, she turned round.

What Trifosa saw then caused her to let out a loud scream. Flavia sat up in fright.

"Whatever's wrong?" she asked.

Trifosa could only point to the coverlet, under which both girls had been sleeping. Scattered all over it were freshly picked bluebells.

Flavia jumped out of bed and stood staring at the flowers, then at Trifosa.

"Then there *was* someone in the house during the night!" Flavia whispered, the colour leaving her cheeks. "But who? And why?"

"Nobilianus," said Trifosa.

It was this incident that alerted Julius to the needs of his daughter, of her loneliness and grief for her mother.

He sent the slaves round the house, strengthening all the bolts and bars and locks, and began taking her to Calleva with him during the week. However, when he saw how miserable she and Hestigys were when apart, he decided that there was only one way forward, and spoke to Hestig.

"I agree," said Hestig. "My son's like a bull on his own in a field. I don't think he'll wait much longer."

"Then they should be married as soon as possible," said Julius. "She needs someone to look after her, and I know he'll take care of her."

In August, at about the time Julius had hoped to be a father again, they were married in the Roman temple by a Roman priest. Flavia wore pale blue and Trifosa, as her flower girl, glowed in green. Both of them turned many heads.

Julius noticed with pleasure that the temple was looking clean and fresh again – obviously, someone had been hard at work there that morning. Thoughts of Jeetuna came into his head, but he dismissed them.

The young couple moved in with Julius and their happiness was evident to all who saw them together. Trifena became a second mother to Flavia, and the two families drew closer as the months went by.

One evening, having said goodnight to Julius after being closeted with him for an hour, and closing the front door behind him, Hestig took his wife by the hand and sat her down on the couch in the triclinium.

"I have just had the most surprising conversation with Julius," he began. "I don't quite know how to tell you."

Trifena smiled and ruffled his hair, which still reminded her of a field mouse, and said, "You don't have to, I can guess."

"You can?" he asked in surprise.

"Yes, I'm not blind," she said. "Julius has asked for Trifosa's hand in marriage."

Hestig nodded, amazed at her perception.

"What did you say?"

"I said I'd talk it over with you. What do you think? He's willing to wait until October next year, when she's eighteen. He is just asking for permission to court her. Of course, there's a big age difference —"

"Nearly thirty years," mused Trifena, "but she needs calming down. He's a good man, he'll look after her, I know, and she'd be safe from that horror, Nobilianus."

"He's lonely," added Hestig, "and he wants more children."

"And she gets on so well with Flavia," said Trifena.

"So we're agreed?" asked Hestig.

"Certainly, we're agreed," replied Trifena, "but I don't know what the young madam in question will say about it."

"We'll ask her in the morning," said Hestig. "I have promised to give Julius our answer as soon as possible."

Trifosa was plainly astonished by the proposal, and not as sure as her parents were of the suitability of the arrangement.

"I like him," she said, "but he's so old." She put her head on one side and appeared to consider the matter. "Would he give me everything I asked for, do you think?"

Trifena said she thought he probably would, but for Trifosa's sake, she hoped he wouldn't. "You'll never want for anything," she said.

"It would be fun, though, to be Flavia's sister-in-law and stepmother at the same time!"

Trifena looked at her husband. "She's not mature enough to make a decision," she told him.

"Yes, I am," argued Trifosa. "I don't love him, Mother."

"He's giving you over a year to make up your mind, dear, but I don't want to force you into anything you're not happy about. He's a fine man, though, and a Roman, and you won't do any better."

"If I say 'yes' now, can I say 'no' in a year's time if I want to?"

"You can't keep stringing him along for a year, Trifosa," her mother scolded her. "If you decide your answer is 'no', you must tell him as soon as you're sure. I expect he'll want to look elsewhere if you refuse him."

"I've made up my mind," said Trifosa. "We can be special friends now, if that's what he wants."

"That's all he's asking," said her father. "I'll walk across and tell him the good news straight away. He said he won't leave for Calleva until he knows."

"I'm sure you've done the right thing, dear," smiled Trifena.

Julius was overjoyed when he received Hestig's reply.

"I'm not replacing Lucilla," he explained, "but I've been so lonely since she left me. We always wanted a son and Trifosa's young and strong enough to fill the house with children, her and Flavia between them."

Hestig held the horse's head while his friend mounted.

"My heart's lighter than it has been since Lucilla died," he called back as he galloped away down the hill.

Julius had asked that the betrothal should be kept a secret until he had a chance to tell Flavia himself. Trifosa tried hard to carry out his wishes, but had been dropping veiled hints to her friend all week, while hopping about from foot to foot.

In consequence, Flavia had to admit to her father, when he finally returned from Calleva and took time to sit her down and tell her the news, that she already had an inkling of the matter.

Her feelings were mixed.

"Sweetheart, I've not forgotten your mother – how could I ever do so? But I am very lonely. It's made worse when I see the happiness you and Hestigys are enjoying."

Flavia kissed him and said she was very glad for them both, although she confided to her husband that she thought her friend was too young and the age difference between them too great.

Hestigys laughed. "My sister's seventeen, going on seven," he said, "but she's got to grow up some time."

Julius lost no time in calling on Trifosa. He had brought gifts from Calleva for her and her parents, and promised to take her there behind him in the saddle one day soon. Trifosa was entranced. Then they walked together round the courtyard and stood by the stone lion fountain, which had been rescued from the previous house and was again installed in a prominent position.

Julius told her of his dreams for the future, which now included her and their children. Trifosa drew back a little.

"Please, Julius, don't rush me," she pleaded, and he stopped in mid-sentence.

"I'm sorry," he apologised.

At that moment the outside bell clanged. A slave answered the door and Africanus walked in. He stopped when he saw them together.

"Africanus!" exclaimed Trifosa. "We have some amazing news for you! I am sort of betrothed to Julius!"

The African stood quite still. "Betrothed?" he asked, as if he could not quite believe what he was hearing.

"Yes, my friend, are you not going to congratulate us?" Julius asked, his happiness evident in his voice.

Africanus seemed stunned. Then, "Of course, of course," he said, and took Julius's outstretched hand. "You deserve every happiness."

"And what about me?" asked Trifosa, pouting a little.

"And you too, young lady," he said, studying her face. "Every happiness – if this is what you want."

"Oh, Africanus, don't be an old grouch!" exclaimed Trifosa. "We can still be friends. Anyway, Julius has said he'll wait till I'm eighteen, haven't you, Julius? We're keeping it a secret until then. He's bought me the loveliest ivory and green silk parasol. Come and see!" and she took his huge black hand in hers and led him into the triclinium.

Hestig came over and watched them go. Julius looked troubled.

"I'd still like to keep our betrothal a secret, for the time being," he confided, "just until *I'm* sure that Trifosa is sure."

"She's got some growing up to do," her father said, "but you're just the man to work the miracle."

CHAPTER 18

"Would you look after the children for me?" Bron asked her mother one afternoon in November. "I haven't been up to the graves for a long time, and I'd like to go."

"In this fog?" asked Trifena in surprise.

"It will hide me," said Bron. "Hopefully, no one in the Temple will see me go past."

"Take care, then."

"I'll only be gone an hour or so," her daughter said, and left.

The fog was thick and Bron used its cover to hurry past the Temple by way of the school, so avoiding the wickerwork god, and on into the wood.

It was quiet in there. No birds were singing. She shivered in the damp chill atmosphere and pulled her cloak tighter around her. There was a constant drip from bare branch to bare branch and the leaves underfoot were slimy wet.

The four plague graves were covered in fallen leaves, which Bron cleared from the grassy mounds.

"You must think I'm very foolish," she said aloud, walking between them. "It's so wet here today I can't sit down – but I wanted to come. Such a long time has passed since we were all together, but I know you haven't forgotten me."

She fell silent then, thinking of the days they had spent together as they trained in Temple and school – mostly happy times. Sorin, with her beautiful pure soprano voice that had ensured her a place in the Temple choir; her other room-mate, little Naila, who had nursed her mother and father and then had succumbed to the pestilence herself; and Edreda, who had started out as Jeetuna's spy but had become a good friend. The fourth mound covered the body of her baby sister, Aelia. All dead, all claimed by the plague, while she had found refuge in Iraina's cell in the wood.

She continued to walk up and down, head bent, trying to decide what to say to them.

"I need to tell you that I'm not very happy – I should be, but I'm not. If it hadn't been for Vortin, I would never have married Soranus – though I don't know who I would have married because there's been no one else. Soranus is good to me and the children, and he loves us, and he's kind and generous, and works hard, and doesn't often get cross – but it's not enough. I see Flavia and Hestigys together, and see how love can be, and what I have is not enough. I'm empty. I need more, but what more I'm not sure – and who can give it to me?"

"I can, Bron."

Bron spun round with horror. Vortin was coming towards her out of the fog. Caught unawares and unprepared, with the thick mist swirling round them, this time she was not mistress of the situation as she had been when he surprised her at the stepping stones four years ago.

"Give me a chance and I will show you I can," he wheedled.

"How long have you been lurking there?" she demanded.

"Long enough to hear your little speech. Come home with me now and let me make love to you. I filled you once and I can do it again."

Memories – the ropes cutting into her young flesh and the gag in her mouth, the terror and subsequent pain – rose up before her like a spectre and she shrank from him in horror.

"Don't come near me, don't touch me!" she warned him.

"But that's just what I had in mind –" he said, "– coming near you and touching you, Bron, all over – like before."

She turned to run but he caught hold of her cloak and held it fast as she struggled to pull free. The brooch at her neck snapped under the tension and the cloak was dragged off her. The sudden release sent her lurching forward and she fell headlong among the leaves.

Scrambling onto her knees then her feet, she turned round, slipped in the mud and sat down heavily. Only the grave mounds separated them.

Vortin bundled her cloak to his chest and came purposefully towards her, but stopped abruptly, then stood as if unable to move, swaying slightly, his eyes fixed, and he spoke to the space between them.

"What are you doing here?" he asked. "Go back to the Temple! Go back!"

Bron stared from where she had fallen. She could see no one. Vortin raised his voice, more nervously now, "Come no nearer! Go away! Go back!"

Then Bron thought she heard singing, a child singing, away through the trees in the fog. The song was plaintive and the voice rose and fell, so pure Bron felt she could see clean through it.

"Sorin?"

She heard a baby's chuckle, and then the unmistakable voice of Naila, *"Get up, Bron! Run, Bron, run!"* overlaid with Edreda's voice urging her, *"Get up, Bron – run!"*

Bron needed no second telling. She stood and ran, back the way she had come, increasing the distance between herself and the obsessive lust of the High Priest.

"Run, Bron, run!"

The voices of Naila and Edreda were echoing in her ears, and Sorin's high soprano lingered among the trees.

When she turned to look, Vortin was standing where she had left him, making no effort to follow her. She did not stop running until she reached her parents' house.

"Bron, whatever's the matter?" Trifena asked with concern. "You look as if you'd seen a ghost – and so cold. Where's your cloak?"

Bron flew into her mother's arms and burst into tears but would not explain.

"You shouldn't go up there if it upsets you so much," her mother sympathised, "or is there some other reason?"

Bron couldn't answer through her sobs.

It was now December and preparations were being made for the winter feast of Unvala. As had happened every year since time began, logs were being dragged up the Temple steps to stack each side of the entrance pillars, houses were being swept clean, extra shopping was running the housekeeping money low, animals were being killed and game birds and domestic fowl were having their necks wrung.

One morning, amidst all this frantic activity, Louca opened her front door and let out such a screech of anguish that it brought her husband, Hoad, to her side.

"By all the gods, Louca, what's the matter?"

Shaking, she pointed. He followed the line of her finger to the plot outside their front door, the grave where their first baby had lain. There was now only a pile of soil beside an empty cavity.

Louca fell to her knees and began clawing at the heaped earth. Hoad put his arms round her and tried to raise her, but she went on scratching and scraping where the wrapped body of their little daughter had lain for the past twenty years – the baby who had been sacrificed on the altar in the wood.

The bloody deed, carried out by Brocchus, had been a bribe to the goddess to send a consort for Nobilianus and an heir to the High Priesthood. The goddess had listened and had sent Bron into the world at the precise moment of sacrifice.

Hoad called a passing neighbour to help him and together they supported Louca into the house and sat her at the table, where her children crowded round and tried to comfort her.

For everyone, it was a horrible mystery without explanation.

Two days later, Veneta set off to Shubinata's temple to collect any curse tablets and offerings left on the altar. The sky was heavily overcast and she was glad of the oil lamp she had brought with her.

It was dark inside the temple, as the large candle on the pedestal had burnt out. She spent some time feeling her way, replacing the candle, then lighting it from the lamp. The welcome flame flared cheerfully and she turned towards the altar.

She was surprised to see there an offering, but a strange one, a large bundle of heavy black cloth. With curiosity, Veneta began to disturb its folds when something fell to the floor. She crouched and had to hunt around with her fingers, as the object was very small. When she did find it and held it towards the light of the candle, she was horrified to see she was holding a bone. It was a tiny rib bone. Putting it to one side, she felt about in the cloth, which she could see now was a cloak. Trembling, she discovered, wrapped in its folds, the skeleton of a baby.

Swiftly wrapping it up again, Veneta sat down on the red carpet, her back against the altar, her knees raised, the bundle in her lap, and tried to make sense of what she held, but could not.

Picking up curse tablets and offerings from the altar, she placed them in a soft skin bag slung over her shoulder, and hurried back to the settlement, the bundle in her arms. She called in on Stalwyn on the way.

"I think it must be Louca's baby," said Veneta, "but why? And whose cloak is it?"

"I may know," said Stalwyn hesitantly. "If you'll wait here, I'll come back shortly with the answer." Veneta nodded and the midwife left the house. She returned with Trifena.

"Please tell Veneta what you told me yesterday," she said.

Trifena fingered the cloak and explained, "Two days ago, Bron went to the graves in the wood, as she does sometimes. She wasn't gone long, but she came running back in such a hysterical state, without her cloak, but she wouldn't say what had happened. She went home, and I still don't know, and I've been worrying about it ever since. Soranus said she hasn't said a word to him, either."

"Is this Bron's cloak?" asked Veneta.

Trifena nodded. "I'll fetch her up here," she said. "It's time we had an explanation."

When Bron arrived with her mother, having left the children with Flavia, she studied the tiny bones. The wafer-thin skull had been broken into several pieces during its disturbance.

"If she'd lived, she would be my age," Bron mused, "and probably married, with children."

"Tell us about your cloak," prompted Veneta, and Bron told them about Vortin finding her in the wood, and leaving her cloak in his hands, and hearing the voices.

"And I heard Aelia – do you remember, Mother, how she used to chuckle so?"

Trifena nodded.

"I believe you, Bron, about the attack," Veneta said, "but we may have to prove it one day and it would be Vortin's word against yours."

"You'll find my brooch up there," Bron remembered. "The clasp broke when he tore the cloak off me."

"It's beginning to make some sort of warped sense," said Veneta. "Vortin probably reasons that he sacrificed this little life for yours, Bron. He is reminding Shubinata that he has kept his part of the bargain and now she must keep hers."

"How?" demanded Bron.

"Every time he has tried to claim you, first as daughter then as his High Priestess, he has been thwarted. This is his way of telling the goddess that he has lost patience."

"Will I never be free of that old devil?" Bron thumped her fist on the table in her agitation.

"It was probably Brocchus who stole the body during the night," conjectured Stalwyn.

"But who put it on the altar?" asked Trifena. "Men aren't allowed in Shubinata's temple."

"Jeetuna," guessed Veneta.

CHAPTER 19

Julius was often in his temple, thanking his emperor-god for his betrothal, and offering gifts, with the plea that Trifosa would grow to feel for him as strongly as he was increasingly feeling towards her.

When in Byden, he spent all the time he could in her company, and when away, thoughts of her lightened his days. He showered gifts on her, which obviously delighted her, though he knew that love could not be bought.

Unaware of the engagement, Jeetuna watched his comings and goings at the Roman temple, and gathered his gifts to take back to Vortin, giving Julius some breathing space, as she had planned. She then began leaving as he was arriving or arriving as he was leaving, as if by chance.

One evening, when he was at prayer and she arrived on some pretext, and made as if to leave, he stopped her.

"Don't go, Jeetuna," he said.

The priestess was surprised at his direct approach, and waited quietly. He was looking at her thoughtfully, and she blushed.

"I need to speak to you," he continued.

"Yes?" she said, and waited again.

"Not here – in private. Is there somewhere we can meet, discreetly, away from the settlement?"

Jeetuna thought quickly and excitedly, then suggested Iraina's cell in the wood.

"No one goes there anymore," she said. "We won't be disturbed."

"I knew you'd think of somewhere," he said. "Is tonight convenient?"

"Very," she replied, breathless at his apparent haste.

"As soon as it's dark," he suggested. "It gets dark early now."

Which means the night is longer, thought Jeetuna gleefully.

"You won't tell a soul?" asked Julius. Jeetuna shook her head and left.

He's forgotten Lucilla already, she exulted, without guilt. *I knew he would!*

She was waiting for him when he emerged from the dark caverns of the wood. He dismounted in the pool of light provided by the candles she had lit outside the cell, nodded briefly, and followed her inside.

The cell was very simply furnished but cosy, with a mattress covered with sheepskins, a chair, table, wooden chest and sheepskin rugs underfoot. Jeetuna had brought fire from the Temple for the small hearth and had lit a large candle in a holder on a stand, which flickered light on to the brushwood walls.

She sat, curled up seductively, on the mattress. Julius chose the chair and moved it so that he faced her, but at a respectful distance.

He began, "Jeetuna, you are a woman of the world, and I know – I remember – that there are fires hot inside you."

Jeetuna smiled. She wondered at his composure and disciplined approach, which was entirely unnecessary as far as she was concerned, but she saw that he was searching for the right words, and they had all night, so she let him continue.

"I loved my wife dearly, and was never unfaithful to her."

"As I know to my cost," interrupted the priestess.

Julius seemed not to hear. "I still mourn her, but life is short and a man – any man – me – I need the comfort of a woman… you know what I mean…"

Jeetuna nodded and wished he would stop justifying his desire and come across for the comfort he was talking about and she was silently panting to give him.

"There is someone I am falling in love with more and more by the day. I believe I have her respect, her admiration, affection even, but I'm not sure that she loves me."

"Why don't you ask her?" Jeetuna suggested, arching her back so that her breasts rose towards him.

125

"Because I am afraid of the answer," he said, like a small boy desiring a treat but expecting to be refused it.

"Then don't be," she coaxed him, but still he did not come to her.

"I thought that, if I paid well, and you wrote a prayer for me to leave on the altar, your goddess might take pity and fill my lady's heart with fire for me."

Jeetuna hesitated. She wondered whether it was really necessary for all this charade, but he pleaded, "Please, Jeetuna, in your faith language," so she got up slowly and went across to the chest.

From it she took a strip of birch wood, shaved so finely that she was able to score it once, twice, and three times so that it folded back on itself and provided four pages on which to write. She then mixed a small quantity of ink in a pottery mortarium – charcoal, water from a phial, and gum arabic. Then she found a quill pen and a small stick of beeswax.

"I'm sure this is not necessary," she told him with some impatience as she brought everything across to the table.

"Just write," he said, equally impatiently, offering her the chair. "You will know what to say."

As he stood close and looked over her shoulder, she rubbed wax over the wooden pages, to prevent the ink from soaking in and smudging. Then she wrote in her flowing handwriting, using Latin characters in the absence of a script in her own language, one small page after another, leaving space for his seal.

"Read it to me," he said when she straightened up.

"Mar pleg, tanum y vesta, ethys suden fwely vethe, gansoll an colon vy, yth ython…" to the end, then translated it for him, and he nodded with satisfaction and thanked her with a warm smile that sent her heart thumping again.

He heated the stick of wax in the candle flame, dripped a blob onto the wood, then sealed it with his signet ring.

"There's only one word missing," whispered Jeetuna, close to him now, "and that's your love's name."

"Your goddess will know," said Julius. "I am very grateful to you, Jeetuna."

"There are ways of showing your gratitude," she whispered again.

"Of course," he replied and fumbled with a cord at his waist, but he was only untying a pouch of coins to give her.

"This gift is to accompany my petition," he said, then laughed. "If it is answered as I hope, I will need prayers for restraint to wait patiently for another year, until she is eighteen."

"What?" asked Jeetuna sharply.

"Trifosa – I have promised to wait until she is eighteen. Then there will be a large offering for your temple on the birth of each baby." He chuckled again. "If I have my way, you'll get rich on the proceeds!"

He lowered his voice. "I rely on your discretion, Jeetuna, not to divulge our conversation here tonight, and thank you from my heart."

With that he had gone. Jeetuna stood where he had left her, his pouch of coins in her hand, her feet like lumps of lead, unable to move, listening to the pounding of his horse's hooves as he galloped off towards the settlement.

When at last the truth bit deep into her consciousness, she exploded into such a rage of screaming and crying that she thought it would never end. Then, with a savage movement of her arm, she swept everything off the table, overturning the candlestand, not caring that the candle fell on the mattress and began burning the coverings. Well fed, the flames rose into the brushwood walls.

She ran outside and one by one hurled the lighted candles into the now flaming interior, until the whole cell was blazing, but not blazing as fiercely as the fires inside her – fires Julius had referred to but had only dimly glimpsed.

Then the roof collapsed into the devouring red and orange flower she had created. She watched and waited until, in swirling hunger, the flower devoured itself, the flames died, and left only charred, smoking remains, dampened by the December air.

The white heat of her anger also quietened into charred pain and a smoking hatred that was not dampened. She crossed to the temple and entered by the door behind the curtains. She fumbled in the shadows and lit a small candle and placed it at the feet of Shubinata.

Then she took two lead strips from the side table, and using the metal stylus also placed there, scratched on them in large, ugly letters.

127

She rolled up both strips and laid one on the altar for Veneta to find and placed the other in the pouch containing the coins Julius had given her. Then she returned to the settlement, not forgetting to take her pottery oil lamp, her plans filling her head.

By now everyone had gone to bed, and by the dim light of the lamp, she hurried along the pathway, skirted the front of the inn, and descended the slope to the forge. It was locked but she searched the ground outside and was rewarded to find a nail and a length of pig iron.

She then walked by way of the craftsmen's compounds on the southern edge of the market place and climbed the slope to the two Roman houses. All was quiet. She cursed Julius under her breath as she passed his, and continued on to Hestig's house. Somewhere within lay Trifosa, the magnet for Julius's love and passion.

Retrieving the lead curse tablet from the pouch, she unrolled it, and without much effort nailed it to the front door, using the pig iron as a hammer.

If one or two insomniacs heard the sounds of hammering, she hoped they would think only that the wind had strengthened and was banging a shutter against a wall.

That accomplished, Jeetuna made her way back into the Temple through the side door and went straight up to the room occupied by Nobilianus. He didn't answer her urgent knocking, and she guessed where he was. Leaning against the wall of the corridor, she slid her back down it until she was sitting on her haunches, and waited for his return, too angry to doze.

In the early hours of the morning, he slowly came along the corridor, half dressed, and let her into his room.

"I'm flattered by your lust for my body," he said with a drawl, "but I've been at it all night and I'm tired and want some sleep. You can sleep with me if you want, but I do mean sleep."

"Shut up, Nobilianus, and listen!" she said sharply, and told him all that had happened that night in Iraina's cell, and since.

"Julius and Trifosa!" he exclaimed, rousing a little. "The sly old fox! He hasn't even given time for his tears to evaporate from Lucilla's tear jar! Wait till she's eighteen, indeed! If you believe that, you'll believe anything!"

128

"What are you going to do about Trifosa?" Jeetuna demanded.

"Nothing much," he replied. "I've quite gone off her lately. They guard her too closely. Flavia, now there's a blonde beauty! A Roman, too! If you'd help me get to her, I'd be happy, and you could revenge yourself on Julius and Hestigys at the same time!"

"How did you know about me and Hestigys?" asked Jeetuna, surprised.

"I make it my business to know," he said. "Now, as I told you, I'm tired, Jeetuna. If you want any action tonight, you'll have to do all the work yourself."

"That's not a problem! My hatred is giving me enough energy for both of us! But I won't be punched, Nobilianus, you're never going to punch me again!"

"Please yourself," he said. "Get on with it, then."

CHAPTER 20

Late the following morning, Trifena received a visitor. Veneta was greatly distressed. In her hand she clutched the curse tablet from Shubinata's altar with Trifosa's name scrawled almost illegibly on it. She also brought news of the burning down of Iraina's cell.

Trifena had been trying to concentrate on her housekeeping accounts, but her mind was on the lead strip Hestig had found nailed to their front door. Comparing them, they found the writing was probably by the same hand. Both bore the accusation, the words written backwards:

"feiht – asofirT"

"But what is Trifosa supposed to have stolen?" her mother asked in anguish. "She's never taken anything that didn't belong to her in her life! And who can want her cursed?"

"Where is she?" asked Veneta.

"Julius has taken her to Calleva for a few days. I know she's young, but Hestig and I trust him," and Trifena told the priestess about the secret betrothal. Veneta said she was surprised but very pleased for the couple.

"Julius will go to the Christian church to contact Asher, and ask if she can stay at Chrystella's, like Bron did when she visited there with her father."

Meanwhile Bron was having an argument with Soranus at the forge. The hatred inscribed on the lead tablet was almost tangible and had unnerved the whole family.

"I want Pulcher to come back!" Bron told her husband.

"He can come and go as he pleases," replied Soranus. "If he chooses to stay away, it's up to him."

"He chooses to stay away because he's not made welcome!" she retorted.

"Well, I don't like him always hanging around you," argued Soranus. "Alon! Come away from the charcoal!"

Bron rescued their son and scolded him for getting his clothes so dirty.

"But I need him – Vortin was outside again this morning when I came out, standing by the grave of Storm. If he can dig up one baby, he can dig up another! He gives me the creeps! I feel safe with Pulcher around when you're not. If he had been with me in the wood the other day, Vortin would never have been able to get that close."

"Pulcher loves you, Bron."

"I know he does, and he would never do anything to hurt me. We're good friends, you know that."

"I still don't want him hanging around!"

"But I do!" and Bron marched out of the forge, taking the children with her.

They seldom had a row, and Soranus was so concerned that he came home at lunchtime to make up, but they continued to argue, and he went back to work without eating, slamming the front door behind him.

Bron went round to her mother's, and passed Jeetuna going in the other direction. The priestess was heavily made up, as usual, and wearing too much jewellery on fingers and wrists, her necklace glinting gold in spite of the stormy sky, which was not allowing any sunlight through. They briefly acknowledged each other, but there had never been any affection between them.

There was something about the priestess that Bron wanted to think about, but her head was full of her row with Soranus, and she paid scant attention to anything else.

"This business of the curse tablet has upset us all," Trifena soothed her daughter. "Don't take it out on Soranus. He's a good husband to you and doesn't need it. And don't set him and Pulcher against each other, either. Neither of them deserves that."

131

"You're my mother, you're supposed to be on my side!" Bron complained.

"I'm on all your sides," said Trifena.

"I'm going to see Pulcher right now," decided Bron and left in a whirl of indignation, her children trailing behind her.

Just over two hours' brisk walking brought Jeetuna to the hovel in the wood. She called Umbella's name and, receiving no reply, entered and found the old woman asleep in her chair by the fire. As Jeetuna shook her by the shoulder, she opened one eye, which glared balefully at the priestess.

"I was asleep!" she said resentfully.

"I need you," replied Jeetuna, without apology.

"Usual first," said Umbella, holding out her hand. Jeetuna obliged.

"What does my fine lady want today?" cackled Umbella, regarding the coins with satisfaction.

"Another potion, like the first," she said.

"I heard it worked well." Jeetuna nodded. "But so many enemies!" Umbella chided, and shook her head. "It's too risky – suspicious. Both women loved by the same man. Too suspicious," and she shook her head again.

In surprise, Jeetuna asked, "How –?" but didn't bother to finish her question.

The old woman looked even more ugly when she grinned. "I see things," she said by way of explanation, "hear things, know things. What I could give you is a potion that will cause her to look elsewhere for love."

"Can you do that?" asked Jeetuna.

"Of course I can – if you are able to get it down her," promised Umbella.

"If you can mix it, be assured I'll get it down her!" hissed the priestess.

"This one'll cost more than you've given me – it's strong magic."

"I haven't brought any more. I thought that would be ample."

"It would be ample if all you wanted was a spell to stop the badgers suckling your cows, but it's not enough for what you're

132

asking. I don't mind being paid in kind – I'll have that necklace you're wearing –"

"No you won't, it's special," replied the priestess, and placed her hand firmly on her neck, protecting the glittering beads.

"Pity," said Umbella, shrugging. "Your silver bracelets, then."

Jeetuna reluctantly relinquished three. Umbella stood her ground and Jeetuna handed over a fourth.

"Wait there," the old woman instructed and retired to the end of her hut. With her back to the priestess, she was busy pounding, diluting and straining. Jeetuna did not know that all this activity camouflaged the simple action of squeezing a few drops of lemon juice into clear stream water and pouring it into a phial.

With trust, Jeetuna took the phial and thanked her.

"You know, you have the semblance of one of us," commented Umbella, looking into the dark blue pools beneath the blackened lids. "I hadn't noticed it before, but since you've murdered –"

"One of us?" repeated Jeetuna. "Who's 'us'?"

"The sisterhood," said Umbella. "You could share the power."

"The power to do what?" asked Jeetuna, intrigued.

"What I do – pills, potions, poisons, making people fall in love, out of love, get better, get sick, die, leave the body, fly –"

"Fly?" asked Jeetuna.

"It's not difficult," said Umbella. "I could do that for you."

Jeetuna was fascinated. "Do you fly?"

"Sometimes," Umbella replied, "at night, when the moon is full enough to see by."

"You grow wings?" asked Jeetuna.

Umbella laughed loudly. "Easier than that. On this." She indicated a besom broom standing propped up against the wall.

"Could you make me fly on it?" asked Jeetuna.

"Yes, but not today. You need instruction and preparation. Besides, you haven't enough on you to pay me, unless I take that necklace."

"You're not having it," repeated Jeetuna firmly, "but I can bring anything else you want."

"Gold will do!" cackled Umbella, as if she were enjoying a private joke. "Come back when the moon is full. Go now!"

Obediently Jeetuna left.

Julius brought Trifosa home three days later. It was Pulcher who noticed the familiar chestnut horse with two riders coming down the slope towards the settlement and ran next door to alert Bron. She came out into the compound with the children.

"Has Auntie Trifosa brought me a doll?" asked Layla.

"I don't know," said Bron, "and you mustn't ask. Little children who ask, don't get."

As the four of them watched, another horse, as black as the cloak that enveloped its rider and draped over its haunches, breasted the ridge and galloped down to the Stan, slowing to a walk as it followed the first horse through the ford. The party dismounted and paid some attention to one of the black horse's rear hooves, then continued up the path, leading their mounts, the black animal obviously slightly lame. Instead of turning left towards those who watched them, as expected, they made for the inn.

"I wonder who he is," said Bron. "Come on, you two, let's go and tell your grandmother that Trifosa is home. You're welcome to come with us, Pulcher."

It was not long before Trifena's slave answered a knock at the front door and Trifosa rushed in, followed by Julius. She ran round hugging everyone, trying to describe everything she had seen and done in Calleva in the company of Julius, and with Chrystella and the Christians when he was at work.

"Bron, they send you their regards," she told her sister.

Once in the triclinium, the family unwrapped the generous presents Trifosa had brought them. There were decorated jet hairpins for Bron, Flavia and Trifena, and gaming boards and bone dice for the menfolk. Pulcher was delighted to be given a wooden scale model of a covered wagon. Layla retreated into a corner to play with her new, painted clay doll and Alon was getting under everybody's feet, pulling his wooden horse on wheels.

Then Trifosa showed the family the gifts Julius had lavished on her.

"You're spoiling her," Trifena told him.

He shook his head and admitted, "I can't refuse her anything," then, more seriously, asked if there was any news about the curse tablets.

Trifena shook her head. "It's still a mystery."

"Do you think Pulcher would guard her when I can't be with her?"

"Ask him," Trifena suggested.

Pulcher was absorbed in studying his covered wagon. When asked, he looked across to Bron. She smiled and nodded, and he agreed.

Watching her young sister still bubbling over with excitement, Bron decided that it was all just a game to her. She had no idea of settling down, looking after a husband and home and having a family, which was all that Julius wanted.

"Oh, Bron, I've been so distracted that I quite forgot to tell you. We brought someone back with us who knows you," Trifosa suddenly announced.

The other horseman? Bron was mystified. "But I don't know anyone from Calleva except Asher and Chrystella."

"He said he met you when you were there with Adrianus Maximus."

Bron knew then. "Legionary Aurelius Catus?" she asked, and again experienced the momentary, exquisite pain in her lower abdomen, as she had done once before when she thought of him.

Julius nodded. "Not a legionary any more – a junior officer now. He said the last time you met you were very young, just married and pregnant and he promised your father he would be of service to you if you ever needed him. He holds your father in great esteem."

Bron looked at her mother. She knew that Trifena would once have blushed and lowered her eyes at the mention of Bron's father, but not any more.

"Julius, would you invite the young man to visit us tomorrow? He is very welcome here," she said.

Bron did not tell Soranus about the visit of Aurelius Catus. They had had little conversation since his comment, "I notice that Pulcher's on guard again," and her defiant reply, "Yes, I asked him to come back."

That night she did not mind when he went to bed before her and didn't even say goodnight before turning his back. It gave her space to think about the evening in the inn more than eight years ago when she had met a young legionary, who had treated her respectfully, like a grown-up, when she was still only a child.

She went to sleep with her head full of pleasure pictures.

CHAPTER 21

Next morning, however, Bron decided she should say something to her husband about the visit of Aurelius and the proposed meeting, and mentioned it as the family ate their breakfast porridge together.

"Not another man concerned about your welfare?" Soranus asked with sarcasm. "How many are we – about seven?"

Bron flushed. "He made a promise to my father," she said.

"I don't remember your mentioning it before," he said dully.

"I'm sure I must have done... you've forgotten," replied Bron, though she knew she had never told him. She had not done so when she first returned from Calleva, and as the years had passed without knowing whether Aurelius was dead or alive, there seemed no point in doing so.

After Soranus left for the forge, she tried to concentrate on her duties around the house, but felt as though she were walking barefoot on hot cinders and moved from one job to another without accomplishing very much.

Just when she felt she couldn't wait a moment longer, Trifena's slave girl appeared in the compound and said that her presence was requested in her mother's house.

She followed the girl there and entered the triclinium, with Layla and Alon on either side of her. Sitting facing her mother, and sideways on to Bron, was Aurelius Catus, his right leg thrust forward, his right forearm taking his weight, listening intently to Trifena. She noticed again that he was relaxed and familiar with their local dialect.

The young Roman was broader in the shoulders than Bron remembered and his muscular arms looked stronger and harder. He was bronzed from his tours of duty in hotter climes. As before, his helmet lay on the couch by his side, and his hair, still disobeying the comb, was blonded by the fierce suns under which he had served.

As soon as Trifena saw the children, she held out her hands and they ran to the couch where she sat and climbed all over her until she settled them one on each side, her arms around both of them.

Bron remained quite still by the door as Aurelius turned towards her and stood. Then she came across to him, round the side of the couch, and he took both her hands in his and looked down at her.

"It's good to see you again, little Bron – though not so little now, eh?"

She smiled. "It *has* been eight years," she said.

"As long as that? I suppose it must be, looking at your children. Then your daughter is eight?"

"No, she's six. My first son died."

"I'm sorry," said Aurelius, "but you have another fine son here," and he reached out and ruffled Alon's auburn hair.

"I thought you were dead," said Bron.

"I'm lucky not to be," he said. "Since I saw you I've been fighting alongside Stilicho."

"Stilicho?" asked Bron.

"He's our great general and led us to victory over Alaric and the Goths – though they fought well, there's no denying, and it wasn't a foregone conclusion. Now we've been sent back to Calleva to rest."

The children were getting fidgety. "I'll take them for a wander while you two talk," offered Trifena. "The girl will bring you something to drink in a while."

"Thank you," said Bron, sitting in the seat her mother had vacated as the three of them left the room. Aurelius sat down again. Delighted, she desired nothing more than to be alone with this young Roman soldier who had ridden for four or five hours especially to see her. She was inclined to exclaim, as when a child, "This is just what I wanted!" but instead she said, "I'm glad you're safe."

"How could it be otherwise?" he asked with a smile. There was a sparkle in his deep brown eyes, which were regarding her with much amusement. " 'May the sun god protect you with his warmth and the water goddess grant you fast currents and fair winds.' Do you remember?"

Bron felt her face burning. "Did I really say that?" she asked, laughing. He nodded. "How pretentious of me! But I was only a child."

"Not at all," he said. "They were beautiful words to bless me with. You see, I am still here, in one piece, so someone must have heard them."

"Has it been bad?" asked Bron quietly.

"No one can imagine, who wasn't there," he told her. "But it must have been so in every battle since time began, and will be so until time ends."

"Have you killed anyone?" asked Bron.

"Many," he replied frankly. "When it's 'kill or be killed', there's no choice. I'm not proud of it, it just happens. The first one was at the battle of Pollentia – I hesitated for a second, but fortunately he hesitated longer. He was younger than I was, younger and more frightened. Then it gets easier, especially when you find yourself treading in a friend's guts, or see his head on the end of a spear, and his mouth running red, not with wine as in the old days, but with blood – then it becomes easy."

Bron nodded. She understood that he needed to unburden his personal nightmares and was flattered that he could confide in her so intimately.

"Your gladius becomes your best friend: get in close, left foot, advance right foot, thrust – in, out, and on to the next – left, right, thrust, under the heart or in the throat, and out again while he's still drawing back an arm to plunge a spear into you – in, out and away – they're dead if you're skilled, but no matter, they'll bleed to death anyway."

He took breath. "I'm sorry," he said and apologised for swearing and for describing the action so callously.

"It's all right," Bron said, "and I'm glad about the blessing."

He brightened up, seeming to cast his dark thoughts aside. "By the way, I've been promoted. It was because of your father's patronage."

"I'm sure it was also because of your bravery," surmised Bron, certain that he had consistently given a good account of himself on the battlefield.

"Well, maybe that too," he acquiesced, "but it happened faster because of your father's letter. So tell me what you've been doing with your life."

"It's as you see," smiled Bron. "Three children are the sum of it."

"And your husband?"

"Soranus is doing very well for us." Bron needed to remind herself and tell him what a good husband and father Soranus was. "He's taken over the smithy. I noticed yesterday that your horse was lame. If he's cast a shoe, Soranus will replace it for you."

"It's arranged that I shall meet him later," smiled the young Roman. "So! You don't need me, that's obvious, but if ever you do, you have only to send a message to the barracks. I haven't forgotten my promise to your father. It's the only repayment I can make him. Of course, I hope for your sake that you never need me."

Oh, but I do, I do! Bron silently cried out as he stood to go. *Please don't leave yet!* She was surprised that he hadn't heard her.

For a brief moment, she wished that Aurelius would gallop off with her on his horse, out of Vortin's reach, then told herself not to be so stupid.

As if reading her thoughts, he sat down again.

"Bron, Adrianus Maximus told me who the father of your baby was. That High Priest – is he still around?"

"Yes," she said.

"Is he of any danger to you?"

"There's nothing he can do to me any more," she said. "I have the protection of Soranus and my family and friends, and Julius Gaius, who will shortly be my brother-in-law."

"Your sister is lovely," he said. "Julius is a lucky man. You haven't any spare sisters, have you, Bron? One you can save for me? One who will wait that long?"

Bron shook her head miserably.

"Oh, well, my bad luck." He smiled and stood up again.

At that moment, the slave arrived with warm goat's milk. Bron hoped he would stay to drink it, but he apologised and said he needed to get his horse shod then return to Calleva. He took Bron's left hand in his and kissed the palm gently.

"I have been recalled to duty," he said, still holding her hand. "Say it again for me – your blessing."

"May the sun god protect you with his warmth and the water goddess grant you fast currents and fair winds," she said softly. Then she looked into his eyes and added, "Please come back safely," and this time found she was saying it aloud.

After he had gone, she sat staring into space, sipping the hot liquid and warming her hands round the beaker. Trifena and the children found her there, and their chatter and quarrelling dragged her thoughts back to reality.

CHAPTER 22

AD 405

It was a carrier passing through Byden early in the year, on his way to Verulamium, who brought the first news of the uprising.

A small garrison of African legionaries stationed outside Camulodunum, most of them one-time slaves but now freed and with Roman citizenship, had staged a revolt. They had broken into a local brewery and consumed quantities of beer and had then smashed up their quarters and walked into town, fighting and looting on the way. More scandalously, they had defiled and gang-raped local white women, the citizens they were paid to protect.

Their grievance seemed to be their inferior treatment when compared with the privileges, as they saw them, afforded to the white legionaries. They complained that they were more harshly treated by the officers, their food and equipment was inferior, and in battle they were always placed in the most vulnerable areas, so suffered more grievous losses.

For three days they had held parts of the town hostage, until they were finally overcome, were dismissed the service, and put to death in gladiatorial combat or by public execution in the amphitheatre. Only a handful managed to escape retribution because of a lesser part they had played in the affray.

It was after receiving this news that people began looking askance at Africanus and no longer greeted him in a friendly manner when meeting him out and about in the settlement. There was a lot of uninformed gossip and some of the more wealthy parents withdrew their children from the school.

All this upset him very much, as his delight was the children and passing on his accumulated knowledge to them. He offered to resign but Veneta persuaded him to stay. She said she was supported in this by Vortin. The High Priest hardly ever spoke to the teacher, but seemed shrewd enough to value his services.

One morning, when Africanus was shopping in the market, a couple of shepherds' wives shouted ridiculous accusations at him, which encouraged a woman standing by to hurl insults at his back as he retreated. A mother whispered to her small son, who immediately picked up a stone and threw it in his direction. The boy's friends thought this was great fun and joined in. Wishing to avoid a confrontation, Africanus tried to dodge the stones and left the area with as much dignity as he could salvage.

"It's time I resigned from the village council," he told Hestig as they walked home together.

"Nonsense! The episode will soon be forgotten, if you can weather the storm."

The big man confided his distress and unhappiness to Trifena as she bathed his cuts.

"You know you have our family's love and admiration," she said by way of comfort, "and you'll always be welcome in this house."

Gratefully he smiled and thanked her, and clasped her small hand between his large ones.

Trifosa was also in the room and he caught her looking at him, but he could not read in her face what she was thinking, and she did not speak.

Three months had gone by, it was March, and Jeetuna still had had no opportunity to administer the love potion to Trifosa. They were never in the same social gathering, so opportunities never presented themselves.

There was only one route that Jeetuna could take and accordingly she made a point of speaking to Trifena's slave at the end of a Temple service. She said she had something to say to the girl, which would be to her advantage, and asked to meet her the following day at Shubinata's temple in the wood.

The slave girl was on time but Jeetuna was ahead of her.

"I have been very concerned for Trifosa," Jeetuna began. "You know about the two curse tablets, one on the altar and the other nailed to your front door?" The girl nodded. "I have prayed to the goddess for Trifosa's protection and she has directed me to mix this potion."

"That's very kind," murmured the slave girl – warily, Jeetuna thought.

"The only problem I have," she continued, with increased enthusiasm, "is that the magic will not work if the drinker realises what she is drinking, so it has to be administered secretly, and as Trifosa and I never seem to meet socially, this is rather difficult. That's why I would like your help."

The slave girl hesitated.

"Be assured," wheedled Jeetuna, "that no harm will come to your mistress. I swear, with the authority of Shubinata and on my own life, that there will be no harmful side effects and it will cause your mistress no hurt."

"If you are sure –" said the girl.

"I am sure," stated Jeetuna. "Now, I don't expect you to do this for me – for Trifosa – for nothing and I am willing to pay for your services. What would you suggest is a reasonable amount?"

Someone had left a pile of coins on the altar as an offering. Jeetuna extracted two of them and proffered them to the girl, who again hesitated.

"Two now and another when you report back to me that you have accomplished what I ask," Jeetuna bribed her. This made up the girl's mind and she nodded.

"Good," said Jeetuna and showed her a phial. "To prove to you that there is no harm in the liquid, I will wet my lips with it myself," which she did.

Appearing satisfied, the girl took the phial from the priestess and secreted it down the front of her tunic.

"Just slip it into any drink you pour for Trifosa. It will water down the taste a little, but other than that, she won't notice."

The girl nodded again and left. Jeetuna rubbed her hands together gleefully, tipped the remaining coins into her purse, extinguished the candle, and also left the temple.

It was now only seven months to the marriage of Trifosa and Julius. The betrothal was still officially a secret, but people in the settlement were noticing enough to guess what was happening, and Julius decided it was time to make an official announcement.

Trifosa was asked by her mother whether she was in agreement. Trifosa thought about wearing the beautiful ring Julius had bought her, and the envious looks of her girlfriends and other women in the settlement, and readily agreed, so the date was set for a reception at which the announcement would be made.

The celebration was to be held at the home of Julius, and Trifena said she was happy to act as hostess, with the slaves of both households working under her instructions, and Flavia was relieved to leave all the organisation to her mother-in-law.

When the invitations were delivered, only Africanus declined to accept, making the excuse that his presence would sour the proceedings and might cause some to stay away. Trifosa asked her father to call on him to ask him to change his mind, but Africanus was adamant.

For many, this was the first time they had been inside the Roman house. As they were welcomed in by both families, there was much laughter and excitement and, Trifosa guessed, not a little envy.

Some assembled in the triclinium. This was a splendid room with walls painted in three horizontal bands, pale green above and below, a red panel between, on which were depicted mythological figures feasting and dancing, and animals and birds, intertwined with scrolls of foliage – motifs that were repeated on the white painted ceiling.

On the floor, a colourful mosaic pictured Juno, the protector of women, Fortuna for good luck, and Mars the god of war, in foliate frames that echoed the scrolls on walls and ceiling.

145

In the courtyard, guests admired the wall veneers in Purbeck marble, the exotic plants, statuettes of gods and goddesses, and concealed trickling fountains.

As was customary, the facilities of the bathhouse would be offered during the evening. Visitors would see that the corridors leading there were painted in blues and greens in which swam many kinds of fish and sea creatures.

Once inside the bath complex, they would enter an almost celestial world where the wall mosaics reflected down into the clear water, which shimmered the reflections back. Light through the green glass in the high windows enhanced the underwater effect, so that bathers felt they were floating in this other world where troubles could be forgotten and from which they were reluctant to return.

"To think that this will all be yours, Trifosa," whispered one of her friends at the end of the evening.

"I hope I'm equal to the task," Trifosa replied, with anxiety.

"He'll help you – he adores you," her friend replied. "You are so lucky! You really have fallen on your feet. He's gorgeous!"

When the guests had partaken sumptuously of fine wines, of which there was no shortage, and had had their fill of hors d'oeuvres, meat and shellfish, and fruit and pies, served on the best red Samian ware, and before they began the bathing sessions, Julius called for silence and said he had an important announcement to make. The room became quiet and those in the courtyard wandered across to the doorway to find out what was happening inside.

Julius walked over to where Trifosa was standing with her friends and took her by the hand and brought her into the centre of the crowd.

"There was a special reason for this reception," he began, "which most of you must have guessed. I will not leave you guessing any longer but will state officially that I have asked Trifosa to marry me, and the dear girl has said she will. The date is fixed for next October, when she is eighteen."

There was a general ripple of clapping and good wishes. Julius smiled.

"Thank you," he said. "We are aware that there is a large

difference in our ages, but we know we are going to be very happy together."

The gathering clapped and cheered again and, at Hestig's bidding, raised their goblets and drained them to the toast, "The happy couple!"

Trifosa tipped up her goblet and the liquid slid down her throat. She was unaware that the slave girl was watching from a distance and in imagination was already spending the three coins.

Then one or two called for the bride-to-be to say a few words.

Blushing and self-conscious, Trifosa told the guests, "No one could have been more surprised than I was when Julius proposed. I am so lucky that he has chosen me, and I will be a good wife to him, but I think he will need a lot of patience!"

Her friends laughed, knowing Trifosa as they did, and her mother said he certainly would.

"I have a little something here," said Julius, looking across to Hestigys, who dived in his leather pouch and brought out the engagement ring. Julius accepted it from him and, taking hold of Trifosa's left hand, slipped it on her third finger. It was made of solid gold and showed a pair of clasped hands. Inside it was inscribed 'Julius and Trifosa 405'.

The guests clapped again and Trifosa's friends crowded round to admire the ring. Trifosa's cheeks burned red from the wine and her excitement and pleasure. Trifena came over and put her arms round her daughter and kissed her. People were shaking Julius by the hand.

"Bron, don't look so anxious," Trifosa chided her.

"I just hope you know what you're doing," Bron whispered. "Marriage is more than a ring and a bed."

The voice of young Hestigys was heard above the general hubbub and the guests quietened.

"My wife and I would like to congratulate *her* father on the excellent choice of *my* sister," he said. "We just hope that he will be able to keep up with her!" The guests laughed again.

"Now Flavia and I would like to make an announcement!" Hestigys continued. He went across to his wife and put his arm round her and smiled down into her blue eyes. The crowd waited expectantly. "We hope to be at the wedding, but may not be, because we are expecting a baby in October!"

Julius uncharacteristically whooped with joy and crossed to Flavia to hug and kiss her, and hugged Hestigys, and the menfolk shook the father-to-be by the hand, and the women crowded round to congratulate the mother-to-be.

Now there was cause for double rejoicing and it was a noisy crowd who left the room to make their way towards the bathhouse, anticipating the prospect of a wedding and a birth in the same season.

Bron was envious. With the way things were at present between Soranus and herself, another baby for them was not a possibility.

"Bron," Soranus said, drawing her to one side, "I have some tidying up to do at the forge. I left my tools out in my hurry to get here on time. I'll go back and clear up. If I'm not home when you want to go to bed, don't wait up for me."

"Can't it wait till tomorrow?" Bron asked him.

" 'Fraid not. Attryde likes the forge kept in good order. I'll see you in the morning," and he kissed her on the cheek and left.

Tears came to Bron's eyes as she watched him leave. She knew that she was in danger of driving him away. She might already have done so. She felt sure that the forge was as clean and tidy as it was required to be, and guessed that Attryde, his benefactor and perhaps already his love, was waiting for him.

Through her blurred vision she saw Pulcher leave the group he was with and come over to her.

"Don't cry, Bron," he said quietly. "Come, I take you home."

CHAPTER 23

Jeetuna decided, now that her mission was accomplished and Trifosa had drunk the potion, to visit Umbella during the March full moon and learn how to fly. She set out without a lamp, as the moon provided more than enough light to show her the path through the wood.

When she rustled the woven-grass door, Umbella called out to her to come in.

"Hello, my dear, I was expecting you," Umbella greeted her. "It's a fine night for flying."

Jeetuna looked at the besom broom standing by the wall.

"Is it safe?" she asked. "Won't I fall off?"

"Not if you hold on tight," chuckled Umbella. "Anyway, if you do, you'll only float down."

"Will you come with me as it's my first time?" Jeetuna asked anxiously.

"Yes, if you want me to," Umbella replied, "to give you confidence. I'll ride behind. Once you get up there, though, you'll be fine. Take the broom and wait for me outside. I'll bring you the brew you have to drink. It won't take me long to prepare it. Payment first, though."

Jeetuna paid, then picked up the besom broom and went outside to the fire. She left Umbella heating a glass container full of a grey-brown liquid in the candle flame.

It was cold outside and Jeetuna pulled her cloak more tightly around her. *Would she really be able to fly?* Umbella seemed confident she would. Once the skill was mastered, she had decided that her first visit would be to the courtyard of the Roman house, and she would slip into the warmth of Julius' bed and by morning he wouldn't know whether his pleasure had been taken sleeping or waking. If she visited him often, and the love potion worked its magic on Trifosa, the girl would soon become just a might-have-been memory.

Umbella emerged from the hut, holding a black pottery bowl in a grimy cloth.

"Drink this," she said to Jeetuna. "Wait till you feel ready, then sit sideways on the broomstick. I'll sit behind you. It may feel awkward at first, but you'll be more comfortable, once you're airborne."

"How high and how far?" asked Jeetuna.

"As high and as far as you like," Umbella indulged her. "Once I see that you're in control, I'll return, but you can stay up for as long as you wish – the broom will bring you home. One other thing – don't look down too often, it may make you feel sick. Now, are you ready?"

Jeetuna took a deep breath. "Yes," she said.

"Swallow it, then – every drop."

Jeetuna sat on the grass, put the bowl to her lips and tipped back her head. The brew was satisfyingly warm on that cold night and tasted of wild mushrooms.

"That was good," she approved as she gave the bowl back to Umbella and wiped her mouth on her cloak, "and I feel relaxed – sort of floating."

"Splendid!" exclaimed the old woman. "You're letting it work on you already. I'm going inside to clean out the bowl. Call me when you want to leave."

Jeetuna eased herself on to her back between the roots of the trees. For a while she was content to lie quite still, her mind drifting lazily from thought to thought, feeling well pleased with the world in general and herself in particular. She was prepared to embrace this new experience – would welcome it and learn and take full advantage of it.

The priestess raised her eyes to the full moon, framed in black by the topmost branches that stretched and clawed fingers towards it. Strangely, the branches began to turn a luminous green and to circle around the bright white face, which smiled at her, and called to her to come.

Then the stars exploded in the vivid blue sky, scattering sparks which also exploded before raining down between the trees, which were changing colour from brightest purple to citrus yellow then flaming orange and cringing pink.

Jeetuna was ready to fly, and she fumbled with the besom broom and called to Umbella, whose voice came echoing, reaching her from somewhere miles below, because Jeetuna hadn't waited and was now rising higher and higher.

The clouds through which she flew, white and grey and black in turn, enveloped her, so that she could see nothing, then suddenly disappeared to reveal the countryside beneath, grass and woods and rivers and towns, all rushing in a continuous stream below and behind her.

Then she remembered what Umbella had told her and looked ahead, flying into a mighty rainbow, which changed her whole body into colours she had never imagined before, chasing themselves through her one after another and dragging her mind along with them.

"I'm flying!" she cried at the top of her voice. "Look at me, Mummy, I'm flying!"

Her cries brought Umbella from the hut. She came over to where the priestess lay with eyes open, one hand on the broom, and put her misshapen fingers on the pulse at the slender wrist. Nodding to herself, her fingers slid under the cloak to the pouch tied at Jeetuna's waist. She undid the knots and removed it from the golden, tasselled girdle, then went back inside the hut to sleep.

It was well into the early hours of the morning when she heard fumbling at the door and opened it to find the priestess crouched on the ground outside, leaning her head against the wall of the hut.

"So, you're back," Umbella said with mock annoyance. "I wondered when you'd decide you'd had enough. Have you brought my broom back?"

"It's over there," mumbled Jeetuna.

"Well?" asked the old woman. "How was it? Did you enjoy it? How far did you go? I flew back after half-an-hour as I could see you were managing fine. You've been flying for about four hours."

"It was wonderful!" enthused Jeetuna. "I can't wait to do it again, but I feel very sick."

"I told you not to look down," Umbella scolded. "Don't worry, it often happens first time. It won't, once you get used to it."

"And I seem to have lost my money pouch."

"You must have dropped it while you were up there. No good searching – could be anywhere."

Jeetuna nodded.

"You'll come again, then?" Umbella asked.

"At the next full moon, and every full moon," promised Jeetuna, then mysteriously, "I have places to go and people to visit."

"Hmph!" said Umbella. "I think you mean one person to visit, am I right?"

"That's my business!"

"Makes no odds to me what you do while you're up there. You'd better get back to the Temple now or someone will start asking questions. The walk back will settle your stomach. If you're sick, don't worry about it. Goodnight to you," and Umbella went back inside the hut.

She hoped she could fulfil Jeetuna's expectations sufficiently to keep her coming back for more, until she could get her hooked on the drug. The plan would need some careful management, but the outcome would be worth it. There were rich pickings to be made and the Temple's coffers must be almost bottomless.

Soranus saw Jeetuna wandering about the settlement as he made his way home from the forge, though she didn't notice him. It was only a couple of hours before sunrise. He was annoyed with himself for having stayed so long with Attryde. However much he enjoyed her company, which he did, and she his, he was still a married man with family responsibilities, though he was not sure whether Bron cared any more.

She was fast asleep when he crept into bed beside her. Her

warmth reached across to him and he wanted to put his arm across her and snuggle into her neck, but he was cautious about waking her and did not want to draw attention to the time of his arrival back in bed. Of course, he could have pretended he had been there for hours, but she would know by the fresh coldness of his body. He sighed and lay still.

Bron opened her eyes. At last he was home. She wondered, if it came to a showdown, whether he would leave her or Attryde. She had lain awake all these hours, imagining them together. She hoped he had washed before he left the widow, before he came back to their marital bed. She thought he might put an arm across her and cuddle up to her, but he didn't. *That was all right, because she didn't want him to, did she? At least she might get a few hours' sleep now, before she had to get up.* But she would have welcomed his arm over her.

CHAPTER 24

The settlement was in an uproar. Hoad and Louca's eldest daughter Carinna, aged sixteen, had been raped.

She and her elder brother had been minding the family's flock of sheep on open grasslands in the valley of the Pegingaburnan, not far from the Roman villa at Aetheling.

It had been raining hard for two weeks and the river was swollen. One of the sheep had slipped down the muddy bank and must have been standing by the edge, in the water, for a couple of hours before her brother found it. By then its wool was saturated and he hadn't the strength to pull the heavy animal out; the more he tried, the more the sheep struggled and the deeper its feet became embedded in the mud.

He left his sister to look after the rest of the flock while he went back to the settlement to get help and bring some ropes. By the time the party returned a couple of hours later, they found Carinna lying whimpering in the grass, hurt and terrified.

"I don't know who he was, but he was so strong," she sobbed. "He was on a horse. He wore a long brown cloak with a hood and had a black cloth over his face so that I couldn't see him. Then he blindfolded me."

"Did you recognise his voice?" they asked her, but she said he didn't speak to her at all.

The innkeeper confirmed that one of the horses was missing from the stable. It was found next day, wandering in the area where the attack had taken place.

Popular suspicion fell on Africanus, in spite of the fact that no one had ever seen him riding a horse. He insisted that, on the day and at the time in question, he was alone in his house suffering from a stomach complaint, but because of that, he had no alibi that could be proved.

Hoad and Louca assured him that they did not suspect him for one minute, but people had not forgotten the uprising of the legionaries in Camulodunum, and subsequently they had developed an irrational fear of black faces. Because of their pressure, Africanus was placed under house arrest and brought to trial before his friends and colleagues on the village council. Hestig presided.

As Carinna had been the only person present and could not make a positive identification of her attacker's identity, except that he was tall and strong, and proof was lacking, Hestig ruled that there was no case to answer and Africanus was cleared of all guilt.

The people in the settlement gossiped about nothing else for several days and the African was forced into seclusion. A week later, taking advantage of the light from the full moon, someone nailed a curse tablet to the front door of his house.

Greatly distressed, he brought it early next morning to the market to show Hestig.

"I'm so sorry, old friend," said Hestig "that people's bigotry and racial prejudice has done this to you."

"I must leave the settlement," said Africanus. "I can't teach any more. If the parents don't respect me then neither will the children, and my being here is only damaging the school."

"Please don't do anything rash," Hestig pleaded with him. "Why don't you go up to the Temple and talk to Selvid and Veneta about it?"

Africanus promised that he would, but promised no more than that.

At that moment, Bron and the children with Trifosa approached the booth. The girls greeted the African cheerily.

"Do you know, Daddy," said Bron, "I can't find any horsehair pot scourers anywhere in the market – a delivery from Calleva has been delayed."

"Pot scourers?" repeated Africanus. "I can make you a couple of those while I'm sitting at home with nothing to do."

"Would you?" asked Bron. "That *is* kind of you."

"There's little else I can do for your family – except taint you all with my unpopularity."

"Is that why you've been staying away?" Trifosa chided him. "We've missed you. I wanted to show you my engagement ring."

"I've had somewhat of a problem," said Africanus, with a residual spark of his natural good humour. "There was the little matter of a house arrest and trial."

"But you stopped coming to see us before that," complained Trifosa.

"Nobody in his right mind believes you raped Carinna!" exclaimed Bron.

"The person who nailed this to my door did," replied Africanus and opened his huge palm to reveal the curse tablet clenched within it.

The girls stared at it, sympathy written all over their faces.

"I know only too well the upset these tablets cause," said Trifosa.

"Africanus wants to leave us," announced Hestig.

"But you can't do that!" said Bron.

"Please don't leave!" echoed Trifosa.

"I've asked him to talk it over with Selvid and Veneta before he does anything rash," Hestig told his daughters.

"Shall we go with you right away?" suggested Bron. "There's no time like now."

"Yes, let's," said Trifosa, "and woe to anyone who sends you so much as a dirty look while we're with you!"

Africanus reluctantly agreed, so with Bron and the children on one side and Trifosa on the other, he went up to the Temple.

"Not everyone is prejudiced against you," Bron encouraged him. "Many of those you've taught respect and love you."

"Including us," added Trifosa.

Bron said she would wait outside as she didn't want to run into Vortin, so Africanus and Trifosa entered and asked one of the eunuchs if Selvid or Veneta, or both, were available.

While they waited, Trifosa said to Africanus, "Do you want to see my engagement ring, or not?"

"I've a feeling you won't let me refuse," he smiled at her.

She held out her left hand and wriggled her fingers about so that the gold caught the light from the torch in the brazier above and flashed back at them.

Africanus took her hand in his and studied the ring and ran a finger over the clasped hands motif.

"It's beautiful," he said. "You're very lucky to be marrying Julius, and I hope you realise it, young lady."

"Of course I do," said Trifosa, tossing her head so that her long hair also caught the light from the torch and shone with bronze and copper and gold.

"Do you love him, Trifosa?" Africanus asked her directly.

"Of course," said Trifosa again, but with less assurance, "otherwise why would I be marrying him?"

"Why, indeed?" asked her friend. "I hope you do, little girl, because if not you should put an end to the engagement. It would cause him great grief, of course, but better that now than a lifetime of misery for both of you."

"What are you talking about, Africanus? Of course I'm going to marry him, in six months' time, when I'm eighteen, so you mustn't leave the settlement because I want you at the wedding."

Africanus thought he would be long gone by then.

When he didn't answer, Trifosa scolded him. "I'm not a little girl any more, Africanus, and you shouldn't treat me like one."

The big man sighed. He was only too aware that she was no longer a child. He wished he wasn't so aware. When he still didn't answer, Trifosa said he was in such a bad mood that she would wait for him outside.

"Don't wait," he said. "I may be some time. Tell Bron I'll bring her the pot scourers as soon as I've made them."

"I won't wait, then!" Trifosa threw back at him over her shoulder as she marched out. Africanus smiled to himself and shook his head at her indignation.

Bron saw the expression on Trifosa's face. "Whatever's the matter?" she asked. "You look so cross!"

"It's Africanus. He makes me so mad sometimes!"

Bron laughed. "I hope you haven't upset him, he's got enough to put up with, without your tantrums."

Trifosa laughed as well. "He knows me too well for that, Bron. He won't leave, will he? I don't want him to leave."

"I think he might," her sister replied. "Let's hope that Selvid and Veneta can persuade him otherwise."

At that moment, Jeetuna passed them on her way into the Temple. She looked rather dazed and tired but acknowledged them both with a peremptory nod then stared at Trifosa intently as if she was trying to delve into her mind.

"Did you notice her jewellery?" asked Trifosa. "All those bracelets and rings and earrings – and that necklace! The sun shone out of the beads! I wonder where she gets it all from."

"Perhaps I am being suspicious, but I can guess," said Bron.

"Where?" asked Trifosa in a conspiratorial whisper.

"She must steal the thank-offerings that have been left on the altar or sacrificed in the Stan mere – you don't think Shubinata gets them all, do you?"

"But don't the women who've given them recognise their own jewellery?" asked Trifosa.

"Perhaps she has them altered or melted down to make something else, or the giver has died, or is too frightened to say anything."

"I'd commit murder for her necklace! Perhaps I'll ask Julius. Do you think he would buy me one like it?"

"Trifosa, don't be so mercenary!" her sister scolded as they walked back to the market. "He should mean more to you than just an endless supply of presents. I hope you won't ask him."

"But if I did?" persisted Trifosa.

"You know he will give you anything you ask for," Bron said.

"Why does everyone keep lecturing me about Julius?" Trifosa pouted.

"Who's everyone?" asked Bron.

"Africanus – and now you."

"We're doing it for your own happiness, little sister."

When they went to bed, Bron told Soranus about their meeting with Africanus that morning and their visit to the Temple.

"I hope he doesn't feel he's got to leave," said Bron. "We'll all miss him so much."

"It's a matter of a man's pride," her husband replied. "We do many things to keep our pride intact. But I agree with you, he'll be a huge loss to the settlement, and a lot of people won't realise it until he's gone."

"But where can he go?" asked Bron.

"I'm sure he'll survive. He should be able to get work in a town, though it may not be teaching. I expect there's less spitefulness in the towns than in the villages."

The African's suspected unhappiness and loneliness weighed heavily on Bron's spirits and she would have welcomed the reassurance of her husband's arms around her, but he had settled down to sleep – as was usual lately, with his back towards her. She cuddled up to him and put one arm under his nightshift and began moving it caressingly down his stomach. Once, that would have been enough, but he muttered, "Not tonight, Bron, I'm too tired."

"You're always too tired," she snapped back at him, "and don't think I don't know why!"

"And what does that mean?" he asked her, sitting up, his voice sounding very controlled.

"You know what it means!" she shouted at him, also sitting up. "She's much too old for you, Soranus! She's an old woman!"

"She's forty-two!" he argued, then regretted saying it.

"So you admit it!"

"Oh, go to sleep, Bron," he replied, lying down and returning to his former position. "It doesn't mean anything – not to me, anyway, and I don't think it does to her, either. You know how much I love you, but she needs me and you don't."

"But I do," whimpered Bron.

"Then, in the name of Ashuba, show it!" he said.

"I thought I was," she said, deflated.

"It will take more than a hand on my belly!" Soranus told her.

159

Bron lay back on the pillows. She thought about the day's events, trying to make sense of why people, herself included, seemed to go out of their way to make other people unhappy.

Suddenly, she sat up again, her back rigid, as if someone had jabbed a needle into her buttocks.

"Soranus! Wake up! Wake up!"

"What now?" he asked grumpily. "I was nearly asleep."

"I should have thought of it before! I've been so stupid! It's been hanging around at the back of my mind for weeks but I didn't have time to sort it all out!"

"What are you talking about, Bron? You're not making sense at the moment."

"That necklace! Jeetuna's necklace!"

"What about it?"

"She was wearing it again today. I've seen her wearing it before – on the day we had the row about Pulcher."

"That was weeks ago," Soranus remarked.

"That's what I said – it's been buzzing round my head for weeks. The necklace is so distinctive – clear glass beads on copper wire, with hearts of gold foil."

"Sounds expensive, but that's Jeetuna!" he said.

"But it was Lucilla's! At least, she bought it as a thank-offering for goddess Shubinata."

"So?" asked Soranus. "Bron, has this got some significance, or can I go back to sleep?"

"Just hear me out, please, Soranus."

He sat up and clasped his arms round his knees. "Go ahead – but it had better be good!"

"I happened to meet Lucilla in the market on the day she died. She was looking for a gift for Shubinata and asked me to help her choose one, which I did. She bought that necklace. Veneta found her dead in the temple later in the day."

"Go on," said Soranus.

"When they collected her body, there was a pouch of coins on the altar, which was a gift from Julius, but no one mentioned the necklace. Veneta said there was another pouch, made of linen,

160

attached to Lucilla's girdle, which contained only a few personal items and some coins. I never thought any more about it, but if the necklace was not on her person, she must have presented it to our goddess. So where was it? Lucilla was going to the temple on her own – she told me – and hadn't planned to meet Jeetuna there. So how did the necklace turn up round Jeetuna's neck?"

Soranus replied thoughtfully, "If Jeetuna had gone to the temple after Lucilla's death, and had stolen the necklace, she would have seen Lucilla's body."

"So why didn't she report it?"

"Unless she got hold of the necklace some other way, or it's a duplicate," suggested Soranus.

"I don't see how that's possible. Lucilla bought it from a pedlar that morning and went straight to the temple. No one else saw it except me –"

"– and the pedlar," Soranus reminded her. "He would have recognised it again, surely?"

"He's not one of the usual travellers," said Bron. "I've not seen him before or since. He told us he was moving on."

Both were silent for a while.

"I first saw Jeetuna wearing it, as I said, on the day we had the row about Pulcher, and I knew something was amiss, but I couldn't quite put my mind to it. Then we had the upset about Trifosa's curse tablets, and Julius took Trifosa to Calleva, then there was the engagement party and news of Flavia's baby, and the rape, and trial of Africanus – and it all got lost in my head."

"What are we saying here?" asked Soranus.

"I'm not sure," replied Bron. "What do you think?"

"We know that Jeetuna must have been at the temple between the time Lucilla presented her gift and Veneta found her body."

"But that's all we know," Bron whispered. "We can't prove anything else."

Soranus was concerned. "Bron, will you leave this to me? I'll speak to your father and brother –"

"Why Hestigys?" asked Bron.

"Didn't you know? Hestigys had an affair with Jeetuna. He

dumped her when Flavia came on the scene."

"My brother and Jeetuna?" gasped Bron. "But she's —"

"Don't tell me – an old woman!" and Soranus laughed. "Oh, my darling Bron, you've still got a lot to learn. Don't tell your mother, though. I think your father knows, because Jeetuna used to make cow's eyes at him, but he wouldn't play along."

They settled down to sleep then, with their arms around each other, but that was all, because the thoughts they were sharing about Lucilla's death lay darkly between them.

CHAPTER 25

The morning sunshine through the open doorway cast Attryde's shadow across the floor. Soranus saw it but did not look round and continued topping up the quenching tank with water. The door closed quietly and, from behind, her arms came round his chest. She hugged him and kissed the back of his neck.

"How's my baby?" she asked.

"Attryde, this has got to stop," he told her.

Attryde moved close up against his back and ran her hands down his body and squeezed him where she knew it gave him pleasure. He put the water pitcher on a stool, took her hands away and turned round.

"I mean it," he said. "Bron has guessed, and I've got too much to lose."

Attryde sighed. "I knew it had to end some time," she said.

"I don't want to hurt you, you're just lovely, but –"

"But you love Bron and the children. It's all right, I know when I'm beaten. I can't fight your family. It was good while it lasted and you haven't hurt me – you're the best thing that's happened to me in years. That wife of yours doesn't recognise pure iron when she has it in her hands. She ought to be more careful with you or she may lose you for good. Will you let me kiss you goodbye?"

Soranus hesitated. "It's all right, I won't eat you," she promised. When he still hesitated, she pulled him to her and kissed him soundly on the lips.

"Phew!" he said and she smiled. "You youngsters think you have a monopoly on lovemaking, but you haven't. I will always be grateful to you for getting me away from the inn. You'll still work here for me, won't you – I promise I'll try to keep my hands off you."

"Yes, of course," he said. "Now, I think we both need to cool down a bit. I have an errand to attend to for Bron, but I'll be back later."

She gave him a hearty slap on his backside and let him go.

Soranus went to the pottery booth to find Hestig. As soon as there was a lull in trading, he confided to him what he and Bron had discussed together the night before.

Hestig looked grave. "But what motive could Jeetuna have for hurting Lucilla?" he asked, avoiding the word 'murdering'.

He turned to face his son. "Hestigys, did she ever say anything to you that might explain it?"

"Why me?" Hestigys looked flustered.

"Come, lad," said his father. "I know about you and Jeetuna." He laughed at his son's discomfiture. "You needn't flatter yourself – she only trapped you after I refused to have anything to do with her! Do you think she would have bothered with the calf if she could have had the bull?" He laughed again. "I'm teasing you, son. Of course I knew – but you had better not tell your mother, and certainly not Flavia."

"Flavia knows already," said Hestigys. "We haven't any secrets from each other."

Hestig became serious again. "As soon as I can, I'll speak to Julius, if I can do so without upsetting him. Perhaps we can get to the bottom of this."

Julius was in Calleva and the opportunity didn't arise for several days. As soon as he returned, he called on Trifosa, then spent a couple of hours in discussion with her father. Africanus no longer joined them in the evenings.

"Julius," began Hestig, "you will think this is a strange question, but please go along with me for now, and I hope to explain later. Have you and Jeetuna ever had an affair?"

Julius looked offended. "Why do you ask?"

"I have good reason," said Hestig.

"Never!" replied Julius. Hestig was relieved but baffled.

"Of course," continued the Roman, "it was touch-and-go one evening down by the Stan, but I managed to escape," and he told his friend about the incident with Jeetuna on the night of the full moon, and what she had said, as far as he could remember. He smiled then. "It was the night Lucilla became pregnant. Will you tell me now why you are asking?"

"I will in time – please trust me."

Hestig was even more worried after his conversation with Julius and spoke to his wife.

"Trifena, I need to ask you a couple of questions about Lucilla. What made her – a Roman – decide to go to our temple to take her thank-offerings to Shubinata?"

"Jeetuna suggested it," Trifena replied. "I went with her first time, when she prayed to the goddess for another baby, then when she became pregnant, Jeetuna said she should go alone to take a thank-offering. She asked me to let her know when Lucilla was going, and I did. Why?"

"Just an idea I have," was all that Hestig would say.

"It's late, I think I'll go to bed," said Trifena.

"I'll stay up for a while," her husband said. "I have some writing to do."

She did not question him as she left, knowing him well enough to realise he would confide in her when he was ready.

However, in the early hours of the morning, she came looking for him and found him still seated at a table in a small room adjoining the triclinium, scratching with a metal stylus on beeswax. She stood behind him and looked over his shoulder as he was rubbing out a word with the blunt end of the stylus, smoothing the wax before writing on it again.

"Still busy? Aren't you coming to bed?" she asked sleepily.

"I've almost finished," he said.

"What are you doing?"

"I am writing down, before I forget, all the times and ways in which we know the hierarchy up at the Temple has broken Temple law," he said. "I have worked from the top down, starting with Vortin."

Trifena sounded afraid. "That's a dangerous document," she said.

"It will be well hidden," promised her husband, though where, he had not yet decided.

"Tell me," whispered Trifena.

He took a deep breath. "Vortin –" he began. "He reinstated baby sacrifice at the time Bron was born, which is against *Roman* law. He transgressed *Temple* law when he did what he did to Bron – we had bought her back and she was no longer Temple property, and also was not yet twelve years old."

"It *was* eight years ago," Trifena reminded him.

"No matter, it happened," Hestig said. "Iraina – consort of the High Priest and only the High Priest – deserting him for a Catuvellauni man and having a family by him.

"Then there's Nobilianus, and all his weird antics such as setting fire to the Temple. Again, he should restrict himself to the priestesses and girls at the Temple, but he wanders as his fancy takes him. His pursuit of Trifosa since she was a little girl and the attempted rape of her in the wood, we know about –"

He was referring to an incident nine years previously. Trifosa had been eight years of age when Nobilianus enticed her into the wood. Very fortunately, Africanus had come across them and intercepted Nobilianus, who had had too much to drink, and rescued Trifosa.

Trifena added, "And his treatment of the girls at the inn, and the bluebell incident, which fills me with alarm every time I think about it."

"Selvid and Veneta –" continued Hestig.

Trifena interrupted him. "There is no complaint against them, they are the only rays of sunshine in the whole putrid establishment."

"But," her husband reminded her, "they have betrayed the faith, now that they are Christians, and are married, which is against all Temple law, and probably they have flouted it more soundly than all the others put together.

"Sharma – we know what Bron and Pulcher saw in the wood – Sharma and Brocchus and their shame. Sharma now has these two

Temple boys running around after him. Vortin seems to turn a blind eye. Yet Vortin needs to watch his back – only he and Nobilianus stand between Sharma and his ambitions to become High Priest. Brocchus –"

"He's an evil man." Trifena shuddered.

"And not a eunuch, from what Bron and Pulcher tell us. He murdered Hoad and Louca's daughter, admittedly on Vortin's instructions, and probably it was he who recently dug up the baby's skeleton. He probably set fire to our house – I'm sure he's at the back of much of the evil that happens here!"

"But there's no proof," Trifena pointed out.

"I know," Hestig agreed. "Then we come to Jeetuna. She should couple with no one except the priests, but she's game for any pair of male legs, of any age it seems."

"You resisted her," said Trifena.

"Yes I did, but then she turned her attentions to –"

"Who?" asked Trifena innocently.

"Julius."

"You mean our son," said Trifena. "I'm not stupid, Hestig, though I didn't know about it until it was all over."

"I'm sorry, dear, I should have realised you knew," he replied, "but I did mean Julius."

Then he told her about the necklace and all the unanswered questions.

Trifena took a deep breath. "I can't believe – are you saying –?"

"I'm not saying anything at the moment, but everything points to murder."

"That lovely woman – and her baby – poor Julius."

"Vortin seems to have lost control up there and they are all jostling for position and doing as they please."

"Have you written all that down?" asked Trifena.

"As best I can," he replied. "Now I will seal it."

He folded the wooden frames against each other, surprised to find that he had covered twelve wax tablets with close writing. Then he tied them with goat hair twine into three packs of four tablets.

Taking one pack at a time, he knotted together the two free ends of twine and passed the resultant loop through notches cut in a small, heart-shaped, open metal container, leaving the knot lying inside it. He filled the container with wax over the knot, stamped his seal on the pliant surface, and closed the lid. He repeated the exercise twice more. Now the wax tablets could not be opened without breaking the seals or cutting the twine and were safe from idle, inquisitive eyes. He placed them in a lead container and closed the lid.

"Where are you going to hide them?" asked Trifena anxiously.

"I'll bury them somewhere in the morning – better you don't know where," her husband said.

"And what are you going to do with them?"

"I don't know yet, but we may need them one day. Now I'm ready to go to bed."

CHAPTER 26

The May full moon brought Jeetuna for the third time to Umbella's hut. The old woman said she was expecting her.

"This time it's different," said Jeetuna. "Now I've got used to flying, I have a visit to make."

The old woman cackled. "Would the Roman house figure in this plan?" she asked.

"Keep your filthy tongue in your head, old woman," Jeetuna rebuked her sharply.

"Just as you please, but whatever your wish, concentrate on it – think of nothing else."

"I've been thinking of nothing else for a week," said Jeetuna. "I'll go outside as usual and wait for you to bring me the brew."

"To do what you want will need something stronger," wheedled Umbella.

"So I suppose it's going to cost me more!"

"Of course," replied the hag with a shrug that was little evident beneath her shapeless clothes.

"How much more?" asked the priestess.

"Double," she leered.

Jeetuna pulled a face. "It will be worth it, won't it?" Umbella asked her. Jeetuna nodded and handed over what the old woman wanted and left the hut with the besom broom. She sat under her favourite tree and, as she had been instructed, thought about Julius.

It was a warm evening and the bright full moon floated magnificently in the indigo sky. An owl hooted in the distance and was answered by another closer at hand, and a bat darted by her and circled the hut.

It's strange, thought Jeetuna, *that there is always a bat or two circling Umbella's hut.*

In a while, the old woman came out and stood above her. She handed the priestess a leaf-wrapped parcel. When Jeetuna opened it, she saw lying against the dark green a whitish powder. Jeetuna looked puzzled.

"Sniff it and eat it," the old woman instructed her. Jeetuna formed the leaf into an open tube, tipped back her head and let the powder slip into her nose and mouth and down her throat.

Coughing and spluttering, she waited a moment and then felt such a rush of euphoria that she smiled broadly at Umbella, who was still hovering above her, and lay back lazily.

"Well?" asked Umbella.

"It's even better than before," gasped Jeetuna, her breathing noticeably faster and shallower.

"I'll leave you to it, then," said Umbella. "Good luck with your quest, and I'll see you in the morning."

She came to the door once and watched the priestess agitatedly pacing backwards and forwards. Finally, Jeetuna lay down again, her mouth and limbs twitching a little.

Later, Umbella went out and laid a hand on her forehead, which was burning in spite of the cooling evening air. She also felt her pulse and, satisfied, returned to her hovel to sleep.

As usual, Julius had spent the evening with Trifosa and her parents. Trifena was showing her daughter how to embroider a table napkin but Trifosa was clumsy with the needle, and when she pricked her finger and blood stained the linen, she threw it down and said she couldn't be bothered any more that evening.

Her mother shook her head and picked the napkin up and looked across to Julius. He met her eyes and smiled with amusement.

"Julius, you shouldn't indulge her so," remonstrated Trifena.

When he felt he could not intrude on their hospitality any longer and he really should leave, he said goodnight to Hestig and Trifena and asked if Trifosa would accompany him to the front door, which she did.

Until now, the couple had had little physical contact. Julius judged that he needed to take their courtship at Trifosa's pace, and she had never shown any wish for more than a platonic friendship.

It concerned him that she seemed quite unaffected when they touched. This happened quite often because he engineered it so, brushing his hand against hers or standing close behind her so that her shoulder and arm settled against his chest; sometimes he had gone as far as lightly putting his arm round her waist.

Every touch sent a shock coursing through his body. He yearned for more, but she displayed no need for his caresses. He comforted himself with the thought that he was so experienced and she was so young, and a virgin he felt sure. So he bided his time.

However, with their marriage only five months away, he decided he should put their relationship on a more intimate footing physically. So tonight, as they stood together under the light from a torch high up on the outside wall of the house, he faced her and took her hands in his.

"Trifosa, I do love you," he whispered to her. "After Lucilla's death, I thought I would never feel this way about anybody ever again, but you have brought meaning into my life once more."

She looked up at him, her pale brown eyes widely innocent.

"I love you, too, Julius," she said, but the words came too easily.

Slowly he drew her towards him until she was close enough for him to put his arms round her. She laid her head on his chest and sighed contentedly. He let her stay there for a few moments before tilting her face up towards his, and he bent his head until their lips were close and closing. She parted her lips a little and shut her eyes and he closed the gap between them. As he transferred his longing to her lips, he breathed in deeply of her youth and virginity, and drew her tightly against him.

Trifosa must have decided that she enjoyed being kissed because she made no attempt to move, and Julius was encouraged to press his lips more firmly against hers, then release his tongue into her mouth.

The inevitable happened and he knew she must be feeling the movement against her stomach. He heard her sharp intake of breath and felt her hesitation. When the movement increased and pressed hard against her, and he had made no attempt to draw away, she sprang back in alarm.

"I'm sorry, Trifosa, I'm so sorry. I didn't mean to frighten you."

"It made me remember… It reminded me… When I was only eight years old, Nobilianus caught me in the wood. My mother said he was a wicked boy for doing what he was trying to do. I didn't know then what he was trying to do, but it was like what happened just then. Africanus rescued me from *him*."

"You're grown up now and you don't need Africanus to protect you any more, because I'm here. You must know, my darling, I would do nothing to hurt you, ever. But being betrothed makes a difference…"

"If it's all right, why were you apologising?"

"I'm sorry, Trifosa."

"There you go – apologising again!"

"Because you're making me as tongue-tied as a schoolboy." He caressed her cheek. "Trifosa, how much do you know about married life? About what just happened?" he prompted.

"It's like the animals," she stated flatly.

"Physically, yes," he replied, "but animals have no feelings for each other as people in love do."

"I'm not sure."

"Don't worry about it," he whispered, taking her in his arms again. "I'll show you once we're married. There's nothing to be afraid of – why don't you ask Bron to explain it to you?"

"I ought to go back inside," she decided, sounding intensely bored by the whole subject.

"Goodnight, then," he said, reluctantly releasing her. "Sweet dreams, my darling, until we share our dreams in each other's arms."

But he could not let her go and pulled her to him again and buried his face in her thick burnished hair and kissed her ear. He would have been even more deeply hurt had he known she was trying to remember how it came about that they *were* betrothed. And where *was* Africanus? Why was he keeping out of her way these days?

Suddenly, Julius shivered and looked up at the moon, which was smiling knowingly at them. Trifosa's eyes followed his. Owls hooted away to the south, and a bat dived above them and circled the luminous circle. Julius shivered again as both saw a strange dark shape pass across the bright smiling face.

"Must have been a cloud," Julius said, and finally let his fiancée close the door on him.

CHAPTER 27

Next day, Julius decided to work from home, partly to keep Flavia company. Halfway through the morning, the bell at the front door clanged, and a slave came to announce the arrival of an unexpected visitor.

"Officer Aurelius Catus."

Julius hurried into the courtyard to greet him. The young soldier strode through the open door and extended his hand to the older man.

"Aurelius, my friend, what a surprise! What are you doing here? I thought you were fighting in Gaul!"

"I should have been but for the gravest misfortune," Aurelius told him. "We were in barracks at Portus Dubris, waiting to cross the Channel, when I was struck down by marsh fever, and the century left without me. Several of us contracted the fever and we were all sent back to Calleva to convalesce."

"Are you quite recovered, Aurelius? You are certainly paler than when I last saw you."

"Well enough," replied the young man, "and getting stronger by the day. However, the town oppressed me so I thought I would pay Byden a visit."

"So where are you staying?"

"At the inn."

"I will not hear of it!" exclaimed Julius. "You will lodge here until you have fully recuperated. I will send one of the slaves with you to collect your things and bring your horse over."

Aurelius admitted he was only too willing to accept the hospitality of Julius and the comforts of his home.

Late that afternoon, after school, Africanus decided there were a few things he needed in the market and it was time he started walking about the settlement again.

It was only a few minutes before he was noticed by one of the cowmen's wives from the poorer end of the village, and she started calling after him, names that made him blush. Her raucous comments attracted the attention of a couple of her friends, who joined in the name-calling. It was obvious that they did not agree with the judgement of the court in finding him not guilty of the rape of Corinna.

He turned to face them, to defend himself, and was aware of Trifosa and Bron approaching with the children. They were deep in conversation and at first didn't notice him, but the noise soon caught their attention and, when they understood what was happening, they hurried across and stood on each side of him.

He did not feel that he could reply to the women for fear of inciting them to further invective, which would frighten the children, so he put an arm around each of the sisters and remained silent. This caused the women to shout louder, and the crowd round them became restless.

Africanus looked across to the pottery booth for assistance, but unusually neither Hestig nor his son was there at that moment.

Aurelius had offered to accompany Flavia to market to help her carry back sucking pigs for the evening meal, leaving Julius to work in peace. As they drew near they heard the commotion, and arrived to find Africanus facing an antagonistic crowd, who were not only showing their mistrust of him but were accusing Hestig's family of befriending a rapist.

Aurelius assessed the situation in an instant and pushed his way roughly through the throng, his arm protecting Flavia, and strode across to the little group. They were surprised to see him and he heard Bron's sharp intake of breath. He turned on the crowd and waited. The women's spiteful haranguing tailed away and gradually everyone fell silent.

"Is this how you treat people in Byden?" he asked them, his voice firm and even, his anger under control. "Frightening children with your cackling and face-pulling? I've seen more courtesy in the arena! Go back to your pigsties!"

Gradually, they slunk away, muttering to each other.

Aurelius turned to Africanus and the sisters. "Are you all right? Are the children very frightened?"

"We're – we're not hurt," stammered Bron. "What are you doing here? I thought – I thought you were abroad."

"It's a long story." The young man smiled at her. "It's good to see you again, Bron."

"You were marvellous!" enthused Trifosa. "Wasn't he, Africanus?"

"He certainly was. Marvellous. Won't you introduce me?"

The introductions made, Africanus apologised for the distress he had caused them, and said this was the reason he had been staying away from the family.

"Come home with me," he invited them. "I would like to offer you my hospitality."

Flavia excused herself, as she still had her shopping to do, and wanted to find her husband. The others followed Africanus as he led the way to his home, heading for the little round house near the school.

Aurelius saw it was like all the other round houses in the settlement. A pig with her piglets and a few chickens in the compound scattered as the party approached.

Africanus led them inside and asked them to sit down while he found a bottle of wine. Aurelius sat on a stool and Bron and the children on the mattress on the raised platform. Trifosa went with Africanus to find and pour the wine.

The house was almost bare of furniture and the only table was covered with an assortment of vellum and parchment scrolls, some in cylindrical containers of skin or woven work, some lying loose or scattered round the table legs.

Aurelius was telling Bron his tale of woe when Africanus and Trifosa returned from the kitchen area with a jug of wine and beakers. Trifosa had prepared two watered-down drinks for Layla and Alon.

"It's so pleasant not to be drinking alone," said their host as he and Trifosa served his guests.

Aurelius was told about the antagonism shown towards Africanus since the uprising of the black legionaries in Camulodunum, followed by the rape of Corinna and the trial, at which he was exonerated.

"I can't stay in Byden much longer," their friend commented. The girls said nothing.

They left shortly afterwards, Aurelius promising to visit him some evenings.

"He seems very lonely," said Trifosa anxiously as they walked home. "Perhaps you can persuade him to stay in Byden, Aurelius."

Aurelius shook his head. "If he feels his time here has come to an end, it's better for him to leave and seek a life elsewhere."

"And when will you leave for your 'elsewhere' life?" Bron asked him.

"As soon as I am recalled," Aurelius answered her. "I will have no say in the matter. Still, I don't think it will be for a month or so."

"Will you stay with Julius until then?"

"For a couple of weeks, I expect, as long as I'm not in the way."

That night there was no satisfying Bron. She lay naked in bed, waiting for Soranus to come close beside her, then covered him with kisses as he feverishly coated himself with olive oil. She laughed and licked it off and would not wait for him to rub it on again.

"Kendrus said –" he tried to explain.

"Kendrus is not here," insisted Bron, "but we are, and anyway you know I want another baby."

"But I don't," he gulped.

"Sshh!" she said, then caressed and fondled and aroused him again, the olive oil left untouched.

He lay back exhausted, and there was no way he could satisfy her a third time.

"I can't, Bron," he said. "Perhaps in the morning."

"Then I'll wake you early."

He drifted off to sleep, wondering what had so aroused her.

"You look tired," commented Attryde when he arrived late for work next morning. "Heavy night?"

"You could say that," he answered, smugness written all over his face.

"Everything all right between you and Bron, baby?" Attryde asked.

"Very all right," he said, "and I wish you would stop calling me 'baby'. I'm not your baby."

"No, you're not," she replied, sharpness in her voice. Sensing she wanted to say more, Soranus waited, but she was silent.

"I've work to do," he told her.

She came close to him and put her arms round his neck. He took them away so she put them round his waist.

"Soranus," she said, "I'm pregnant."

"You're what?" he asked, stupidly.

"I'm pregnant."

"The hell you are!" he said. "Who's –?"

"The father? You, of course. There's been no one else."

Soranus stared at her. "But you told me you were barren!"

"I thought I was. I've never fallen before, truly."

"Anyway, you're too –"

"Old?" She finished the sentence for him. "Some women do have babies in their forties and it looks like I'm one of them."

"Are you sure?"

"Yes. I've been to see Stalwyn."

"You'll get rid of it, of course," he said.

"No, I won't, I want this baby – our baby. It will be all I have left of you when you've gone."

"By all the gods, how am I going to tell Bron?" he agonised.

"I don't know and I don't care. You should have thought of that before you jumped into my bed."

"She'll go mad!" Soranus said.

"She can do what she likes," retorted Attryde and walked out of the forge.

He followed her into the house. "I'm sorry, Attryde," he said contritely. "It's been a shock. Are you well?"

"Sick," she said.

"You can't possibly keep the baby, you know that. For one thing, you'd have to bring it up on your own –"

"Plenty of women do. If necessary, I could go back to work in the inn – though, of course, if you moved in with me, I wouldn't be on my own."

He remained silent.

"So I'm good enough to bed but not to wed," she said. "Oh, it's all right, Soranus. I never expected you to make a commitment. I know you love that wife of yours."

"She's been pleading with me, but I haven't let her have another child. This news will play havoc with my marriage!"

"I don't care about your marriage, Soranus. That's between you and your beloved Bron. You'll just have to sort it out together. I'm not aborting our baby to save your marriage and you can't make me! Give her another one if that's what it takes."

"How can I tell her?" he asked helplessly.

Attryde shrugged. "You'll just have to pick the right moment."

"But there won't be a right moment."

He sat with his head in his hands.

"It's strange," mused Attryde, "how quick men are to take their pleasure but they never seem to think there'll be any consequences."

CHAPTER 28

Trifosa jumped out of bed that morning with a mission of her own. After lunch, she went to her father's stall and asked Hestig for one of his pots, but would not tell him why she wanted it and would only say that it was for a surprise.

She went down to the Stan and filled the pot with clear, cool water, almost up to the brim, knowing that she was bound to spill some before it reached its destination. Then she went along by the stream, picking wild flowers and some of the beautiful wild grasses.

On her way up the slope towards the school she was passed by the children heading homewards. There seemed to be a lot less of them than there used to be.

Arriving at the house of Africanus, she knocked at the door, but receiving no reply, moved across to the Temple and sat on the steps. She had to sit there for about an hour before she saw Africanus enter his house.

She then walked across to the front door and knocked again, the pot of flowers in her arms. When he opened it, he was obviously surprised to see her standing there, but also pleased, she thought.

"Hello, Trifosa," he said, "this is a welcome visit. What brings you here?"

Trifosa suddenly found herself tongue-tied and a little embarrassed. *What if he felt offended by her gesture?*

"I've brought you these flowers," she stammered uncertainly, holding the pot out to him with both hands. "I thought your room needed –" She stopped. "Brightening up" is what she was going to say, but again wondered whether he would take offence, and who

180

was she to decide whether his room needed brightening up or not? The only thing she was certain about was that Africanus liked flowers.

She continued to hold the pot towards him, her arms beginning to ache. Seeing them sag a little he took the pot from her and looked down at the gift, a tenderness in his eyes that surprised her.

"It's a beautiful gift," he said softly, "and I do appreciate your kindness, little lady. I'm not quite sure where I will put them –"

"You could put them in the hearth," she said, "so wherever you are you will see them and think of me."

He said nothing. She would have been surprised if she had known the reply of his heart: *Trifosa, I don't need a pot of flowers to make me think about you.*

"If you invite me in," suggested Trifosa enthusiastically, "I'll arrange them for you. They've got a bit tangled on the way up here."

"I can't do that," he said.

"Why not?" she asked him. "It would only take a few minutes."

"Trifosa, you don't understand. I can't invite you into my house. For one thing, it will do your family no good if you are seen talking to me. You know how unpopular I am at the moment – you saw what happened yesterday. And secondly, it would do your reputation the greatest harm. Apart from anything else, if people should see you, a young woman, coming into my home, when everyone knows you are betrothed to Julius –"

"Oh, that!" said Trifosa. "What nonsense!"

"It's not nonsense, Trifosa," he replied. "You're young and you don't yet know how cruel people can be. It's for your own protection that I won't ask you in, but I *will* put them in the hearth, and I *will* think of you every time I look at them, and I won't rearrange them because they're perfect just as they are. Thank you again for your kind thought, and now you really should go."

"But, Africanus –" she remonstrated with him.

"Just go, Trifosa, please just go!" He went inside and closed the door on her.

Trifosa felt tears stinging her eyes at his rejection, but she pushed her hair away from her face and turned and walked back down into the settlement, her head held high, just in case he was watching her from his window. If she had turned round, she would have seen that he was.

Soranus had left the house in such high spirits that morning, a wide grin on his face, but he crept home after work and let himself in quietly, hoping Bron wouldn't hear him.

"Soranus, is that you?" she called from the kitchen.

"Yes," he called back. "I've come to collect my towel. I've decided to have a bath, so I'm going along to your mother's."

"Your meal will be ready in an hour."

"I'll be back by then."

He escaped before Bron saw him.

He lay in the hot water and contemplated his stupidity. It was bad from whichever angle he looked at it. He knew that Bron would scream and shout at him, and rightly so. He had been refusing to give her a baby since Alon was born, in spite of her entreaties, and now he had given a baby to Attryde. *What a fool he had been!* But hadn't she told him that she was barren, and hadn't Bron called her "old"?

He wished he could share his dilemma with someone who would tell him what to do. Perhaps Hestigys could give him some advice. After all, he had had an affair with an older woman, though Jeetuna had not got herself pregnant.

"You look as if you need this relaxation," commented his father-in-law, slipping into the water beside him.

"It gets the iron grit out of my pores," said Soranus.

After a plunge in the cold pool, he dressed and crossed to the Roman house. A slave answered the door.

"Is your young master in?" he asked. Flavia came across the courtyard.

"Hello, Soranus," she welcomed him. "Come into the triclinium. Hestigys will be here at any minute."

"How are you, Flavia?" he remembered to ask her.

"Never better," she said. She certainly looked radiant.

"You're looking forward to the baby?"

"We can't wait," she replied.

Soranus had forgotten to ask Attryde when her baby – their baby– was expected. Perhaps she could yet be persuaded… But he guessed it was a forlorn hope. Soranus suddenly thought about his mother, Campania, and knew she would be disgusted with him.

Hestigys came in then and they shook hands.

"Hestigys, can I have a word with you in private?" he asked.

"I'll go and keep Aurelius company," offered Flavia. "It's a warm evening – we can sit in the courtyard."

"Aurelius Catus?" asked Soranus. "Is he here?"

"Yes, didn't Bron tell you?" asked Hestigys in surprise. "He's staying for a couple of weeks, recuperating from a fever."

"Perhaps it slipped her memory," Soranus said. It was strange how news of Aurelius always slipped Bron's memory.

"That's not very likely after the trouble in the market," said Hestigys.

"What trouble?" asked Soranus. Hestigys frowned and wondered what game his sister was playing.

Flavia left the room.

"What trouble?" asked Soranus again, and Hestigys told him about the incident with Africanus and the part Aurelius had played in protecting him, the girls and the children.

Soranus remembered Bron's hunger for him last night and again this morning, and tried to make sense of it all. However, whatever her reason, it was unimportant compared with the news he had to break to her.

Hesitantly, he told Hestigys, and asked how he could best tell Bron.

Hestigys shook his head. "There's no best way, you'll just have to say it straight out. Soranus, what were you thinking about?"

"You're lucky it didn't happen to Jeetuna!" retorted Soranus.

"She was too experienced for that –"

"So should Attryde have been," Soranus agonised.

"– and I wasn't a husband and father then," Hestigys said, and grinned as he added as an afterthought, "and I wasn't married to my sister!"

183

Soranus arrived home late and his dinner had spoiled. Bron had thrown it out to the pigs.

"There's bread and cheese if you're hungry," she told him.

"I'm sorry, Bron," he apologised. "I just got talking to Hestigys and forgot the time." He paused. "I met Aurelius Catus. You didn't tell me he was here, or what happened in the market yesterday."

"I thought it would worry you," she said lamely.

The children were in bed and the house was quiet. On another occasion, he might have pursued the matter. He gulped.

"Bron," he said, "I've something to tell you. Come and sit down."

She sat and looked at him anxiously.

"What's the matter?" she asked. "What's wrong?"

Hestigys had advised him to come straight out with it and that is what he would do. There was no other way.

"Bron, dear, you know I love you and the children more than anything else in the world."

She nodded.

"What I have to say is difficult – nigh on impossible – to tell you."

He mustered all the courage he could and blurted out, "Attryde is expecting a baby!"

For a moment Bron did not comprehend. "She should be so lucky! Who's the father? It won't make any difference to your working at the forge, will it?"

Soranus didn't answer. He just watched her face as the significance of what he had told her gradually sank in.

"Not you, Soranus? Please, please, not you!"

When he still didn't answer, she began to cry, and her crying became hysterical until she was beating him on the chest with both fists and screaming at him.

"Have you given her a baby? How could you, Soranus? She's too old to have a baby! It should be mine! How could you? How could you?"

After a few minutes of screaming and hitting him, during which time he did not attempt any defence, she exhausted herself into silence. He reached out towards her.

"No, don't touch me! Don't ever touch me again!" she screamed and ran out of the room and out of the front door.

Layla appeared, woken by the noise, followed by Alon.

"Where's Mummy gone?" his daughter asked.

"It's all right, she'll be back soon. Go back to bed both of you, and I'll come and tuck you up."

Bron didn't come back all night. In the morning, Hestig arrived at the door.

"I thought you ought to know that Bron is with us," he said. "Trifena will be along soon to take care of the children so you can get to work. You must patch this up between you, whatever the trouble is."

"That's not going to be easy," Soranus said.

When Trifena arrived, he left for work. He was late unlocking the forge, but it couldn't be helped.

Attryde came across from her house and greeted him with a smile. It was a relief to him to be with someone cheerful, even though she was the cause of his woes.

"How are you?" Soranus asked her.

"We're fine," she said.

"Bron's left," Soranus said flatly. "She's gone to her mother's. She didn't even take the children."

"The invitation still stands to move in with me."

Soranus shook his head. "Thanks, but no. By the way, you haven't told me when the baby's due."

"Stalwyn thinks it will be at the time of the Unvala fires."

Soranus returned that evening to an empty house. He prepared and ate a light meal, then went to see Hestigys.

"I don't know what to do," he said in despair.

"Do you want me to go and plead for you?" asked his brother-in-law.

"Would you? Thanks, Hestigys. I'll owe you one."

Hestigys returned ten minutes later. "Bron says, 'If Soranus has anything to say to me, tell him to come himself and not send his messenger'. Sorry, Soranus, I did my best."

When Soranus arrived at the house of his in-laws, the children

185

were already in bed. Trifena took Hestig by the arm and led him into the courtyard, leaving Bron and her husband alone in the triclinium. Both were silent for a while.

"I think you have something to say to me," Bron began icily.

"Only that I love you and the children. Attryde means nothing to me. I know it, she knows it, and so should you. Nor do I mean anything to her, though –"

"Though what?"

He couldn't resist saying, "She said I could move in with her if you didn't want me."

"And?"

"I refused, of course."

"Have you finished with her for good?"

"Yes, but she won't get rid of the baby, though I asked her to."

"How utterly selfish you men are!" Bron accused him. "How can you even suggest that a woman kills her own baby, just because it's convenient?"

Soranus felt and looked ashamed beneath her scorn. "I must take some responsibility for what's happened," he conceded, "so I'll have to stay at the forge and continue working for her."

"What are we going to do, Soranus?"

"We're going home, Bron – and if you want another baby, you can have one."

"No more olive oil?"

"No more olive oil," he repeated, then remembering Bron's way of dealing with it, grinned, "– more's the pity."

Bron threw her arms around him and hugged him.

"We'll pick the children up in the morning," she said. "Let's go home."

CHAPTER 29

Jeetuna kept diligent watch on the Roman temple. On a bright morning in late June, she was rewarded with the sight of Julius and his young friend, Aurelius Catus, making their way past the wickerwork god, up the white steps and through the columns towards the altar of Honorius, emperor of the western empire, proclaimed a deity.

She hurried across the intervening ground and quietly followed them in. They were kneeling at prayer and did not hear her. In the past, she would have been licking her lips at the image of the handsome, young tousled-haired legionary, but these days she lived, ate and slept only with fantasies of Julius.

She had not been able to reach him during her last full-moon flight but determined that it was only a matter of time. Once he had spent all night with her, he would forget his slip of a girl fiancée, his virgin Trifosa.

The family slave had given Umbella's innocuous concoction to Trifosa at her engagement party and on a couple of occasions since. Jeetuna was waiting for the magic to take effect and for the girl to be casting her virginal net elsewhere and abandoning Julius.

As she stood concealed behind one of the columns, she took pleasure in studying him, his light brown head lowered in prayer, his broad back and shoulders filling his toga. She could see that on the third finger of his left hand he wore a gold betrothal ring, similar to the one she had seen Trifosa wearing, but wider. She concentrated her mind on the ring and cursed it.

After spying on them for a few moments, she made a slight sound, causing the two men to turn their heads. On seeing her standing there, they both jumped courteously to their feet.

"Jeetuna!" exclaimed Julius. "Are you here again?"

She had no excuses today, she brought no flowers, she carried no cleaning implements, so all she could answer was, "Yes."

Julius said, "May I introduce you to Officer Aurelius Catus, a friend from the Calleva garrison?"

Aurelius nodded towards her respectfully.

"I apologise, I didn't mean to disturb you," Jeetuna said.

She was aware that Aurelius was studying her intently. She recognised a young man of the world who would not be unaware of her predatory ambitions. She lowered her eyes before his unblinking gaze and murmured, "I'm sorry again to have disturbed you. I will withdraw."

However, she had come to make contact with Julius and would not leave until she had done so.

"Julius," she said, "your marriage is drawing closer."

"Yes, indeed," he replied with enthusiasm. "Less than five months now."

"I hope Trifosa realises how fortunate she is to have won such a noble man as yourself."

She noticed some hesitation before Julius answered modestly, "It is I who am fortunate, in that she and her family accepted my proposal."

Jeetuna glared. Aurelius came to the assistance of his friend.

"I would judge they have a very happy future ahead of them, lady, and I only wish my own future contained such bright promise."

"I'm sure you're right," she said. "How could it be otherwise?"

She looked at the young soldier, sensing that if she attempted a move that threatened the happiness of Julius and Trifosa, she would have him to deal with.

"I will pray for your future," she told him, "that you achieve success on the battlefield and return unscathed to settle down with a wife and family."

She flung a look at him, indicating that the last thing that interested her was his return, unscathed or otherwise.

However, he posed no real threat. It was only two days to the full moon and her monthly visit to Umbella, and in anticipation she smiled a little smile, which only touched the corners of her mouth. Then she left.

Aurelius wondered why she had come. He had seen the way she devoured Julius with her eyes. He had looked at Julius to see if he recognised the danger, but he appeared not to do so. Aurelius smiled to himself. Julius had not a thought in his head that did not concern Trifosa.

All the same, Aurelius thought he should warn his friend. "There goes a dangerous woman. She is planning something. You need to watch your back."

"Oh, she's harmless enough," Julius told him. "Come, let's finish our devotions then we will call on Trifosa before I go back home to work. It's a fine day so you may want to take your pleasure elsewhere."

"I'll wander round and check what's happening in this great metropolis," Aurelius said with a grin.

After a stroll about the settlement and lunch, Aurelius decided to visit the forge. He was inclined to have a new pendant added to the decorations on his horse's harness and had decided on a bronze representation of Medusa with snakes writhing around her head, to turn away any evil eye.

When he entered the forge, Soranus was hard at work hammering out a poker, its point representing a stag's head with pricked-out eyes and a curved antler sweeping backwards, a practical shape for controlling logs on a fire.

He was surprised to see the young man's employer sitting on a stool. She was busily sewing and he wondered whether she was keeping an eye on her investment. To Aurelius's inexperienced eye, the garment she was making looked small enough to fit a baby.

Aurelius greeted her with a nod and she smiled back at him. He explained his wishes to Soranus and they discussed the pendant for a few minutes until the blacksmith understood exactly what was required. Then Soranus returned to his work.

Attryde laid the garment on her lap and watched him with obvious pleasure. The young man's chest was bare, his skin glistening with sweat, and the muscles in his strong biceps were tightening and loosening magnificently as he wielded the hammer on the anvil.

Aurelius, with time on his hands, also watched, mesmerised by the ringing beat of the hammer on the iron. Even while Soranus was rolling the shaft to the next position, he tapped the hammer lightly on the anvil, never compromising the rhythm.

Attryde stood up to ease her muscles and Aurelius thought she looked as if she were in the early stages of pregnancy.

At that moment there was the sound of running feet and children's excited laughter as the door opened and Alon and Layla ran into the forge, closely followed by Bron.

She stopped with surprise when she saw Aurelius and smiled at him with undisguised pleasure. Then she darted a look at Attryde, who stared her out, and Aurelius thought he could have cut the atmosphere between them with one of the new knife blades lying on the bench. He looked from one to the other and it did not take him long to surmise the cause of the antagonism.

"I have brought you some lunch," Bron said brightly to Soranus.

"He's already had lunch," stated Attryde. "As he hadn't brought any with him, I provided it."

Bron stood holding out the package towards her husband, and hurled the knife-blade glare at Attryde again.

"It's all right," said Soranus, "I'll eat it, I'm still hungry. Well, not hungry, exactly," he hurriedly corrected himself, seeing Attryde's expression, "but I can always eat, as you know."

Aurelius wondered with amusement whether Soranus would have to eat two lunches every day for the next six or seven months.

Bron put the package down on the side table. She was obviously in no hurry to leave and Aurelius guessed she was staking her claim at the very centre of Attryde's domain.

"Alon, come away from the charcoal!" ordered Soranus.

Bron caught hold of their son and brought him struggling to the doorway.

"He doesn't learn!" she grumbled to her husband.

"Now look how dirty you are, Alon," scolded his father. "How many times do we have to tell you?"

"I'd better take him home and clean him up," said Bron. "Come along, Layla, we're going home."

"I want to kiss Daddy goodbye," complained their daughter.

"I'm too dirty," said Soranus. When he saw her wrinkle up her nose in disappointment, he relented. "Oh, come on then, see if you can find a clean spot."

They had all forgotten about Attryde, who stood by, watching the sort of domestic scene that is enacted many times a day in every family. She sat down heavily, deflated, unable to compete.

Aurelius, the observer, wondered how it would be when Attryde's baby arrived.

He escorted Bron and the children home. She asked him in for a cold drink, and he accepted. She washed Alon and changed his clothes, then sent the children outside to play.

"He'll be just as dirty again in ten minutes," she commented, with resignation.

"I'm glad to see you looking so well," he said. "I still feel a responsibility towards you, as your father asked of me, but it's not necessary – is it?"

"You mean Attryde? You noticed?" Aurelius nodded. "It was – an accident – it won't happen again. She has been very kind to us."

Aurelius thought that she had certainly been very kind to Soranus.

"If you were my wife, Bron, I would never look at another woman for the rest of my days."

Bron blushed and admitted, "I was being rotten to him – I can't really blame him." She brightened. "But everything's all right again, and he's said I can have another baby. I'm sorry. I'm sure you're not interested in babies."

"Wives and babies don't enter a career soldier's thinking. Those who marry local girls unfortunately often desert. There are plenty of camp followers, of course, but most of them are dirty and diseased. And a lot of the men have mistresses settled in the towns. I'm sorry, I shouldn't be saying these things to you."

Bron changed the subject. "Have you seen my father lately, Aurelius?"

"Not since we were all together in Calleva. What a little girl you were then! He entrusted you to me and I have never forgotten my promise to him."

"But you can't help me while you're abroad fighting, except to come home safely," said Bron.

"You're the second woman to say that to me today," he said and told her about the meeting with Jeetuna in the Roman temple. Then the conversation turned to the marriage of Julius and Trifosa.

"Will you come to the celebration?" asked Bron.

"Yes, if I am still kicking my heels in Calleva," he replied. He stood to go.

"You can stay longer if you wish," invited Bron. "I didn't get round to giving you that drink."

He grinned. "Must think about your reputation!"

She went with him to the front door and he strode off down the slope towards the stream.

He turned once and saw her watching him, hesitated, then looked at the children playing with their friends along the pathway. They waved to him and he waved back, then he turned again and went on his way.

Umbella was amused that, this month, Jeetuna hadn't waited until the moon was full. It was slightly less than completely circular.

"Anxious, aren't we?" sneered the old woman as the priestess approached in the late afternoon.

"I'll have that new stuff again," said Jeetuna, "and I'll take some away with me. It takes too long walking out here, and I don't seem to be able to locate the house I'm looking for when I fly. It will be better to start much nearer. I'll take away as much as you've prepared. I can pay."

"Now you're talking!" said Umbella gleefully, adding, "I'll always have more, whenever you want it. Show me what you have brought from the Temple as payment."

To herself she exulted, *You're hooked, my beauty! And I'm going to bleed you dry!*

CHAPTER 30

"Push, Flavia, push!" cried Stalwyn.

"Not much longer, my darling," encouraged Hestigys in tears from behind the birthing chair, his arms locked tightly under his wife's breasts. "Stalwyn, is there nothing more you can do for her?"

"I've done all I can," replied Stalwyn helplessly. "It's up to her now, and the goddess!"

"Bron!" Hestigys appealed to his sister. "She's too weak to push!"

"We've been praying for hours," Bron told him, "but I'll try again. Hold on, Flavia, please hold on, just a little longer," and she ran back to her mother and sister, who were on their knees at the house shrine.

Ten minutes later, the cry of a baby brought them rushing back into the bedroom. Hestigys was holding a bundle in his arms.

"It's a girl! A beautiful girl! And she's perfect!" he told them with great excitement. "Oh, my clever darling!" and he kissed Flavia and their daughter until he felt he had no more kisses left in him.

Stalwyn prised the baby from him and began wrapping sheep's wool round her. "She's arrived too early. She's so small, too small," the midwife whispered to Trifena.

Hestigys ran out on to the pathway. "It's a girl!" he shouted to anyone who would listen. Those passing smiled and shook his hand and congratulated him and wished the family well.

Flavia's father was there now, standing with his arm around Trifosa, looking with such pride and concern at his daughter as she lay in bed.

Julius had confided to Trifosa that he had seen Lucilla struggle in childbirth and could not bear to watch his daughter suffer so. He had been walking round the settlement during the long hours of Flavia's labour. Trifosa also heard Stalwyn whisper to Trifena that Flavia could not have held on for much longer.

The girl stood watching the scene before her, appalled. Was this what Julius had in mind for her? She could die producing his babies!

Trifena looked at her daughter's face and took her by the hand.

"If Julius can bear to let you go," she said, "let's organise something to eat and drink – we would all benefit from it. And I think we should leave Flavia and Hestigys and the baby alone for a while, so she can have some quiet, and they can all get to know each other."

"Daddy!" Flavia summoned enough energy to call her father over. He took his arm away from Trifosa's waist and knelt by the side of the bed, smoothing the tangled blonde hair, wet with perspiration.

"You've been so brave and I'm so proud of you," he whispered. "My granddaughter is beautiful."

"We're going to name her Lucilla, after Mummy."

His eyes filled with tears and he turned to share his happiness with Trifosa, but she had already escaped into the kitchen.

For a while life became more hectic for everyone in the family. Flavia needed nursing back to health and there was the baby to be cared for in the meantime. All helped as best they could and were fully distracted and occupied.

Julius was delighted to have a baby in his house and nursed little Lucilla as often as he was able. At times, Trifosa felt as though she had a rival for his affections. She told herself not to be so mean of spirit, but she watched him as he walked backwards and forwards, cradling the baby, and realised that she was about to marry a grandfather. And she wasn't yet eighteen years old!

Sometimes he put Lucilla into her arms. Trifosa hoped she made the right noises and assumed the correct expression, but she always handed the baby back as soon as she could.

She knew this did not go unnoticed by Trifena, who had probably confided her fears to Bron.

She guessed what her sister would say: "Don't worry, Mother. It will be different when the babies are her own."

About a week later, Veneta left the schoolroom after school and went to the Temple to find her husband. Selvid could see that she had been crying.

"Whatever's the matter?" he asked with concern.

"Africanus and I have had a long chat. He is aware why so many of the children have been taken away from the school. The roll has dropped so low that we can't ignore it any longer. Vortin has told him: Leave or be thrown out! How can Vortin treat him like that?"

"Leave the school?" asked Selvid.

"The settlement," replied Veneta. "People will realise once he's gone how much he did for the community, especially the children. I won't be able to manage the school on my own."

That evening, Africanus called on Hestig, and they were closeted together for about an hour in the triclinium. Trifena wondered what they were talking about. Hestig then requested her to join them, and despatched a slave to ask Bron and Hestigys to come as quickly as possible.

Only Trifosa was absent. She had left the house earlier with Julius, in great excitement as he was taking her to the inn to consult a jeweller from Calleva. They were choosing a wedding gift for the bridegroom to give to his bride. Trifena whispered to her husband that Trifosa was bound to be very upset about Africanus leaving, and it would be a shame to spoil her evening with such tidings. So Hestig agreed not to send for her, in the circumstances. Trifena breathed a sigh of relief.

"Africanus has some very sad news for us," Hestig said when the family had assembled. "I will leave him to tell you himself."

"I love Byden and its people and I have taught many of them, you three children included," Africanus began. "By the way, where is Trifosa?"

"She's out with Julius," Trifena explained. "They're choosing a wedding gift for her."

"Of course." said Africanus, then continued, "Recently, there have been problems, as you know. I have always done my best as I saw it. However, so many children have been taken away from the school that the income from fees has dropped drastically, and Vortin has issued me with an ultimatum – either I go voluntarily or he dismisses me! It wasn't unexpected, I have been thinking of leaving Byden for some time. Vortin just brought it forward."

"You're leaving us?" asked Hestigys.

"Yes, there's no reason to stay any longer."

"When?" asked Bron.

"Now – tonight," he replied. He turned to Hestig. "I'm taking many of my scrolls with me, but I can't take them all, so you are welcome to any I leave behind. There is a great deal of knowledge contained in them."

"I remember my first day at school," Bron reminisced with a smile. "I thought you had the most beautiful voice I had ever heard in my whole life – all three years of it! You took us on a nature ramble in the woods, and then we played *terni lapilli*. I thought it quite remarkable that we all won a game each – quite amazing!" Africanus smiled. "Then there was my time spent in the wood during the plague, when you came every day to give me a lesson – from a distance, of course. Dear Africanus, I learnt everything I know from you."

"You exaggerate." He smiled. "But perhaps *nearly* everything." They all laughed.

Their laughter masked the sound of the return of Trifosa and Julius.

"This sounds a happy gathering!" exclaimed Julius as they entered the room. "Are we missing a party?"

There was silence until Hestigys said, "Not so happy – Africanus is leaving us."

"Tonight," added the African, "as soon as I have thrown a few things into my pack."

Trifena saw Trifosa's face become a mask, without emotion, and could only guess what her young daughter was thinking and feeling.

Africanus explained briefly what he had already told the others. He didn't look at Trifosa, only at Julius.

"I'm very sorry to hear it," said Julius sincerely. "I know things have not been happy for you recently."

"I have been so loath to go, but now I have no option. However, I take so many happy memories with me that they will last a lifetime, no matter where I end my days."

"Have you any idea where that will be?" asked Hestig.

"Not as yet," he answered, "so it will be no use sending out a search party! I will just wait to see where the road leads. But I will waste no more of your time. It is no use prolonging goodbyes. Please let me see myself out. Just stay quite still. I want to remember you all as you are."

But they did not heed his words and first Bron then Trifena threw their arms round him and hugged him and left tears on his tunic, then the men shook him vigorously by the hand and clapped him on the back.

Only Trifosa did not move. She appeared glued to the spot. Africanus came to her.

"Goodbye, young lady, be good – no more climbing trees! And be happy!" and he was gone.

Suddenly, Trifosa catapulted back to life.

"I can't let him go like that!" she cried, and ran out of the room, frantically calling him to wait a moment.

Julius looked surprised and the others embarrassed.

"He was her tutor for many years," Trifena explained hurriedly, "and they were good friends."

A few moments later Trifosa returned, her cheeks streaked with tears.

"I know he heard me but he didn't wait," she said. "He's gone. I think I'll go to bed, if you will all excuse me, I have a splitting headache," and she left the room. The family looked at one another and obviously all felt that she had behaved very badly.

"I'll go home now," mumbled Julius.

"Were you able to decide on your gift?" asked Trifena, trying to lighten the gloom.

"Yes, we chose earrings," he replied, but did not elaborate further.

When Bron and Hestigys had also left, and with Hestig asleep in bed beside her, Trifena listened anxiously to her daughter crying. She was about to go to her when the crying stopped and there was silence. Trifena sighed. She was always very perceptive where her children were concerned and hoped that, in time, with marriage and a family, Africanus would become a less acutely painful memory for Trifosa.

Next morning neither she nor Hestig mentioned the events of the previous evening. Their hearts were heavy at the loss of a dear and respected friend, but they remained silent on the subject and Hestig left for the pottery stall as usual, collecting his son on the way.

Trifosa had not put in an appearance and her mother decided to let her sleep in for a while. However, when there was still no sign of her by mid-morning, Trifena sent the slave to wake her up.

The girl returned running, screeching that her young mistress was not in her room, that her bed had not been slept in, and all her costly jewellery was lying in a heap on the bedcover.

With deep apprehension, Trifena rushed past the slave to her daughter's bedroom. What the girl had not noticed were two letters, one hastily scrawled on vellum addressed to Trifena and Hestig, and another on tablets, sealed, and addressed to Julius.

With trepidation, Trifena sat on the bed and read their letter:

Dear Mummy and Daddy, it breaks my heart to leave you, but it would be broken forever if I stayed. I am going after Africanus. I think he may be making for the Ridgeway and I hope to catch him up.

I realised tonight what I have known for a long time but would not admit: that I love him. I can't face my future without him.

You know I have never loved Julius, but I was dazzled by the presents and jewellery. I understand now how little they mean to me because I am able to leave them all behind.

Trifena picked up her daughter's gold engagement ring and fingered the clasped-hands motif, in reality so drastically torn apart.

I know I will be hurting Julius. He has been so kind and loving towards me and he does not deserve this, but better to leave now than that I should come to hate him, which I would in time. Please return his jewellery and give him my letter.

If I do not find Africanus, or if he will not have me and sends me home, I will destroy this letter, and you will not be reading it. Then I will marry Julius like a dutiful daughter and settle down and be miserable for the rest of my life and probably be glad to die in childbirth, and you will never know how I really feel.

Give my love to Bron and the family, Hestigys and Flavia and the baby. I cannot bear the thought that I will never see you all again, but perhaps that will not be so. I love you dearly.

Your disobedient daughter, Trifosa.

Trifena smiled at the closing words, in spite of her tears, and sat on the bed for a long time, staring at her daughter's handwriting and at the pile of jewellery, which in haste had been tipped in a heap. She thought she would untangle it before returning it to Julius.

Poor, dear man! How could they tell him? Fortunately, it would be Hestig's task to take the letter and jewellery to him, and not hers.

Hestig! She must send him word, then inform the rest of the family. But perhaps she should wait. Perhaps Trifosa would get lost in the wood or would not find Africanus or he would send her home. He was an honourable man and would send her home, surely.

But even as she thought all this, she knew it was a forlorn hope. Africanus loved her daughter. Trifena had known it for a long time.

But what sort of future would Trifosa have with him, a black man with no work, a mixed marriage, babies of what colour? The world was so prejudiced.

However, Trifena knew about love – of the passion they would have for each other now, and of the quieter, enduring love that hopefully would see them through all the pain in their future.

Of course, they could go after her and bring her back if they could find her, but what good would that do? Trifena realised that she would have to live the rest of her life without her spirited youngest child. Trifosa was the second daughter they had loved and lost.

Opening the door, she called to the slave to fetch Hestig home, then burst into a torrent of tears.

CHAPTER 31

The news about Trifosa and Africanus spread round the settlement faster than the plague, and the family was censured for allowing such a scandal to take place. However, Hestig was a well-respected council leader and it was easy for people to transfer the blame of the abduction on to Africanus – if not abducting, exactly, he had obviously enticed Trifosa away. What he had used as enticement, when she had everything she could want from Julius, no one thought to explain.

Work was again an escape for Julius and he went back to living in his town house in Calleva for most of the time, visiting Byden only occasionally to see his daughter and granddaughter.

On one of his brief visits, he brought Aurelius with him for company. The young man had been promoted again to a higher, though still junior, rank and then grounded for a while behind a desk, administering the affairs of the garrison in the absence of a senior officer. More and more fighting men were being withdrawn from duty in the area.

Julius had avoided all contact with Trifosa's family since her elopement and spoke to his son-in-law, Hestigys, only when he had to, not wishing to cause a rift between himself and his daughter.

Aurelius lost no time in visiting Hestig and Trifena on the evening of his arrival. He hoped that Bron would be there, but she wasn't. Next day he went to the forge and chatted to Soranus for a couple of hours while he worked, and met Attryde again, now in her fifth month of pregnancy, but Bron did not put in an appearance there, either.

He enquired about Attryde's health, and whether the forge was busy, and how were the children, before he plucked up courage to ask about Bron.

"She's very well – missing her sister, though," Soranus told him.

"A very sad affair," Aurelius commented. "It has destroyed Julius. He is quite suicidal."

"He'll recover," said Attryde. "One has to. Life goes on."

Aurelius deliberately passed Bron's home on several occasions, and once saw the children playing outside, but could hardly loiter for long without attracting comment.

He knew that, even if Bron saw him stroll past the house, she had no plausible reason to invite him in.

Eventually, he had to return with Julius to Calleva without meeting her.

Jeetuna was beside herself with glee and on her visits to Umbella heaped money and jewellery into her hands as thanks for the potion provided for Trifosa to drink. Of course, Umbella never informed her that the liquid had consisted only of stream water and lemon juice.

The priestess considered that Julius was now vulnerable enough to succumb, though it was difficult to arrange as cajole and plead as she might, her broomstick had never flown her to the Roman house as she had intended.

Frustrated, once again she sought consolation in her companion, the white powder bought at some expense from Umbella, and soon was in a world of her own where even inanimate objects came to life and catapulted about in a madness of luminous colours. Her only anxiety was the number of insects crawling up her arms.

Veneta was struggling to keep up standards at the school now that Africanus had gone, and Vortin allowed Selvid to spend much of his time there, not wishing to lose any more school fees. Veneta also enlisted the help of a few of the pupils who had left school recently and who showed an aptitude for teaching.

Vortin had never appointed a High Priestess to replace Iraina and seemed less and less interested in the rituals, leaving Sharma with the responsibility, and for much of the time was not aware of the details of day-to-day happenings. He was sixty-five years old and slowing down mentally and physically, though his passion for Bron burnt as fiercely as ever, fuelled by her absence, as she kept well out of his way.

He had little contact with his son. Nobilianus spent most of his time with the girls in the Temple or at the inn, or prostrate on his mattress, sleeping off the effects of his nights' drinking bouts. Sharma made sure that he was kept well supplied with beer and wine. That way, he was less trouble to everyone, except the girls.

One night, having left the inn, roaring and singing, he stumbled his way across the market toward the Roman house, where he knew Flavia would be asleep inside.

He woke the family with his noise. Against all odds, the baby had survived and was thriving, and her lusty cries added to the commotion Nobilianus was making. Hestigys threw on some clothes and went outside.

He found Nobilianus slopped against the wall of the house, and as he watched, the High Priest's son collapsed in a heap. Hestigys tried to get him on to his feet, without success, so he walked down the slope and, with many apologies, wheedled Soranus and Pulcher from their beds.

With difficulty, the three of them manhandled Nobilianus down the hill to the stream, and dumped him in it.

"That should sober him up!" said Hestigys with satisfaction, slapping his hands together as if to wipe every vestige of Nobilianus off them. "I'm at my wits' end to know what to do to make him leave Flavia alone!"

Nobilianus woke up, wet and shivering, next morning. He wondered how he had got into the water and seemed to remember people and voices and white faces, but could not be sure. A day later he developed a chill and stayed in bed until he was better, which gave everyone relief from him for ten days.

About the time he was up and around again, Hestigys arrived home unexpectedly during one afternoon, accompanied by Aurelius. Flavia was putting Lucilla down to sleep after an afternoon feed. She was startled to see them and knew at once that something was amiss.

"Darling, Aurelius has ridden over from Calleva with news of your father."

"Something's wrong?" she asked in alarm.

"He's not at all well," explained Aurelius, "in fact, he's very ill. His doctor wanted to send for you. We're not sure what the trouble is, but he has a fever and has stopped eating. He has been in bed for a week and is so thin."

"I know what's wrong with him," cried Flavia, turning to her husband. "It's your sister's fault. He doesn't want to live."

"I'll take you to Calleva at once," said Hestigys, putting his arm round her shoulders. "I'll ask mother if she will look after Lucilla." He saw the look on his wife's face as she was about to protest. "We can't take her with us and risk her getting sick," he said. "I'm sure Stalwyn will be able to arrange a wet-nurse while you're away."

Flavia nodded.

"Aurelius will stay with you while I go across to the inn and ask if a carrier is leaving for Calleva shortly. If not, I'll hire a wagon."

She nodded again and he left. Aurelius answered her questions as best he could but was interrupted by the arrival of Trifena, who came immediately Hestigys had called, to take Lucilla home with her. Flavia was in tears at having to leave her baby behind but Trifena assured her that Lucilla would be well cared for, and if there was any problem, they would send for her immediately.

"Are you coming with us?" Flavia asked Aurelius.

"I can't," he explained. "I rode my horse very hard to get here and he cast a shoe. Soranus is resting him overnight while I stay at the inn and I'll collect him in the morning and ride back."

"Stay at the inn? Nonsense!" protested Flavia. "You must stay here. The slaves will look after you. Just ask them for whatever you need."

Hestigys returned with a hired horse and wagon, and the young couple left almost immediately.

CHAPTER 32

Left to his own devices, Aurelius wandered across to the inn for his evening meal and returned to the villa later. Having nothing to do there, he called on Trifena and Hestig, and the two men spent the evening gambling.

He was still there when Bron arrived. As she entered the room, his eyes met hers and held them for a moment before he nodded briefly and turned back to his game.

She said that Soranus had told her of the urgent visit of Aurelius and the reason, and she was calling to ask if her mother needed any assistance with the baby. Stalwyn was there with a wet-nurse, and Lucilla had fed satisfactorily but was a little fractious, so Trifena was walking up and down with the baby in her arms.

Bron took Lucilla to give her mother a rest. She bent her head over the little bundle, talking to her softly, and the baby quietened but fidgeted and turned her head and nuzzled into Bron's breast, looking for another feed.

"She still seems hungry," said Bron.

Aurelius raised his head and could not take his eyes off Bron with the baby against her breast. He broke out in a sweat, and cursed himself for acting like a menopausal woman. To hide his confusion he poured himself another glass of wine and gulped it down, then made a wrong move and lost all his counters.

"My game, I think," smiled Hestig. "Shall we play again?"

"Certainly," agreed Aurelius.

"I must be getting back," Bron said.

Aurelius yawned. "On second thoughts," he said, "I'm feeling rather tired, and I hope to get away early tomorrow morning. I think I'll go too. I'll walk Bron home."

"Have a safe journey," said Trifena. "No doubt we shall hear any news. I feel so sorry for Julius and can't help thinking that our daughter has had a lot to do with his illness."

"Have you heard from Africanus since they left?" Aurelius asked, and Trifena shook her head.

"We don't know where they are or how they are faring. It worries us so."

It was only a short distance to the little round house which was home to Bron, and Aurelius dawdled to make the walk last as long as possible.

"How ill is Julius?" she asked.

"I don't think the illness is too serious," Aurelius answered her, "but he is not rallying, not fighting it. He just lies there. My hope is that Flavia will be able to put some life into him."

"It's true what Mother said, it's all the fault of my sister. Love can be so cruel."

Aurelius shot a glance at her, but her head was bent and he could not see her face. There seemed nothing more to say to each other and they walked the last steps in silence.

"So, you'll be going away again tomorrow?" asked Bron as they reached her compound.

" 'Fraid so," he replied and took her hand and placed the back of it to his lips and kept it there, looking at her seriously all the while.

She ran her other hand through his blonde tangle. Her soft laugh smothered him like a nest of pillows. "Do you never brush it?"

Aurelius took her fingers out of his hair and transferred his kisses to the tip of each finger in turn.

"That's one of the things I'm waiting for you to do for me," he said quietly.

"I must go in," she said very quickly. "I hope you have a good journey back. Don't stay away too long," and she turned and left him.

He walked round the settlement for an hour before returning to the villa and going to bed, only to lie awake staring at the dark ceiling, knowing that Bron was lying next to her husband not very far away.

She was turning this way and that, keeping Soranus awake.

"What's the matter?" he asked her.

"It's a hot night," she said.

"You'd be cooler if you kept still."

He was fast asleep when an hour later she decided she could not lie there any longer and needed some fresh air. Throwing a light shawl round her shoulders, she quietly let herself out into the compound.

She was not surprised to see Aurelius already there, sitting on the wall, with only a bedsheet wound round him like a toga. Neither did he seem surprised to see her. It was as if they met by arrangement, although nothing had been said.

Nothing was said now, but he took her by the hand and together they walked down to the Stan, across the stepping stones and into the tall grasses on the other side of the stream.

"Where?" he asked.

"The mere," she said, but they did not get that far. Within a few yards they stopped, again as if by instinct, and turned to each other, and ran their hands over the contours of each other's bodies, and sank down among the grass so that it covered them completely and they were in a cool green world where nothing else and no one else mattered.

Except that thoughts of her children came into Bron's mind, and behind them a picture of their father, but she pushed their silent reproach from her.

Bron was wearing only her nightshift and Aurelius would not wait for her to take it off but was kissing her thighs and stomach and all that was in between, then nuzzled his head between her breasts. Her nipples stood out strong and hard to tempt him, and she sighed a long, deep sigh. He pulled off her shift then and wriggled himself higher to reach her lips.

Then he knelt beside her while she pulled away the sheet wound round him. She felt a shudder go through his body and they could wait no longer and were unable to hold anything back from each other, giving and taking without stint.

"Aurelius, my own darling," she whispered.

"I love you," he said, coming to life again.

"I've loved you since the day I met you in the inn at Calleva," she told him.

"Show me again how much!" he pleaded.

They rolled over in the grass and afterwards lay quietly together in each other's arms.

"What are we going to do?" she asked him. He didn't answer. "Aurelius, what are we going to do? I can't leave my children, or Soranus, however much I love you."

"I can't ask you to do that, darling Bron. Where would we live? I won't let you become a camp follower, that's not for you. I don't know what we're going to do."

"The answer is 'nothing', isn't it? This is all we have now, and for the future being together as often as we can."

"If I could, I would marry you before the gods, but I can't. Oh, I can't get enough of you," he whispered. "What am I going to do, Bron? I just can't get enough of you!"

For Bron, this time their union was like no other. She burst into tears and moved off him and sat beside him and held him in her arms as if she would never let him go.

"Whatever's the matter, darling?" he asked.

"That was –" she sobbed, "that was the first time ever my body – you know – moved inside."

He looked at her in amazement and was ashamed that he had assumed so much and hadn't asked her.

"How is that possible?"

"Vortin," she continued to sob, "he was so cruel and rough and I resisted him then and the memory of him since. So I have dammed everything up inside, but you have let the flood through."

"Do you think – with Soranus?"

"I don't know," she said. "If I do, he will wonder how it happened. He may be suspicious. I hate deceiving him."

"It's too late for that now. You can't tell him."

"No. Aurelius –"

"I must take you back," he said, standing up, trying to ignore the way her eyes lingered on him, and reaching for the sheet. "You may be missed."

Reluctantly she replaced her nightshift.

"Aurelius, please –"

"No," he said firmly. "There isn't any more time. You leave first. I'll wait awhile before I go back."

She left him then, with a last lingering kiss, feeling as if they were one whole, complete unity that was being ripped apart. She wished she had told him what she had always said when a child, that he was just what she had always wanted.

Soranus was still asleep when she crept back to bed. In the morning, her union with Aurelius seemed like an impossible dream, except that she was very tired and a little sore.

Aurelius would be well on his way to Calleva by now. She could not eat breakfast or lunch and wondered how she was going to remain sane until she could lie with him again. She also wondered how she was going to keep looking her husband and children in the eyes and carry on as usual, and felt utterly miserable, but not soiled. Her love for Aurelius was too pure to make her feel soiled.

During the afternoon, Pulcher called on an errand. He regarded her with love, as always, but she thought she also detected reproach in his eyes. She could not meet his gaze and looked away. Did he know? It would not surprise her. His voices always seemed to tell him not only everything she did but also what she was thinking.

CHAPTER 33

Hestigys and Flavia returned ten days later, bringing Julius with them. He had begun to eat in response to his daughter's entreaties and his doctor said he was now strong enough to travel.

Flavia left Hestigys to put him to bed while she went to fetch Lucilla home. The baby had not thrived as well on milk from the wet-nurse but happily picked up immediately Flavia was feeding her again.

It did not take long for Jeetuna to become aware that Julius was in the settlement and the circumstances of his being there and she rallied sufficiently between her drug taking to walk to Shubinata's temple and pray for his full recovery.

So far, she had been able to hide her addiction from everyone. She sought Vortin's permission to visit Julius and take the best wishes of the Temple and to ask if there was anything they could do to help or if there was anything he needed, and Vortin acquiesced.

Jeetuna waited around until she saw Flavia go out with her baby then knocked on the door and announced her presence to the slave.

Julius received her kindly and did not seem to blame her that the prayer she had supposedly offered to Shubinata on his behalf, to woo Trifosa's love, had not been effective. He was sitting in a chair in the courtyard with the slaves passing backwards and forwards as they performed their tasks around the villa.

He offered her a cold drink of apple juice and they sat chatting amiably in the warmth of the sun. Jeetuna thought that here was contentment and closed her eyes for a few moments, trying to imagine what it would be like to live with Julius. When she opened them he was looking at her.

"Are you feeling all right?" he asked.

She smiled and replied, "I was just thinking how lonely it must be here for you without Lucilla and –" She left the sentence unfinished.

He finished it for her. "– and Trifosa. We should have been wed in a month's time."

"I'm so sorry," said Jeetuna, reflecting that, now she had murdered Lucilla and sent Trifosa away by enchantment, he was suffering the loneliness she had engineered, and fully intended to fill, in whatever capacity he would have her.

Of course, once she moved in, Flavia and Hestigys and the baby would have to go. However, she must proceed carefully so as not to arouse any suspicion or antagonism. She kept the conversation in friendly vein and they chatted about his work and general affairs in the settlement and in Calleva.

She also thought it expedient to apologise for her outburst by the Stan on the night the travelling players had visited.

"It's all right, Jeetuna. That was in the past, in a previous life as far as I'm concerned, and of course you were still in an emotional state after being hypnotised. Please forget it – I have."

When she rose to leave, he seemed genuinely disappointed and asked her to come again any time, and she said she would.

Unfortunately, she had stayed a little too long and passed Flavia at the front door.

"What did she want?" asked his daughter suspiciously.

"Vortin sent her to ask if I needed anything."

"I hope you told her 'no'," Flavia said sharply. "We make sure you have everything you need."

Julius smiled. "I did say just that," he replied.

Jeetuna came once a week after that, then twice, and stayed longer. Flavia was aware that Julius looked forward to her visits. He started sleeping more restfully and eating larger portions and began to put back some of the weight he had lost. Flavia confided her fears to Trifena.

"I don't trust her," she said. "She's too sweet by half. I'm sure she's got her own agenda concerning my father. Hestigys is anxious, too. He knows her – quite well." She paused with embarrassment.

"It's all right, dear," said Trifena and kissed her daughter-in-law on the forehead, "I know about Hestigys and Jeetuna."

"I'm glad," said Flavia with some relief. "I hate secrets in families."

Trifena too was worried and later spoke to Hestig.

"It makes sense," he said. "She tried it on once before with him, but he rejected her. Since then she's got rid of Lucilla and their baby, and with Trifosa also gone –"

"She couldn't have had anything to do with that," protested Trifena.

"Maybe not, but it has served her purpose. Now there's no other woman to stand in her way."

"Except Flavia."

CHAPTER 34

AD 406

Attryde had a difficult labour and Kendrus finally performed a successful caesarean section. Her baby was born in January, a little girl with a mass of dark hair, looking like both parents. Attryde named her Obrina.

Soranus was as nervous as he had been with all his children but had not attended the birth, although he asked his mother, Campania, to be present in his stead.

After the baby was born, he briefly visited mother and daughter in their house opposite the forge every day without telling Bron, though he thought she guessed. He was surprised that there were no outbursts of jealousy and recrimination. In fact, Bron had been extremely taciturn lately.

Bron's baby was born in late March, a little boy, the smallest of all her babies, whom they named Darius. Soranus was delighted at having another son. He had forgotten his reluctance to have any more children and walked around for some weeks with a grin from ear to ear, having proved to the world that he was capable of producing babies so easily.

When Pulcher came to see his new godson and Bron laid the baby in his arms, he studied the little features intently and looked up at her, an unspoken question in his eyes. Bron turned away. Even if he had asked outright, she could not have told him for sure who was her son's father.

Of course, the people in the settlement gossiped about the arrival of the babies within three months of each other. It was not always possible for Attryde and Bron, each with a young child strapped to her back or slung in front, to avoid each other in the market or along the paths. At these times they would pass without a word, Bron with guilt, and Attryde probably unwilling to cause any more trouble in the family of her young employee. However, if there had been any sign at all of a rift in their marriage, Bron knew that Attryde would gladly welcome Soranus into her home.

Julius was taking longer to convalesce than anticipated, and as he had not been to Calleva since Flavia and Hestigys brought him home, and as Aurelius had not visited Byden in the last nine months, Bron's lover was completely unaware of the birth of her baby.

She had plenty to do and think about during the day, but there were times when she lay awake at night, longing to feel again the complete fulfilment she had experienced with Aurelius inside her.

She enjoyed Soranus, their lovemaking now spiced with the knowledge that another woman would have him, given the glimmer of a chance. However, she held herself back and physically had shut down again, separating her experiences with the two men she loved.

Therefore there was no difference for Soranus to notice, and as he had accepted the way things were from the beginning of their marriage, he did not look for anything more from Bron.

While at work in the heat, or while shoeing a horse with smoke in his eyes and the reek of burning hoof in his nostrils, he would reflect how Attryde had abandoned herself to him in a way Bron never had. This intrigued and excited him, but he had made a promise to his wife and intended to keep it, though at times Attryde made it very difficult for him.

It was difficult now, with her sitting on a stool in front of him, bare breasted, feeding the baby. He was glad when the bellows boy came in and she covered herself up.

CHAPTER 35

Pulcher had decided long ago that nothing in this life or the next could even remotely approach the ecstasy of watching Bron bathing.

He gazed and worshipped as she paddled about in the cold flow of the Stan, envying the clear water that splashed her honey-coloured skin, the droplets cooling the hills and valleys of her young body.

She crouched, as smooth and rounded as the pebble she was choosing, then stood and stretched to hold it against the sunlight, with very little hidden from his view and left to his imagination.

He would have been alarmed and she less playful if they had been aware that two pairs of dark eyes were violating her privacy and relishing every movement of her young, naked body.

Climbing the low bank, she reached for her towel, rubbed herself and her thick, black curls dry on its rough weave, and quickly dressed.

A cock pheasant flapped noisily from its cover, raucously protesting at being disturbed by the breeze that rustled through the bramble bushes.

He saw Bron jump and look nervously around. She would be checking to make sure that Vortin was not concealed nearby and seeking comfort from the sight of his own dwarfish figure on the opposite bank. She knew that he would never allow the High Priest anywhere near her, although at that moment his eyes were modestly averted and directed up the hill towards the settlement.

When his gaze was lured back, she was shaking her curls dry.

About to return by way of the stepping-stones, Bron still looked uncertain. Whatever it was she then heard caused her to spin around in alarm. Suddenly, two young Roman legionaries sprang up from the tall grasses edging the stream. As she turned to flee, shouting desperately for help, one threw his arms around her, encircling her waist, while the other clamped a hand over her mouth.

Screaming for help for the girl he loved more than life itself, Pulcher began hobbling up the hill towards the market, all the while cursing his deformed legs for their lack of speed.

When he looked back, Bron was still grappling with her kidnappers, struggling and kicking. In spite of her spirited resistance, they found no difficulty in tossing her up on to the saddle of one of their horses, which must have been tethered out of sight in the trees, and when he looked again, they were galloping south-eastwards, in the direction of Calleva Atrebatum.

CHAPTER 36

Bron lay on a mattress on a low wooden bed in a small room, where the two legionaries had left her. A tiny barred window was letting in fresh air and she was cold.

At first they had gagged her and bound her hands together, though they had not tied her to the bed as Vortin had done. However, one of them had returned an hour later and released her, and after looking at the fear in her eyes, would not look at her again. He returned once more, bringing black bread and ripe strawberries and a pitcher of water with a beaker, which he left on a wooden chair. He came again, and with obvious embarrassment, pushed a chamber pot under the bed with his foot.

Throughout, he had said nothing and each time seemed glad to escape from the room.

After using the pot and eating the bread and strawberries and having a drink, she felt more relaxed, though she told herself she should not drop her guard.

Wandering over to the window, and standing on the chair, she saw that she was on the third floor of a large flint and stone building adjoining the town walls, which were made of the same materials. Her window overlooked a large area. She guessed it was a parade ground and she was in a barracks block. However, she had not seen any other legionaries when her two kidnappers had smuggled her up the stairs and into this room.

This was explained later when there was a commotion below and through an archway marched a century of soldiers. Their helmets and segmented armour glinted bright silver in the setting sun, and the leather strips hanging from their belts were slapping against legs covered by woollen tunics, the metal ends jangling and clinking against each other.

She watched as they were lined up before their officer, harangued for twenty minutes, then dismissed. No one looked up to see her arm frantically waving through the bars.

She heard some of them clattering up the stairs and talking and laughing as they passed her locked door, but no one attempted to come in, and the noise quietened as doors banged behind them. Later, they returned along the corridor in twos and threes on their way out. She dare not attract their attention then for fear that, if discovered, her plight might become worse than it was now.

She continued to lie on the mattress, wondering where her two kidnappers were and how long it would be before they returned to do whatever it was they had in mind when they seized her. There was only one outcome she could think of realistically, and knew she was no match for two of them.

Her breasts were painful and still leaking milk and she expressed some as best she could into the chamber pot. This made her think of her baby and the children, for whom she yearned. Pulcher would have raised the alarm and Soranus, who she knew would be beside himself with anxiety and anger, would be leading a party searching for her, but whether they would find her she was not certain. Her only hope was to convince these two young men that one of their officers was a friend of hers and would wreak punishment on them if they violated her. Aurelius must be in the garrison somewhere.

Tears came to her eyes. She had not seen him for over nine months and she could only think that he was bored with her or, worse, despised her after she had given herself to him so completely. However, he had made a promise to her father and she felt sure he would honour it if he could. Perhaps, though, he had been drafted abroad and had not been able to send her word before he left. He might even be dead by now.

She could feel her muscles gradually stiffening after the hard ride. It grew dark and still they did not come to claim her.

Lysander and Decimus, the two young legionaries who had captured Bron, had accompanied their comrades on a tour of the inns. When groups of them left to visit the brothels, her kidnappers returned surreptitiously to the barracks and sat on the edges of their adjacent beds, facing each other, discussing Bron and what to do with her.

Both were eighteen years old. They had been excused duties while recovering from the same fever that Aurelius had contracted, which had taken months to make its way round the garrison. Before resuming duties on the following morning, they had taken a leisurely ride and had reached Byden in their wanderings.

Having dismounted and watered their horses at the Stan, they had tied them to some spindly trees and sat down in the grass to eat the food brought with them, then had dozed in the April sunshine. Bron had disturbed them when she came to bathe.

Peering through the grasses to find out who had woken them, they were delighted to see this lovely girl only a few years older than themselves, and had stayed hidden, spying on her. With winks and grins and nudges, they had dared each other in whispers to creep up on her and steal a few kisses before making their getaway, but this had developed into the lustful idea of kidnapping her. They waited till she had dressed before carrying out their plan.

This empty room was used only for visitors or sick legionaries and, frequently, by those who smuggled in their girlfriends. Now that they had Bron imprisoned, they were not sure what to do with her. Rape could be a capital offence and, when it came to the point, they had little nerve and little inclination to take a girl who was not willing.

"If she is willing," reasoned Lysander, "we won't be raping her."

They had drawn straws to decide who should go in and take off her gag, and it had fallen to Decimus. However, he had seen the fear in her eyes. He thought of the sisters he had left behind in Naples and had no heart for the violation, and retreated as soon as possible.

"Well?" asked Lysander on his return.

"I didn't ask," said Decimus.

Decimus again drew the short straw when they judged it was time to take in some food and the chamber pot.

"Ask her this time," instructed Lysander, but again Decimus had not found the courage to speak. He looked at Bron and saw how beautiful she was and knew there must be a man somewhere who was breathing fire at her disappearance. He also noticed that her tunic was stained with milk and felt miserable at the thought that there was also a baby who needed her, and again retreated in confusion and guilt.

"I'll go this time," said Lysander after they had returned from wandering round the town. He was excited at the prospect of persuading Bron into compliance and could not understand the reluctance of his friend. They had brought back some sweetmeats to tempt her.

All was quiet in the barracks as he unlocked the door and went inside. She seemed to have mustered up some courage and regarded him evenly.

"What's your name?" he asked her.

"Bron," she said. "What's yours?"

"Lysander," he replied before he had thought about whether he should tell her or not.

"Why have you brought me here?" she asked.

"What do you think?" He grinned at her, displaying more bravado than he was feeling.

"As yet I have come to no harm," she said, "except that you have frightened the wits out of me. Please release me and there will be no repercussions, I promise you."

"What repercussions could there be?" he asked.

Bron could not but hear the uncertainty in his voice.

"First of all," she replied with confidence, "I am a friend of one of your junior officers, Aurelius Catus."

Lysander stared at her.

"It's true," she said. "My father is a Roman and was provincial governor of Eboracum. Officer Aurelius Catus is a friend."

"You're Roman?" Lysander was now very apprehensive.

"Half Roman," she said. "My mother is Atrebatis. Our ancestral home is Byden and Vortin, the High Priest there, will leave no stone unturned until he has found me, added to which I have a husband, a

221

father and a brother who will also not rest till they have rescued me. So you see, you are in some difficulty if you attempt to lay a finger on me."

Lysander looked at her and judged that some at least of what she said was true. He nodded and retreated.

Now it was the turn of Decimus to ask what had happened. Lysander related to him all that Bron had said.

"We must get her out of here!" said Lysander, panicking.

They heard the first of the legionaries returning in good time before 'lights out'.

"But how?" asked Decimus. "If we release her, how can we get her back to Byden? We're on guard duty first thing in the morning."

"Well, we can't take her home tonight," said Lysander, "not after 'lights out'. We will have to think about it tomorrow."

The barrack rooms began to fill with returning men. The last two to throw themselves on the empty beds in the room occupied by Lysander and Decimus were extremely merry.

"How could you afford all that drink on our pay?" enquired Decimus.

"A stranger was buying, a local man," was the explanation. "He was asking whether anyone had seen a girl being brought into town by two legionaries. He would have paid well for any information, and the beer was loosening our tongues, but none of us could help him. Good luck to 'em, I say, if they can get away with it!"

"He was asking about Officer Aurelius Catus," said the other. "No luck there, either, as the officer's away for a few days. The man left the inn when we did."

Lysander and Decimus exchanged worried glances and said nothing.

When news spread of the abduction of Bron, everyone in the settlement was stunned. They had never had trouble from the occupying forces previously, although legionaries often passed through on their way to larger towns. Any rowdiness had been contained in the inn.

Hestig reminded Trifena that rape was treated seriously under Roman law and a convicted soldier could have his nose cut off, but she replied that he was being naive and it was well known that the law was not so vigorously invoked when the girl was local and not Roman.

Vortin ordered that all horses in the settlement should be commandeered and Soranus, Hestig, Hestigys and most other able-bodied men set off for Calleva, the Ridgeway and all surrounding areas, but returned that day and the next without news. There had been no sightings of Bron and her two attackers, or no one would admit to having seen them, and it seemed that they had completely disappeared.

CHAPTER 37

Both legionaries had difficulty sleeping for thinking about Bron lying in the room along the corridor.

They were not the only ones who weren't asleep. Two legionaries at the end of the barrack room had smuggled a girl in and the noise they were making was keeping the other six awake, until someone shouted at them to tone it down.

However, the girl's presence gave Decimus an idea, which he shared with Lysander before they went on guard duty next morning. They woke the girl and a whispered conversation took place.

"I need paying," she told them.

"Of course," said Decimus and together they found sufficient coins to satisfy her and handed them over, with a key.

Bron, meantime, had slept only fitfully. During the night, she had been expressing her milk at intervals, and when the chamber pot was full one way and another, all she could do was throw the contents through the barred window.

She was glad she had had a strip bathe in the Stan before her capture but by morning was feeling grubby and hungry. Her tunic had been laid over the chair to dry during the night, but the milk stains were still evident.

At least, the two legionaries had left her alone, and if they had not taken her so far, she guessed that their nerve had failed them and they were unlikely to do so now. Perhaps today Soranus would find her, though she couldn't think how.

She dozed again and was awakened by the turning of the key in the lock. The sun was streaming in through the window and it was obviously well past sunrise. She bounded over to the chair, threw on her tunic and was hurriedly knotting her girdle when, to Bron's surprise, a girl aged about seventeen came into the room, closing the door behind her.

"Hello," the girl greeted her, "I've come to get you out of here."

Bron studied her suspiciously, wondering what new twist in her fortunes this presented. The girl wore a long grey cloak but revealed a flash of bright green beneath it. Bron had had sufficient contact with the girls in the Temple to know what profession this one followed.

"How?" asked Bron, looking into a pair of grey eyes.

"Just stay with me and do what I do," the girl said. "Here, put my cloak round you. By the way, what's your name?"

"Bron. What's yours?"

"Jannica. Have they tired of you?" Jannica looked surprised and Bron felt flattered.

"There's more to it than that," she said.

"You can tell me later. Just follow me, and don't speak unless you're spoken to – your speech is not common like ours and you'll make the guards suspicious."

Bron smiled. "I can talk common if I need to," she said, changing her accent.

They left the room, Jannica closing the door and leaving the key on the inside, then crept along the corridor. Suddenly, the notes of the wake-up call rang out from a bucina blown on the parade ground below. As they passed a couple of barrack rooms, the men were stirring and Jannica put her finger to her lips.

"If they see *you*, you'll never get out of here," she whispered.

They descended the stone staircase. Two sides of the square parade ground were formed by the fifteen-feet-high town walls and were patrolled by guards. Fortunately, however, they were looking out towards the country and did not notice the girls as they sidled through the shadows alongside the walls.

At the guardroom under the archway they were met by Decimus. Lysander was inside, distracting the attention of their fellow sentries. Decimus let them pass without comment, looking decidedly relieved, Bron thought.

They crossed an outer courtyard to a further archway in the walls, through which they could glimpse the town. Here they were not so lucky. A burly sentry barred their way.

"And where do you two little ladies think you're going in such a hurry?" he leered at them.

"Back into town." Jannica smiled brightly at him.

He looked from her to Bron and decided to have some sport with at least one of them, preferably the dark one. He was off duty soon.

"And supposing I don't let you through?" he asked, and called to one of the other sentries who was inside the guardroom.

"So, what have we here?" asked the second sentry, lounging against the door jamb. He was a swarthy man with the look of the southern Mediterranean about him.

"One each is what we have," grinned the first. "Come inside, ladies. We're off duty and off to bed soon. We'll take you with us."

"We've been here all night," protested Jannica. "Fair's fair, soldier, we need our sleep."

"Of course you do. We'll let you sleep – eventually – won't we, Naseem? I'll have the dark one. I know you prefer pale-skinned women."

"Need some warming up," replied the man called Naseem. "I'm always cold in this god-forsaken country!"

"If you let us pass, we'll be back later," offered Jannica.

"Why go, if you intend coming back?" asked the first man.

"We haven't spent all our pay yet! We can give you girls a good time," wheedled Naseem persuasively.

"The best!" agreed his friend.

"It's strange that I'm never stopped from coming in, only from going out!" complained Jannica.

Bron felt it was time she took a hand. She drew herself up, looked at both men without fear and said in her best accent, "My name is Bron. My father was governor of Eboracum for many years and I am here at the express wish of Officer Aurelius Catus. You will find yourselves in great trouble if you don't let us pass!"

The two men stared at her, clearly amazed by her haughty speech and bearing, and obviously wondering if what she was saying was true. Jannica also looked impressed and both girls watched the men's expression change from arrogance to uncertainty and then to apprehension.

"We don't believe you, but you can go. With a pedigree like that you're probably no good in bed anyway and only fit for the officers. The other one can stay, though. She's one of us."

"We both go or neither of us goes!" Bron said.

The men hesitated. "Oh, lah-di-dah!" the first man jeered. "Get off with you! The other one stays!"

Bron walked into the guardroom, to the surprise of the other two men sitting there. They were flicking two coins into the air and betting on which way up they would land. She sat on a bench.

"Both or neither!" she repeated.

The first guard stormed in after her and would have grabbed her by the arm if she had not fixed him with a supercilious stare. He dropped his hand.

"Oh, very well," he acquiesced. "You can both get the hell out of here!"

Without needing to be told twice, they scuttled through the archway and out into the town.

"You were marvellous!" enthused Jannica. "Was it all true?"

Bron laughed. "Most of it."

"Usually, I would have stayed," said Jannica, "but it made a change to see them back down. That felt good, though if I did it too often I'd get a bad reputation and would lose my job. But it did feel good!"

She led Bron through the wakening streets of Calleva and along a couple of narrow alleyways. Bron noticed that they were now following a line of bare footmarks painted on the pavement slabs, which led to an open doorway.

"It's not what you're used to, I know," Jannica apologised, taking her through it, "but I don't know where else to take you."

"It's all right," Bron assured her. "I feel safe here."

They mounted the stairs to the second floor. The noises coming from the various rooms reminded Bron of the time she had spent with the girls in the Temple. Jannica knocked on a door and was invited inside. She closed the door behind her and left Bron standing in the passageway.

A moment later she opened the door again and invited Bron in. The room was well furnished with a lot of tapestry wall hangings, embroidered covers and cushions, and woven rugs and sheepskins. A table served for both conducting business and eating meals, judging by the writing materials and household ware scattered over it. A cubicle in the corner was curtained off.

A tall imposing woman of about fifty years stood on the far side of the table. She had grey hair piled on top of her head and secured by ornamental hairpins, and wore plenty of make-up. Her blue tunic was well cut. Obviously, there was no lack of money here.

"Bron, meet Luenda. She's our 'mother'," Jannica said, "the only mother most of us have got."

"Will we be paid for helping you?" Luenda asked.

Bron knew that if Soranus could not afford whatever the woman demanded, Hestig would.

"You'll be well paid," she promised.

"What do you need?" asked the woman.

"A wash, and some food, then I want to go home to my husband and children," Bron answered her.

Luenda nodded. "Take her along to the bath suite, then downstairs for breakfast," she told Jannica.

Bron took off the cloak and Luenda studied her thoughtfully before turning again to Jannica.

"Did you get any sleep last night?"

"Enough," Jannica replied.

"Good. When you've organised Bron's breakfast, go back to work."

Jannica took Bron to the baths and both enjoyed a hot soak, the steam room and a cold plunge, and took advantage of a massage from a blonde girl who had no clients at that moment.

Then they went into a room on the ground floor at the front of the property, which served as an eating house for those using the facilities, and also for passers-by. Jannica left her then.

"If you need me, I'll be in the display room across the passage

228

for a while, but after that I'll be upstairs and you won't be able to get hold of me – not while whatever's-his-name's got hold of me, at least."

"Then we'll have to say goodbye," said Bron and held out her hand. "Thank you for your kindness. I hope Luenda gives you some of the money she'll make for returning me home."

Jannica smiled. "No matter – I didn't tell her that the legionaries paid me for getting you out of the barracks!" She winked and left the room.

CHAPTER 38

"Sit down, Bron," said Luenda when Bron entered her office again. "I have a favour to ask you." Bron waited. "I know you want to get home as soon as possible but –" She paused, then continued in a rush, "I have never been one to mince my words so I will come straight out with it and say what I have to say." She paused again. What she said next amazed Bron.

"Two weeks ago one of my girls died, three weeks after giving birth. Normally, we're not sentimental about such things but she was a good girl, and I think her baby daughter brought her the only real happiness she ever knew. The poor little scrap has ceased to thrive. We've put her to three wet-nurses but she continues to go downhill. I'd like to give her to you to feed for the next few days. I notice that you've recently had a baby yourself –"

Bron smiled happily and nodded. "A boy, Darius," she said.

"Is he well?" asked Luenda.

"He was putting on weight by the day, until I was kidnapped," said Bron. "I just hope that they've made good provision for him since."

"Have you any doubts?" asked Luenda.

"No, except that I'm his mother and I'm not there," replied Bron. Luenda indicated that she understood.

"You look strong and healthy and you come from a farming community. I can't help noticing that you have a lot of milk – it's very obvious from the way your breasts are leaking. It may be that you're just what this little thing needs."

Bron looked surprised at her concern.

"I know, perhaps I'm getting soft in my old age, but that's the size of it. Will you stay with us for a few days?"

Bron hesitated. This served her own purpose well but she had to make up her mind whether to indulge her need for Aurelius and dally here for a few days, neglecting her own family, or go straight home as she should.

"I'll do this for you on two conditions," she stipulated.

"Which are?"

"First that you will get a message to my husband that I am well and safe but delayed in Calleva for a couple of days, and secondly –" She hesitated. "Two, you find out for me where Officer Aurelius Catus is and inform him that I am here."

Luenda looked at her keenly.

"He's a friend of my father," Bron explained, "and has become my guardian."

Luenda knew every man in Calleva, almost without exception. "He's young to be your guardian," she commented.

Bron felt herself blushing and again adopted a haughty stance, which she realised didn't fool Luenda for one moment.

"My father was governor of Eboracum and helped Officer Catus to promotion," she said. "In return, he promised to look out for my welfare."

"I know he's away for a few days," Luenda informed her, "but I'll find out when he's due to return, and yes, we'll send a message to your husband. Of course, we won't tell him where you are, so if he comes looking, he won't find you. I'll make sure you get home safely."

Bron trusted Luenda to carry out her promises. However, if she found herself in any danger, she knew she could contact her Christian friends, who would look after her. She could have done that anyway, but she guessed they would not help her to meet Aurelius, and that was uppermost in her mind at this time.

The deal having been struck, Luenda asked Bron to follow her. She led her out of the house and through the crowds to a street a couple of blocks away, and stopped outside a single-storey house with thatched roof and small, thickly-glazed windows.

Luenda knocked at the low wooden door, which was opened by a woman. She looked as old as fifty, but Bron judged her to be about thirty-five. Three children, probably all under five years of age, were clinging to her legs and she had a sleeping baby in her arms.

"Is this the baby?" asked Bron, but Luenda shook her head, and without a word the woman led them into the room in which all the family lived, ate and slept.

In a corner on a bundle of rags lay a new-born baby who was crying incessantly. Bron was glad the room was so dark because it hid much of the dirt and grime, stale food and worse that Bron could partially see and certainly smell.

She picked her way warily across the room and without more thought scooped the baby up into her arms. Luenda and the woman watched. The baby stopped crying for an instant then started again.

"She's hungry," said Bron. "How often have you been feeding her?"

"As often as I can," said the woman.

"Before or after your own baby?" asked Bron sharply.

"After, of course." The woman hissed in her ear, "She's only a brothel baby."

Without another word Bron crossed to the door, relieved to escape into the fresh air.

"I'll send someone round with your last payment," Luenda told the woman and followed Bron out.

"I was glad to get out of there!" exclaimed Bron, looking at Luenda reproachfully.

"It's the third wet-nurse we've tried in two weeks," repeated Luenda defensively. "There's a lot of need for their services in the town and the women with a surplus of milk are thin on the ground."

"And thin in the milk, I should think," commented Bron acidly.

"Well, if you can suggest what else we could have done, I should like to hear it!" snapped back Luenda. "Do you think we don't care? It's not often we have the problem, but this baby would just not be aborted, no matter what her mother did. Sometimes it happens so. This time the baby lived and the mother died."

The baby was a little quieter now that they were in the fresh air and on the move.

"It has cost me a lot of money," continued Luenda. "I've not only lost the services of my girl but we also have a baby to support."

"What will you do with her?" asked Bron.

"Sell her, hopefully, if she lives," replied Luenda. "There are some rich women in the town who are childless and occasionally come to us to buy a baby, though I know of none at the moment. Failing that, we'll have to give her away. We'll make sure it's to a good home, as far as we can judge."

Bron looked down at the wizened little face and was filled with pity.

"I'll see what I can do for her," she promised. "I'll feed her as soon as we get back. Can you give us a quiet room somewhere?"

Luenda said she could.

When they arrived back at the brothel, Luenda sat Bron and the baby in her own room while she set about organising a quiet one for them both.

When she returned, having prepared all that was necessary, Bron had already fed the baby and was smiling.

"It took a while to get her on to the breast," she said, "but I managed it in the end, and my goodness, wasn't she hungry! I feel a lot better, too. She's asleep now but I'll feed her again when she wakes up."

"Well done!" said Luenda. "Come with me."

The room made ready was on the second floor but at the back of the building, overlooking a quiet courtyard.

"If you go down the back stairs," Luenda told her, "there's a door that leads directly into the courtyard. You can walk with her there in the sunshine at any time and you won't be disturbed. You may need some sleep now. You'll have nothing else to do here except look after the baby. You know where the bathhouse is. The girls will make sure you are fed at regular intervals. They'll bring clean napkins and swaddling."

"I have never swaddled my babies," said Bron, "and I don't want to swaddle this one."

"As you please," said Luenda. "If you have any clothes you want washed, the girls will also do that for you, and lend you anything you need in the meantime." She smiled. "I suggest you let them have your tunic straight away and have those stains washed out."

Bron laid the baby gently on the mattress on the bed then stepped out of her tunic and handed it over.

"Now I'll go and organise the errands I promised you," Luenda said. "I'll get a message to your husband and I'll find out when Officer Catus is due to return."

"By the way, what's the baby's name?" asked Bron.

"She hasn't been given one," said Luenda.

"Then I shall call her Gift," decided Bron.

CHAPTER 39

The morning after Bron had been kidnapped, Jeetuna saw her opportunity and moved in on Julius.

Although in a drugged state, she had planned her move very carefully. She slipped into the villa unnoticed during all the comings and goings and made straight for his bedroom.

He was having his breakfast when he heard her calling him. He came out of the triclinium and followed her voice, and expressed the greatest surprise at finding her naked in his bed.

What followed was confused in the telling. Unknown to Jeetuna, Flavia was in the baby's nursery. Hearing raised voices, pleadings and angry exchanges, she went across to his bedroom and found her father and the priestess arguing. He was telling her that she was only a friend and didn't she realise that any attempt at such a relationship would incur Vortin's wrath?

Jeetuna was kneeling on the bed and flaunting herself so brazenly before Julius, having taken his hand in an attempt to guide it to her body, that Flavia, with unaccustomed anger, launched herself at the priestess. Such a tussle developed that Julius had to separate them. At this point, Flavia punched Jeetuna twice, so hard that she caused a broken tooth and a black eye.

Then Julius ordered the priestess from the house. She would not have gone had not Hestigys fortuitously returned at that moment and physically ejected her, throwing her clothes after her.

Utterly humiliated, Jeetuna dressed haphazardly in the compound and ran down to the Stan, to staunch the blood in her mouth, bathe her eye and generally clean herself up. Then she slunk back to the

Temple by way of the wooded areas and went to her room and locked herself in.

Late that afternoon, a carrier brought word to Soranus that Bron was in Calleva and was well and unharmed. He said she was being cared for by friends and would return in a couple of days, after she had recovered from her ordeal. Vortin called off the search.

"She must be with the Christians," guessed Trifena. "Don't worry, Soranus, I'm sure she'll be back as soon as she can."

"But if she's well and unharmed, why hasn't she come home immediately?"

"Perhaps she's not quite as well as she would like you to believe. Give her time, lad. She'll be home. She wouldn't leave the children for longer than she has to."

When there was no further word and she had not returned by late afternoon on the following day, Soranus saddled his horse to ride over to Calleva. Attryde told him he was a fool and that Bron obviously didn't care about him and the children or she would have come home sooner, but he said he was going anyway.

"So once again I come a poor second to your wife!" she called after him.

When he arrived in the town late that evening, he asked the way to the Christian church. He found a worshipper there who said that Asher, the pilgrim, was away on his wanderings and directed him to Chrystella's house, as she was one of the Christian community.

Chrystella welcomed him warmly but was surprised by his enquiries as she didn't know that Bron was in Calleva.

"Where can she be?" he asked wildly.

"I can't think," said Chrystella. "Have you tried the barracks?"

She offered him a meal but he would not wait and thanked her and left.

At the first guardroom he made further enquiries. Naseem was on duty again.

"A dark girl, you say? There was one here yesterday morning. She spun a line about her father being the governor of Eboracum—"

"That's her!" cried Soranus. "What happened to her?"

"We let her go, if that's what you mean. I swear we didn't lay a hand on her!"

Soranus gave the guard a coin. "I believe you," he said. "Do you know where she went?"

"She mentioned Officer Aurelius Catus, but she was with a girl from one of the brothels."

Soranus was perplexed but asked directions to the brothel. "Is Officer Catus in Calleva?" he asked.

"Not as far as I know," replied Naseem. Soranus thanked him and left.

He found his way to the footsteps painted on the paving slabs and went through the open door. A very young girl came out of the room on his right and asked if he had visited before. He shook his head and said he wasn't there for the usual reason but wanted to speak to the mistress of the house. The girl went upstairs and returned with Luenda.

She greeted him warmly until he explained his errand, when her attitude changed. He thought it was because she was not going to make any money out of him.

"I know of no such young woman," she said. "If she isn't a prostitute, I can't think what she was doing coming out of the barracks early in the morning. None of my girls has mentioned such a person. If you are her husband, I suggest you go home and wait for her there. No doubt she'll return when she's ready."

With a heavy heart, Soranus made his way round some of the inns and drinking places but no one had seen Bron, and he finally gave up and rode home through the night.

Luenda did not tell Bron that her husband had called there, looking for her. She reasoned that Bron was in no danger and would be returning home soon enough. Until then, Gift needed her.

Aurelius returned to Calleva next day. Luenda had left word for him in the junior officers' mess. After he had been to the public baths and changed his clothes as necessary and cleaned his uniform, he called at the brothel and was greeted by Luenda. She knew him well as he had been a regular visitor, more so during the last few months.

In answer to his questions, Luenda told him what had happened to Bron. She led him to the back door.

"They're in the courtyard," she said and left him.

Quietly, he opened the door and stepped out into the courtyard. For a while he remained hidden behind a flowering cherry tree in a large ornamental urn, his gaze transfixed. Bron was walking backwards and forwards, smiling down at the bundle in her arms and talking softly. It was not the first time he had watched Bron with a baby. Again, he felt sweat break out on his forehead. Luenda had told him about this baby so he knew its history. However, Bron had milk in her breasts and was able to feed her because she had had a baby of her own – recently, Luenda said. He did the calculation and wondered.

The nine months since he had last seen Bron had seemed like a lifetime. She was the last thought in his head before he went to sleep, and when he lay awake through the dark hours of the night, she filled his fantasies. Every day, when his thoughts were not occupied with his duties, and often when they were, his mind capriciously recaptured visions of her and his heart and body ached with longing.

But she was married with a family and he could only hurt and disrupt them all, and he was not willing to do that, even for his own indulgence. To satisfy his craving, he had been visiting places like this wherever he was stationed, and although it meant he was not spending his nights alone, there was no joy in his encounters, and they didn't heal his heart or fill the void in his life.

When he could bear it no longer, he stepped out from behind the tree and spoke her name. Startled, Bron looked up, and with a cry of joy ran to him. His arms went round her and they kissed hungrily, the baby between them. Bron began to explain.

"I know, Luenda told me what happened to you. You may be sure I will be dealing with those two young men. Is there somewhere more private where we can *talk*?" Bron recognised the euphemism for what it was.

"I have my own room," she smiled. "I am being treated like a queen. Come, we won't be disturbed there."

They made their way up the stairs, Bron leading him by the hand, and into her room, which she had made as cosy as she could. She laid the baby in a wooden rocking crib then sat on the bed and invited Aurelius to sit beside her. They felt as awkward with each other as two first-time lovers. His arm went round her and she laid her head on his shoulder.

"Bron," he said, "Luenda tells me you've had a baby."

Bron nodded. "A little boy, Darius."

"I didn't know," he said.

"How could you? You haven't been to see me in nine months."

"You know what I'm asking."

"Yes, and I don't know, honestly I don't. Soranus thinks Darius is his son and, of course, he may be, but he was small and could have arrived before full-term. He could be yours, dearest. Aurelius, have you fallen out of love with me that you haven't been to see me?"

"Oh, my darling, how could you think that? It's because I love you so much that I haven't been to Byden. When I'm with you, as now, I think it's not possible to live without you, but I must because you belong to someone else, and Soranus is a good man. I can't look after you and the children as he can. My career is the Army and I could be recalled to Rome and to the fighting at any time. It's impossible, so I have to keep away, though it destroys me."

Bron put her arms tightly round his waist and he lay back upon the mattress and brought her down with him. They shifted around until they were lying side by side, then neither moved.

"Bron, are you going to let me make love to you?" he asked.

"I've never made love in front of the children," she answered him.

"But she's not your baby," he reminded her.

"She feels as if she is."

Five minutes later he swung his feet to the floor and stood up.

"It's not working, is it?" he said.

Bron knelt up and clung to him, her arms round his thighs and her head against his waist. He had no need to tell her that he wanted her, because she could feel the protrusion beneath his uniform, but she probably realised he was not going to do anything about it. He had a question to ask her but was reluctant to hear the answer. Bron read his thoughts.

"It's not been the same with Soranus," she said. "There has been only that one time, with you."

"Then at least we have that," he said. "I'll order a wagon to take you home tomorrow morning. Don't stop me now and don't come after me," and he left the room.

When Jannica brought the evening meal, she found Bron sobbing, the baby in her arms. She put down the tray and went to find Luenda.

The older woman sat on the bed beside her guest. "What's wrong, Bron? Doesn't he love you any more, is that it?"

"The trouble is that he does love me, and I love him, but we met too late."

"Love!" exclaimed Luenda. "Better off without it. It's a prison where everyone suffers. Better to take what you can from it and leave the rest alone."

"He's sending a carriage for me in the morning," Bron told her. "Gift is doing well. She should be all right if you can find a better wet-nurse – there must be someone who's lost her own baby."

"You've been so good for her, Bron. Thank you."

"I hate leaving her," said Bron, "but I must go home to my own baby and the children." Then she asked quietly, "Tell me, Luenda, what is she to you?"

"Her mother was also a brothel baby. Nothing I tried would abort her, either. Gift is my granddaughter," she said.

CHAPTER 40

An enclosed carriage arrived next morning. Bron kissed Luenda and Jannica goodbye and said she would visit them if ever she were in Calleva again. Then she clambered into the vehicle and the horse set off towards the north.

When they were about a mile from Byden, Bron saw Pulcher in the distance, sitting on the grass by a milestone. She guessed he had been there since they had received her message, waiting for her return, only leaving his post to sleep at home during the hours of darkness.

He took no notice of the carriage as it rolled nearer, obviously expecting her to return in a wagon. It was only when it drew level and the horse was reined in, and Bron pulled back the curtain and called to him, that he realised she had at last returned, safe and well.

He clambered to his feet in haste and came running over, his face alight with happiness, and reached his hands up to take hold of her outstretched fingers.

The driver moved the carriage over to the milestone and, using the stone as a mounting platform, Pulcher climbed up inside. He was set down a mile further on before they crossed the Stan, and hurried off to his house, trying not to attract any attention.

The carriage continued on its way along the path through the settlement and stopped outside the forge. Bron got down, thanked the driver, and hurried inside.

On seeing her, Soranus dropped the file with which he was smoothing a horseshoe and rushed over to her. Their arms went round each other and he began to cry. Neither of them noticed Attryde leaving quietly with her baby.

He locked the forge and, with their arms still around each other, they walked towards their house. Everyone they met on the way stopped to enquire how she was and to say how pleased they were to see her home. At the pottery stall, her father and brother hugged her and Hestig left to tell Trifena and to ask her to collect up the children and take them to their home.

While they were on their own and before the family arrived, Soranus told Bron how he had been like a wild man while she was away and of his abortive trip to Calleva. Bron was able to say honestly that Luenda had not informed her of his visit, but she decided not to say more until the whole family was gathered and she could say it all once and get it over.

It was not long before Layla and Alon came rushing in, looking for their mother, and Bron filled her arms with them. Then she took her sleeping baby from Trifena.

"He looks well." Bron laughed. "I don't think he's even missed me."

While the children played at her feet, calling for her attention at frequent intervals, and she fed Darius, she related all that had happened to her, only leaving out the details of her meeting with Aurelius.

Then they told her about the extensive searches Vortin had organised and how he had sworn to bring the two legionaries to justice.

"Daddy, please, I don't want any more trouble. They are very young, and they didn't hurt me. Please speak to Vortin about it."

"I'll try," Hestig promised.

They also told Bron of the scandal concerning Jeetuna.

"She hasn't come out of her room for three days now," said Hestig.

"It's time for the children to eat," announced Trifena, "and you must be hungry, Bron. By now, there'll be a meal waiting for us at home, so let's all make our way there, and you can all have an early night. I'm sure you all need one."

"Before we go," said Bron, "there's something I have to tell you. It's not an easy thing to say, and you're all going to be very cross with me, especially you, Soranus, but I couldn't help it, I really couldn't, and I hope you'll think I did the right thing when you see –"

"See what?" asked Trifena.

"This is all very mysterious, darling," said Soranus. "What mischief have you been up to now?"

Instead of answering, Bron went to the front door. She smiled at Pulcher who was waiting there, and asked him to come inside. When the family saw him, there was a stunned silence.

Bron took Gift from Pulcher's care and gave her to Soranus, whose arms went round her automatically, though he was gaping at Bron.

"Soranus, darling, I couldn't help it. Look at her, she's so tiny, so vulnerable. I couldn't leave her in that place. She needs a family. *She needs us.* I couldn't leave her behind."

"Oh, Bron!" her mother reproached her.

"Soranus, say something," pleaded Bron. "Look at her, just look at her!" Soranus did so and she could sense that her battle was almost won.

"Bron, you should have asked first. You can't manage two babies, one not your own. It will be like having twins!"

"I will manage," she said. "Other mothers do."

"We can't afford another baby!"

"We won't have to. Luenda said she will send money over every week. She would also like to see her occasionally."

Trifena took the baby from Soranus and walked over to show her to Hestig.

"Soranus, if it's really too much, I can send her back. The carriage won't leave until I have your answer. The driver is waiting at the inn."

Soranus hesitated then gave in. "All right, Bron, you win, as long as you think you can manage. I'm so pleased to have you home, I can't refuse you anything – it won't last, of course!"

They all laughed and Bron hugged him and told him how lucky she was to be married to him, and meant it. Trifena introduced Gift to the children and they gave her a kiss, as instructed, then went back to their game. Finally, the party made its way to the small villa and Hestig left to give the driver, who was waiting at the inn, the good news to pass on to Luenda.

Vortin called during the meal to see Bron and even he was made welcome and given a glass of the best wine. Bron thanked him for organising the search parties and introduced him to Gift. For an hour or two the passions between them, of hatred on her part and lust on his, were laid aside, though she was careful not to be left alone with him at any time.

Vortin returned to the Temple to be told that Jeetuna had still not opened her door. He went to bed, his head filled with visions of Bron, who in her happiness, surrounded by those who loved her, with her babies in her arms and her children at her feet, seemed to him more desirable than ever.

He also had to decide how long to leave Jeetuna before breaking down her door.

CHAPTER 41

The priestess remained deaf to all bribing, wheedling and ultimatums. When they broke in seven days later, her room stank of urine and excrement, and there were flecks of white powder over her filthy bed, the furniture and floor.

She showed no trace of the beauty she once had in such abundance. Her eyes were dark and sunken, her face lined and grimy round swollen lips, her hands and nails filthy and her hair, once the colour of wheat, was dank and matted.

She was taken away by the women and cleaned up, and under the care of Stalwyn, nursed back to some semblance of health. Veneta visited her every day to try to drag her mind back to reality, and made some progress, though her withdrawal from the drug was terrible to watch, and Veneta was exhausted by the daily battle for Jeetuna's body, mind and spirit.

The priestess was not allowed back into her room until it had been thoroughly cleaned, fumigated and redecorated by men from the village.

Jeetuna's humiliation deepened as she imagined them gossiping to their wives each evening and receiving many a meal from nosy neighbours on the strength of their first-hand knowledge of her plight. The story would balloon as it was repeated over and over again to those who would listen, who would be almost everybody. Many would gloat, especially the jealous women, but she hoped there would be a few who would feel compassion at the loss of her dignity and beauty.

One afternoon, on instructions from Sharma, Brocchus led the eunuchs through the woods to Umbella's hut, approaching quietly so as not to forewarn the old woman. When they flung open the door and burst in, they found her dozing in a chair, her long and untidy grey hair tangled about her. She had no opportunity to escape.

While two of them pinned her arms behind her back, which caused great pain and provoked her into crying out in anguish then complaining bitterly, the others ransacked the hovel. With foresight, they had brought torches, which gave sufficient light to set about their task.

Brocchus ordered them to drag down all the herbs and plants that had been strung up to dry. Then glass bottles containing brightly coloured liquids were swept to the floor from shelves and table. They did not all smash on the beaten earth, but their contents spilled out so that the eunuchs' feet and sandals looked as though they had been wading through rainbows. Drawers were emptied of their paraphernalia and discovered packets were ripped open, their contents tipped into the running liquids. Then Brocchus ordered the party to turn its attention to the boxes and wooden chests piled high in one dark corner.

His eyes gleamed in the torchlight as each container was thrown open, to reveal the revenue from Umbella's clients. The good luck charms, figurines of Ashuba and Shubinata, shoes, written blessings, strangely-shaped and patterned stones, animal skulls and the like were discarded, but the piles and piles of coins, jewellery, the parcels of precious metals and stones, and valuable artefacts were all tipped into three chests.

Still Brocchus had not found what he was seeking.

"Where are they, old woman?" he shouted at her.

Umbella played the innocent.

"Everything I have, you see there," she bleated.

He ordered the eunuchs to pull her arms and shoulders back until her elbows met. There was a loud crack and a scream of pain from the hag.

Brocchus walked over and brought his face close to hers.

"All the things Jeetuna brought you!" he rasped at her. "Where are they?"

Umbella was still defiant. "There is nothing else."

Brocchus slapped her hard on one side of her wrinkled face and her head stayed twisted to one side.

"Tell us, and you save your life!"

"There is nothing –" He slapped the other side of her face and her head twisted towards the opposite shoulder. Her bottom lip was bleeding and a great red weal had appeared across one cheek.

"I go free?" she asked. Brocchus nodded.

Suspiciously, she tried to make doubly sure. "You speak the truth?" Brocchus nodded again.

"Buried outside, under the fire," she at last whimpered reluctantly.

"Don't let her move!" he ordered and strode outside, beckoning the remaining eunuchs to follow. They pushed over the triangular support, and the cauldron and its contents were sent flying into the trees. With branches in leaf, they beat out the flames and scattered the ashes. One of them fetched a bucketful of cold water from the wall of the hut, and swung it backwards before flinging the contents over the area, to cool the ground. Having searched about and found a couple of spades lying in the undergrowth, two of them began to dig.

It was not long before spades struck wood and metal, and a large chest was uncovered. More digging, some heaving and dragging, and the chest lay on the ground before them, leaving a large, empty cavity in the earth.

Throwing open the lid, Brocchus found what he had been looking for – all the items Jeetuna had stolen from the Temple. The gold gleamed in the afternoon sunshine. Brocchus rifled through the piles. Some of the goods had disappeared from the Temple a long time ago, but many had not been missed as they had never reached the treasury in the first place.

"Shall I tell them to let her go now?" asked one of the party.

"Certainly not!" replied Brocchus. "She's not going anywhere – at least not under her own volition – and then not all of her. We won't be able to carry her body back to Sharma as well as everything else. Tell them to bring her out here!"

Without compassion, Umbella was dragged from the hut by her

broken arms. She was screeching at the top of her voice one minute and pitifully pleading for mercy the next.

"I told you where it all was," she cried. "You said you'd spare my life!"

"So what? You told me there *was* nothing else – and I said you'd go free. So, we were both lying! Lay her face down on the ground!"

"No! No! Have mercy, Brocchus! I've never harmed you. I could help you – give you love potions for your young men, keep you virile – whatever you want!"

"Throw her down!" ordered Brocchus again. "Sit one on each arm, one on each foot, and one on her legs! And hand me that spade!"

"Brocchus –" remonstrated one of the eunuchs.

"Keep quiet and there'll be gold enough in your pouches by the time you get back to the Temple. Turn your faces away if you're squeamish."

Umbella, her voice rising in a crescendo, began damning Brocchus and the eunuchs with such vituperation and such powerful curses that they began to shake and loosen their grip on her. Seeing this, Brocchus knocked her senseless in mid-screech with the handle of the spade.

There was a sudden, unexpected silence. No one moved or spoke. Then Brocchus raised the spade above his head with both hands and brought it down edge-on unerringly on Umbella's neck. Her long flowing hair was cropped and her head rolled free, its eyes staring and mouth open.

At that moment, a cloud of starlings rose squawking high above the trees and flew away to the north.

"Our work here is done," announced Brocchus. "Throw her body into the pit and find a sack to put her head in. We'll take it back to show Sharma. Oh, and set fire to the hut."

Having been alerted by the flock of frightened birds, and noticing the smoke spiralling above the distant canopy of branches and leaves, a crowd was waiting for them in the settlement. The party made straight for the Temple. Between them, the eunuchs carried four chests of treasure. They also carried a sack that leaked blood.

Perhaps it was the memory of what Jeetuna had been, and because most of the treasures had been recovered, that caused Vortin to stop short of evicting her from the Temple. However, he stripped her of her priestly office and she was relegated to the ranks of the temple prostitutes.

"Where you belong!" Vortin told her. "I should have done it years ago!"

Jeetuna finally pulled her reason together and became so surprisingly subdued that Veneta reported to Vortin that all was well.

However, all was not well. What motivated Jeetuna now was revenge on as many people around her as she could reach, beginning with Julius, and she calculated that trouncing Flavia would destroy several of them in one stroke, making it an effective starting point.

She had not long to wait.

CHAPTER 42

Flavia had recently discovered that she had an aptitude for creating pleasing designs from nature with which to decorate the pottery Hestig and her husband made and sold. She had taken to wandering round and about the settlement with her wax tablets and stylus, reproducing flowers and leaves and natural patterns, to paint them later on pots and pitchers, plates, bowls and beakers before their final firing. The decorated items were popular and sales increased.

It was two weeks after the great May celebration of Rosalia, when the families honoured their dead at the sacred pits near the Stan mere, the pool of spring water on high ground to the west of the settlement.

Jeetuna came out onto the Temple steps for some fresh air and noticed Flavia pass by with her wax tablets under her arm. Unusually, her young daughter was not with her. Jeetuna watched as she made her way through the gap in the bank and across the ditch towards the lynchets. She hurried upstairs to find Nobilianus, who was sitting on his bed using his dagger to whittle a piece of wood into the shape of a buxom female figurine.

"Nobilianus, you once told me that it would make you happy if you could get to Flavia. I can tell you where she is at this moment, and she's alone."

"So where is she?"

"I've just seen her leave the settlement through the west bank, and it's my guess she's making for the wood to do some sketching. If you go now, you'll catch her up."

Nobilianus caressed the wooden figure with his podgy fingers, then, without a word, inexplicably grasped his dagger and stabbed it into each breast before throwing the damaged carving onto the bed. He returned the dagger to its leather sheath slung round his waist and stood up.

Jeetuna was surprised when he then unlocked the door of a small cupboard and pulled from it a ground-length brown cloak with a hood, and a piece of black cloth.

Her memory flew to the rape of Louca's daughter, Carinna, and the only description she had been able to give of her attacker. Nobilianus looked at her enquiringly.

"She's nothing to me," shrugged Jeetuna. "I won't tell, whatever happens."

"Then wish me luck!" He laughed and left the room.

For about thirty minutes Jeetuna lay on his bed, with which she was entirely familiar, holding the damaged wooden figurine in her hands, then could contain her curiosity no longer, put it on the table, and followed him.

Nobilianus left the Temple by way of Vortin's private door behind the altar and walked quickly past his father's house and so into the wood. It took him some time to locate Flavia, but he finally saw her sitting on a tree stump, her hands busy with a stylus on pliable wax.

Usually her blonde hair was cut short but lately she had let it grow longer, and as she bent her head over her work, a lock of it was falling across her face, hiding one cheek. One foot was out of sight beneath her, but from the light blue folds of her under-tunic the other foot emerged, encased in a blue square-toed shoe. She was leaning slightly forward, the wax tablets resting on her knee. Her arms were encased in the long sleeves of her dark blue over-tunic but Nobilianus remembered they were white and soft and firm and he imagined them round his neck.

He had already disguised himself with the cloak and hood and had tied the cloth round his face. He called her name, the sound muffled, and she looked up, startled. He drew in his breath when he saw her eyes, as blue as the bluebells he had scattered over her bedcover the night he had visited her and Trifosa while they slept.

He approached quickly through the trees. With a cry of alarm, Flavia jumped up and turned to run. It took him only a few steps to reach her. His arms went round her waist and he lifted her off her feet, carrying her deeper into the wood. She struggled, pushing his arms away, kicking and screaming at the same time, so he dropped her and fell on top of her, trying to put his hand over her mouth.

For a while they rolled together over tree roots and fallen branches, Flavia trying to stand up and Nobilianus determined that she should not. Once, she managed to cling to the trunk of a small tree and pull herself away from him, but he slithered towards her, hands reaching. She bent one leg up to her waist and delivered a resolute backward kick, towards his face. Her foot made contact and he yelled and his hands involuntarily flew to his chin and cheek. As she scrambled to her knees, he grounded her again, face down.

Selvid's task that day was to take a party of eunuchs back to the sacred pits and clear from the mounds the dead garlands and posies of flowers left there after the Rosalia festival. They also needed to collect together the remnants of the picnics left for the ancestors, which had been partially devoured by them, the birds and scavenging animals, and cart them away by wooden wheelbarrows to a compost heap in the wood. The compost was used as fertiliser on the lynchets.

Among the pits, Selvid lifted his head and listened.

"What was that?" he asked the eunuchs working with him. They had been busy trundling the wheelbarrows across the chalky ground and had heard nothing.

"I thought I heard a scream," said Selvid, but the men laughed and said it was the breeze, or the nymphs at the pool or the murmuring of the dead.

"I must have imagined it," he agreed. "Take a sack and go over to the mere and collect the offerings dropped into it, then you can go back to the Temple and hand them over to Sharma. It won't take me long to finish here."

"If you don't arrive back, we'll send out a search party!" They laughed again and left him.

Nobilianus had pushed Flavia's tunic up. He had his hands round her waist and was fumbling with the laces of her underwear, but was in too much of a hurry to untie them, so tried tearing the linen, but it held firm.

Flavia, choking with her mouth full of leaf mould and dirt, managed to turn onto her back, arms flailing. He pinned her down and now was kneeling over her. She brought her knee up and again made contact. With a howl of pain his hands flew to his groin. She tried to move away, but his knees were planted on her tunic on each side and she couldn't. He bent over her again, his face close to hers, and with lust dulling his pain, attempted to kiss her. She brought up her right hand and tore the cloth away.

For a split second there was silence between them, as if time held its breath.

"Nobilianus, you monster!" she accused him.

"Damn you, Roman bitch!" he shouted at her, still in pain. "Damn you with your blue eyes and innocence! Hestigys won't want you any more after this!"

Finally, the linen gave way under his frantic tugging and at last, with noisy exultation, he knew Flavia as only her husband had known her.

She continued to resist him, but the ferocity of his attack left her semi-conscious, and when he had no more energy he found a short branch and used that instead. Flavia passed out.

Nobilianus sat back on his haunches, breathing hard. Finally he stood, looking down at her. The mist cleared from his eyes and with it the mist in his head. He noticed the blood on his hands. The perspiration running all over his body turned icy cold, and he shivered. He began to realise what he had done. Then, with only one thought in his head, and that was to flee, he gathered together his cloak, the black cloth, and the clothing he had discarded.

He was about to take flight when Jeetuna came out of the trees. Her face was ashen. She must have witnessed his frenzied attack but had done nothing to stop it.

"You can't leave her like that," she said. Nobilianus stared at her. "She recognised you, didn't she?"

"Yes, but –"

"Can you imagine what her father will do when she tells him who did that to her? In the name of Ashuba, she's a Roman! There's nowhere you can go where Julius won't find you! He'll hunt you down till the day he dies and Hestigys after him! And don't imagine that your father will save you, because he won't!"

"But what can I do?" blubbered Nobilianus, now in terror.

"There's only one thing you can do. You'll have to kill her!"

"I've – I've never killed – killed anyone!" he stammered.

"So now you have to!" Jeetuna was relentless. "You've got a dagger. Kill her then go back to the Temple as if nothing had happened. Nobilianus, pull yourself together and kill her! She's half dead already. You'll be putting her out of her misery. Do you think she wants to wake up and remember what you did to her?"

Nobilianus pulled the dagger from its sheath and looked at it.

"Do it!" commanded Jeetuna.

He raised his hand and brought the dagger down between Flavia's bare breasts, where he judged her heart to be. She convulsed and lay still.

"Again!" Jeetuna whispered in his ear. "Make sure of it!"

He pulled the dagger from the soft flesh, closed his eyes and plunged it in a second time. Then he dropped the dagger and ran. Jeetuna walked over and looked down at Flavia.

"Not so beautiful now, are you?" she sneered. "We'll see what your father and husband make of this!"

She was about to pick up the dagger but thought she heard noises coming towards her, twigs breaking, and quickly vanished through the trees.

"So what if they find it?" she thought. "It isn't my dagger."

Selvid was on his way back to the settlement and would have passed within a few feet of Flavia's body, but a slight movement, a receding shadow, caught his eye and he turned his head. He stopped and, curious, went over to look at what was lying beneath the trees.

What he saw filled him with such horror that the memory stayed with him for the rest of his life. There was a ringing in his ears and an ache in his head and he reached out one hand to steady himself on a tree trunk.

Among broken branches, disturbed leaves and scuffed earth lay Flavia, her long blonde hair tangled with last year's leaves, her face dirty, her arms and legs at strange angles. There were signs of blood high up on the insides of her legs and two lines of congealing blood running from wounds between her bare breasts and another trickle from her mouth.

He bent down and gently pulled her tunic over her as best he could. He knew she was dead but felt for her pulse and listened to her heart, anyway. There was no sign of life.

He sat and cradled her head in his lap and the tears flowed down his cheeks. Who could have done this to so beautiful a girl? How could he tell her husband and her father, both of whom adored her, and who would care for her baby now, little Lucilla?

He knew he should run to get help and organise a search party, but shock and distress kept him there for a long time. It was then he saw the dagger lying in the grass near the body. He laid her head down gently and leant over and picked it up and stared at it. The blood on it was still sticky.

It was in this position that two of the eunuchs found him. He looked up at them, the dagger in his hand. They stared in disbelief at the horrific scene they had chanced upon.

"Selvid, what have you done?" they accused him.

"Done? Why, nothing. I found her like this." He was suddenly aware of the dagger in his hand and dropped it as if it were a lump of hot metal.

They came over and he stood up.

"We must get help," he said, "and send out a search party. The killer may still be in the wood."

They stood one on each side of him, took him by the arms, and walked with him back to the settlement. He made no attempt to free himself.

"You can't possibly think that I had anything to do with it!" he protested.

"It looks bad," said one of the eunuchs.

"We must take you to Vortin," said the other

"Ashuba, help us, I have no stomach for this," added the first.

"But we are wasting time, we must search!" insisted Selvid, whose brain was beginning to function more clearly.

"We will do whatever needs to be done," they told him.

They took him to Vortin and explained what they had seen. The High Priest told one of them to fetch Hestig from the pottery booth, without saying anything to Hestigys. Sharma and Veneta were also summoned.

When all had gathered, the two eunuchs repeated their story. Selvid protested his innocence and Veneta pleaded for his release, but he was taken to the prison in the market building, because it was a civil offence.

Then Hestig was given the heavy task of telling his son and despatching a message to Julius, who had returned to his work in Calleva several weeks previously.

Veneta was sent with Brocchus and four of the eunuchs to bring the body back in a wooden box. She returned in tears, holding against her heart a wax tablet incised with a delicate design of white woodruff, their smooth leaves whorled round square stems. Grief and shock rendered the party speechless, except for Brocchus, who remained unaffected.

Meantime, Jeetuna was relishing the imagined grief of Julius and Hestigys when they heard the news. Additionally and surprisingly, she had caught Selvid in her net, and therefore Veneta. Four in one stroke! And she had done nothing amiss, only spoken a few opportune words to that crazy Nobilianus.

She knew he was cowering in his room. Perhaps he would be the next to fall! That left Vortin and possibly Sharma – she would decide later. There were a few more on her blacklist, notably Bron, who had always been a rival when it came to Vortin's passions.

It had all been so easy!

CHAPTER 43

The courtroom above the covered market was full of spectators for the trial of Selvid, and the hubbub was deafening. When Hestig and members of the council entered, however, a hush fell in which you could have heard the wheat growing.

Hestig took his seat in the centre of the long table, facing the people, the councillors seated on each side of him. He rose to speak.

He saw his son in front of him, sitting with Julius, and in the row behind them, Trifena with Bron. Vortin was not present but had sent Sharma in his stead. Hestig was surprised to see the tall figure of Asher standing at the back with a woman who was a stranger.

Selvid sat apart on Hestig's right, with Veneta sitting as near to him as she could.

"Fellow inhabitants of Byden, friends," Hestig began, "you know why this court has been convened. This is a very sad occasion for all of us, and especially, of course, for the family and friends of Flavia. Selvid has been accused of her rape and murder and we are here to see that justice is done, without bias either way, dealing only in facts that can be proved, or a probability so strong that it must be true. We cannot give a guilty verdict using evidence that is only a possibility.

"As you know, I am – was – Flavia's father-in-law. For that reason you may think that I should not be leading these proceedings. I can only say that I will have no input into the discussion of the councillors on guilt or innocence. Julius and Hestigys are agreeable to my taking this chair. However, if there are any objections, please voice them now."

Everyone waited. Hestig hoped that he was respected as a man of honour. He had been accused falsely on two occasions, years ago for the murder of Septima the prostitute and later for the theft of the council's funds, and of all the councillors he would know best about lawful procedures. No one objected.

He thanked them for their confidence in him.

"Now we come to the councillors. Julius is not allowed to serve as he is the father of the victim, and neither can Kendrus, our doctor, as he will be called as a witness, so we have elected the jeweller and the beekeeper in their places. The other councillors you know as honest tradesmen. Has anyone any objections about the ability of these seven men to come to a just verdict?" No one had.

Hestig then addressed the accused. "Selvid, answer on oath – did you murder Flavia?"

"I swear by the one true God that I am innocent of this terrible crime. How anyone could think –"

"Thank you, Selvid. You will have your chance later. First, we will call Flavia's husband, now widower, my son, Hestigys."

Hestigys rose from his seat and stood to the left of the table, facing the people. He swore by Ashuba that he would tell the truth, then asked for a chair. Seated, and obviously in great distress, he related why Flavia had gone on her own into the wood that day a week ago.

His mother had called unexpectedly, he said, and had offered to look after the baby for a while, and Flavia had welcomed the opportunity to take her wax tablets and stylus into the wood to sketch designs from nature with which to decorate their pottery. He laid on the table the wax tablet incised with the woodruff design, which Veneta had brought back from the wood and had returned to him.

"Thank you, son," said Hestig gruffly.

Hestigys, now in tears, returned to his seat next to Julius.

Hoad was at the door of the council chamber and was asked to call in one of the eunuchs who had found Selvid with Flavia's body. He told his story with the help of Hestig's questions, followed by those of the councillors. He went out and the second eunuch was called. His story supported the first, and he also left the room.

Then Kendrus was called. He had examined Flavia's body as it lay in the Temple and was about to describe the fearful injuries she had suffered and to state the reason for death, when Hestig raised his hand and stopped him.

"For mercy's sake," he explained, "I must give my son and Julius the option of leaving the room before you give your evidence."

Hestigys left but Julius stayed.

When Hestigys returned, Julius was weeping and being comforted by Louca, who was sitting on the other side of him. Hestig allowed a short interruption to the proceedings while Hoad brought him a beaker of water and he struggled to recover his composure.

Then Hestig said that, after the murder, he had asked for a thorough search of the area to be made and this had been carried out by his son-in-law, Soranus. The young man was called and, on oath, described the scene as he had found it after the removal of Flavia's body. There was the disturbed state of the area and blood, he said, and he had found Flavia's stylus. He had also found a short branch with blood on it.

Kendrus was recalled and asked if, as far as he could judge, Flavia had been attacked with the branch. Kendrus said no, but from his examination and dirt and flakes of bark found in Flavia's body, he could guess how the branch had been used. Grim-faced, Soranus and the doctor then left the room.

By now, they had all heard as much as they could take in one morning, besides which everyone was beginning to feel hungry, so Hestig allowed a break for lunch, stipulating that all those involved in the trial should not leave the building, but that food and drink should be brought in for them.

When everyone had reassembled, he asked Selvid to stand.

"You have heard all the evidence, Selvid. Do you still maintain your innocence?"

"Yes, as God is my witness," he said.

"Then tell us in your own words exactly what happened that day."

Selvid did so, every now and then looking over to Veneta for support. She smiled and nodded encouragement.

"You have our full attention, Selvid, and the whole afternoon – and tomorrow, if necessary – to place before us your defence," Hestig told him. "You may call your first witness."

Selvid asked that the eunuchs should return, one at a time, to say why they had gone back to look for him in the wood. They gladly related how he thought he had heard a scream while they were still working among the pits, and their jest about the wind and nymphs and dead ancestors talking to him, and their teasing promise to search for him if he did not return in a reasonable time.

"Of course," said the carpenter, "you could have pretended to hear the scream."

"But I had no way of knowing that Flavia had gone into the wood, so why should I have concocted a lie about hearing a scream? As it turns out, it *was* a scream I heard, and I only wish I had investigated at the time. I will never cease to reproach myself for ignoring it.

"Also, as I knew the eunuchs would be coming back for me if I delayed, why would I stay so long with Flavia's body and risk being caught?"

"Why *did* you stay so long?" asked the wheelwright. Selvid told him that shock and grief had immobilised him.

"But you had the dagger in your hand," persisted the beekeeper.

"I had only just noticed it and picked it up," said Selvid. "I have another question for the eunuch."

Hestig invited him to ask it.

"Did you see me that day, or have you ever seen me, with a dagger?" The eunuch shook his head. "When you searched me, did you find a dagger holster on me?" The eunuch said he hadn't.

Selvid recalled Soranus and asked him if he had found such a holster or pouch at the scene of the murder. Soranus said he hadn't.

"I have never carried a dagger and I wasn't doing so on that day," insisted Selvid. "If I was carrying a dagger, where was the sheath? There was no sheath because there was no dagger."

Hestig thought he had made his third good point.

"What was my motive? I would have needed a reason to kill her."

One of the councillors suggested that lust was a motive. Selvid vehemently denied this.

"It seems that I now have the choice of risking my life or my priestly office," he said to the councillors. "What I have to say will surprise you all, I know, and I also know that I will not be able to serve you in this community any longer, certainly not in the way I have done in the past. Before I make this statement, I apologise to the council, to you people, and above all to Vortin and my colleagues at the Temple."

He crossed to Veneta, took her hand to bring her to her feet, and stood with his arm round her waist. There was a surprised murmur from the crowd.

"I have to tell you that Veneta and I were married in Calleva seven years ago. We are happily married. I had no lust for Flavia, whose family are my friends."

"You lie!" shouted Sharma. "Priests are not allowed to marry! It's Temple law. It's Ashuba's law!"

"But we are no longer subject to Ashuba's or Temple law," countered Selvid. "In fact, neither of us believes in Ashuba any more. We became Christians before we were married in the Christian church."

There was uproar in the room and it took several minutes before Hestig and the councillors were able to quieten Sharma and everyone else sufficiently to make themselves heard.

"Whatever you feel about this," Hestig told the people, "is irrelevant in this case. Your outrage will have to be addressed after the trial. May I remind you that we are dealing with facts here. Selvid, can you prove what you are saying?"

"Yes, I can," said Selvid. He then called Asher. "You will remember Asher, the Christian, from the time he has spent among us."

Asher confirmed all that Selvid had said, as did his companion Chrystella, who was called to make a statement after him.

Selvid completed his case by calling a few inhabitants of the settlement whom he had helped at various times and who gave him good character references. It was hardly necessary, as all the people knew him well.

"That completes my defence," he announced, "except to say that you all know that I am incapable of committing such a terrible crime. Julius and Hestigys," and he addressed himself directly to the two men, "you must know I couldn't have done it."

"You may return to your seat," Hestig told him.

The councillors then withdrew to discuss their views and decide on their verdict. They returned in a very short time and resumed their seats.

"Please give us your decision," Hestig requested.

The ropemaker had been deputed to speak for them all.

"We have unanimously decided that Selvid is not guilty," he told the court.

Again there was uproar, with people cheering and clapping. Veneta was tearful. A large group surrounded Selvid, all wanting to shake his hand. He finally made his way over to Hestig and the councillors to thank them, then turned, and found himself facing Hestigys and Julius. They both hugged him.

"I never thought for one moment that you were guilty," said Julius.

"But who is?" asked Hestigys. "If I find him, I'll kill him with my own hands."

Selvid and Veneta did not return to the Temple that night. They accepted an invitation from Julius to stay at the villa with him and Hestigys as house guests, until they had decided their future.

CHAPTER 44

Sharma hurried back to the Temple immediately after the trial to inform Vortin of the verdict and of the betrayal by his priest and priestess.

Vortin lashed out at those within reach, who happened to be Sharma's two young assistants, and cuffed them both around the ears. Sharma jerked his head towards the back of the Temple, and they scuttled off to hide in his apartment.

Vortin obviously felt threatened and acted from emotion rather than reason and ordered the entrance doors to be slammed shut and locked, keeping out the world beyond. Sharma persuaded him to leave the side door open so that men visiting the second floor could come and go without hindrance.

"We need their gold," Sharma told him.

Next morning, Selvid and Veneta came to the Temple doors and banged loudly. When, eventually, Sharma let them in, they asked for Vortin, but the High Priest would not speak to them. They were accompanied by the eunuchs to their rooms to collect their personal belongings only, and were then escorted out without seeing the High Priest.

Their exit was accompanied by the sound of sledgehammer blows on stone as the Christian altar in the little round temple was smashed to smithereens.

"Vortin, we should discuss the situation rationally," advised Sharma.

"Then come to my office," growled the High Priest. Once inside, Sharma closed the door.

"First of all, we should open the Temple again," he argued. "The people need to worship and take part in the rituals. If we abandon them now, we could lose them altogether to this Christian religion, besides which we want their offerings."

"Very well," agreed the High Priest. "We'll open the Temple this afternoon, but we have to show them who is master here."

And who is master here? thought Sharma. *Certainly not you, old man.*

Aloud he said, "We need to strengthen our position. You must find another High Priestess, Vortin. We should also choose two priestesses from among the girls in training, and another priest from among the boys."

"Have you any suggestions?" asked Vortin.

"The two whose ears you boxed yesterday. They are eighteen years old now and have always been willing and eager to please," – only Sharma knew the extent of their willingness to please – "and rather than choose between them, why not allow them both to take over duties?"

"Very well," agreed Vortin, "and I leave it to you to find two girls of aptitude. I trust your judgement, but remember that their duties include my bed as well as yours."

Sharma was pleased with the way his plans were progressing. He needed those around him he could trust when the time came to oust Vortin and proclaim himself High Priest in his stead. Besides, he had long promised his boys a reward for their subservience over the years, and this was entirely suitable.

Vortin continued, "As for my consort, there is only one young woman I desire in that high office and you know who she is."

"Bron," answered Sharma, choking on the name. *Old fool,* he thought, and realised he must make his move sooner rather than later.

"There remains the problem of the school now that Veneta has gone," Vortin said.

"There are three one-time pupils who have already been teaching under her supervision," Sharma reminded him. "They will have to continue for the time being until we find a replacement for her and Africanus."

These decisions made, Sharma left to find his boys and Vortin found a eunuch and gave instructions for the doors to be re-opened later in the day.

Meanwhile, Nobilianus was in his room, keeping out of the way of those on the lower floor. He had hoped that Selvid would be convicted of the rape and murder of Flavia, putting an end to the matter and protecting his own identity, and was terrified to discover that this had not happened.

He knew from overheard conversations of the women in the Temple that there was a great deal of anger in the settlement over Flavia's death. This had progressed into fear. Young women were afraid to walk alone in local woods and fields. However, if anyone suspected him – *and why should they?* – there was nothing to link him to the rapes.

Of course, there *was* one person who knew the truth and that was Jeetuna. He was aware that she had told him of Flavia's whereabouts, not for his gratification but for hers, to avenge herself on Julius and Hestigys.

That made no difference, though, to the fact that she had witnessed the incident. She had no reason to tell, but if she were given a reason, *might she not...?*

News of the reward reached the ears of Nobilianus within hours of its being offered. Julius was willing to give a substantial sum to anyone providing information that would bring Flavia's murderer to justice. Jeetuna now had a reason.

Next day, a group of councillors entered his room, in spite of his protests. They would not say who had sent them. Hestig approached the low cupboard and asked Nobilianus to unlock it. He did so with ill grace. They rifled through spare candles, clothing, a couple of parchment scrolls and various small gifts for the girls at the inn, but found nothing incriminating.

The women gossiped that Julius had returned to Calleva with Asher and Chrystella. He had given the villa to Hestigys and little Lucilla and had left saying that Byden had devoured the three women he loved, and destroyed him.

Three days later they heard that he was dead by his own hand, having plunged a pugio, a Roman dagger, into his chest twice, imitating the injuries that had killed his daughter.

Nobilianus guessed that Jeetuna's revenge was sweet and she must be revelling in it. However, she still posed a threat to him.

He sat in his room, brooding over the package he held in his hands, his thoughts as black as the mind-blowing powder in the package was white.

He had found it in Jeetuna's room, carefully wrapped in a leaf, after she had been evicted and before anyone arrived to clean up. Nobilianus screwed up his nose and face now at the thought of the stench and filth in the room at the time. He knew what the powder was and the power it contained because Jeetuna had confided in him.

That night, he visited the girls along the corridor and asked for Jeetuna's favours and said he would stay with her the whole night. She was apprehensive and afraid of him until she saw the white powder lying on the open leaf in the palm of his hand, then everything else scattered from her mind. She reached out to take the leaf from him but he closed his fingers round it. She grasped his fist and wrenched at it then tried to prize his fingers open.

"On one condition," he said. "I want to see you fly, Jeetuna. You did tell me you could fly, didn't you?"

Jeetuna nodded, her eyes on his closed hand.

"If I go downstairs in about an hour's time, you can slip out after me when no one's looking and meet me outside. I will have a broom with me, and the powder. Then you can show me how you fly. Is that a bargain?"

Jeetuna nodded again. She would have done anything to get her hands on the powder. He put the package back in his pouch.

"Now," he said, "I will give you a night to remember for the rest of your life," and he laughed. It amused him to make love to her that night. He was even quite gentle with her.

She tried once or twice when he was most vulnerable to steal the package from him, but he was too aware to allow that to happen.

About an hour later, when all the women were otherwise occupied,

Nobilianus left the room and crept down the iron staircase and out of the Temple by the side door. A crescent moon hung above the tiled roof. He found the broom where he had propped it against the wall, and waited. Ten minutes later, Jeetuna joined him.

"Give it to me!" she demanded.

"I have an idea," he said. "It would be better to launch yourself off a platform – give yourself more height – wouldn't it?"

"Yes," she answered doubtfully, "but there is no platform."

"Ah, but there is," he replied. "Over here!"

He led her to the base of the wickerwork god, trailing the broomstick behind him. The god towered high above them, legs apart, arms stretched out – Vortin's threatened instrument of death.

"Come on," invited Nobilianus. "We'll climb the ladder to the platform in his chest. That should be high enough. Follow me. Of course, you don't mind heights, but be careful you don't fall!"

Any apprehension Jeetuna might have felt was smothered by thoughts of the white ecstasy. Nobilianus left the broomstick behind without Jeetuna noticing and together they climbed the ladder on the left side of the god, higher and higher, passing the gates to the platforms in the god's left leg, his thigh, his abdomen, and so up to his chest. Above them the crescent moon hung silently, for the moment the brightest object in the sky.

Nobilianus opened the gate that led to the platform inside the wickerwork.

"What a view!" he exclaimed.

In the dim light they looked down on the tiles of the Temple roof, black now but red by daylight. In front of them lay the open square of the market place with the covered market, council chamber above, the inn to their left. Scattered about in profusion were the simple round houses of the people, the large white Roman villa that had witnessed Jeetuna's final humiliation standing prominently to their right.

"Look, Jeetuna, look at the view!"

But Jeetuna had only one thought in her head. "The powder!" she pleaded.

He teased her a little, passing the package from hand to hand

and round behind his back and over his head, out of reach of her grasping fingers, but finally he relented and gave it to her. She pressed the powder into her mouth and breathed it up her nose, and licked her fingers. He caught hold of her as her legs buckled, and guided her slowly to the floor.

For a few moments he contemplated her, remembering the times when he was just a boy and she had pledged her loyalty to him and had kissed his ring. He began to feel sorry for her, until he remembered the knowledge she possessed and the danger she presented while she was still alive.

"Fly, Jeetuna, fly!" he whispered then. "Fly out of your life and out of mine. Goodbye, my sweet."

He stood up with neck bent because the roof of the cage they occupied was not high enough for him to stand upright. Then he left the platform through the gate and climbed down the ladder, chopping through the rungs as he went, using a small axe that had been slung on his belt.

When he reached the ground, he picked up a torch he had left lying beside a lamp and lit the oil-soaked linen. The torch burst into flame. Then he ran to the legs of the giant god and set each alight. The wicker was brittle and flared immediately. He flung the torch high, and before it fell, it set a thigh alight. Then he crept quietly back to Jeetuna's room.

It was not long before someone outside shouted "Fire!" and began pounding the huge gong. He heard the girls and their clients hurrying from their rooms, and someone banged on Jeetuna's door.

Nobilianus opened it and asked sleepily, "What's up?"

"There's a fire somewhere!" he was told. "Everyone should get outside!"

He joined the crowd that had now gathered in front of the towering wicker figure, though all stood at a distance because of the heat.

"Has anyone seen Jeetuna?" asked Nobilianus. "She's missing." One or two shook their heads.

"Look! Someone's up there!" a man shouted.

"Is the fire appliance coming?" Sharma asked.

Then one of the girls cried out, "She's up there! Isn't that Jeetuna up there?"

They all craned their necks to look skywards. Now the moon was hidden by clouds of grey smoke. A lone figure knelt on a platform high above them, holding on to the willow weave in front of her.

"Come down the ladder, Jeetuna!"

"By all the gods, Jeetuna, climb down the ladder!"

But Jeetuna took no notice. Instead, she called gaily to the horrified crowd below, "I'll fly down! Fly down!"

"You can't fly, Jeetuna!" someone shouted back.

"The smoke has addled her brain," commented a woman grimly.

A man tried to climb the ladder but was beaten back by flames and, anyway, the rungs gave way beneath his feet.

The fire appliance arrived and willing hands pumped, but the spouts of water made no difference to the fire, which was well in control.

"Watch me flying, Mummy! Flying! Flying!" Jeetuna was laughing now with pleasure as she repeated the word over and over. The people looked and waited in silence, knowing there was nothing more they could do to help her.

Smoke reached the lone figure and smothered her, hiding her from sight, and the drugged voice was billowed away with the leaping sparks in the thick grey swirls. As the crowd watched, the orange flames reached towards the platform.

Then suddenly the smoke cleared and Jeetuna, choking but still laughing, with arms outstretched and calling to her mother, took a great leap from the platform, down into the flames. There was one high-pitched, heart-stopping shriek that became a scream, then nothing more.

Jeetuna had taken her first and last real flight.

The silent onlookers stared as the flames rose higher. Smoke began pouring out of the god's mouth, his nostrils, his eyes. Through the smoke came the flames, until the face was eerily lit, eyes shining red, wide mouth grinning. Then the head too was fully alight.

For a moment there was a pause, while the onlookers all held their breath, then the whole construction collapsed, devouring itself in an inferno of splintered, blazing wood and a downpour of burning, golden sparks.

The crowd moved further back. No one spoke. Gradually the

flames died down until all that was left was a blackened circle of smoking rubble, amongst which lay Jeetuna's burnt and misshapen body.

The people stayed quiet, shocked and horrified, trying to come to terms with what they had just witnessed. Then they turned on Vortin, who was standing on the Temple steps, apart from the crowd. The god he created had killed. The people's faces and accusations were so angry that he retreated inside.

"Go home, all of you!" commanded Sharma. "There's nothing more can be done here. Go home!"

"She left the room while I was asleep," Nobilianus repeated over and over to anyone who would listen to him. "What could have made her do such a thing?"

"It must have been an accident," said one of the Temple girls. "She must have gone up there with a torch and dropped it by accident."

"Yes, that must be so," said Nobilianus and turned towards the Temple to go inside, "but why was she up there at all?"

"That's something we will never know," said the girl.

Hestig stood and gazed after Nobilianus. His thoughts were his own, but there was no proof.

CHAPTER 45

It had been several months since Trifena had worshipped at the house shrine, months that had witnessed Bron's kidnap, Flavia's murder and now Jeetuna's death.

She decided once and for all to have it out with Ashuba and purposefully headed for the triclinium and pulled back the curtain, black in colour, which had replaced the red curtain burnt in the previous house. There were no flowers on the altar, no gifts as before, only candles, which had never been lit and which she did not light now.

She dispensed with kneeling and stood squarely before the god and his wife and looked up into his face. He looked down at her.

"I want to know, Ashuba – are you the true god or is there one greater, like Veneta says? Are you all-powerful? Or powerless, unnecessary, irrelevant, knowing nothing about us, having no interest in us – in fact, just a lump of stone?"

Her questions became more demanding. "And how about you, Shubinata? Wife? Goddess? Or stone, without mind or heart, carved at the whim of man for his own ends? Fabricated to command power and wealth for the privileged few, keeping the people in bonds, denying them freedom and thought for themselves? Are you both powerless before this Christian god of love? What are you?"

Did she imagine it or did Ashuba's eyes begin to glow, deep in their sockets, the glow becoming a spark and the spark a red fire, as in the Temple when she first arrived in Byden, when she had asked him what he wanted from her? Again she felt her spine tingling as if she had sat in a patch of stinging nettles.

"No!" she cried. "Not this time! Then you had a baby killed and you took Bron from me! Never again! You don't reign any more, not in this house!" and she swept the lumps of carved stone from their places and they fell to the floor with a crash and lay chipped and cracked on chipped and cracked tiles.

Hestig hurried in to find out what had caused the noise and understood immediately what had happened.

"My sentiments exactly," he said. "I was not sure how you felt about it, our old religion. I'll get it all cleared away."

Trifena hugged him. "Such a sense of freedom!" she told him.

Sharma chose the great Midsummer Festival to make his move. Between them, he and Brocchus had persuaded the eunuchs that there was no longer any place for Vortin in the Temple, that he was too old at sixty-six and was not capable of offering them any viable future.

Sharma invited them to consider the man's record: he had relinquished his High Priestess and had not replaced her because he was still lusting after Bron, who hated him and would never consent to become his consort, and never came near the Temple, anyway. He had allowed the pillar of the school, Africanus, to leave and had not sent to bring him back. He had not prevented his priest and priestess, not only from committing sacrilege and marrying, but blasphemously denying the true religion of the settlement. He had allowed Jeetuna to defile herself and Temple property and had stood by as she burnt herself to death. He had not kept his son, Nobilianus, in check, and finally, he had incurred the anger and recriminations of the people.

In other words, he was no longer fit for the office of High Priest – but Sharma was. Under Vortin's nose and with his permission, he had replaced Temple staff with those loyal to himself and they would prosper as Sharma prospered.

By ridding the Temple of Vortin – and, it went without saying, that crazy Nobilianus – Sharma would earn the approval of the people and they would again bring their treasures to fill Temple coffers and elevate the religious community. In time he would replace the High

Priestess with one of the young priestesses-in-training – not this year, but certainly next year. Then there would again be sacred babies, conceived as before on the altar at the great Midsummer Festival, to follow the high priestly line.

The eunuchs were convinced by the arguments and the Temple women did not care which men were in office, they were still men, except that they would be glad to get rid of Nobilianus.

So the eunuchs and those in training were issued with their orders, except for Sharma's two young followers, now priests, who were allowed to stay out of the way in case of bloodshed.

It was the day before Midsummer Day and Vortin was at prayer at the altar. He had been on his knees for half an hour when Sharma, Brocchus and the eunuchs came to arrest him. At first he did not seem to realise their intent, but when he saw their grim faces and their purposeful advance, he tried to flee, but was caught and tumbled to the ground. His legs were tied together and his hands behind his back, and he was ignominiously manhandled to his house.

There he was untied and told he would remain under house arrest, guarded day and night. In the meantime, food and drink would be sent in, and occasionally a girl. Sharma considered that would keep him quiet and amenable until he had decided what to do with him. Realistically, there was only one end in view, but Sharma wanted to take his time and think things through. It may be that Vortin could serve some useful purpose, even now.

Nobilianus gave in without a struggle and was confined to his room under the same conditions, except that none of the girls would agree to entertain him. Sharma accepted their decision and commented to Nobilianus that it was his own fault and his hard luck.

All that day, Sharma chose to carry on as normal, and people coming and going in the Temple noticed nothing amiss, as Vortin was so often absent, anyway.

Next morning, Sharma instructed the eunuchs to carry the great gong forward to the top of Temple steps and bang it continuously, changing over as each one became exhausted, until all the people had assembled in the open space in front of the building, or as many as could be spared from their work.

A large crowd attended and the gong was silenced, its rhythmic clang still echoing in everyone's ears for some time, quietening them and allowing Sharma to address them.

"People of Byden, I have called you together with a serious purpose. You already know that great changes are afoot." He spent a long time reminding them of Vortin's failings.

"Was there ever such failure on the part of a High Priest, ever such weakness, such betrayal, such –"

"No!" roared the crowd, not waiting for Sharma to finish his sentence.

"All that is now remedied!" shouted the priest. "Vortin and his vile son Nobilianus have been arrested and are under guard. I am taking his place as High Priest!"

Instead of the cheers Sharma anticipated, the people hushed. Obviously, they had not expected this.

"You are wondering about my authority to take such a drastic step! My authority is Ashuba, mighty Ashuba, who at the altar has personally guaranteed me his blessing." *If Vortin can continually claim Ashuba's approval, why shouldn't I take advantage of the people's gullibility?* he thought. "My second authority is the great Book of the Altar. Translate it into the vulgar tongue, Brocchus!"

Brocchus had in his hand one of the scrolls taken from the clay cylinder that lay on the altar. Dramatically, he unrolled it and read the passage that had caused him several hours of searching to find.

"Listen, my people, and take heed. Bow your knees and your necks before your great sun god, Ashuba, god of light, who warms you and feeds you and demands total obedience.

"Listen, my people, to the abominations of Ashuba, which are punishable by disaster, disease and death:

"It is an abomination to betray your god, who will not overlook your fault.

"Betrayal comes by denying your god lives and reigns with power.

"Betrayal comes by rendering less than total commitment to your god and his Temple.

"Betrayal comes by disobedience to his will.

"Betrayal comes by obedience in body but disobedience in heart and mind.

"Betrayal comes by ignoring his ancient rituals of worship and service.

"Betrayal comes by running with his enemies."

Brocchus paused. "Shall I read further, Sharma? "Betrayal is the first. There are thirty-two abominations."

"No, that will suffice."

Sharma turned to the crowd. "There you have it," he shouted. "Betrayal!"

"Betrayal!" chorused the people dutifully.

When Sharma had dismissed them, they quietly returned to their homes and work, seemingly stunned at his news and needing time to mull it over.

As they dispersed, Brocchus and those eunuchs not occupied with guarding Vortin and his son came down into the crowd and arrested Selvid and Veneta. People around them were taken unawares and, as Sharma had anticipated, were too surprised to offer support. The couple made no attempt to resist and were led away into the Temple. They were shut in Selvid's old apartment and the door was locked.

Hestig did not hear of their arrest until next morning and he at once went up to the Temple and demanded to see Sharma.

"They are Temple staff and they will stay here under arrest until I decide what to do with them," announced Sharma. "Vortin was weak and did not punish them for their betrayal. I intend to do so. They stay under guard."

He would not be moved and Hestig left the Temple not knowing what to do next.

"My dear, your time has come," said Trifena. "You must call a meeting of the council and get them to agree to mobilise the people to rebellion. Dig up the list of offences you buried and read it to them. Speak to the people – they trust you and will follow you. Let *them* decide what is to happen to the hierarchy up there. Then let the council govern until you all have had time to plan the future. *Now* is the time to act, for you to act, Hestig."

He looked at his wife with admiration. "Do you think I am up to this?" he asked her.

She kissed him. "I know you are."

The council met in secret in the triclinium of the Roman villa, at the invitation of Hestigys. His father had retrieved the written list of offences and now discussed it with the other members, who without exception agreed that it was time to act.

The names of all the male inhabitants of Byden were written down and each councillor was allocated a number of them to contact.

"While this is happening, life in the settlement must continue as normal," said Hestig, "so that no one at the Temple is suspicious."

"Is everyone trustworthy?" the jeweller wondered.

"There are one or two who may not be," replied Hestig. "I will have a word with the innkeeper and ask her to make sure they are otherwise engaged with the women when we attack."

"What about our families?" asked the carpenter.

"We must allow each man to decide about his own womenfolk and children," advised Kendrus. "We will need the women solidly behind us – I know my own wife is – but there are a few who cannot bridle their tongues."

"You will need a plan of attack," said Hestigys from his voluntary sentry post in the doorway.

"Come, Son, and join us, and say what you have on your mind," invited his father.

Together they agreed a strategy and fixed a date for the uprising.

"Then what happens?" asked the beekeeper.

"Sharma – Brocchus – all of them must have a trial," replied Kendrus, "so everyone can see that justice is being done."

"But what can we do to punish them?" asked the wheelwright.

"Why not let the people decide that also?" suggested Hestigys.

CHAPTER 46

The day appointed, a day in July, was warm but wet. The rain had been constant since morning and now, early evening, though it had stopped, the pathways were sodden.

Hestig related later with much amusement, something he'd certainly not felt at the time, how everyone in the attacking force left his muddy shoes or sandals in the portico before entering the Temple.

"They were so quiet, no one inside heard them coming," he recounted, and laughed, "but they took so long removing their footwear, that all of them could have been cut down in the portico and killed in their bare feet!"

The largest force gathered at the front entrance, with smaller forces at the side and rear doors.

The Temple soon swarmed with the invaders. Sharma and his staff were engaged in carrying out their devotions and duties and were taken completely by surprise. All were soon under arrest and securely bound, nervous before the menace of farm implements and kitchen knives.

Each was taken to his own apartment and placed under guard, which changed hourly. Sharma's men who were guarding Vortin and Nobilianus were replaced by the council's men. The prisoners were informed of the changeover. Vortin at first thought he was being rescued, and was delighted and expressed his gratitude, but was soon told that that was not the intention and he would remain a prisoner.

Selvid and Veneta were released.

Some of the settlement's women, who followed their menfolk, were despatched to tell the girls on the second floor what had happened and to warn them not to go downstairs until they were given permission to do so. It was the time of day, between late afternoon and early evening, when they had no clients with them.

Mischievously, the girls invited the women to look around their rooms. With curiosity stronger than modesty, some accepted the invitation, and later descended the stairs chattering animatedly and possessing much more knowledge than they had when they climbed them.

"What's it like up there?" asked the guards, men of the village, who had been placed at the bottom of the staircase.

"Never you mind!" was the unsatisfactory reply they received from the women.

The girls did all they could to entice the hourly replacements to climb the staircase. One young lad actually got as far as the fifth step before his companion noticed and spoke sharply to him, and he came down, shamefaced. Finally, the girls gave up and went to bed.

Hestig and the council entered the Temple early next morning and prepared to receive the whole population of Byden, to put Vortin and his staff on trial, and discuss the future of the settlement. The torches round the walls were kept burning, but the candles on the altar were extinguished and the altar remained strangely dark.

The large table from Vortin's office was placed before the altar and the members of the council sat with their backs to Ashuba. The people had never seen anyone turn his back on their great god and whispered their fear of retribution, but were encouraged by those who were not so in awe of their traditional religion, which had so often failed them.

Hestig looked again at the bare feet of the crowd and shook his head in resignation. He knew they had been very brave on the previous day and had taken over the Temple without bloodshed, and he was very pleased with them, farmers and tradesmen and craftsmen as they were, without any military ambition or prowess. He was very proud to be leading these people, his adopted extended family, and vowed to himself that he would do his very best for them.

Vortin was the first to be brought from his enforced imprisonment and stood before the people. A list of accusations against him was read out and witnesses given opportunity to confirm each reprehensible action. The final person to speak was Hoad, who related the killing of his baby daughter twenty-one years ago, on the night of Bron's birth, and the digging up of her body two years previously, both incidents obviously ordered by the High Priest.

However, when everyone thought that the list was complete, Bron was called. She came forward nervously, and Hestig knew she was not relishing the evidence she had to give.

Her first accusation concerned the attack on her in the wood, when Vortin had wrenched the cloak off her shoulders, the cloak that was later used to wrap round the baby skeleton. Veneta produced Bron's brooch, which had been snapped off during the tussle and which she had later found near the children's plague mounds, as Bron had described. Vortin claimed that was only circumstantial evidence and was not proof, which the court had to accept.

Then to a hushed crowd, Bron related in a whisper what had happened the night before she left the Temple, at the age of only eleven years. Several times Hestig had to ask her to speak up. Soranus brought her a chair and asked to stand by her while she completed her statement. This was allowed, as he too had questions to answer about the circumstances of his marriage to Bron. Pulcher was also called, having helped rescue Bron from Vortin. The people cheered when they heard that he had knocked the High Priest out and broken his jaw. The account ended with the birth of Storm, the son of Bron and Vortin.

"They're lying!" shouted Vortin, breaking his silence. "They have connived together against me, you all have! I've heard nothing but lies this morning from all of you!"

"Is this your defence," asked Hestig, "that none of this is true? The people have witnessed these happenings for the most part, and as for the rape of Bron after she had been bought back and was still under-age, you have heard the evidence brought by Pulcher. I too could give evidence if I was not heading this trial."

"Pulcher dotes on the girl! Everyone knows that! And you are her father! Of course you're going to back her up. Prove it, prove it if you can – but you can't, because it never happened!"

"Oh, but it did, and I *can* prove it!" Trifena was edging through the crowd of people, who were making way for her. In her hand were several pieces of torn paper that she placed on a wooden chopping board. She laid it on the table, arranged the pieces, and turned the board round so that it faced the councillors.

"What is this?" asked Vortin. "What evidence have you faked?"

"It is the letter," Trifena told him, "that you wrote to Bron on the occasion of her marriage to Soranus, before Storm was born. In her anger, my daughter tore it up, but I have kept the pieces these nine years."

"Kendrus, please read it to the people," Hestig requested the doctor.

Kendrus picked up the board and read: " *'Darling Bron, I have already given you my wedding day gift, the most precious I possess, so that now our baby grows inside you. Stay well.'* The note is signed 'Forever, V'."

A murmur bubbled round the crowd like the bubble of the Stan over the stepping-stones when the water was running high. All eyes were on Vortin.

"V?" he asked. "Who's V? It could be any of her lovers."

"I was only eleven when you raped me in the Temple," Bron said evenly to him. "I had no lovers. I wasn't sure what the sexual act was till you took me."

"There's no mistake, it's your writing," said Kendrus, and passed the board along the line of councillors.

"I think we can regard the case proved against you, Vortin," said Hestig. "You have ruled this settlement with greed, lust and cruelty for over thirty years and it's time to put an end to your reign. Take him back to his house!" he ordered the guards.

"Just a moment!" Everyone looked surprised that Bron was speaking again, her voice louder and clearer than it had been while giving evidence.

Trifena was still standing at the front of the crowd.

"Bron, no!" she called to her daughter, having guessed what Bron was about to do. Hestig was puzzled.

Bron ignored her mother and continued, "I have a confession to make."

Now Hestig realised what she was going to say, and also tried to stop her, but she shook her head.

"Help me, Soranus," she pleaded, and he took her in his arms. She leaned against him for a moment while the people waited expectantly, then gently took his arms away and walked to where Vortin stood, a guard on each side of him, and faced him squarely.

"Vortin, I am making this statement because guilt has eaten away at my conscience these seven years and it will be a relief to confess. I want everyone to know, and above all I want you to know.

"You intended to take Storm into the Temple as your successor when he was three years old. You told me you were even going to take away the name of your other son, Nobilianus, and give it to our baby. You intended to train him in your ways so he would follow your precepts and become a second you! My baby, my first son – a second Vortin!

"Not only that, but you would have taken me with him to become your High Priestess. You would have taken me away from the husband you made me marry to save your reputation, and parted me from my daughter and the baby I was carrying.

"Soranus did not want to marry me. He was young, only fourteen, yet he gave up his freedom to give a name and a home to me and your child. He became a father to Storm in more than just a name. But you cared about none of that."

Vortin interrupted her. "Bron, my love, my life, my lust – oh, I don't mind admitting it now, now that you have told everyone how I enjoyed you that night – you are getting hysterical! What has this to do with anything?"

"It has to do with everything!"

"Bron, you don't have to do this!" cried Trifena again.

Bron turned to her. "Yes, I do, Mother."

She took a step closer to Vortin and looked up into his face.

"I killed him! I killed Storm! I loved him but I murdered our baby!"

There was an eruption of disbelief from the crowd. Vortin stared at her.

"What do you mean, you killed him? He died in his sleep, you said so! Kendrus said so! Of course you didn't kill him!"

"Oh, but I did," Bron replied and described how she had taken the pillow and placed it over Storm's face until all life had been smothered out of him.

When she had said all she meant to say, she would have collapsed if Soranus had not caught her and held on to her.

Meantime, Vortin was being dragged from the Temple. He was screaming at Bron.

"He was our baby! My son! My son! How could you, Bron? But we can have other sons! We can have another baby! You and me, Bron! You and me!"

Bron was crying now, her hands covering her ears so that she should not hear what Vortin was shouting at her. His voice became muffled as he was bundled out of the back door.

Hestig stood and the people quietened, waiting to hear what he would say.

"I have to tell you that Bron speaks the truth," he said. "She has described how she murdered her own son, and why. You all know she loved Storm, in spite of his parentage. We will pause the proceedings now so that the councillors may confer. If they decide to discuss this matter further in open court, I will relinquish my position as chairman. Please all go home now and return when you hear the gong. It is our intention to stand Nobilianus before you this afternoon."

When the court reassembled, the people still excitedly discussing everything they must have been saying all lunchtime, they were carrying an assortment of chairs. They had obviously decided that the proceedings were going to take a long time and no one wanted to miss a minute by getting too tired and having to go home.

Bron and Soranus sat before the people, holding hands. Kendrus stood in the chairman's place, with Hestig relegated to his left. The crowd quietened expectantly.

"The councillors have conferred," Kendrus announced, "and

282

agree that, up to the moment of the murder, Bron had been an exemplary mother, especially considering the circumstances of Storm's conception. Though murdering her son could never be condoned, it is recognised that she was acting under extreme provocation and was trying to protect her family. She has also carried her guilt all these years. In the circumstances, we have decided to take no action against her."

There were murmurs of approval from the crowd. Kendrus held up his hand for silence and continued.

"However, we are critical of Hestig and his family for keeping the matter secret, though again we understand the reasons. In the circumstances, we wish to relieve him of his position as chairman of the council, but have agreed to take the opinion of the people. Anyone may speak."

Several men spoke, registering support for the family. Infanticide was not uncommon, though unofficial, and would have passed unremarked if it had not been for Bron's public confession.

Groups conferred together and finally the woman who sold pulses stood and said it seemed to her that no one wished Hestig to be replaced.

"Times are changing," she said, "and we need leadership we can trust."

Everyone voiced approval, and clapped when Hestig resumed his seat and Bron and Soranus took their chairs back into the crowd.

"Thank you," Hestig said, "on behalf of my daughter and my family. Now it seems time to call Nobilianus, but before we do, I would like to speak to you about Jeetuna.

"I know we were all shocked at the horrific death she suffered, and we are still not sure how it happened, and may never know. However, if she was brought before us today, there is a charge she would have to answer, and I am glad that Julius is no longer with us to hear it."

Hestig then explained why he was suspicious that Jeetuna had committed murder. Lucilla had bought the necklace of glass beads containing gold foil as an offering to Shubinata only hours before she had been found dead in the temple in the wood. Several of the younger women nodded in agreement when he said that it had later been observed round Jeetuna's neck.

"All those closely affected are no longer with us, and speculation is idle," Hestig continued, "but it may be that rough justice was being administered by the wickerwork god. Now we will see Nobilianus."

Hoad and the butcher were sent to bring the young man to the court, but came clattering back down the staircase without him.

"He's in no fit state," Hoad declared, "he's shaking too much to stand up straight and is being violently sick."

The crowd murmured their disappointment. They were having a day's holiday and were enjoying the spectacle being paraded before them. The council members conferred.

"He'll keep for later," Hestig announced. "We will now see Sharma and Brocchus together."

Sharma was brought in, protesting loudly at his treatment. Brocchus remained silent and aloof, a supercilious smile on his lips. Everything he had done had been on someone else's orders, and Hestig guessed he would say so.

It was difficult to bring a charge against Sharma. He argued that he had served the Temple with dedication and had carried out his duties conscientiously, supplying whatever Vortin was lacking. He insisted that his takeover was necessary for the maintenance of the strict observances at the Temple and the welfare of the people, turning aside the anger and retribution of Ashuba.

Dramatically, he gazed up at the great stone god towering above the dark altar and said he would pray for forgiveness for the settlement once he was free to resume his High Priestly duties.

Hestig asked him to step aside for the time being and make way for Brocchus.

The eunuch stood, tall and erect, cloaked in black, intimidating, theatrically fixing his dark eyes on individuals in the crowd, causing them to shrink visibly as if trying to hide inside their own clothes.

Whatever their crimes, those who had already been accused displayed human weakness that the people understood, but here was someone who practised evil for evil's sake, and enjoyed it.

"We all know you, Brocchus," Hestig began, "and what you are.

Your crimes are many. We know you murdered the baby daughter of Hoad and Louca. However, the murder of Septima, the prostitute from the inn, the theft of the settlement's money when it was in my charge, the fire that destroyed my house and killed young Vitius and our slave, Bettina – none of this can be proved against you."

"Whatever I have done has been on the orders of Vortin and Sharma, who were obeying the will of Ashuba," stated Brocchus without emotion. "Any guilt is theirs, not mine."

"So you take no responsibility for any of your actions?" asked Hestig.

"None," replied the eunuch.

"I think there is one for which you must take responsibility," said Hestig quietly.

Kendrus walked to the altar and took hold of the clay cylinder. He removed the cap and took from it one of the scrolls, which he brought to the table. The wheelwright held the carved wooden baton at one end and rolled up the parchment as Kendrus scrolled through, finding the passage he had previously noted.

"You will remember this, Brocchus," Kendrus said, "as you were reading from it only a few weeks ago, during the trial of Selvid. It is one of the Abominations of Ashuba, the tenth in fact – the tenth, Brocchus.

"'Listen, my people, to the abominations of Ashuba, which are punishable by disaster, disease and death:

"'It is an abomination to–' "

"What you are accusing me of is a lie!" shouted Brocchus, with a passion that clearly surprised the people, who as yet did not understand what the accusation was. "Sharma, I have served you well and loyally all these years! Speak on my behalf!"

"What Brocchus says is the truth," said Sharma, flustered.

Still no one in the crowd understood what was happening.

"Bron, are you prepared to give evidence?" Hestig asked his daughter. She hesitated. Pulcher stepped forward.

"Not Bron – I say," he insisted, and Hestig nodded.

In his own words, with halting speech, Pulcher described how, twelve years previously when only a child, Bron had wandered too far into the wood and had come upon Sharma, Brocchus and Vitius, the young priest-in-training, who had later been burnt to death in the fire. As he described what she had seen, and he had witnessed also from his hiding place, Bron bent her head in shame before the pictures in her memory. Pulcher said how in distress she had run away and he had found her later tearing her arms to pieces with a flint.

There was no sound except for the heavy breathing of Brocchus.

"There is only one way to ascertain the truth," stated Kendrus. "Brocchus, I am asking you to disrobe."

The eunuch, who was not a eunuch, struggled and had to be held down while his clothes were pulled off him, but proof of his duplicity was there for all to see. The crowd looked on in amazement and no one said a word.

He was allowed to robe again and Sharma's two young priests were called to give further evidence. They were reluctant until they were promised their freedom in return for their statement, and then they held nothing back. Most of the people looked sickened by what they heard.

Both were allowed to collect their personal belongings from the Temple and were asked to leave the settlement immediately. It was rumoured later that they had fled to Calleva. If that was so, they disappeared forever into its shadows.

CHAPTER 47

The council met again next morning in the council chamber. Elation at the success of the proceedings of the previous two days had been replaced overnight by concern at the responsibility placed upon them by the people, and concern at the grave decisions that had to be made about the future of those convicted.

"We've all got businesses to run," complained the carpenter. "We can't afford to be spending so much time on council matters."

"We've agreed to close the Temple for the time being," said the jeweller, "but that poses the question of what we do with the eunuchs who have not been accused of any misdemeanours –"

"And what do we do about the girls there, and the children, and the school?" asked the beekeeper.

"Then we have to decide how to punish Vortin and the rest of them, and we still haven't managed to get Nobilianus out of his room."

"It's too much responsibility," said the wheelwright.

There was a dejected silence. Apparently, everyone felt the same way.

"Come," Hestig encouraged them, "we have a great opportunity here to start afresh. This is no way to set out on such an adventure. One decision at a time. First, the children and the school."

By the end of the morning, they had decided to ask Veneta and Selvid to continue overseeing the care and education of the Temple children. There would be no further intake of pupils for the time being.

The Temple would be closed to all religious observances. The eunuchs and the women would be offered the choice of a handsome grant from the Temple coffers and their freedom, or a regular wage in return for keeping the Temple in good order and looking after the physical welfare of the children and staff who remained.

"And the prisoners?" asked Kendrus.

"I don't know how you others feel," said Hestig, "but I propose we let them all go free and give them enough money to get them away from here to another settlement. What harm can they do us now? Their world has crumbled. No one wants them back. Let them go!"

"But they deserve punishment!" argued the ropemaker.

"I agree with Hestig," said Kendrus. "What else can we do with them? Kill them?"

"Why not?" questioned the carpenter.

"How?" asked Hestig. "Who would carry out the sentence? Will you?"

The carpenter looked uncomfortable.

"Under Roman law we are not allowed to exact the death penalty," Kendrus reminded them. "Anyway, there's been enough killing in Byden lately."

There was further discussion, but finally they decided that they did not want to enter this new phase of life in Byden with more bloodshed.

Their last decision was to officially invite Hestigys and Hoad on to the council.

Trifena was impressed with the progress the men had made. "You've done well," she told her husband when he came home for a meal. "There's only one thing you've overlooked."

"And what's that?" he asked.

"The people need a religion."

"That's women's work," he said. "What do you suggest?"

"We could ask Asher to come back and talk to us again."

"Find out what the other women in the settlement want, and if you are all in agreement, we'll arrange it," he said.

Next day, the guards were relieved of their duties. Sharma and Brocchus were given sufficient money for their immediate needs and they left together. Vortin was unusually submissive and went without a backward glance. He did not ask to say goodbye to his son.

Nobilianus had not been tried but everyone knew many of his excesses and guessed there were more. He complained that he was still sick, and had to be forcibly evicted from his room. He collapsed on the staircase and was half-carried, half-dragged from the Temple, a pouch of coins thrown after him.

As he made no attempt to get up from where he had been dropped on the steps, a horse was brought from the inn, he was bundled on to it, and it was given a hearty slap, which sent it off at a gallop towards the wood.

The people collectively heaved a sigh of relief and returned to their normal daily working lives.

One afternoon the following week, Veneta decided she should dismantle Shubinata's temple in the wood. She took with her the three eunuchs who had opted to stay on.

When they went inside – the first time that men had been allowed to enter – Veneta was surprised to see that some of the altar curtains had been pulled down and were lying in a heap on the red carpet, almost as if they had been used for a makeshift bed. They could all guess who had used them.

Together the working party rolled up the carpet, folded the curtains and draperies, collected up the candles, stacked up the few items of furniture and took an axe to the wooden altar. Finally, they lifted the stone statue of the goddess off her pedestal and threw it into the trees. Then they loaded up the wheelbarrows they had brought with them.

"I'll finish sweeping up," Veneta told them, "then I'll lock the door and follow you back."

She completed her work and locked the temple door and set off along the path towards the settlement.

She had not gone far before a feeling came over her that she was being followed. She stopped and looked behind but could see no one. A few minutes later she again sensed that something or someone was shadowing her among the trees to her right and keeping abreast of her.

It must be a deer, she thought nervously but was not able to calm her heart, which was beating fast, or slow her breathing.

She looked around again and could see nothing unusual, but quickened her pace, anyway.

Suddenly he stood in front of her, barring her way, a figure wearing a long brown cloak and hood, a black cloth covering his face. She gasped and stepped to one side but he stepped in front of her. When she moved the other way, he again blocked her escape.

She remembered the description that Hoad's daughter, Carinna, had given of her rapist, and Jeetuna's statement, and later the unsuccessful search for the cloak and cloth in the cupboard.

"Nobilianus?" she asked, and the figure just laughed.

She turned to run but he was upon her. His arms came round her to stop her flight and he brought her to the ground. She remembered the horrific description of the attack on Flavia that Kendrus had given in court and redoubled her efforts to get away, but she was no match for his strength and weight bearing down upon her, pushing her face and the palms of her hands into the beaten earth of the pathway.

She had just about given herself up for dead and worse when his weight lightened. His body and legs were still covering hers but he seemed to have raised himself up on his hands and arms so that his chest was lifted off her shoulders. She managed to raise her head from the pathway and let out a piercing scream.

"Quiet!" he hissed at her, "or I'll silence you like I did Flavia and Jeetuna!"

He got off her and stood and she rolled onto her back and looked up at him. He had his head raised as if he were listening. Then she heard it too – men's voices and the sound of their approach, not on the pathway, but brushing through the long grass and nettles between the trees.

She scrambled to her feet and took off into the undergrowth, sobbing and gasping, until she stopped by a tangle of fallen branches to draw breath and take stock of her situation. Thankfully, Nobilianus was nowhere to be seen.

Suddenly there were shouts. "Look! Over there! There's

someone through the trees! Hey, you, come here!"

Veneta ran again. Fortunately, the green and brown colours of her tunic mingled with the natural shades in the wood and she was practically invisible as she wove in and out of the trees. It wasn't long before she found herself back by the tangle of branches and realised that, in her panic, she must have stumbled round in a circle. She dropped to her knees, using the branches as cover.

At some distance several men were shouting. "I've got him! Spying on us, were you? Thought you couldn't be seen in your cloak with your face covered up! Shows how wrong you were!"

Then she heard terrified squeals, like sounds she had once heard being beaten out of a cornered rat. There was scuffling, and the unmistakable whine of Nobilianus, pleading for pity. The men were laughing now.

"See how he grovels! He eats the dirt! Stand up, man! Get him up on his feet and bring him over here!"

Three men appeared on the path a few yards ahead of her, dragging Nobilianus between them. He looked about to faint and they threw him to the ground. Veneta held her breath, but they were much too occupied with taunting their victim to notice her.

She had never seen men like them nor their strange dress before. All three were unusually tall and their fair hair fell to their shoulders. Their sandals were Roman-style and their legs bare below leather trousers pulled tight at the knees. A short-sleeved grey woollen tunic was worn over the trousers and each had the hide of a calf slung from one shoulder, across the chest and caught in a belt at the waist. From these belts hung sheaths for daggers and knives.

Nobilianus was now curled up on the path, trying to protect himself as all three of his captors took delight in kicking him forcibly in the buttocks, the back, the stomach and ribs, his head, and finally his groin, returning to their attack again and again. He writhed in agony, screaming all the time and, when they finally stopped, began to blubber and sob and cry. Monster as he was, Veneta could not help feeling sorry for him.

The tallest of them unsheathed a long curved dagger, which he whirled and flashed in the sunlight above his head, then slashed through the air in front of himself, causing his companions to jump back in alarm, out of his reach. The man was enjoying this display of his prowess and laughed heartily.

Veneta crouched lower, closed her eyes and bent her head and prayed. Moments later she heard a scream, such a scream that it sent a cold surge of horror through her. But it was cut off before it reached its climax. She dared to look up.

"That's done for him!" the tall man exclaimed with great satisfaction. "Vortin wouldn't be best pleased to have him running back to the village with tales of spies in the vicinity! Nothing's going to stop Vortin taking revenge –"

"Or us the spoils of battle!" interrupted one of the other men.

The priestess stayed quite still in the same position, hardly daring to breathe, as they strode off, still laughing. She remained in her hiding place a long time and only when she judged it safe did she creep out towards the body of Nobilianus.

The cloth was pulled away from his sickly, contorted face. His eyes were wide open and stared at her, unseeing. His mouth gaped in mid-scream, and an open wound slit his throat from ear to ear, and was filled with dark, drying blood.

She untied the knot, pulled the black cloth free, and placed it over his face and grinning neck, then ran back to the settlement with her news.

While Stalwyn stayed with her and washed her grazes and cuts, listening to the details of what she had endured, a party of men left to bring the body back to the settlement.

They laid it on the Temple floor and examined the contents of a pouch tied to the black leather belt. In it they found a crudely carved wooden figurine of a woman, bearing two stab marks in the breasts, similar to those found on Flavia's body. The wood was smooth where it had either been well oiled or stroked often. With disgust, they threw the brown cloak over the body.

Hestig was summoned and with him came his son. A circle of people had already gathered round the covered corpse.

Hestigys pulled the cloak off the body and tossed it to one side, then drew his own knife and, yelling loudly, would have attacked dead Nobilianus in a frenzy of grief and revenge, had he not been restrained by his father and friends who were standing by. His near neighbour, the beekeeper, took him home.

Veneta insisted on speaking to Hestig privately and he came to see her and Selvid in their rooms. She again related all that had happened but this time added a clearer description of the three strangers and repeated their words about Vortin, which up to now she had not revealed.

Hestig looked grim and asked her not to say anything to anyone else until he was ready to tell them, as he did not want to panic the people.

Obviously, Vortin was planning to return and it seemed that he would not come alone.

CHAPTER 48

AD 406

Summer returned in September. The new, wheeled cutting machine that the farmers shared had brought in an early harvest, leaving the field colours shading from gold through to dark yellow and dark brown. Where the land between the lynchets had been ploughed but not planted that year, the light brown soil was flecked with lumps of white chalk, which looked like a scattering of blossom.

After having consulted the council, and calling the people to the Temple steps, Hestig asked Veneta to repeat what she had overheard in the wood. Vortin had recruited friends from elsewhere, he warned those gathered, and would be returning to exact revenge.

Accordingly, he reintroduced the military training sessions in the market place during the evenings while it was still light, but with more purpose and focus than before, and this time with weapons, which Soranus spent day and night hammering out in the forge. The men were shown how to practise killing sack dummies filled with straw.

Kendrus and Stalwyn spent hours tearing up linen for bandages and slings, stacking splints made by the carpenter, preparing figwort for healing wounds, comfrey root plaster for broken bones, and other ointments and medicines, and storing neat alcohol for anaesthetics and wound-cleaning.

Hestig dismissed the idea of using the inn as a casualty centre, because it would probably be at the heart of the fighting, so Stalwyn cleared their wooden table and generally prepared their house to receive Byden's wounded and dying.

"It is hateful to have to do all this," Hestig told his wife, "but there is no knowing what Vortin will attempt and we must be prepared."

"Will he come for revenge or for Bron?" Trifena asked anxiously.

"Both, I expect," Hestig replied. "I have spoken to Soranus about it. We should be making plans for her escape, but where would she go? She has four children to think about now."

Some relief from thoughts of battle came with the arrival of Asher, at the request of the women of the settlement. He stayed at the Temple. The stone representation of Ashuba had been broken up and removed and the altar lay bare.

"I'm impressed with the speed with which you've made all these changes," he told Hestig.

Most of the settlement came to hear him speak that evening, ready to consider any new religion that would fill the gap left by the destruction of the old.

"Please sit down," he said, addressing them from the Temple steps. Most of the crowd sat expectantly.

"Until now, you have been used to the idea of men, particularly the Roman emperors, becoming gods, but I will tell you about Jesus Christ, who was God become man."

The people were so intrigued by what Asher was saying that only a few at the back of the crowd noticed the arrival of a visitor, who had walked over from the inn. Hestig was one of those who noticed.

He watched as the visitor's eyes searched the faces in the crowd until they finally rested on Bron. Appearing satisfied, Aurelius turned towards Asher, now paying attention.

"First, though, I want you to be less afraid. There is no need to take off your shoes when you enter the Temple. There is no need for animal sacrifices or any other sacrifices – no crippling thank-offerings and elaborate rituals and observances – because you cannot earn your way into heaven. Heaven is God's gift to you. So stop being so afraid of him, relax, you have free will – come to his altar if you want to, stay away if you don't. But I tell you this, once you have fallen in love with God, you won't be able to stay away!"

"We're human," called someone from the crowd. "We can't love God."

"Why not?" countered the old pilgrim. "He loves you!"

"Prove it!" shouted someone else.

"I don't have to prove it," Asher called to him, "because Jesus already has. He died a terrible death for you, crucified by his own people with the help of the Romans, so you can have all that freedom I was talking about."

"How can death give life?" was the next shouted question.

"You're a farming community – you see it happening all around you!" Asher shouted back. "You plant a seed, the seed dies, and a plant grows!"

Another heckler objected, "He didn't die for me – I never knew the man!"

Asher explained, "All wrongdoing merits God's punishment." The people nodded. They were used to a doctrine of punishments. Asher continued, "But Jesus took the punishment instead of us – in other words, God suffered his own punishment."

"That may be," countered the previous heckler, "but I didn't ask him to. I don't need a scapegoat. I've never done harm to anyone. I've never done anything wrong."

Asher ran down the steps, surprisingly sprightly for an old man with cranky knees, and hurried across to the man who had objected, took him by the hand and pumped it up and down enthusiastically.

"I'm so honoured to shake your hand, friend," he enthused. "It's the first time I've met someone who's perfect!"

The man and the crowd laughed good-naturedly and Asher mingled with them, answering their questions as best he could. These ideas were new to them and needed thinking and talking about.

Bron was standing with the adult members of her family around her, including her husband, and Aurelius judged that it was not a good time to break his news to her. It could wait till morning; that way, it would shorten the time that remained to them to bid each other goodbye.

He wanted to look his best for her, but slept very little that night, and got up next morning tired and apprehensive and dreading what the day would bring.

He hated the subterfuge but didn't know how else to contrive a meeting with her alone. Accordingly, he called at Pulcher's door. The dwarf was surprised to see Aurelius standing there but invited him inside.

The Roman explained his mission and Pulcher nodded.

"I swear to you that I will not harm her and will make no attempt to take her with me, no matter how I feel," he pleaded. "I know her place is here with her family and among her people."

"Pulcher understands."

They waited till they saw Soranus leave for the forge then the dwarf walked over to Bron's front door and knocked. She was busy grinding corn and was looking harassed when he interrupted her.

Layla and Alon were quarrelling over a set of wooden building blocks Pulcher had made them, and Darius and Gift, "the twins" as people called them, now six months old, were both crying.

Bron smiled in spite of the noise. "Soranus was glad to leave for work this morning!" she said.

Pulcher took her hand off the handle of the quern and sat her down.

"I haven't time for a chat," she told him.

He shook his head. "No chat," he said. "Bron, Aurelius here!"

"Here? Where?"

"My house. He wants to see you."

"I can't go, Pulcher. You know I can't. It's over between us – well, not over, exactly, but impossible. Please tell him – ask him – to leave me in peace. Be gentle with him, though."

"Bron, I think you go," said Pulcher. "Important you go. I look after the children."

Bron studied his expression then stood up. She took off her over tunic, which was stained where Gift had puked up some of her feed, and shook out her curls.

"Do I look halfway respectable?" she asked Pulcher.

He smiled and nodded and she left.

Aurelius was behind the door, impatiently waiting for her, and swung it open as she tapped softly.

"Bron, you've come!" he exclaimed with pleasure, shutting the door behind her. "I wasn't sure you would!"

"I said 'No', but Pulcher said it was important."

"It is."

They stood looking at each other, neither knowing how to continue. He was thinking that this vision of her would have to last him for the rest of his life. He gently drew her into his arms. She made a token resistance then submitted.

"Bron, my darling girl, there's no easy way of telling you this."

She looked up into his deep brown eyes and must have read there what he had come to say.

"When?" she asked.

"The day after tomorrow. Our recall to Rome came through yesterday. I couldn't go without seeing you to say goodbye."

She uttered a strangulated noise at the back of her throat.

"We are all going," he continued, "the entire Calleva garrison. We will leave behind only a few old soldiers to clear up the army's affairs, some sick in the hospital to follow on later, and a few who have married Atrebatis girls and have bought themselves out."

"How can I let you go?" Tears began to wet her cheeks.

He smiled ruefully. "Like those we leave behind, I feel old, and sick, and married to an Atrebatis girl," he said.

She ruffled his hair, which he knew always gave her supreme pleasure. He produced a comb and she tidied it for him while he held her tightly round the waist. He had to keep reminding himself that Roman soldiers don't cry.

"It serves no purpose in prolonging this," he said gruffly. "You know I will love you for always. If I had my way –"

She nodded.

"Be strong for both of us and go now," he said.

"I can't, not yet. Just one last kiss, Aurelius, just one more."

"I love you," she whispered as they parted to draw breath. "Please live, Aurelius, and wherever you are throughout your life, when the moon is new, look up and remember me, and my eyes will meet yours there. Now I will go –"

"Your blessing, Bron, I can't leave without your blessing. Say it for me – please," and he prompted her, " 'May the sun god protect you –' "

" '– with his warmth," continued Bron, "and the water goddess grant you fast currents and fair winds' – and bring you back to me one day, my dearest boy," and she left him and went home.

When Pulcher returned to his house ten minutes later, there was no sign of Aurelius.

The young soldier was not in a hurry to abandon Byden and the girl who was tearing his heart to shreds. He spent half an hour idly chatting to a carrier who was leaving later in the day for the garrison in Calleva and helped him load his cart with boxes of soft fruit and vegetables and loose potatoes, apples and pears brought in by the local people.

When he could delay no longer, he collected his horse from the inn stable and led him down the slope to the ford.

After crossing the ford, Aurelius mounted and let the animal walk at an easy pace up the hill and over the ridge.

CHAPTER 49

The council had posted sentries at strategic points on the boundaries and it was two of these young men who brought Vortin in during the morning, at about the time that Aurelius was knocking on Pulcher's door.

"We didn't arrest him," explained the herdsmen when Hestig and other members of the council arrived at the Temple. "He came to find us – he seemed to know we wuz there!"

The councillors exchanged glances. It seemed that Vortin, and whoever had come with him, knew where the sentries were posted. Hestig thanked the men for a job well done and sent them back to their stations.

Vortin looked round the interior of the Temple. "I see it didn't take you long to make your mark here," he snorted with disgust.

"An improvement, I would say," replied Hestig, wondering why the deposed High Priest had wandered into the enemy camp. "What are you doing here? We told you not to come back."

"Since when have you told *me* what to do?" Vortin challenged him.

"Since the people rid themselves of the corruption of your regime and elected us, the council, as responsible for their welfare – since then, Vortin. I repeat, why have you come?"

"I don't care for your tone," said Vortin, "but will overlook it. I have come in peace to claim what is mine by right."

"You won't get your god, your Temple or your religion back!" Kendrus told him.

"I'm not interested in those things," retorted Vortin.

Hestig knew what was coming. The other men were not so aware.

"Then all that remains of yours is your despicable son," snapped the beekeeper.

"Ah, Nobilianus. Where is he? Still here?"

"He was killed in the wood a few weeks ago by three strangers," the wheelwright told him, without emotion.

Vortin looked surprised, but displayed no grief. "So that's who it was," he said, more to himself than to those around him.

Kendrus continued, "If you are interested, which you don't appear to be, his body is buried in the wood, away from the settlement he terrorised, and far from any decent being he could still corrupt from his grave."

"So be it," said Vortin, "he probably deserved it."

Hestig faced him squarely. "So what – or who – have you come to claim?" he asked.

"You know very well, Hestig – your daughter. I have come to take Bron away with me. I will make her my wife and treat her well and you will be suitably recompensed for your loss." There were gasps of incredulity from those listening.

"Bron is not for sale," Hestig said.

"Oh, come now," laughed Vortin. "Accept the deal while it's still on the table. It won't be there for long."

"Hestig is right," Kendrus said. "There is no deal."

Hestigys and the four other members of the council loudly voiced their support.

"You obviously have not considered the consequences," Vortin explained with mock patience.

"Which are?" queried Hoad.

"I will take her by force," Vortin stated simply.

The carpenter laughed. "You and who else?"

"I have – friends. In fact, quite a few friends. They will stop at nothing if it is worth their while. You cannot possibly have hidden all the Temple treasures."

Hestig smiled. That was exactly what they had done. An army of them had removed every bag of gold and jewellery, artefact and vestment and buried them in pits all over the area. Vortin saw the smile.

"They will find it all," he said.

"As head of the council, I am asking you now to leave us in peace, Vortin. You will not have Bron, so get that through your skull."

"Would you sacrifice the whole settlement for one young trollop?"

He had touched a sensitive nerve. While Hestig knew the family would fight for Bron's safety, he was not sure how far the settlement as a whole would be willing to sacrifice their own families for his. Kendrus came to his rescue.

"Unless we make a stand on this issue, we will not be able to make a stand on whatever else you throw at us. Begone, Vortin!"

"I came in friendship to warn you all," said Vortin, "so on your own heads be it!" and he turned and stalked away.

"I fear the worst," said the beekeeper as soon as he was out of sight.

The carpenter sounded perplexed. "But who are these friends of Vortin? Where do they come from? I didn't know he had any such *friends*."

"It is my guess," Hestig replied, "that when he left here he made for the village where he sat out the plague, among the Dobunni people to the north-west."

"But they don't look for trouble any more than we do," Kendrus pointed out.

"No, but many of our tribal villages are being infiltrated by the fair-haired men."

"The Saxon warriors?" asked the carpenter. "Folks say they'll commit any crime if it's made worth their while!"

"Then may God – whichever one he is – preserve us from the English!" the beekeeper prayed fervently.

"I'm so sorry," apologised Hestig, "that it's my daughter who has caused the problem, but it's not her fault."

"We all know that," Hoad assured him. "Don't I, more than most, remember the night of her birth? She has never been to blame."

"We must be ready," said Hestig. "They may be upon us at any time, and we don't know how many. Hestigys, sound the alarm. While you do that, I will make sure your mother and baby Lucilla are hidden. The rest of you go home to make sure your own people are safe, then assemble in the market place with the fighting men, and stand in your divisions according to our drill."

Each family had rehearsed its own precautions in the event of an attack, to be put into operation once the warning gong sounded. Some of the women and children would hide in pits, if they had them; some would flee to the woods; others had decided to stay where they were. No one panicked when the gong boomed. Its deep resonance was caught and held by each wall before being bounced off to the next, all round the houses. Everyone knew what to do.

Hestig ran home to Trifena, who cared for Lucilla while Hestigys was at work, and together they hurried to the Roman villa. At the last minute, Trifena retrieved a small bundle, which she hid in Lucilla's blankets.

They arrived at the same time as Veneta. She had left the Temple children in the care of the women and the eunuchs.

"We have our own methods of luring them away from the fight if they attack the Temple," one of the girls had told Veneta. "It will slow them up, if nothing else."

"I've come to help," Veneta said to Hestig. "Selvid's gone to the market place. He wants to fight alongside all of you."

It was not long before Soranus and his mother, Campania, brought Bron and the four children to join them and they all hurried to the bathhouse, which was furthest away from the front door.

"I've got to go now and make sure that Attryde and her baby" (Soranus had never said "our" baby in Bron's hearing) "are hidden. I'll come back if there's any danger to you, I promise," and he was gone. Hestig went with him.

As they left, they found Pulcher at the front door and let him in.

Hestig had prepared his troops well. All the fit men of whatever age had assembled in the market place and he despatched some of them under section commanders to vulnerable areas on the boundaries. The councillors knew that this was a fairly pointless exercise as the enemy could swarm in between the patrols. However, this was a first line of defence.

Other groups were deployed around the settlement, concealed wherever there were shadows. They had all acquired any weapons they could lay their hands on.

The women sharpened kitchen knives and prepared in their own way.

CHAPTER 50

They had not long to wait. With whoops and yells intended to frighten away any opposition, and nearly succeeding, a horde of tall, blonde warriors came pouring out of the wood from all directions. After brief skirmishes with the small groups on the boundaries, where they did not get all their own way, they arrived in the settlement.

They made straight for the Temple, where Vortin had told them there was treasure enough for all, and were enraged to find the coffers and cupboards empty. The eunuchs took several of the invaders by surprise and quietly strangled them as they had been taught.

A few noticed the staircases on each side of the entrance doors and began to climb them. At once the girls appeared at the top, three on each side, calling and waving, flashing bare legs and thighs and breasts, so that the men fought to get into their rooms, forming a disorderly queue on the stairs.

The noise allowed Sunina and another of the girls to lead a column of children from Selvid's rooms, where they had been hiding, out of the rear door behind the altar and into the house that had been Vortin's. They climbed down the wooden steps into the cellar, where once Bron had been held a prisoner, just as they had practised. Food and water for them had been stored there in readiness. Sunina went back up the stairs to replace the carpet and pull the table over the trapdoor, then left silently.

The children were now behind the attackers' lines and as safe as they could be in the absence of fortified shelters. Until now Byden had been a peaceful settlement without need for defence.

Sunina returned to the Temple to discover that some of the men, angry at not finding the treasures Vortin had promised, had set fire to the draperies behind the altar and to the carpet leading from the front entrance. The girls and men were clattering down the staircase amid shouts and raucous laughter, and tumbled out into the fresh air. The girls quickly disappeared along the pathways, luring some of the men away to their deaths.

Vortin appeared on the steps of the Temple and tried in vain to bring order to the proceedings but the fighting men were uncontrollable, oblivious of the orders issued by their officers before battle.

"Remember why you are here!" Vortin was yelling at them as he ran down the steps towards the market. "Find her! Find her!"

Skirmishes were taking place all around. Fires were beginning to blaze in many of the houses.

The butcher's wife, a large woman, defended herself by wielding a heavy iron pot, which she brought crashing down on the head of her assailant, knocking him out. A young woman and her small daughter were being dragged up the Temple steps by a hefty man who was yelling obscenities at them in a foreign tongue. A little boy, barely a toddler, was sitting on the bottom step, crying and holding out his arms to his mother.

Suddenly the gong was pounded: once, twice, three times. There was a momentary lull as people looked up. Standing at the top of the Temple steps was the tall figure of Asher.

"Stop!" he cried to the leering man. "Leave them be! Where is your compassion? Stop this madness!"

"Out of my way, old man!" cried their assailant in his Nordic dialect, dropping his prisoners' arms and standing to face Asher. The woman clutched her daughter then ran down the steps to scoop up the toddler and escape to safety.

Asher descended the steps and stood his ground, watching the woman out of the corner of his eye, but was not prepared for what happened next. The man bent down and picked up a broad sword with two sharp cutting edges, which its now-dead owner had dropped, and with a swift lunge pierced the left side of Asher's chest. The old man collapsed, and as the stranger pulled the sword from the quivering body, bright red blood spurted high and spattered the hide slung from his shoulder.

Cursing, the foreigner bent to pick up a small object that the sword had dislodged, which had dropped onto the step. It was a small rectangular bronze brooch, its fibula now broken off. The brooch was engraved with a green fish, standing proud of its red background. The man hurled it from him in disgust, looked in vain for the woman, wiped the sword on Asher's stained tunic, and ran down the steps to rejoin the affray.

Soranus knelt by the body of his victim and withdrew his dagger. He looked around him. Although they lacked experience, the discipline of the men of Byden and their determination to defend their homes and families was producing formidable opposition, and their line was holding. Vortin's force had only just reached the market place. However, realistically, Soranus guessed that the line would be broken and the settlement overrun in a couple of hours.

He noticed that it wasn't only the yellow-grey smoke drifting across the village that was blocking out the sun. The sky had darkened and he felt the first few drops of rain.

There was a yell above him and a man twice his age launched himself at him. The enemy was pot-bellied and flabby and fell heavily when Soranus rolled out of the way. Soranus killed him, too. It had been easier than the first time, but he still hated doing it. At least he was fighting for his own, but these men were willing to kill for money, and when there was little chance of being paid, they killed anyway.

His thoughts flew to Bron, the reason for this attack, and the children, and he knew it was time to fall back and go to their defence.

Section V

AURELIUS CATUS

CHAPTER 51

Aurelius was not sure for how long he rode, widening the distance between himself and Byden, but when he reached the next ridge, he reined in and patted his horse's neck. Then he stood up in the stirrups and swivelled round to have a last look in the direction of the settlement.

The sky had grown suddenly dark and he thought he detected a few drops of rain. The clouds were even darker above the ridge he had left. They were very low and rolling fast. As he looked, he came to the surprising conclusion that the dark billows were not clouds, but smoke. When dull red began to tinge the black, he knew Byden was on fire!

He wheeled his horse round and set off at a gallop back the way he had come. As he careered down the hill towards the settlement, seeing the fires now close at hand and hearing the shouts and clamour of fighting, his only fear was for Bron.

He reached the ford and swung down off his horse, which he hurriedly tied to a tree, then splashed through the water and ran up the slope. The door of Bron's house was swinging open and there was no one inside. He banged on Pulcher's door without result, then ran to the villa. He nearly collided with Soranus at the entrance. Soranus stared at him, obviously surprised to see him in the settlement.

"Is Bron safe?" Aurelius gasped.

"Yes, but I've come to hide her and the children where Vortin won't find them, though I don't know where." Soranus was coughing in the smoke.

"Is Vortin responsible for this?" Soranus nodded.

As no one was answering their frantic knocks, the two men together charged the door once, twice and three times before it gave way under their combined weight.

"This way!"

Soranus led him to the bathhouse where the women and children were gathered. Pulcher was trying to occupy Layla and Alon by playing word games with them. "I spy..."

"Bron darling, it's time for you to go!" said Soranus.

"But where, how?" she asked helplessly.

Aurelius moved from behind her husband and she noticed him for the first time.

"I thought you'd gone," she said.

"I saw the fires and came back to help," he told her.

Soranus heard the familiarity and tenderness in their voices and looked from his wife to Aurelius and back again. It was not difficult to see how it was between them, and he sighed.

"I have a plan," Aurelius told them. "It's not perfect, but it's the only one I can think of."

He explained what he had in mind.

"First we've to get you away into hiding, Bron. Perhaps up at the mere?"

"It's the first place Vortin will look," said Soranus.

"Where then?"

"There's plenty of undergrowth between the Stan and the mere – perhaps somewhere there," suggested Campania.

"Under cover of the smoke we'll get a cart away," Aurelius said thoughtfully. "One of the carriers was loading up at the inn and he may not have been able to leave yet. If the cart is seen and searched, they'll find only fruit and vegetables in it. I will pay the carrier to wait over the other side of the ridge, and as soon as it's dark, I'll find you and take you to wherever the cart is hidden."

They thought it might work and no one had any other suggestions.

"Then where?" asked Bron.

"Calleva," replied Aurelius.

Soranus shook his head. "If Vortin can't find Bron in Byden, Calleva is the next place he'll look."

"But he won't be able to get past the Roman fortifications," suggested Trifena.

"In a couple of days' time, the soldiers won't be in Calleva, Mother. Aurelius and the whole garrison have been recalled to Rome. There'll be no protection there or anywhere else."

There was silence, during which Soranus found himself wondering how Bron once again possessed knowledge about the garrison that no one else had.

Then Aurelius said quietly, "It seems I must take them with me, to Rome if necessary."

"Soranus –" said Bron, turning towards him.

"It's out of the question! I couldn't possibly let you go. There'd be no knowing when we'd meet again. No, Aurelius, the answer's 'No!' "

"It seems Vortin will stop at nothing till he's found Bron," countered Aurelius. He looked straight at Soranus. "If she were mine, I'd let her leave."

"But she's not yours!" snapped Soranus.

"You're wasting time," agonised Trifena. "Bron's in danger while you two are arguing."

"I swear I'll look after her and the children," Aurelius promised, "and bring them home just as soon as you send word that it's safe."

"Send word? How could I possibly send you word? Once you leave here, I'll never see her and my children again. You know I'm right."

"I'll come back, Soranus – I'll make you that promise. If it takes a lifetime, I'll come back." Soranus knew that Bron was speaking from her heart and meant it.

"Why not go with them as well, son?" Campania asked him.

He turned to his mother in great distress.

"I must stay here to fight with our friends – this attack would never have happened if it hadn't been for us – I can't run out on them – and I have Attryde and our baby to think of. They have no one else."

"Someone's got to decide, and quickly," pleaded Trifena.

With a head that was pounding and a heart as heavy as lead, Soranus dragged his will to a decision.

"Aurelius, I need a few moments alone with my wife."

"There's no time!"

"That's why I need to talk to her. It seems you may have her for the rest of your life."

Soranus drew Bron apart and took both her hands and clenched them in his fists against his chest. He looked into her face and told her how much he had loved her since he was a little boy, and always would, and there had never been any other love in his heart.

With an unsteady voice, he said he was releasing her from her marriage vows so that she should feel no guilt. While saying that, he withdrew the iron ring from her marriage finger and slid it on to the third finger of her right hand.

She threw her arms round his neck and said she couldn't leave him, and his arms slid round her waist and he kissed all of her that he could – her hair and ear and cheek and neck.

"I remember Umbella's warning," Trifena agonised, though no one was listening to her, "when she stopped your father and me in the wood the day we arrived in Byden. She said people would curse the day I returned with my 'mongrel child', my half-caste Bron, unleashing sword, fire and total destruction. She may be dead, but it has all come true – today is the day – and I am to blame!"

Aurelius came over to Soranus and said he had to take Bron now, without any more delay. He prised her fingers open and took her arms away from her husband's neck.

"I'll always talk to the children about you, Soranus," she sobbed. "I won't let them forget you."

Clinging to his children, kissing first one then the other, Soranus was also crying.

"Take them, Aurelius. Be good to them."

He rushed out, taking his mother with him.

Still sobbing, Bron kissed Trifena and was about to say farewell to Veneta when Hestigys hurried in. Bron ran across to her brother.

"We're leaving for Rome!" she told him.

"Veneta," he implored, "please take Lucilla and go with them!"

"I can't leave Selvid," Veneta said.

Hestigys hesitated then put his arm round her shoulders.

"Selvid is dead, Veneta. I saw him go down. I went to help him, but he was dead. I'm telling you the truth. I really am so sorry. He was a fine man and you can be proud of him. Please take Lucilla and go. I'm staying to fight on. There's nothing here for me anymore. It doesn't matter what happens to me but she has her life ahead of her."

Trifena watched her friend's face drain of all colour, and transferred Lucilla into her arms.

"Veneta, she's yours now, she needs you," she whispered. "There's something wrapped in her blanket – they may come in useful."

"I can't manage four children on my own!" Bron said.

"Of course, I go with you," offered Pulcher, "but not Rome – my voices say no welcome for me there."

Trifena gave him a small bundle to carry. "Pulcher, Bron will need these," she said.

"What is it?" asked Bron.

"The amber and pearl necklace and all Vortin's gifts. I've kept them for you. I'm not sending my daughter off to strangers empty handed!"

"Mother, I love you. Tell Daddy I love him. How can I leave you all?"

"Go, Bron, go now!" said Trifena, "And –" She paused, then breathed softly, "– if you meet your father, tell him – tell him I haven't forgotten him."

She threw her arms round her daughter and the children, then turned her back so that no one would see her tears, as if anyone needed to see them to know that they were flowing down her cheeks.

A moment later, Trifena and Hestigys were standing alone. She had the sudden knowledge that she had lost her third daughter.

"Mother, I've got to go back to the fighting," Hestigys told her.

"Don't worry about me, son – I'll hide in the hypocaust. Find your father and look after him – you're all I've got left now."

CHAPTER 52

Bron left first with Layla and Darius. As she went, she bent down and hurriedly scooped up a handful of earth from the grave of Storm, her first-born. At a loss to know what to do with it now she had it in her hand, Aurelius took it from her and promised to keep it safe.

A few minutes later, Pulcher followed with Alon and Gift, then Veneta crept out with Lucilla, who had to be carried as she was not yet walking. The last to leave was Aurelius, and he made his way by the lower paths to the inn.

Bron walked as quickly as she could with Darius in her arms and Layla running by her side, but without panic, hushing her daughter's questions as they went. They kept in the shadow of the boundary bank, passing behind Pulcher's house and the house and straw hives of the beekeeper, and so down to the Stan, crossing well above the stepping-stones at a point where the slack, clear water came up above her knees and to Layla's waist. Her daughter was complaining bitterly about the cold water, but stopped when she heard the fear in her mother's voice as she was told to be quiet.

They walked upstream a little way, as arranged, then sat on the bank and waited for the others, stung by nettles, scratched and bleeding from the long, thorny arms of the bramble bushes, which were searching for fresh soil to root in, and shivering from the wet and cold and fear.

Pulcher related later that he had arrived at the stream holding Alon by the hand and with Gift in his other arm. When they waded in and the water was creeping up Alon's chest, the boy began to scream, screams that Bron heard and which brought her to her feet with anxiety.

The only way Pulcher could calm Alon was by turning back to the bank they had just left. It was not an easy task, as Pulcher himself was not very tall and was having to hold Gift above his head. All they could do was wait until Veneta arrived.

This she did quite soon and they solved the problem when Veneta took Lucilla and Gift across in her arms and Pulcher gave Alon a piggy-back, which stopped the little boy's tears and brought a smile back to his face.

They soon found Bron, and the party of three adults and five children continued on their way, travelling southwest. They made slow progress as they scrambled through the trees and helped the children clamber over dry branches and other obstacles that strewed the ground.

After half-an-hour, they stopped to draw breath and sank down on a patch of soft ferns. Only the three babies were warm and dry. They could not light a fire for fear of drawing attention to their whereabouts, but fortunately the sun was escaping erratically from behind the passing storm clouds and Layla and Alon were persuaded to run around naked in the warmth while their clothes were draped over bushes to dry.

As the women rested and the children picked blackberries and stained their faces and fingers purple with the juice, Pulcher said he had to hide their tracks, and ran back to the stream. He found a small branch, and by walking backwards and swinging it from side to side, tried to disguise the inevitable swathe they had made in the grass and undergrowth as they passed through it.

The noise of battle from Byden increased and subsided at intervals.

"Surely they can't hold out much longer!" said Bron. She put an arm round Veneta, who was weeping by her side.

"Selvid will always be remembered," Bron comforted her, "for the gentle and kindly man he was."

"And I should not be grieving so," Veneta answered her, "because he is at peace now with our Lord, but how can I not grieve when I love him so much?"

Pulcher returned and they decided it was time to move on again. Layla and Alon refused to put on their clothes, which were still wet and cold, and Bron hadn't the heart to insist. Instead, she took off her outer tunic, which Pulcher slit into two with his knife, and they wrapped each child in the material and tied it round as best they could with bindweed and Bron's and Veneta's girdles. Pulcher bundled up the wet garments and took them with him.

When they next stopped, Veneta remembered what Trifena had told her and looked for the package wrapped in Lucilla's blanket. From it she pulled a pair of chained gold cloak brooches and handed them to Bron.

"They were my mother's," Bron told her, inspecting them. "Daddy bought them for her last year when they had been married twenty years."

"That's a long time," said Veneta. "I wish Selvid and I had had as long together."

"Soranus and I have been married for nine years," said Bron with nostalgia. "We had our crises as we grew up, but it has been a good marriage, and I'm very grateful for it, and for our children."

Lucilla was crawling about and had found a hard, light brown oak apple, which Veneta had to take out of her mouth. Layla and her brother were studying a small toad that had wandered into view. About four inches long, it was musty green with black patches all over its body and had two shiny black eyes. It was not very anxious to move further.

Bron was scolding them for poking it when they heard the sounds of cracking twigs.

"It must be Aurelius!" exclaimed Bron. "We'll be all right, now!"

But it wasn't Aurelius. It was a dark-skinned man, not at all like the fair ones among Vortin's rabble, and he was wearing the tattered remnants of a Roman uniform.

"Deserter!" Pulcher whispered. He laid his hand on a stout broken branch that lay in the grass by his side.

"So, who's this I find?" the man asked in Latin. "Is it possible that it's the little lady herself?"

To his surprise, Veneta answered him in his own language, and

317

held a conversation with him, then translated for the benefit of Bron and Pulcher.

"Vortin is going mad trying to find you," she told Bron. "The fighting is almost over and the Byden men have capitulated."

"Never!" exclaimed Bron.

"Not possible!" chorused Pulcher.

"He has offered a huge reward for you, Bron, and has sent out groups of his men to look for you all over the area. This man says there are others behind him and he is ready to take you back before *they* find you and try to share the reward money."

As if to underline his intention, their would-be assailant drew his gladius, the short sword Aurelius had described as being so effective, and stood before them with legs apart, gripping the bone handle so tightly that his knuckles stood out white against the natural suntan of his hand.

Pulcher expected at any moment to be stuck through like one of the straw-filled sack dummies, and the women pulled the children to them, but in fact this Roman had no inclination for killing. If the young, pretty one would come with him, he said, he was prepared to spare the others.

Bron saw his hesitation and relaxed a little. As she did so, her right hand unclenched and she realised she was still holding her mother's gold brooches. She held them out to him.

He took them and turned them over in his hand.

"Real gold," said Veneta.

He put them in his scabbard. "Not enough," he said.

"How much is Vortin promising you?" asked Veneta.

"A bag of gold," he replied.

Bron looked at Pulcher and indicated with her eyes what he should do. Surreptitiously, he reached a hand into the bundle Trifena had given him, which he had placed on the grass beside him when he sat down.

"Don't trust Vortin," Veneta was saying. "He'll never give you a bag of gold. He'd rather kill you first."

Out of the corner of her eye, Bron saw Pulcher's fingers searching around in the bundle, trying to distinguish its contents. She knew he would find a silver bracelet, hooped earrings with their pendants, another pair of gold brooches, a glass phial of incense, the gold betrothal ring with clasped hands and the tiny gold torque Vortin had sent for Storm.

There was also the necklace, the amber and pearl necklace.

At that moment, Gift woke up and began to cry. Taking advantage of this, Pulcher picked her up from the grass and handed her to Bron, the baby concealing the necklace in his hand. Bron saw the flash of amber and understood Pulcher's intention and took it from him. He didn't want to alert the hopeful hostage-taker to the possibility that there were other treasures where the necklace had come from.

She reached a hand to the back of her neck and brought it away with the necklace grasped in it. She handed it to the man standing above them. His eyes gleamed as he examined it.

"Real amber, real pearls – priceless," Veneta told him, "but don't let Vortin see it because he gave it to her."

The Roman sheathed his sword.

"No chance of that," he said, "because I won't be going back – except to tell the rest of my party that there's no one here."

"Then go quickly," Veneta urged him, "as we are expecting one of your officers from Calleva to come for us soon to take us to safety."

That galvanised the man into action. Desertion was punishable by death, without appeal.

Gift's whimpering had woken Darius. Lucilla was crawling round Veneta's feet.

"You'd better feed those babies and keep them quiet!" he advised, and vanished through the trees.

"I can't feed all three!" wailed Bron. "I'm not a milk-pumping machine! Lucilla will have to be weaned, and overnight!"

Pulcher found a piece of stale bread he had in a pouch and gave it to Veneta. She cupped her hands as Bron expressed some milk, which soaked into the bread. Veneta further softened it by moulding it in her hands, then gave it to Lucilla to suck and chew on while Bron fed the two babies.

They listened intently for any sound and at one time heard some thrashing about in the undergrowth, and feared that the Roman deserter had not kept his word, but the sounds gradually receded and all was quiet.

"So the necklace my father gave my mother has bought my freedom for a second time," Bron mused.

They stayed where they were and it grew dark, except for the ominous red glow from the settlement. The adults were fearful about what had happened there and about the fate of those left behind, but no one said a word. The children slept, cuddled up to Pulcher.

"I'm so hungry," said Veneta.

"Aurelius will never find us tonight," Bron said.

CHAPTER 53

But amazingly, he did. They heard him, calling softly as he came. His horse's footfalls were barely discernible beneath the rags he had wrapped round its hooves. When they answered, he dropped the leading rein and tumbled through the trees and into the open patch of grass where they sat.

"Oh, Aurelius, we're so glad to see you!" said Bron and began to cry. She was exhausted by the lack of food, the cold, the fear and the responsibility of the children. 'A man in a million' Veneta called him.

"I was lucky," he told them. "I met a deserter on his way to – well, wherever he was going. He had got hold of some wine from somewhere and was drunk and was wearing your necklace round his throat. Of course, I thought the worst and would have killed him on the spot, but he just laughed and told me where you were hiding. He described you all so accurately and said he didn't kill women and children and –" Aurelius stopped. The man had said "freaks". "– and babies, and you had bought your freedom. He could have been lying, but I believed him and let him go."

"How is it, in Byden?" Bron asked anxiously. "Have you seen my parents or Soranus and Hestigys?"

"No, I haven't," answered Aurelius, "but then I've been too busy. All I know for sure is that the Temple is well on fire. There is a cart waiting for us over the ridge, but first you must all eat."

He went across to his horse and returned with packets of bread and cheese and tomatoes and apples. He had even brought wine. The innkeeper had raided her girls' rooms and had also sent an assortment of warm clothing.

Bron could not stop crying, she was so tired, so he lifted her onto his horse, Veneta behind her. He gave them the three youngest to hold, then woke the sleeping children and lifted Alon onto Pulcher's crooked back, then bent down so that Layla could climb onto his, and in that fashion they turned to travel south, leaving the wood and moving out into the open countryside.

The carrier was waiting for them and helped lift everyone except Pulcher into his cart, where they gratefully snuggled down onto the soft woollen blankets the innkeeper's wife had provided for them, which the carrier had been sitting on, to avoid suspicion.

"You should be safe, ladies," said the carrier. "I was stopped once, but they let me go when they searched and found only fruit and vegetables."

Aurelius mounted his horse.

Bron suddenly remembered Pulcher, who was standing forlornly by the side of the cart. She clambered across and put her arms out towards him. He reached up and held them.

"Pulcher, come with us!" she pleaded.

"No, Bron. Rome not my home. You don't need me anymore, you have a true husband."

"You will always be my dearest friend –"

"We must go, Bron," Aurelius said anxiously.

"I will never forget you, never –" she cried as the cart began to move. "One day I will come back, I promise, I promise!"

"I love you, Bron," Pulcher said, releasing her arms.

"Aurelius, stop the cart! Let me kiss Pulcher goodbye!"

Aurelius nodded to the carrier and the old man pulled the mule to a stop. Bron reached over the side and took Pulcher's face in her hands and kissed his forehead, cheeks and finally his lips. Then she drew back and the cart moved forward again.

He stood with his fingers on his lips as if to prevent the kiss from escaping. The distance between them increased. On the crown of the ridge, Aurelius turned in his saddle and waved, then gave the Roman salute of respect.

The dwarf stood long after they had disappeared, until he could no longer hear the sound of the hooves and rattle of the cart. He was conscious only of a gaping wound where his heart used to be. Bron had taken it away with her and he knew the wound would not heal until she brought it back.

As he crossed the stepping-stones on his return into the settlement, he saw two figures on the other bank, silhouetted against the red and orange glow of the fires. Hestigys reached out and guided him onto firm earth.

"Have they gone?" he asked.

"Safely away," replied Pulcher.

"Veneta? How was Veneta?"

Pulcher turned to discover who was asking the question and was amazed to see Selvid standing there.

"Tired, hungry, afraid – in tears. We thought you dead."

"I always promised to get her away to safety if ever she was in danger and I knew she wouldn't leave if she thought I was still alive," Selvid explained. "I'm sorry for asking you to lie, Hestigys."

"I didn't lie for *you*, Selvid, but for Lucilla and for me. My only regret is that Vortin has escaped."

They turned to walk up the slope towards the burning village. On the crown of the hill, the Temple stood, a blackened, smoking ruin.

By the light of the fires that were destroying homes and livelihoods, they saw the wounded and dying of both sides lying around them and recognised faces and bodies of neighbours and friends.

"Hestigys, please –" It was the jeweller's wife. "I can't carry him, please take my husband to Kendrus."

Hestigys and Selvid walked across to her and lifted the injured man between them.

"Just look at his hands, his dear hands that fashioned the most exquisite designs!" she cried. "Look at his hands!"

They looked and looked away again and began the slow walk to the house of Kendrus and Stalwyn, leaving their friend, the dwarf, standing alone.

And Pulcher, overwhelming grief weighting and stiffening his grossly twisted body, resolved that, whatever the devastation caused by Vortin and his rabble, and whoever had perished and whoever had lived, Byden would be rebuilt and there would be a home waiting for Bron whenever she came back to him.

To be continued...

Author's Notes

- Part of a bronze Medusa's head in a circular frame was found with a metal detector. The head showed an elongated eye and deeply grooved hair, probably depicting writhing snakes. It was broken but could have been part of a harness decoration. *p189*

- A bronze fish brooch was found in the plough layer. The outline of the green fish stands proud of its red background. It is similar to another found in Kent, and four or five others of differing designs have been discovered in the south of England.
The fish was adopted as a Christian emblem. *p307*

- Skeletons of babies are being found all over the site. Some will have been prenatal, others stillborn, some newly born. Only one adult skeleton has been discovered – an elderly male lying in a crouched position in a shallow grave.

The Medusa medallion with break clearly showing. The right side was found; the complete circle has been reconstructed by Jeffrey Wallis of Archaeofacts Silversmithing, Oxford.

The Christian fish brooch.

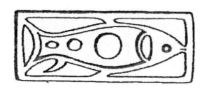